RICHARD RATHWELL

THE BUSH

Hank the aid detective

BLUE ORANGE
publishing

To Wife and Children

First (Test Mouse) Edition
Published 2004 by Blue Orange Publishing Limited
London UK

The Bush copyright 2004 Blue Orange Publishing

All rights reserved. This publication may not be reproduced,
Stored in a retrieval system, or transmitted, in any form or by any
Means, electronic, mechanical, photocopying, recording or
Otherwise, without the prior permission of the publishers.

Printed and bound in Great Britain by
Antony Rowe Ltd., Chippenham, Wiltshire

THE BUSH

I

There were ten columns of women. Each column had fifteen women; each dressed in an ankle length royal blue skirt made of shirt cotton and each in a brick red blouse. They all had white head ties and not a hair showed. They were arranged by height with the shortest at the front. The square on which they stood was hot and windless. The fine white sand lay undisturbed. There was one very short woman who shifted herself to stand on one foot then another. The rest were motionless. The sky was without clouds.

Madame Youngo came onto the veranda through her office door. She was a tall woman and heavy set. Her head tie was elaborate and fringed. She walked slowly to the only high backed chair in the row of chairs facing the square. The chair was woven from thin wicker. It was positioned in the precise middle of the veranda in the shade from the overhanging roof. After smoothing the wrinkles from her brocaded and embroidered silk 'up and down', she sat.

On each side of her, and slightly behind, sat six male teachers, three to each side, all dressed in white smocks and leggings. They were on green plastic chairs. Standing at the right end of their chairs, still on the veranda but at the end, was a man in green military uniform holding a long cane in one hand. At his feet was a small stool. On the other end of the veranda was a short man in a colourful yellow flowered shirt and with him was a dog. He held a metre long cardboard tube.

The square had low cement buildings on three sides. Each too had a veranda. They were all painted dark green. The roofs were of dull grey corrugated tin, striped with dust filled rivulets. The square was open on the side opposite the veranda of Madame Youngo, of her office, and of where the male staff sat, mopping their brows with white neck scarves.

Beyond the open side of the square, past the rows of women, were two lines of palms bordering a gravel path which stretched the distance to an open gate in a tall chain linked fence. Clusters of other green buildings were to the left and right of the palms and of the path. A dark mustard coloured plain sloped downward from outside the fence. It stretched miles and miles to a ring of mountains floating over the plain in the heat haze. The plain was dotted with green and grey patches, some trees and to the far right in a slight depression was a village.

Behind and above Madame Youngo's office, only one half mile behind opposite the plain and the far ring of mountains was a sudden and isolated mountain. It was every shade of green and was topped by a mist. From that direction came the hum of insects and the twitter of lizards. Other than those sounds and that one small woman there was only quiet and some heavy breathing in the square in the heat.

The two male foreign guests were, of course, within the office but could see the assembly through the glassless windows. The assembly could see them. It was proper they should be there and in any event it was cooler inside. The seven female teachers were in a classroom facing the square to the left of Madame Youngo. Two veiled and one unveiled face could be seen against the dark through the empty window frame.

Chatter arose and then stopped in that dark room as Madame Youngo, glancing from side to side, lifted herself from her chair and took one step towards the square on the veranda. This step took her from the shadow of the overhanging roof of her office directly into the sunlight.

"You are ladies of the night," she said softly through tight lips.

A low moan rippled through the columns of women. But not one mouth was open. Then the shorter woman gasped.

"We have seen you," Madame Youngo now shouted. "All of the world has seen you!" She then gestured to her flanking male teachers. They all nodded. Then quietly, conversationally, she added, "We have seen you in the bars and the brothels; we have seen you with corner boys on motor bikes. We have seen you with brown bottles."

From the folds of her jacket she took a sheet of yellow paper. There was another moan. It came both from the square and from the room of female teachers.

"We have your names!" The man with the cane moved from his position to the side of Madam Youngo. He placed the stool behind her and to her right. "We have all the evidence! The truth will come out!

"We are building a new country of discipline and freed from corruption. And what are you doing? You smell of guilt! You have come here from every corner, tribe and people because our leaders, especially my husband, the Governor, wish you to be the teachers of a new nation. They have sacrificed for you. You are failing them. Because of this we will beat you on your bare bottoms." There was then a return to silence. No movement or sound, only lizards twittering.

"Step forward as I name you." The man in green shifted his cane from his left to right hand.

"Fatima, drinking, eight smacks." Fatima was quite small and near the front of the second column. She strode with shoulders back and arms straight down along her sides; behind her hips her palms were open. She stood directly before Madame Youngo who looked down on her from the veranda and then returned to her list. Fatima closed her eyes and lowered her chin.

"Aisha, drinking and vomiting, ten smacks." Aisha was much taller. She joined the queue beside Fatima standing to Fatima's left. Aisha glanced once at a motionless male teacher on his plastic chair on the veranda directly before her and then looked down at the sand.

"Patience, Joy and Charity, drinking and swearing with corner boys. Eleven smacks each."

The line expanded and stretched along the veranda to Madame Youngo's right as Madame Youngo read the names from her list. The queue finally was composed of eleven women.

"Before the beatings we have a lecturer from the health ministry," said Madame Youngo. She then stepped directly backwards and, while smoothing her dress behind, sat down on her chair. Every face in the queue to her right remained looking downwards.

All the other eyes looked to the man with the yellow shirt and the dog. He moved to the centre of the veranda, stepping over the stool and around the man in green with the cane. The dog followed. Bowing slightly to Madame Youngo the man with the cardboard tube and dog turned and began to speak to the square. The dog sat at the feet of Madame Youngo who glanced forward at the mountains.

To the women his words were incomprehensible. He was speaking in English, a lingua franca compulsory to all there but in the accents and tones of the far south and the city. It sounded like a pot boiling over with man squeaks inside. There was a collective sigh of despair from the square through pinched and sometimes trembling. lips. Some eyes looked upward into the sky.

He was the wrong kind of fat. The wrong kind of short. He was not bride fat or thin fat or no meat fat. He was pork on a stick fat, sweat in the office fat. He was the kind who looked at women improperly and would not give presents. He was from the south and probably had evil eye.

For some in the square he was also a fatal destiny. He was the "press your stomach man" come to check for pregnancies which were against school rule number seventeen.

The southern man took a rolled paper from the cardboard tube. After first giving the cardboard tube to a staff man in white, who received it right-handed without facial movement, the southerner gestured towards the dog with the rolled up paper from the tube. His voice lowered into an intimate growl, projecting several bass bleats. He then unrolled the paper quickly and gave out a loud barking sound as he showed it to the women.

It was the picture of a dog's head. The dog's mouth was open, covering two thirds of the poster. There were dozens of uneven teeth and fangs, dripping on bottom and top. A tongue stretched out between teeth and back into a dark, endless hole. An amount of runic writing surrounded the head.

The southern man became silent. The women, nearly each and every one, said "My God" or "God Save Me" in her own tribal language or in the local market language. It sounded to themselves like many cats and cows in distress together.

The man from the South laughed in a kind of satisfied triumph. He then shouted "Rabbits" three times. Many of the women knew what a rabbit was. It was a foreign animal not unlike a Grasscutter. It could be edible but it was in the Christian gifted books mainly as something that talked. It was sometimes magic. It was one of those amazing things to be memorised in a list of amazing things in case of an examination like "hydroplanes" or "suspenders". "Rabbits", to the cleverest women, was misspelt over the devil dog in red letters on the poster.

The man from the south then spoke some dramatic sentence, a slogan, in an artificially deepened voice. It was a sentence using the word "disease", a word they all understood on the square. They knew "sexually transmitted disease". He gestured towards the dog, rotating his hand at the wrist and wriggling his fingers. At this the smaller woman at the front of the queue of those to be beaten cried out in alarm.

The dog, startled, barked sharply and leapt to his feet facing the smaller woman. She screamed out with an urgent and long staccato cry of terror and warning. She then turned and ran weaving between two lines, looking over her shoulder and holding her head tie, finally running directly into another taller woman standing five women back in the middle row. That woman went backward into the one behind her who herself was then already turning to flee.

The dog barked again and leapt from the veranda in pursuit of one woman then another. The line of those to be punished evaporated. The dog snapped with happiness as the square cleared.

Some ran out of the open side, some fled into the green classrooms through door and window. From among those that ran through the open side of the square some turned to the clusters of buildings to the left, and some to the right, and some went down the road between the palms and through the gate in the chain linked fence. A watchman in green, who had been lying across the entrance at the gate, got to his feet and shouted, clutched out and grabbed as women ran past. He caught one but she twisted and spun out of his hands. He then stood motionless, hands at his sides, as the others flew by into the plain.

There were white rubber shoes, white sandals and head ties in the sand. Some small oranges and foil wrapped sweets had fallen from where they had been concealed in skirts and blouses. Heavy footprints and indentations created a chaotic map from the square. The dog was gone but barking was heard to the left from behind the classroom blocks. Some women had gone straight through the classrooms and out the windows on the other side. The dog had followed. The women teachers had disappeared.

The male teachers remained motionless through this as did Madame Youngo. The two male foreign guests came out from the office and stood at the edge of the veranda watching the last running women go. Madame Youngo rose to her feet as the last woman left the square and raced down the emptying path. She turned to the men in white on her left.

"You will go quickly to return those who have run to the village," she said. She turned to her right. "You will get those who go to the church and from the drinking parlour." She then shouted to the women across the corner of the square. "Go to the hostels and bring them from there to the food hall, check under each bed, beat them if they do not come." To the Southern man she said, "Find the dog and take him away." To the man with the cane she said, "Go quickly to the police station and tell them what has happened. Then go to your house. I will send for you there." To the two foreign men she said, "Come back into my office."

Jack Wesley was one. He was a teacher seconded to the school to upgrade the training in classroom skills for the student teachers. He also taught theatre arts and some extra literature classes. He was gaunt from a local diet, tanned and dirty of hair and skin. His white pants were houseboy clean and sharply pressed as was his checkered shirt. He was a man of thirty, notable because of bloodshot eyes. The other man was the aid director, Hank Rousseau. He was buttoned into a many-pocketed light beige military suit. He was about the same age as Jack, but blonde to Jack's brunette and overweight.

Hank went through the door first. Jack took a final look back at a now deserted square and then came Madame Youngo, following, and gesturing to the two dark burgundy coloured, cracked leather looking armchairs facing her large metal green desk. The men both sat heavily and deeply into their chairs. The upholstery rasped.

The office had electricity. Madame Youngo switched on the tall freestanding senior service fan next to her desk. It burst into a whirring clatter. Purple and green lights flickered from the base of the fan as the fan head rotated swiftly, jerking in a narrow arc aimed at Madame Youngo's high backed chair behind her desk. Yellow papers first rose swiftly into the air and then flew, on reaching the main stream, above the chair into the far wall. They slid out of sight.

Madame Youngo turned off the fan lights at the controls on the stand under the caged blades, lowered the fan speed and repositioned the fan head to point at the leather chairs and at the guests. She then sat down.

"That whole thing in the square was quite odd," she said. "But it is always strange on the first day of term. But everyone seems a little tense."

"Rabies is a frightening disease," said Hank. "The health ministry is right to educate about it."

There was a sudden, stuttering series of pops. The lizards stopped humming, the dog stopped barking. The fan whirred on.

"Now they have shot some," said Madame Youngo. The dog barked again once and then stopped altogether. "I am surprised the women were able to run so fast since it is very hot and the death of the dry season. Good for them."

"Of course they will not be so slow as you people. They are used to the seasons. We used to call you people honey because you were slow and dirty in the hot season. We also called you mashed potatoes but I think that was for other reasons.

"It must be hard for you to move and think now but never mind. The rain is almost here; soon you will be cold and fast again. It might come today or even tomorrow after the dancing as it does. Until then we still must plough on with our duties."

The three then sat in silence for a moment. They were overlooked by the portrait of the Governor, the husband of Madame Youngo, from a place on the wall behind her. The Governor smiled broadly while sitting on his own high backed wicker chair in his black suit and narrow black tie. It was the senior staff issued photograph. In the corner of the photo was the red and black logo of the National Redemptionist Party, a black arrowhead on red with the words underneath in green. "Discipline, Progress, Faith, Truth". The popping noises continued in a long burst and then they too stopped.

"We will deal with that when it comes," said Madame Youngo, "but first our pressing business, one thing at a time.

You are a manager Mister Hank, you must understand that. Let us proceed as scheduled.

"You are highly welcome here, Mister Hank, on your visit of inspection. I welcome you on behalf of the school, myself and the Governor. We are very grateful that you and your agency have sent Mister Jack to us and that he is teaching us all of the latest foreign ways. We are happy for the resources you have brought to our institution. We hope that Mister Jack can remain here and that the project money can continue to a successful conclusion."

Hank spoke in formal reply: "Madame, my agency is happy to work with you in partnership in this period of difficulty. We have made educational improvement one of our five priority areas and this project is one of our most successful interventions. We value our relationship with you, with the institution and with the Governor." Hank paused, this prompted by another deeper sound outside, which was followed by some indistinct shouting. "Education is the main factor which can build democracy and further economic development."

"Mister Hank," said Madame and her voice softened, "there is one thing I would like you to do while you are here to investigate Mister Jack. Mister Jack and I have spoken about this and we both believe it will further the project. It has to do with the objective of building links between the institution and the community." Jack shifted himself in his chair but remained staring at the portrait of the Governor as he had for Hank's speech. Hank glanced towards him and then focussed again on Madame Youngo. She continued, still softly.

"We have a problem with community relations. Not a big one but annoying. As you know this institution has women from all over the north. They are from many tribes and of all religions. However there is actually only one who is local and she is from the mountain." Here Jack and Madame Youngo glanced directly at each other. Hank looked at them both briefly. "The rest are from the interior or the river valley."

"Only one of our staff, Mister Jules, is local. He was with the school when it was run by the nuns and before it was taken over by the state. The rest of the staff are from the ministry. Many are actually from the regional capital. They are sent from the Governor for their rural service. What has happened is that, unfortunately, we have encountered a problem with the local community and it needs someone impartial to mediate. You can help us with this. Our staff and I would have a bit of trouble dealing with local people due to certain local historical factors."

"The villagers are Chembe," said Jack.

"And you could help us immensely, your visit comes at such a fortuitous time," Madame continued. "You are well placed."

At this point two women marched by on the veranda followed by two of the men in white. Their footsteps thumped. It was the very short woman and a tall one. The three in the office ignored them.

"I am sure the Governor and the ministry would be very pleased if you could help us."

"And what is it you would like us to do?" asked Hank.

"Actually only you can do this Mister Hank. Mister Jack cannot. The Chembe feel that Mister Jack may sometimes favour the girls in the institution. I think, as you know, he is too close to the locals. Also he has the recurring fever and cannot see things through sometimes. Do not worry Mister Hank. What I am asking should not take too long, it is a simple thing and would give you a chance to learn more of our simple ways. We are sometimes such a primitive people."

"Madame," said Hank, "I know you have a degree from a university in my country."

"It is where I met the Governor," said Madame and smiled. Jack shifted again and the chair rasped.

"You see, Mister Hank, it is a small thing really, as these things go. The misunderstanding started when the women decided to cook some of their own home food behind one of the hostels. They know they should not do this, the food hall food is adequate, but someone, probably a boyfriend or staff member, smuggled some to them. You know they sometimes cut holes in the fences. The watchman cannot be everywhere.

"The fire got out of their control in the grass; they were burning cow dung. It burned up the slope to the forest edge on the mountain. The smoke hung right over the school, over the church and into the village. In the rainless season this can happen so swiftly, even without wind. The fire ran from place to place. By sad chance in doing so the fire burnt several shrines and destroyed several grave sites of the Chembe, or so they say."

"No one knew they were there," said Jack.

"No one really knows what is on the mountain," said Madame Youngo, "but this has created a sort of situation where the Chembe say they will immediately destroy the school and punish us all unless we pay compensation. They have done this sort of thing before. They have some old guns and their bows. We are a bit concerned. They have some other issues as well."

"What do they want?"

"They are asking for fifty fat cows, ten thousand in hard currency and a concrete shrine to be built in the market next to the well."

"They expect to negotiate though," said Jack.

In the corner of the room a lizard suddenly darted along the wall above the portrait of the Governor. It turned the corner and darted along and then down the adjoining wall like a raindrop. The lizard was burgundy coloured, the same shade as the chairs. It was a chameleon. It flowed over the window ledge and was gone. There came a twitter from outside. There was then a clattering round of the deeper sounds.

"The soldiers must be back with their little armoured car," said Madame Youngo. "Now we will not be able to sleep."

"You get used to it," said Jack.

"But how can I negotiate Madame?" Hank said. "I know nothing of the incident. I do not know the Chembe. I know nothing of your customs."

"Mister Hank. It is no problem. You do know our budget. It is only necessary to listen and say that we cannot pay whatever they ask. Make some offers but conclude nothing. Go away without giving expectations. The form and look of the thing only is very important to them, as is your being there as from another world. They are bush people. It is a kind of ritual to them. The ritual is most important. It is a respect. You have come in your four wheel drive and you have your flag. They will wear their beads and carry special knives. They will throw bones.

"I will send our Chembe staff man with you as a translator and he will tell you what to do and explain what is happening. You can put all this in your reports to your headquarters. It will be a great experience; you will not have to conclude anything.

"The Governor will send his men up in a few weeks from the capital and conclude everything. Mister Jack has told me you negotiate with local families when your staff in the capital kill animals when driving or cause accidents. He says you are very experienced and a good conflict manager."

"Thank you Jack," said Hank quietly.

Madame clapped her hands loudly and suddenly. Both men started. "Tea!" she cried. In an instant a short and chubby man came through the door. He had on a plain white shirt and black trousers shiny at knee and buttock The door and frame were dry and warped. The hinges screeched on opening and closing.

"Three teas," said Madame Youngo to the man who stood silently just inside the doorframe. "This is Jules," she said to Hank. "He is a good man from the Chembe themselves. He has been here all his life except for his training in the capital. He teaches geography and helps me in the office. He was deputy to the old mother nun."

"Aim high," said Jules looking straight ahead.

THE BUSH

Hank nodded towards Jules. Jack winked at him. "After tea, Mister Hank," Madame continued, "you will go to meet the Chembe elders. They are waiting for you. Jules will stay with you for the meeting and bring you back. You can sleep in the staff compound in the house of Mister Jack tonight and return to the capital tomorrow. I will send a small girl to tell Mister Jack's houseboy to cook meat."

"But I expected to return today. They expect me at my office. We have meetings. We have a security situation. All I really wanted to do was to discuss your letter about Jack and go. I just wanted to check some of the project inventory in the stores too," said Hank.

"No, no," said Madame Youngo. "Never you mind. Forget that. Let bygones be bygones. Our partnership is much too important to be spoiled by such trivialities. Forget the letter. Stay with us through today and help us with our real problems. And never mind your office. They will understand. We value the real expert help from you people. It is crucial to our development. We thank you so much." At that, Jules opened the door and departed. On opening the door squealed. It was left opened.

Madame watched Jules depart and then, unfolding her hands on the desk, turned to face Hank. Her voice raised itself in pitch but she still spoke softly.

"I must go now to deal with some other urgent school matters as you must appreciate. Please excuse me. When Jules returns with tea he will brief you more in detail. Jack also knows of some of the other issues. Jack and I have agreed the course. When you get back from the elders Jack will help you sort those ones out here. You can use my office for that. It is only for a few additional needed interviews with some of the girls." Madame rose from her chair. She inclined her head slightly to the portrait and walked from the room.

"You are a bastard," said Hank then to Jack. "What is going on?"

"You cannot say that," said Jack. "You can only evaluate me formally at the proper time. Don't forget you are the Country Director. You must follow the rules. You know that. I passed my performance review and the new headquarters desk accepted my interim report. You have nothing on me. I have the right to decide the project implementation in the field. I can suggest how you support me in the field and make whatever requests which are necessary. We do not have to like each other or even understand each other, Hank. We just do the project as it is. The field person decides always."

"Jack, be serious. You do not know a thing about the project design, teacher training or community development. What have you committed me to? And why were you sent here anyway? Did some mad floozy at personnel do it? You were basically a physical education teacher. Probably not a good one. All you are here for is inter-racial sex and native beer."

"Put that in writing," said Jack. "Send it to Headquarters. Let the desk at home see that. You know you have to support me. Youngo and I have now agreed an action. She is the project beneficiary. You cannot ruin the relationship with the Governor either. Hank, I always thought you were an unimaginative podge. Your inflexibility will ruin the project and our position."

Both then stared silently at the Governor until Jules returned with the tea. Jules put the tray on the desk and sat in Madame's chair. "They are very hot teas but sweet," said Jules, gesturing at the three small glasses on the tray. He looked directly at Hank.

"Did Madame tell you about the witchcraft? I would guess not. But I will. Oh, I will, I will, never fear. Measure the cloth before you cut it. A stitch in time saves nine." He laughed.

"No she didn't, Jules," said Jack, "she only mentioned that there are other issues in general. She had other things on her mind."

"I will now tell you something about the Chembe," said Jules to Hank, "and a little about the Mountain. Then we must go to the meeting place as they are waiting. We will take the path by the church as the soldiers are now in the village."

"Perhaps you should call in at the church on the way back," added Jack. "It would be a good courtesy and, after all, the Father was part for some of the incidents, not just the drinking, and he knows some of those involved."

"We shall do that!" said Jules. "It will not take long. A bird in the hand is worth two in the mountain bush, by God! Yes it is, that bird." There were some more pops, quite distant, and a thump.

"It sounds as though I have a lot to do already without seeing the Father," said Hank.

"No, no," said Jack smiling and nodded towards Jules. "It is no problem. The Father is working in Aid, too. That must be interesting. He can fill you in on the local situation. You must do it. It would be very sensitive to the local situation. Madame Youngo would like it." Jules smiled at this.

Hank turned towards Jack and said softly, "Perhaps Jack I should take you back to the capital to the country office with me after this for a few days. It is what I have been thinking. It might be a good thing to do now since I have transport. You could use a few days away. Stop you from going bush. It has been a little hairy here. I may want to have a meeting on the security situation here with you and the other staff. I am sure Madame will let you go for a few days. You know I have responsibility for staff security, Jack. It's in your contract." Jules then glanced from one to the other. He winked at Jack.

The green head of a lizard bobbed up and down in the window frame. Each of the men in turn took a glass of tea from the tray. Each sipped. The tea was now no hotter than the steel desk. The fan throbbed. Jules sat back, relaxing into the high backed chair. Jules spoke.

"You must know something about the Chembe if you are to handle this thing well. We are a small people and, to you, in a corner of the world with no news or information. But some of you people have studied us and written some books and sent some copies. But I guess everyone gets studied. They don't get in the news though.

"Madame Youngo has locked the library from the women but Jack and I have keys so we can prepare classes. The school rubbish is also kept for burial in the same building. I read all the books. There are thousands. I open the crates. We have all the studies of the area in learned journals in the school library with boxes and boxes of gift and Aid books sent to us even from the time of the nuns. Everyone has wanted us to be educated. Hundreds of books on how to build canoes, how to cook with moose, aphorisms for the infirm, romantic poems of the New World, "A Theory of Planets Colliding". We also have our own stories from our memories. A few people have written down versions of these.

"We think we came here from a kingdom on a big river. But lots of other tribes around here think that too. It could have been the Ancient Civilization or the original river of Adam or some river that is gone now maybe when the continents divided. We brought a seedling from our sacred tree, our board thing, a few masks and some of our animals. There was no one here except for the small people on the mountain but they did not farm and had no metals. We didn't fight them and they traded their herbs to us. We planted our tree at the edge of the Mountain and began to farm.

"We thought all the other people around us were devils and very disgusting the way they dressed and ate. We did not like the way they married and talked. They, on their side, called us witches and liars. In fact the tribe in the area around the town by the mountain range call themselves "Bechembe" which means "not Chembe".

"We fought them all, even the Jukawa. You probably know about the Jukawa from the edge of the desert who conquered everything and built some cities and universities. This was long before foreigners. They had factories to make soap and cloth.

People used to say "God Save Us from the Jukawa!" They conquered everything. Then one day they just stopped and went home. It seems a mystery why. They were very clever. They knew about the stars and chemicals. But they went home. No one knows what they found out or learned or saw to do that. They never beat us.

"When you people came we thought you had no legs and were dead. That is because of your skin and trousers. You looked like people in our night-time marching societies who dance on stilts. Some of our oldest men think it is still colonialism and the time the dead arrived and go down on knee when one of you drives by. Our uncles killed a few of you in your tents in the independence time. Our young people are joining religions that say you are very wicked. Very wicked indeed with your sisters and your drugs. Also cooking your enemies in ovens. How did you do that Mister Hank? What kind of ovens were they?

"We were astonished by your love which you invented to cover sin, betrayal and treason and also your motors. We thought these were all because of no legs or laziness. When our men of magic looked at you carefully to see the spirits of your ancestors they could see nothing. We got used to this. But, never fear, it takes all kinds to skin a cat and we actually like some of you now. Some of you try to behave properly. But you can't of course. We called you "lords of the east" and when you found out you liked that. But we meant you made noise at dawn with radios. One man from you studied our songs and our dances. He wrote what you call a treatise and transcribed them. They influenced your avant-garde popular music. Then another found out they were really marching songs of occupying troops. Our masks caused a lot of confusion.

"One of your governments gave us a tribal medal in one of your wars. We had attacked a supply train. We did it because a small boy had noticed black and white cows in the railway cars. They looked delicious and we made their skins into drums. In fact that type of drum is one of the things we are thinking to sell to tourists. If the bridge is repaired and the troubles stop.

"We have a big potential and want to prosper. The stream from the Mountain has mud the colour of empty sky. It is the mud of diamonds. There are tall golden trees on the other side of the Mountain that are as hard as iron. There are birds in the forest which are red and green and talk. They have crowns of pink feathers. No one has seen such birds. Have you seen them Hank?

"The Elders you will see are the main Chembe. They are the guardians of our tribe and this village and its future. They make the laws and have maps to secret places. The groves and clearings. They keep the masks and accept people into the societies. One is the pastor of the new village church, the House of the Apocalypse. It is one of our own churches. Another is for the religion of the east. A very pure form. These pray all day and dance too. This one makes charms from pages of the book. We still have our queen but she lives away from the village by the forest and only sells things like medicines. We like her very much. She makes some gin, too even though the police say she can't after all those Bechembe died. But she uses it to bottle her worms which stop fever and bone pains. One of our good worms especially, the one the doctor who came called "Nematode". We call it "woolly worm".

"The Elders must guard the shrines and the land. Treat your Elder as you would yourself. That is why they need to be talked to. The things have to be made fair and true. Alright that is everything about the Chembes. Any questions? That took longer than I thought. Let's go. I sent a small girl ahead to say we were coming and just now. Waste and haste are brothers. No questions then?"

"I don't think so Jules, thank you. That should do." Hank said evenly. "Jack, we will talk later."

II

They left through the open door and walked across the square. The sun had lowered a little but it was still hot and harshly bright. A few shoes and other objects remained in the square. In the far corner three small girls were sweeping it with twig whisk brooms.

As they walked along the road between the palms Jules pointed out the library building to the right and the hostels to the left. The gate had been closed after the girls had run through but was opened for them by the watchman in patched military green. He had a small bow over his shoulder and a machete in his belt. His sleeping blanket was to one side near a ring of stones for cooking. His pot was near the blanket on which was his quiver of arrows.

The plain was very dry and shimmering in curtains of rising heat. Jules paused at the gate, listening. He did not take the main road which went straight from the gate towards the mountains down the slope. Along that road, to the far right some distance from the gate, the roofs of a village could still be seen in the depression wavering in the heat. Some sounds of singing or shouting could be heard. There were moving figures on the road.

The village was near a thin line of pale green, the route of the seasonal river. Against that line smoke could be seen rising in the haze. The fields nearest the village were baked chocolate and mustard in colour. Between the school gate and the village were expanses of tall grey grasses. They did not stir.

Near the gate stood one twisted tree, leafless at the crown of tangled branches. Twigged pear shaped nests hung on viney strings, to the sides of which clung yellow birds spinning and weaving. Past this footpath led along the outside fence to the right of the gate and onto this Jules, leading Hank, turned.

The fence stretched to their right; the path followed it rising up an arm of the mountain into the heat. Hank and Jules walked it with heads down. After some distance the fence stopped and turned towards the main mountain. Here they looked up. Both men were panting.

The green buildings and the square were now visible back through the fence below in the distance across open stony ground. Hank's four wheel drive was parked behind Madame Youngo's office. The health ministry van was gone. Three small knots of women in blue and red were being shepherded by men in white towards a big building near the square. One man raised his arm and lowered it. Another knot of women was running up the path from the village towards the gate. A man in white ran behind them. A flat topped vehicle moved slowly behind this man in white.

There was a section of the institution beyond the square towards the far perimeter fence that could be seen from the corner of the fence at which Hank and Jules now paused. Towards this far perimeter fence was a section of the compound which was itself fenced off from the rest. Here there were twenty white bungalows. This section had its own gate across which lay the tiny figure of another watchman. Behind this part of the compound was a ridge. The whole institution lay within and filled a kind of plateau, a dinner plate on a shelf bitten or collapsed into the mountain behind, all held slightly above the plain on two sides by the arms of green ridges from the mountain and all enclosed by fence.

On the inside of the fence Jules and Hank had reached, at the corner where it turned towards the mountain, was a clump of trees like cypress with white bark. It was the old border. A narrow gully ran along outside the fence here from the direction of the mountain down into the plain. The path crossed this gully by slanting abruptly down one side and going straight up the other. Before descending into the gully Hank and Jules stood on the crest while three brown and black snakes, each an arm's length long, slid on the flat and stony floor in the cleft upwards towards the mountain. The two then descended and climbed the other side.

The far side of the gully was much higher than the one they had descended. In fact, it was part of another arm angling and sloping from the mountain. On top of this, in a clearing surrounded by a circle of white barked trees, each with protruding grey roots, was the church. It was perched on a high edge of the ridge to face down to the village. The large area around it was bare but for clumps of both fan-shaped and hand-shaped ferns growing from stony blue-grey mossy patches in the dark red soil. Towards the mountain and up the ridge these patches blended together and joined. The ferns became thicker and taller. Then the forest began.

The church was honey coloured, constructed of small, sandy, soft and hard yellow square stones left rough. There was a plain belfry open on four sides at the top within which hung a small black bell. Below the belfry through the tower three steps led through an open door to a dark interior.

The main roof was of tin. Behind the church towards the mountain was another tin roof on a building the same size as the church and made of the same materials but with no belfry. From this building came the sound of opera. The soprano was distinct over the low thrumming of a generator. A path led directly from the church door down the ridge in the direction of the village. It crossed the path from the school directly in front of the steps. Another path went from this junction around the church to the building behind. There was no fence between all this and the mountain.

The cloud from the mountain had extended to overhang the church and its buildings behind which were consequently in shadow. Under the cloud it was noticeably cooler. A wisp of breeze blew.

"The season is almost over; soon we will have rain," said Jules. "The hut of the elders is just over this ridge. When I was a boy, I used to come here by the church to look down on the grasses below after a burning, to see the long boas moving back and forth majestically. Only time really to see them is after a burning. Also, in the rains you could see herds of the bony cows and the nomads on the old paths. They still drive them around the mountain across the border to sell.

"You know we have more snakes per acre than anywhere else in the world? It is in a book on the region in the library. It was all studied just after the war. They hired counters. There is a place in another continent which was close but we beat them. We also have more varieties. Once one of the elders held a meeting to change the name of our village to "Green Snake". He thought it would be good for tourists. The name now means "Green Place". The community didn't want to do this even though the Bechembes called their town "Green Place" too in their language. But that is in their own language after all which calls everything small. Ours actually means "Greenest Place". A rose by any other, what say?"

"Can we go slower?" said Hank. "I feel like I'm moving through jelly. I can't see where we're going from the sweat in my eyes. I can only see what is in front of my feet."

"It will rain soon," said Jules, "then everything will be so wet you will be able to see for miles. You'll be able to fly along all the paths after the rain. Your feet will drink the puddles. Wet birds are faster in the night we say."

The path led over the crest of the ridge and down into a narrow v-shaped cut into the mountain. The ferns grew more densely beside the path. They had thicker stems. There were dead slugs on the path and dried flat worms.

The plain below was obscured. Beside the pathside ferns, past the church, there were small branched bushes with tiny leaves. The grasses amongst these bushes were greener and broad leafed. There was the occasional chatter of some animal further back on the mountain. There, the trees were much taller and dark under their crowns. Some dried vines roped out of the tree tops to the sloping floor which themselves were clustered with smaller branched plants. There were other more wooden chatters in the closest tree tops.

The pair turned to their left and moved downward into the cut more towards the plain. They moved from under the solitary cloud into sunshine and into an empty bright heat as the path narrowed among taller ferns. After a while there appeared ahead at the end of the path a whitewashed reed and twig thatched hut of dried mud. There were several half gourds drying on the roof. The hut was round windowed as though black eyed, each window closely spaced on the side of a small pointy topped door.

In front on stools behind a low table sat three men in voluminous white and blue red vested local dress. The table had on it a one ring gas stove resting on a frame above a blue gas bottle. On the ring was an aluminium saucepan. At the side of the gas bottle were five clear glasses. There was a white plate of plain biscuits. Facing the three men, on the opposite side of the table, were two empty stools. Around the base of the stools entwined carved snakes. The man in the centre of the three had a horned and holed wooden sceptre. The other two had fly whisks with beaded handles. Below their gathered gowns, each seated man showed black trousers falling sockless around non-laced black shoes. All three men were bald on top and had patches of side hair above their ears the colour of a tin roof. They were very thin.

Jules stopped before them and the table, behind one of the empty stools, and Hank moved up behind the other.

"I will now introduce you," said Jules to Hank. "This will take a few moments as I must do the greetings."

"I know some greetings from my language class," said Hank.

"Whatever you do, do not use those. This is Chembe."

A long conversation ensued of rising interrogatives batted back and forth between Jules and the Elders. At one point they all looked at the sky above. At another, they all looked at Hank.

"All right. That one is over. They say you must make the compensation they demand or they will burn the school. They say do not talk to the police as they are all Chembe.

"They say the army will not care about this dispute. They also say you are very welcome here and come in the sight of God and offer tea and biscuits. They say the women trainees are witches and whores except perhaps for the sincere religious ones but they are very few and who knows their hearts."

"Tell them I will have tea," said Hank and sat down. Jules stood and himself served the tea from where it was stewing in the saucepan to each of the Elders in turn and then to Hank. He filled his own glass and sat down. Each of them then flicked some of the floating leaves and stems from the top of the liquid and each sipped. The glasses were set down. On offer from Jules passing the plate all declined a biscuit.

"Now Jules," said Hank while looking straight at the man with the sceptre, "translate what I say exactly. I will pause after each sentence. Do not change my words and ask me if you do not understand them. Translate their replies exactly. If I do not understand them I will ask you. All right?"

"Yes Mister Hank."

"Tell them I have no money. Yes, I am from the agency that repaired the well in the village and gave the grinder. But I have no money and neither has the school." Hank stopped. Jules nodded translated. Then Hank went on.

"The things we did before were because Mister Jack asked for these things as part of his project and mine to help the school develop and be more part of the community. They were things for the project.

"Mister Jack is our local man. I am only here to speak from the middle. I cannot give you anything today. The money is almost gone. It cannot be forever. I can only ask you to forgive the women who burned your ancestors as it was an honest mistake and an accident. There is burning every year. Accidents must happen." Hank looked at Jules. "Is that too much?" Jules shook his head and translated. After this Hank went on.

"The school is very important to us all as it will create teachers to build the nation. The women there are patriots who are dedicating their lives to raise the nation up. They are being given the latest methods. They will create education, the most important thing in life. You must forgive them." Jules translated. The man with the sceptre replied and Jules translated that to Hank.

"He says that the women are mainly whores who are sent here by their husbands while they find other wives or are unmarried ugly women from the plains who are sent here to learn to read and use a fork so they have a higher bride price. He says that Mister Jack got the well repaired because his houseboy, who is the brother of his girlfriend, asked him to. The grinder is being used by the military administrator sent from the interior ministry who is a Bechembe. He charges others to use it. Mister Jack drinks beer with him. He says there is only one Chembe in the school and she is in fact a special Chembe and is from the mountainside. The language in the school is foreign and not from the region. No one understands it. The teachers are drunks and womanisers. Madame Youngo is a snake. Her husband is a tyrant. The school kitchen does not buy meat from the village like the nuns did. There were never as bad burnings as this year. He says they did not want your project; they wanted someone to be trained in carpentry to make coffins. He says he knows some of your language from the army."

"Will you take less compensation?" asked Hank speaking to the Elder directly.

"We will take twenty cows and five thousand dollars and a shrine," said the Elder.

"I have no budget for that and neither has the school. Will you take some roofing tin and a bit of fence?"

"Do you have grain, flour or cloth? What about your four wheel drive?"

"There is royal blue and red cloth. They need the flour at the school. The four wheel drive is the agency's." The other two Elders swished their fly whisks. They clicked their tongues. The man with the sceptre went on.

"How much roofing? We want thirty Moodoos."

"I do not know what a Moodoo is. There is enough unused in the stores of the roofing that we have donated for two buildings the size of a classroom. We also have some sports equipment, team shirts and shorts — you could start a village soccer team — and there are some sets of encyclopaedias in Spanish as well as flip charts."

"What is a flip chart? Roofing, fence and cloth are not enough. We will still burn some buildings."

"What if they buy meat and vegetables from you and the teachers do not drink in the village?"

"We want them to drink in the village."

"I will give you one hundred dollars as well of my own money and so will Mister Jack."

"We also want you to judge the dancing tomorrow. You must bring Jack, too. The Bechembe will be there. We have heard the Governor might even come. If you do this the event will be a success."

The bargaining went on until the afternoon. The light became lemon on the white of the hut. The sky had tiny high white smudges.

Hank and Jules then concluded the offer of compensation. No bones were thrown but the whisks swished. All still was to be confirmed by Madame Youngo. The two had to hurry to depart as night fell swiftly. They went through the long departure ritual again in Chembe. They then turned and left without glancing back. As they went up a path they heard a bottle being opened.

"We can interview the women by good light," said Jules as they hurried along the path. "Madame Youngo has electricity in the office from the generator at her house. Mister Jack will be there. But first we will stop by the Father's house. He will be at the dancing tomorrow, too. I am glad you are staying another day. I didn't get to tell you about the mountain. Well God be praised. There has been no shooting for hours. It doesn't pour but it rains. Why do you think they settled so easily?"

"They seemed excited about building supplies."

When they reached the church the door was closed. The light in the building behind was bright orange. Jules led Hank around the back to the Priest's house. The path of white flat painted stones that led around the church wall went first to a small door in the back of the church and then to the Priest's front door. The cloud on the mountain had extended slightly and was quite dark. It covered part of the plain but not the village. It missed the school below to the left. But the school buildings now had shadows and were magnified in pink and brown. The Mountain was black behind.

Hank knocked. The door was carved with a plain cross. It had large black metal hinges. Footsteps approached immediately. The door was opened by a small boy in khaki shorts and white shirt. He looked at the two and turned back into the house saying nothing. A freestanding whitewashed wooden partition faced the two. It left openings on each side and reached almost to the ceiling. The boy had gone to the left. Directly onto this partition was painted a depiction of the last supper. The figures were in mainly primary colours and in local dress. The saviour looked Chembe, round faced and short. Judas was tall and wore a suit. There was a lion under the table. The interior, extending grey behind the partition, had a musty vegetable smell like husks.

The small boy returned on the left side of the wall followed by a man in black surplice of Hank's height but much older and heavier. He wore at his breast a wooden cross on a silver beaded chain. You could not see his legs as the surplice's cloth swished on the concrete floor. His hair was thin, white and yellow, combed in that style of extending from a part over the left ear across a bald spot to the other ear. His face bloomed with irregular light pink patterns under eye and around nose. He had two chins below an underbite. Each chin was precise and rolled from ear to ear on a thick neck.

"Oh my!" he said, and his voice was a sudden gargle from a time of unuse. "Look at that!" He pointed over the shoulders of Hank and Jules towards the church. They turned. A brown shape was just turning the church corner on the back of the church to creep along the wall on the far side of the path from which Jules and Hank had just come. It was long armed and twisted its shoulders as it turned. It dragged a leg. The creature looked purple and gold in the light reflected from the church wall. It disappeared along the wall into black shadows in the next instant. Then it appeared again loping suddenly away from the wall, angled itself forward and hunched over, scurried to the incline and into the path into the cut. It disappeared over the edge into the ferns.

"Heading for the dry stream and up the Mountain I suppose," said the Father thickly. He spat past Jules to the path side. "Well, come on in. You must be the Aid director. Hank isn't it? Youngo sent a small girl to tell me you might be coming. I am Father Buchanan. And hello Jules old man!"

The voice, warmed up now, had settled into a low and sputtering wet grate. The Father turned and they followed him to the left around the divider, past the Last Supper and into the main room. The small boy closed the door and then followed too.

The room was very large. It was panelled in a dark gnarled hardwood. On the high ceiling there were three big stationary fans hanging on brass coloured chains intertwined with black electric cord. The fans had each four long uncovered blades made of varnished hardwood. Further in, the air smelled sweet from absent flowers.

The main room was the width of the house and extended half the length. It was huge and echoing. It was also quiet, hot and seemed because of its size almost empty. There were two windows, one on each side at the far end of the room, as there had been in the same position in the church in front. These were clear glassed and, though curtained in gauzy cotton, beamed pillars of light red and dusty light to the floor. The windows behind the curtains were frozen outward at an angle, secured by a metal arm between the window and the frame. The curtains did not stir. Outside the red beams the room was grey. From the windows, evenly spaced towards the front door along the wall, were free standing lamp stands topped with beige and fringed octagonal covers. Each had a wire at the base through the wall.

The far wall had three doors. Between the right one and the centre was a grandfather clock which ticked hollowly. The wall to the right had six tall glass doored cupboards in pairs on each side of each lamp stand, and these also were evenly spaced. Four of the cupboards had books aligned in rows interspaced with grey boxes on their shelves. The other pair contained small masks and shiny stones as well as bits of dried wood. One shelf had a small stuffed animal which looked like a tiny deer, and a skull.

Facing away from the cupboards and the left wall was a familiar looking burgundy sofa of cracked leather and two high backed wicker chairs arranged in a semi-circle around a square planked black painted table. This configuration was a small island in the large room facing a short black leather box, opening at the top on a propped metal tube, standing on four curved legs. Inside the box was a turntable on which was a record on which record rested a thick needle protruding from a heavy arm.

From the box a black wire extended through its own hole in the wall. Some reddish light could be seen through the hole around the wire. There were two large black and white traditional cow skin carpets in front of the sofa. One was under the table and one was under the curved legs of the box. Father Buchanan gestured to the wicker chairs. He sat on the sofa. The sofa made a sticky, crackling sound.

"Silly old thing, this couch. I should get rid of it but it belonged to the old Fathers. It was part of a set. Chairs belonged to them, too. Only thing left from the old mission after that fire. Well, welcome to my world!"

He then spoke to the small boy who had placed himself next to the black box. "Go outside and turn on the generator. Then say we want tea and the cake." The boy departed towards the middle door in the far wall. His footsteps echoed in the room.

"We will have light and music, dear guests. And some cool. It is hot and soon will come the unforgiving mosquitoes.

"Keep an eye on the woods," he shouted to the small boy as the boy closed the middle door. The Father then turned to Hank seated on the wicker chair on his left.

"You have been to the house of the queen. Did you see the old fairy?" The father laughed, a sound like a basin emptying. Hank stared at the Father. Jules spoke quickly to Hank into the silence from his chair opposite. His voice was raised slightly and so it echoed slightly.

"Yes, Mister Hank. It is actually her house. She was inside all the time. She listened. It is the house in which the Chembe keep their masks. She lives there because it is near the beginning place of our tree and also the stream. She sells her things from there too and also at times our native beer. She stays inside. All our women like to hide inside." Jules had leaned forward while speaking. He now sank back into his chair and sighed. He glanced towards the Father. Jules was frowning.

"Jules," said the Father, "you should educate our guests more. You are the one that knows." He turned again to Hank.

"He sometimes keeps secrets, does our Jules. Used to work here, you know. He lived at the queen's house, then here. Sang a bit at service. Keeps secrets, he does." He turned again to Jules. "Always thought you were spying a bit for your mother, I did. Wouldn't put it past the old fairy." There was then another gargled laugh followed by a small cough. The father then spat on the floor.

"Father, I brought Mister Hank here so you could explain some of the recent happenings. He is investigating for Madame Youngo. You can explain the recent situation to him better than me," said Jules. The Father laughed.

"The queen is your mother?" Hank said to Jules. "You mean, you are the son of the chief? I didn't know. Jack didn't tell me."

"No, no, Mister Aid director," said Father Buchanan. "You have the whole thing confused! The queen does not marry. Well, she does actually and then every year and only symbolically. The chief is someone else. He is appointed by the government. He is a fine fellow. Comes to the church. He is unrelated to Jules except nominally his father. Has eleven wives. Not really wives the way we mean, of course; marriage here it is a kind of traditional welfare system. He is the one supposed to marry the widows of close relatives. Take care of them. The women demand it. Marries the wives of brothers and uncles and some of the wives of his father. Not his mother though of course. My houseboy here is the chief's grandson but he is his own grandfather, too. Quite complicated. He drew out the family tree for me one day. Took me hours to understand it. I sent it to the Archbishop. We couldn't find the sin in it. But the boy certainly knew who his own mother was and her mother before her. He is a bit secretive on fathers though.

"That old bugger chief mainly uses all his wives for farming. Especially for ploughing. He has lots of fields. He also runs the beer parlour. The chief is long time partner of the administrator. They distribute the seeds from the government. They run the co-operative store near the market. Not that there is much in it.

They administer the free market, with the religious police and with the societies of course. They give out the licences. Both are very wealthy men. The chief has a wonderful big whitewashed compound. It has a mud relief of a lion on one wall painted over in gold paint. Has testicles on it the size of pumpkins.

"Well, I will tell you all about the witchcraft, but first we will have some tea. After that I must check the church see if any of your women are hiding in it. We don't want more incidents. If there are some hiding then that beastie will have frightened them out of their wits. It went right by the window. First I'll check the church then we will have some cake. We must keep living.

"I really laughed when I heard about the school opening. We all did. You would have to know the place and love it, Hank, to see the funny side. To you it must have been very strange, even terrible. But to us, not really that but wonderful. Imagine a ministry of health official actually invoking the cemetery dog of death. That is very funny! Typical thing that." The father laughed and coughed.

"There might be a mate to the beastie that we saw wandering hiding around the church as well. That poor beastie looked as though it was badly hurt. Mad to get away. Been shot most likely. Probably going to the mountain and up the stream for the millipedes. Rub them on the fur you know. Stops the flies and maggots. Probably wants a good roll in the mud at one of the pools higher up. They are there all year. Fed from an underground lake, I think. It will eat a bit of the clay from them especially if it has a stomach wound. Looked like a leg though. It'll get a few of the grey monkeys to give it a smell. See how bad it is. Probably could use a bit of the special rock in the river cave. Lots of animals go there to heal. Saw an elephant going up once. Get the sodium and so on. Then will have a little vomit. After a week it will be as right as rain. Healed and forgiven.

"It is a wonderful place here, Hank. I have found true peace here. I love it." Hank looked around the room. He sneezed.

There was a gusty bang outside followed by a low throbbing thump. The smell of diesel suddenly permeated the air combined with that of urine and wet straw. All six lights went on, at once, radiating a custard glow into the pink light from the windows. The huge fans accelerated into life. They clicked elegantly and softly as a cooling breeze swept the room. From the black box a loud quack was followed by an alarmed yelp which then diffused and calmed itself into a high soprano. The opera about the counterfeit queen, the prostitute.

A slim tall foreign woman entered the room from the back at the middle door. She giggled as she glided across the floor as she balanced a large glass bottomed tray on outstretched arms. The tray had one plate, a black box and a silver teapot with three flowered cups and saucers. The flowers were roses. The plate was of plain beige cakes in squares piled to three stories. The box was empty and contained dozens of empty crinkled black paper envelopes in nests around its inner edges. The nests, however, smelled of chocolate. The woman was wearing a short flowered chintz dress with puffy sleeves and square collar. On her feet were canvas red shoes. Above each ear was a burette adorned with a plastic white daisy head with an orange centre. Her hair was black but with a white widow's peak.

"Ahh, Florence thank you! Now we are alive again! You will close the window from the mosquitoes, won't you dear?" said Father Buchanan.

"You two enjoy this while I check the church. Florence makes the tea hot and sweet. The cakes are hers, too. I won't be a minute." The woman put down the tray in the middle of the square table with the silver pot on Jules' side. She twirled and walked to the end of the room and drew back the curtain of the window on the left side. She lifted the securing arm from its anchoring stud on the sill and pulled the window closed. She then secured the arm in the locked position and drew the curtain.

She giggled again and glancing back at the Father glided across the room to the other window and repeated the operation. She then exited through the third door after glancing over her shoulder. Father Buchanan watched her and then swept his hand in an arc above the tray and grunted. The soprano ended and a chorus began.

"From none of the senses is the truth pure," said Jules.

The father rose to his feet and left the room swishing around the partition. The door to the outside opened and closed with a soft click.

"Who was that lady?" said Hank to Jules.

"It is Madame Florence. She was a teacher at the time of the nuns. She came from the islands. She was once the deputy to the Sister when I was just a young boy. She did the beating. She actually beat Madame Youngo when she was a young girl here. It was just before she graduated. The same day actually. Madame Florence is a helper to the Father now. It's normal." Jules poured tea. The chorus sounded as if marching.

"And Father Buchanan? Who is he?"

"They call him the Bacon Priest. He came here just before the civil war. He supervised the building of the school and the church after the fire destroyed most of the old mission. He has been here with us all the time, mainly, since. But sometimes he used to go back to his country during the war and do a tour. He gave lectures to raise money to do projects back here. He got the young women in the school to sew lace for sale overseas. He imported oxen.

"He arranged for food supplies to the Chembe even though most of the war was in the south and they had no part in it. He used to go on secret missions to some of the tribes to arrange future reconciliation. He would report to his government and to the church. He taught religious studies in the school. Taught the goods and bads of different faiths. He even used to speak about the animists. He also taught literature. He invited scholars from his church and from the universities he visited to stay here on their field trips. They were scientists of all types and some were doctors. They would stay for a month or so and ask the Chembe questions. They would walk around in the heat. One even climbed the Mountain. They watched the animals and brought back plants to the Priest's house. They talked all night with Father. They would treat us for diseases, when we queued up at the church front before the service, with spoonfuls of stuff from bottles.

"The Mother nun, Sister Savonarola, was his partner in Christ. She was sent to be the manager of the school and of the projects. She started the girls' brigades and built the library. She got new seeds and domestic appliances. She also got jazz instruments sent from parishes in developed countries. She was given a large car sent by boat and then driven here. It was the gift of a church in the capital of the world. She even had Hambone Jones here for a visit. She drove him in her car all over the region. The roads were good then. Hambone played saxaphone in schools and churches. He played on our traditional dancing day. Sister stood behind him as he stood in the centre of our field for ceremonies pouring loveliness from his trombone into the sun, with sister holding a parasol over his head. The Bechembe won the dancing that year.

"Sister and Hambone, and the school, were in several magazines. She published a book of poems called "The Secret Book of The Wedded Heart". It was based on mystical things from the other religion or something. How she and Father would enjoy the music here on an evening. She played the liquorice stick. Do you like jazz, Hank? My, that woman could play and sway!

"It changed after the civil war with the new government, Hank. People weren't interested in us here. No one really bought the lace any more. A lot of it is stored in the old domestic science building. This has been closed up for ages. The appliances in it are all broken. The oxen disappeared. They may have been eaten. The Chembe never liked the food he brought, especially the bacon.

"Everyone said the school was to be nationalised and so the old smaller fence was built and the trees cut down. The women who came then to teach were more often from other faiths. It was required. I had been trained in the capital and was appointed a Deputy. I had to help right away with the locals who were suspected of stealing most of the old fence and some other burning in the past. I got some back. Necessity invents its mother.

"The few Chembe who had been religious in that way stopped coming to church when the organ broke. They had all gotten yellow gowns and loved to sing the ritual. Then the broken organ disappeared too. They think that was the Mountain people, although that is unlikely. What would they do with it?

"After a slow torture of memorandums and decrees, the state finally took over the school completely. That is when your agency built the first part of the new fence.

"Sister Savonarola went home where, we heard, she had died. We also heard that she left the church, too but we don't believe it. Madame Youngo took over the jazz records and the school, on the day of the nationalisation, and also some furniture from the Priest's house. This had broken Sister's heart. A bird in the hand is not in the bush.

"Madame Youngo had first come back here as an administrator soon after she returned from University. She disagreed with Sister on everything. She wrote reports to the capital. She was married by then and had taken her husband's faith. He spoke at the launching of the nationalised school.

"But even before the end Sister was more and more bitter and moody. She had the girls beaten more often. She drank a bit of whiskey. She would play her instrument in the office. The car broke down and there were no parts to fix it. She had fights with Florence who had moved from the staff compound here, to the Priest's house. Sister moved to the compound. She visited the queen and bought her beer.

"Madame Florence was still teaching "Home and Beauty Skills" at that time. Sister hated this. Madame Florence didn't stop teaching until Sister had left. There was a lot of trouble over that class from some of the parents and husbands. There were quite a few rumours but the Father defended Madame Florence when they complained."

As the Father opened the door he coughed, saying, "Alright there then, no beasties or women. Seems to be a bit of a fire in the village though." Father Buchanan walked into the room to the gramophone. The female voice was lamenting. He deftly lifted the heavy arm and placed it on its rest. He turned a knob in an array on the front. All rotation ceased. Voices could be heard from behind the middle door for a second. There was a woman's raucous laugh, then the voices ceased. One of the dusty beams from the window momentarily flashed bright red on a stone in one of the display cases against the long wall behind. This startled Hank and Jules who both looked about. Father Buchanan returned to his sofa. He poured himself a tea in the silence and took up a piece of cake.

"Tell me son, how do you like our little country? How's the old Aid game these days?" growled Father Buchanan.

"Well sir," said Hank, "I do like this place despite the problems. It isn't my first posting or my first love but I really like the people here. I know some people are not fond of the place and consider it a hardship posting but I really find it interesting. It is remarkable how people keep going no matter what. And, of course, there is a fascinating mix of culture. A sort of melting pot, really, as the old saying goes. Study in contrasts.

"As for Aid, I must say that this gets a bit more difficult every year. Sometimes it is hard to see what we are really doing here but I suppose we have to have self doubt to keep a bit sharp. But sometimes we get a bit disappointed like when we lower a water table or introduce a crop without a market. I often end up doing things which have nothing to do with Aid at all."

"Quite!" said the Priest. "The old study in contrasts. History repeating itself. Doomed to reoccur and all that. Bit of the inexact science in a melting pot. Melting away as they all mess about, I say. No one appreciates it though. Or places like this. Don't know here is even here, really. Could boil over at any time the old melting pot. No one knows. Not newsworthy. Different world really. Bit of fun though. Better than selling arms or drugs," added the Father. "Now let's get to your witches. Serious stuff. I suppose Youngo has you investigating the stabbing. You are to be a neutral voice and so on. A hired innocent. A good thing too. But she certainly tries to keep her bottom clean."

"I am not sure what I will be investigating, Father. I am supposed to see some girls in her office. It has just been sorting out a fire so far. I negotiated the compensation. There has been nothing about witches. However, whatever it is I will do it. I must make sure the project continues and Jack is alright, although I must say, the way the politics are going we may have to wind some things down. I feel as though I am a kind of Alice. I've been sort of drawn in. I really have to get back to my office, too. We are having an assessment there. Quite a few meetings."

"Quite! Reassess. Wind down the old nation building. They don't want it anyway. Have their own ways." The Priest put down his tea cup. "It was still hot. Quite hot and very sweet thanks be. Good! Now let us talk about the witches. This must be what Youngo has in mind for you.

"In my day witchcraft was against the school rules. We would not tolerate it. One bit of a hint of witchcraft and you were out. Now though, old Youngo says it doesn't exist and so the whole thing has been relaxed. This is really not the time for that. Almost the rains. Beginning of term.

"Every term some women come to the school early before school starts. They are allowed to sleep in the hostels. So some of these women noticed that locks of their hair have been cut in the night. Then, there are things in their porridge. They see someone stealing their footprints after they go outside to the toilet. They report it to the guard to tell staff but nothing happens.

"Then three of the women go to Youngo in a group. They go right to her house in the compound. The little watchman lets them through. She is sitting under her roof on her veranda near her water tank. She is drinking a bottle of beer and she is wrapped in a fluffy towel. No head tie, no hair extensions. I think she may have a bit of a bald spot. Her housemaid is clipping her toenails. A tall girl walks right up to her and says 'Madame there are witches and you do nothing!'

"Naturally Youngo screams at them and flies up slapping them all on their faces like a drummer. The towel flies off. They run like mice before the cat out of the staff compound and back to their hostel. Madame arrives at the hostel with the old sergeant and his cane and his stool about half an hour later. She is gowned and sparkling. She has them all beaten bare bummed.

"She says to each one as they lie over the stool: 'You do this from tribalism and envy. God will punish you. You are saboteurs and provocative. Gold diggers. Predators. You make the nation ashamed. You are as wicked as a pot of snakes. You are ugly girls.' Naturally I hear about this as one of the girls is among the dozen who come every week with permission to service and to confess. I am their Father. I went to see Youngo and spoke to her about an investigation as a more professional way of handling the problem than beatings. This would clear the air. Establish if there was witchcraft and settle everyone's nerves. See who is doing what.

"I suggested Youngo get a foreigner to do it. Not me or Jack as we were involved. Usually since the nationalisation Youngo would wish to beat me out of her office. She is a bitter thing. She would never listen to a thing I said. But this is a bit of an awkward incident now, as the women were saying that the little Chembe girl was the witch. Youngo has to take that seriously and handle it carefully or the flames will dance. Are you following this Hank?

"Right after that the fire took place. Then next day they found poor Chastity in the morning stabbed through the heart, in her bed, with a plain bone knife. Her eyes were open and her hands were clasped around the handle. All the blood had dried."

The middle door at the end of the room opened. Madame Florence came through with an armload of pressed white sheets. She went into the door on the left and closed it softly. Each of the men took a cake from the tray which was now emptied.

"Chastity was the sister of the tall girl who bearded Youngo. The girls to the right and left of her bed had heard nothing. One of those girls was that same sister. The guards had seen nothing. There were no footprints near the hole in the fence beyond the Hostel. Nor by any of the holes in the fence.

"Chastity's father and two uncles came for the body. They brought their religious man. Her intended husband was with them. But they only arrived three days after the death as her village is in the river valley, quite a distance. They had only heard about what had happened two days after the death although this was a reasonable delay to expect, I thought, because although Youngo had sent a message the same day as the body was found, her messenger went by the minibus and it broke down. The family were of a different mind. They didn't believe about the breakdown. Strange deaths must have strange explanations here. The family told the Chembe chief that the body had been interfered with. Some parts were missing. Perhaps it had been in a ceremony.

"The body had been kept in the cooler in the co-operative in the village. The cooler does not get very cold and the administrator had only the plastic packaging the village grinder came in to wrap the body in. This plastic did not go all the way around so he added some blankets. One blanket was decorated with some geometric designs. This caused a lot of confusion.

"The family took the body away in their own village administrator's pick-up. The father and intended husband together with the religious man were in the back with the body on a mattress. The uncles and mother were in front. The local Chembe police had a roadblock that day outside the village towards the Bechembe town. It was right by the Mama Wuta, the green stagnant perennial pool, made by the road construction crew that everyone says is haunted by a drowned child. The police stopped the truck there and were very rude. They made all of them get down. They pointed their guns at them and asked for papers. Anyway, it's said they tried to remove the blankets. The religious man shouted at them. Perhaps the police wanted money. The family went away very angry.

"The soldiers patrolled the road up to the gate to the school the next day in their armoured car. The police all had to stay in their little office behind the co-op. The soldiers went back and forth slowly all day between the school and the village. The car crew was replaced every few hours by fresh soldiers brought in a jeep from the barracks in the Bechembe town. They are from a southern unit, the ones who are nicknamed "Kill and Go". I held a service here in the church but only three girls came. Two days later you arrived for the opening ceremony."

"Madame Youngo had sent me a letter complaining about Jack." Hank turned to Jules. "Jules you knew about this? Of course you did. And Jack too!"

"Just so," said the priest. "I know about that letter, but never mind that now. I will tell you what Chastity told me. That's the main thing you need to know.

"It seems the anxiety had been going on all week. The staff and the women were returning to the school in dribs and drabs. Each day some new woman or a staff member would arrive at the gate in the minivan with their chest or case and the guard or some small boy would carry the luggage to the hostel or the staff quarters. There were new faces in the food hall every morning. At night the boyfriends would come to the holes in the fence for last good-byes or to give gifts. They take the bus to the town and come out at night in taxis. The taxis park in the village and the drivers drink beer.

"The boyfriends walk up the path or go through the fields to the fence. Some are married men. Some officials can be seen. Once in a while there is a brother or house guard sent up to spy. They bump into each other in the night in the fields or by the fence. They bribe the guard. It's called the love run. Happens this time of year. Messengers appear also from home villages with packages of food. The night is filled with whistles and movement. The hostels are hot but still the women hang their extra sheets between the beds on the clotheslines that stretch from wall to wall. This is for privacy and to open their presents. Bit of inferno those hostels, especially at night. I leave it to your imagination. There's lots of whispering and scurrying. Unfamiliar faces.

"It is a strange place for the new women and the new women seem strange to the veterans. There were also more than the usual lights and fires on the mountain at night those days, as I remember. And of course some of the animals and reptiles use the school grounds at night as a way to migrate up to the mountain. Streams of them. The little rodents of all types and some of the worms too. You have to be careful as you walk around.

THE BUSH

"The day before the fire, there was a flight of thousands of heavy moths like small birds which flew from the forest around the church and down over the fence into the schoolyard, just as the women were going from the hostels to the food hall for breakfast. They flew all around the women. Quite a few women had arrived by then and there were a lot of screams and batting about. Some of them picked up small stones and dirt and hurled it. Some ran back to the hostels and some into the food hall. I heard this all myself even up here and it brought me out of my door to see what was going on. I think a few moths actually knocked off some head ties. May have gotten into some hair.

"The moths turned left in a body and swept around the food hall and into the trees beyond the back fence. It looked like someone was shaking an old curtain of lint. They sounded like dried leaves in the wind. When they settled up in the forest they hung from the crowns of tall trees like snow. Next day they were gone, of course.

"That morning in the food hall an unusual thing occurred after they all had gotten their food from the pots and settled down. Chastity was sitting beside her sister, silently eating her porridge, still trembling, I wouldn't wonder, from the moths; all the prayers by Madame Youngo had finished when one of the staff stood up abruptly from his place at the staff table at the head of the hall. He stood stiffly until those scattered in the hall became completely silent. It was so unusual."

Madame Florence came out of the left hand door and went back through the middle. She carried a bundle of greyish sheets and a pair of black shoes. The men watched her in silence. When the door closed the father continued.

""There is no truth to the rumours about myself and Hope," he said. "None of you should say any more about these. You should seek the truth only from facts and not conspire. I know who you gossips are." He then sat without eating. The room was frozen. Chastity said he looked as though he was asleep or stunned. She said he had spoken as though he were drunk. Hope, of course, is Chastity's sister.

"Then all faces turned to Hope. Hope rose to her feet and fled the hall followed by Chastity. They returned to the hostel where some small girls were on their beds crying. Probably because of the moths." The priest coughed but only dryly and continued.

"Chastity's and Hope's beds were side by side. Hope flung herself on the bed and wept. She said that the gossip behind everything was the little Chembe day student. She said it was jealousy and rejection. Hope knew the word would get back to her family. She was promised to a customs official, a cousin, who was from her tribe. She made Chastity promise to tell no one or, at least, to tell no one the truth. The cousin was a vicious man. He'd been in the army before he joined the customs. Hope said she had seen the little Chembe girl talking with a lizard on a classroom wall. She had seen her at night creeping behind the fence, on the mountain side. Even though the little thing slept in a house in the forest, in fact was the only girl who didn't sleep in the dormitory hostels, Hope had seen her in the night at the end of her bed.

"Chastity told me that she had seen the Chembe girl roasting strange meat with the gate guard on his fire. Not baby monkey or any ordinary bush meat but something that smelled sweet. She was sure that the Chembe had been in Madame Youngo's office telling her about when the Christian girls went into the village to the beer parlour after service. Hope had been sweeping in the square when that happened.

"She said that birds flew to the Chembe girl when she ate alone behind the classroom. A mule deer had called to her from the fence. But that was not all. When Hope had been back in her village she had been taking clothing to wash by the river in the evening or for some other reason. She had to pass the bad bush by the river where her tribeswomen used to throw the twins. She saw the Chembe girl flying in the clouds."

"The signature of God is in all things," said Jules. A lizard chattered outside. "Not in his words but in our deeds."

"Thank you Jules, you listened in church!

"Hope told Chastity that she did not know the staff man at all. She had never even made a smile for him. The man the Chembe was after, and was jealous about, was another man. They talked all day on the bed. The next day Chastity was dead.

"I believe you are probably to interview Hope and then the Chembe girl today. There has been all sorts of talk at the school and in the village. There needs to be a report. Of course the Bechembe are involved. The staff teacher who confessed is confined to his house. He is of the other faith. The local religious man has visited him there. The staff man is from a tribe who live beyond the Bechembe. Quite a tall man. The religious man spoke yesterday in the market square against harlots and prostitutes and enemy faiths. You won't speak to the staff member of course. He may have been taken away by now. Anyway, all sorts of talk. There will be quite a few people here tomorrow for the dancing. It could be a bit tense." A rising giggling laugh came from behind the central door at the end of the room. The clock clicked and ticked in the chocolate gloom.

"Well that's all I know. Chastity was very upset when she spoke to me. She was a good girl, a woman really, looking forward to her marriage and teaching. She was a bright and literary girl. She acted like an angel in the play Jack put on about Salome. I used to speak to her sister and to her after every service. Delightful girls. They came back here to the house. Sometimes they danced to my records. Jules would know I was a kind of guardian to them, as I have been to others. A friend really, more than a Father. They needed the support as they are so few in Youngo's place like that. They are meant for a larger world.

"She liked music. She loved fun. She was very upset that so many of the other girls were changing their faith. She thought it was only to get husbands and because they couldn't wear the foreign fashions. She was contemptuous of the ones who had changed from her village. She said they were from ignorant families who shot at the moon during eclipses to stop it being eaten or who burned down hotels at the end of religious festivals. There were often quarrels between the women in the hostel at night.

"I must say that she did come back here once after drinking in the village. I cleaned her up before she went through the fence. She was not an angel. There was a complaint made to me next morning by an Elder that someone had vomited in the village well. There may have been some of the staff there, too, at the time. But classes had not started yet and she was very ashamed when I saw her. She asked forgiveness. These are young women and they are passionate with life. They spend the school break as free birds in their towns and villages and then have to adjust, in a few days, to the Youngo regime with its rules and cossets. I blame Youngo really. It is a horrible killing, killed like an animal. That poor girl. Her poor family." He leaned back into his sofa, his nostrils twitching.

"The proof of the pudding is in the baking; life goes on and on no matter what," said Jules.

"Thank you very much Father," said Hank. "This is all very helpful and illuminating. But my oh my! What am I supposed to do with it? I did need some filling in and I thank you. It is a surprise though. But all I can do, you must admit, is listen. I can't take sides. I don't know anything about this kind of thing. I'll go down to the girls and listen to them make some sort of report, I suppose. I can't get too involved because I am from the agency.

"I don't know what else Madame Youngo wants really. I guess it is the look of the thing. A show of objectivity. But I am sure the rest is a police matter really, or traditional thing, or if some people don't trust the police then some part of the government should get involved. I'll just note what the women say. Everyone will know the foreign man spoke to them and that is that. I think I'll limit the discharge of my responsibility that way.

"The main thing is to make sure mine and Jack's project is O.K and everyone knows it is. Also, I've agreed to stay and judge the dancing tomorrow in the village. I'll be the honoured guest. Jules says it is a big occasion every year for decades.

"But we really must go now, Father. It is getting quite dark and you know the night comes suddenly. If we can borrow a flashlight I would be quite grateful."

The Father was thanked for the tea and cake. Greetings were extended to Madame Florence beyond her door. The Father left for a moment through the left door and returned with a large flashlight. He tested it. He told Hank to leave it for Madame Youngo as it was hers anyway. Jules and Hank parted from him on the white stoned path. They circled the church in the gloom. A weak orange light streaked the sky on scattered clouds radiating from behind the mountain. The bottom of the gully was in shadow. The school compound was a cluster of black boxes.

There was a white, yellow and red glow at the edge of the village from which black smoke extended towards the far mountains in a slanting arc. Along the fence in the distance the gateman's fire sparked. The grasses were a grey waving carpet on the plain. Things scurried, puffed and squeaked on both sides of the path and beyond the fence as the two walked swiftly along its length.

"There is wind in the sky from behind the mountain," said Jules. "It is sent by the rains, they are waking."

They greeted the watchman and turned down the path to the school square. Lantern light flickered in some of the staff houses. A bright lemon light shone in the largest one nearest the square and in the main office. The office light cast long pale rectangles onto the sand. A generator was humming. Three small black figures ran from the office against the light along the veranda. They hopped down and disappeared behind a classroom. Jules and Hank both then ducked down at a whirring sound of a cloud of tiny black bats high above.

"Is there still fruit on the mountain?" said Hank.

"They are looking for the cows," said Jules. "The cows will have ropes of dried blood at their necks in the morning."

"I read that some tribes used to believe that the night bats are souls of the dead. Is that so, Jules?"

"No; for us it is usually the moths."

Nearing the office they could see Jack seated behind the desk on the tall backed chair. A tall woman in the school uniform sat in the other. She had a sheaf of yellow foolscap on her lap. The other tall backed chair had been brought into the room from the veranda. It was against the far wall facing the windows on the square. The fan was rotating at its slowest speed. A mosquito coil was burning in its little plate on the desk as the bitter smell of it extended to the square. The woman and Jack both rose as Jules and Hank entered.

"May I present Miss Hope, Mister Hank," said Jules. "Miss Hope, this is Mister Hank who is the chief of Mister Jack. He has come all the way from the capital to talk to you which is why Madame Youngo was pleased you did not go with your family. It was for her sake and for that of Mister Jack. We are pleased you stayed. We are deeply sorry for the poor dead one.

"Mister Hank is here to ask you about the events lately. Madame Youngo said I should tell you to answer him honestly for the sake of God and the Governor and your dear dead sister, who is, we are sure, with God right now whole and restored." The woman curtsied slightly to Hank, looking downward to the floor. Jules motioned Hank into the empty tall backed chair. Jack sat down and then Jules sat noisily in the empty armchair. The woman remained standing. Jules nodded to Hank.

"She is good in English, Mister Hank."

"Please sit down," Hank said to the girl and, as she sat with eyes still cast down, he turned to Jack and said, "What the devil is going on in the village? Did all the girls get back? What was that shooting? Where is Madame Youngo?"

"Madame Youngo has gone to the village with some of the staff. She told me to tell you to carry on. The dog got out the gate and the soldiers shot it. I don't know what the other shooting was. Not all the girls came back. Relax, Hank."

III

I am Hope. You can call me Hope. Hope is my name for all the registrations. But I also have my birth name and my small name for the village. There is also my tribal name and the name I will have when I will say my new faith at my marriage. The secret birth name is from my mother to fool the evil spirit who is envious of the beauty of a child. It is in the language of women from the time we had queens. It means "To die in the quiet of the storm". "Hope" is what my mother and father wanted to give me, as a gift, and is their feeling for me. I am writing this for Mister Jack. It is a gift to him. I write on the paper my father bought me.

My nickname is "Storyteller". It was mine as a small girl. My sister, Chastity, was given the name "Mangoes" but that was when she went to school. She is my twin. I had that name too. When she was small Chastity was "Knife". She was then thin and bony like me. When I marry I will have the name of a wife of the Prophet and Redeemer and so will Chastity.

Chastity is my holy twin. She is gifted to me by fate. She is my dearest womb friend. I will be forever true to her. Because she is so much to me I can write her story for the world to see her true character despite all her temptations and all the gossip. I hope my story can be a poem, a song, a movie. It will be like the novels read by Mister Jack about family and love. This will show all how we women are and how we suffer. We suffer more than Oliver Twist or King Lear or Madame Heathcliffe or our great nation and Governor suffer which things we learn of in school. I will show that Chastity is a clever tall girl and proud. She is the tree of fruit of her father and grandfather, of her mother and grandmother.

I am writing this novel book also for my teacher Mister Jack. It is his present. He said to write a holiday story so I would not forget. By doing so I know shall praise him. His language is pure as the purest of tongues and his skin is as soft as this paper. He knows all the foreigners but he is their tallest and smartest. Some are as pigs but he is as a king. He is visited by new vehicles. He will return to his land of green hills and strong music and the best markets. He should take this with him to his country. It is a land of constant water where many get rich as my mother's brother's wife's cousin on the other side of my family. I long to see it. Although some say she is a witch. My mother says she is a doctor.

I want him to know of our ways and to love us and I want to show him he has taught me well. Also he must know how we are, for none of us is what we seem. Mister Jack teaches me Methodology about teaching aids for lessons, theatre arts and English. He teaches us the sentence. It is like a magic. He is fixing our school. We all love him. He is our master and lord. Our duty is to please him. He has explained to us how to teach the making of a novel book and about journals. He has taught us about plays and writing in the voices of others. He says my sister and I are remarkable and smart. When I told him after that class that I will go to the hostel and write a novel book he marvelled. He said it is not what he intended but more. But, why not? Our lives are like the great stories. It is then what I am doing on this the very paper my father bought me.

The first man to call Chastity friend, ally and pal was John. She gave him her permission. He said that he loved her and that her eyes killed. He told her that the hair on her smooth body magnets all boys around her. She was cream and butter. Chastity did not heed him on this type of word. She knew it was hard to know what boys mean and she would not be confused. She sang her own song to herself that God would send her suitor and she would hope in God.

Piccolo and John would walk to the primary school with Chastity and me. We were still small enough to have to carry our sitting stones on our heads and our piece of sugar canes in a hidden plastic. Piccolo would call my sister lovely and his ally too. But John would say that she was not Piccolo's wife, or even practice wife and that Piccolo should go away or he would give him a heavy blow. Men are as jealous as women.

My sister told them that they should shut their marathon talk. They were wasting their time as only God knows her true suitor.

Piccolo always had money in his pocket from his father's coat. He said that if Chastity would befriend him he would give her the money.

Chastity said that she was finished with small, silly boys since a long time in her heart. She danced on the road and sang that she did not care for those who need her love. The head of Piccolo was down in shame. John laughed at him. Piccolo was a soft and funny boy. He died with a fever.

John then said to Chastity that she had a bad behaviour. He said to Piccolo that he should forgive Chastity because she was young. But later I know he agreed with Piccolo for a plan to share her. This was even before our breasts and menses had arrived. John is now in the customs.

John asked me what kind of girl my sister is to refuse to befriend a good looking boy like Piccolo. Later I know that the boys went to the bush doctor with Piccolo's money to get medicine to rub on Chastity's body to make her follow them. On the way to the doctor the toe of John hit on a stone and began to bleed. He said to his friend Piccolo not to look and that the blood was like water on a mountain. Piccolo said to his friend that this is a great pity and is the result of beauty which is a magic. There are terrible things the result of beauty.

They entered the small house of the doctor. This house was near the bad bush and the swamp. It always frightened us all. The doctor sat on her bed with her beer in hand. He said he knew their mind of their coming. She told them that the highest man in the city of the high comes to her for treatments. This man had many wives but no power. She had given the man useless medicines as he was wicked. She told the village men the location of his house. She told them they were small boys. She took the money and gave them only beer.

When we were in the last days of school Chastity and I went to the homes of our aunts and their society sisters. They gave us new pens. We had on our dresses bought from the town and they praised us and stroked us. It was the first dress where I did not share the cloth. I said I wouldn't and so did Chastity. It was a special day for each only.

The aunts made prophecies based on the stories of our girlhood. Mine was of the time I chased a red goat who had entered our field *after the ewes. The one for Chastity was of the time she found the dried bone of the monkey. This is how we are. We women live lives of great secrecy. We have mysteries and trickery. But when we see certain things they are a fate and there is nothing you can do. You are a woman. If you see a cow dancing in the morning sun you will marry the one that burns in your heart. If you see a green eyed lizard you will die by the hand of a jealous person.*

Then we went to the centre of town for the examinations. All the world was there. We sat on the cement sides of the trench from the clinic to the river. Our feet were in the water. There were lines of us boys and girls along the trench. We sisters were the ones who looked the best. We were so smart, as smart as southerners. We had watched all of the programs on beauty. We knew the fashions of foreigners. Our family had the most electrical things bought by our father from the traders from across the border or from gifts our uncles, especially the youngest one.

The teachers walked behind us all leaning over every one in their turn. They helped us to open the blue packages in plastic from the ministry. They helped us to read the instructions. They patted our heads. There was the favourite of Chastity and the fat headmaster. I liked the same favourite, a serious one who had studied in the town. The headmaster was too familiar. We spread open the packages on our knees to write in the blanks. The inspectors from town all sat in their chairs under the market tree. They were to ensure the customs of the examination. The village fathers approached them one by one. They talked to them one by one softly and gave bottles of beer.

Chastity and I were the biggest girls there. We wrote gracefully with knees together. Our hair was plaited in swirls. We had white ribbons. Chastity hummed and sang but did never cry out at the questions like the others. We were sugar and sweet cakes to all. We were the sunny memories of the examination day. The other girls had envy. Our aunties had pride and threw out their bosoms. They called out to us as we wrote and praised us using our small and big names. They no longer used the just small nouns of our language to praise us. It was another sacred day of becoming women. Our value was increased by many animals. They were thinking the secret praise names that cannot be uttered aloud but are kept to call heaven.

The rural fathers had come the night before with their burning torches from the hills and the farms. We saw the lights on the road. Now they stood further, behind the teachers, away from the tree at the edges of the market. They stood in silence staring at their rough sons and daughters with their tongues between their teeth. They had eyes for us town sisters too. The village women ululated when a teacher stopped in their pacing to help their own child. We had the confidence. My favourite helped me.

Our aunt had said that morning to Chastity and I that you are now women and to come and place our hands on her bosoms. Your ears are mine today, she said, as I am your aunt and mother. She told us to not let any man ruin us as the family have paid for us to pass the common examinations with the suffering of their hands and backs. They wished us to go to the teacher school. She warned that many men are roaming about searching for women but not to marry them but to ruin them. She said she was our sister and mother and that we are delivered of her sister who had no abortion. She said to watch for devils as they seem beautiful but have no souls, only wicked spells. She told us not to do witchcraft on men in case it bounces onto others. She knew that God shall guard us. We also must be smart.

She told us to remember the vulture eats between his meals and that is why he is so well fed. She taught us a secret and useful song. My aunt warned that an education makes us both smart and stupid, better and ill, especially when we eat new things. My aunt did not go to school. Her sister had but had been shameless and my uncles did not speak of her or where she disappeared to.

The parents escorted us home after examinations to our feast. As we ate my sister said to father that she was frightened because John wished to marry her. She thought John would force her and bring a shame. She had dreamed of rags in the bad bush. She wanted father to pray to God and tell her uncles. Piccolo had told me of a potion John had but I had not yet told Chastity, as I had sworn not to. A fate is individual and everything is fate.

THE BUSH 55

Father said that it was funny to hear a small girl tell a joke. Things would not go like that. He had purchased the mathematical equipment for school already. He had purchased the compass and the foolscap. In a week they would take the bus to the school and the admissions officer. He can register us both as one. There will be no marriage except that arranged and only when Chastity was finished schooling. There will be a proper bride price. The world was becoming newer. He said we are a new family for the nation. This is how my father spoke. My sister thanked my father. I do not think John had respect but my sister kept her shame.

The admission officer was dressed in white and sat on the veranda of the school. He feasted his eyes on the beautiful flowers that had come there. He was a beautiful hairy man, fat and smelling sweet. He told us not to hide our faces. He handed each of us a paper to write on. Our fathers made a line to pay him the admission and the paper fee. Some of the girls paid it themselves and some did not have to. This man became our teacher for mathematics and a favourite of Chastity's. This is the man who kissed my sister one year later. It was behind a classroom. It made the flesh and body of my sister shake. She ran from him saying that she had to go to class. In class the test was "girl is to woman as boy is to blank". My sister cried there and was later beaten for class disturbance.

The man gave her a piece of paper one day. It was answers for a test. Another day he put money into her hand as she walked across the school square. I saw it very clearly. I told her that I thought the man loved her and that she was not to be too shy. We were guests in his school. I told her that she should thank him for his kindness. He was as good a choice as any. One day that teacher gave me sweets and a fruit.

We were always tested. The teacher would say one day what a word was and test us the next. Like "humanitarian": Was it an ape, a poison fruit, a person who does not want others to suffer? We discussed this. I told my sister that her teacher was a humanitarian. My sister did not agree. She said she needed only little help for tests and knew the names of capitals and presidents. She wanted to go to foreign places. This was not true; she did not know all these things.

Chastity, even when she was helped with answers and grades remained stubborn. She was still with her shyness and rudeness. She used to sing her song that God was good and that if you follow his way he would do a favour. She sang so the teacher would hear her. I told her she should cook some of our food for the teacher on our own hostel fire. She must love him for the simple reason that he loved her. This is our way. I knew she could be as happy and fat as a new baby born. She was still a young girl and frightened of being active. This made her haughty and proud. She was frightened of being under pregnancy.

Then there came a day which was in the dry season. We had not seen the wet for a month. Our throats were paper and our clothes were dusty. The soap dried on our elbows as we bathed from pails. Chastity was always coughing. We all were coughing that day as flights of thick grasshoppers had settled one after another on the school fields. They rubbed their legs and vibrated in the dust but made no sound. We had to sweep paths through them as they died. There were many whirlwinds in the dust outside the fence. Some were very tall and carried sticks. They spoke coldness and temptation. We saw the mathematics teacher behind a classroom with a small girl. They were ankle deep in insects. I asked my sister how she expected to achieve her ambition with a mind so stubborn and selfish, creating want but giving nothing. Did she see what had happened? Another was taking from her tree. She did not see it even then. She said she could take from other trees.

Two years later a foreign man came to the school to teach the older girls to be teachers. He looked like our picture of the explorer of the Antarctic. We marvelled when we saw him. I determined to take him from his wife but we never saw her. I would write the wife a secret note to kill her heart and sign it "Mangoes!" I would walk before her in my new town dress to freeze her body. When I told Chastity she pinched my arm and told me to remember my aunt and the family.

THE BUSH

My sister and I studied hard and we became more of women. We laughed at the small girls. We saw our menses every month. We each had our small girls for our washing and plaiting our hair. There was no jealousy or gossiping left in the hostel against us because of our heavy blows and the tongue of Chastity which was like a cow skin whip wet with water.

We received news from home of our intendeds. The families had been active and our market had increased. Chastity cried the tears of the bride all night. None of the other boys or men from our home came to our fence with presents any longer. There were only our little cousins, the messengers from our uncles. We felt the cold winds from the mountain more because of our new sizes and shapes. The cotton uniforms were tight and thin on us. We were now allowed to leave school for the church each week and, after that, the village. We talked to the Priest about ways of the world. We gave thanks to God as we passed every examination. Chastity stood as a tower and tree in every school assembly. I stood by her. We will be teachers.

We returned to our homes for the last holiday before our last year. My mother told us of one of our village girls who went to a school in the capital who was so clever that she needed only three years of school instead of four. The other girls had poisoned her. Another had been caught on "press your stomach day". She had completely disappeared. Many people in the village had begun to think that school was for wickedness and that their next daughters would stay at home or go to religious school in the village no matter what the country needed. One little girl was kept by a farmer always in the house but she fell pregnant too. People say it is to a lizard. Tragedy happens to the beautiful and young. Some say we are in a time of evil spirits, envy and gathering of abominations.

My mother told us to follow her advice, no matter how bitter, because we were the most precious. She told us we must not knock our feet on life. She warned us of false men who would not help a woman or respect her with big dowries. Such men did not care about divorce and kept trying week after week for the return of Bride Price even if it was nothing. She told us that a man who cared not for cows was *impotent.* She made us swear on her bosoms to be smart in the school in all ways, in the ways of our village. She told me not to use the words I was learning in my mind. She said we must ask the priest every week for advice as now was the most dangerous time for women. She wished us to live the life we deserve after school and not have to squat down and urinate in the fields. She would go to the doctor to get us bags of charms to protect us. She had already brought a drink which tasted like excreta. Chastity gulped it down but I spit it out and mother cried. We told mother everything about our school.

Mother said there were two things. There are those that you say are and show like the flashing of eyes in the sun; but those are the things that bring danger and death. There are the other things which must be only done in shadow as a bush cat does. These are the things that bring life. These things were for the hidden world and not to be in this. We were crossing these back and forth. She feared for us.

She said that there are things that frighten us and the things that we really do. The things that frighten us are just comical. They are silly when you really look at them. Not all things though, some are terrible, she was talking of those things that frighten us only.

If we really see them they are much less than what they are or how we imagine them in the other places. People, said mother, are the same way. The people we see as gods are just comical in masks but others around us are as terrible as a strange forest. These things have gotten too much power and they confuse us. That is because they are like us.

She said that as a girl she was frightened of killing the rats that came into the house to take the fruit. She was frightened of pregnancy and of her father. Look at her now, the main things of life were easy. It was easy to kill, it was easy to birth and her father and ours were as babies. This sounds different in our own language but I thought it was good advice. You must do what you must without fear no matter how frightful it seems.

My mother wept and wept all that night and said she sent us to school years ago like baby cows still shining in placenta and we now had returned like witches in storms who wanted all the electrical things that few had, that we sang evil foreign songs and begged father *for coloured shoes. We corrected our father and mocked him as he watched football on his new television.*

She sent us to our aunts to learn the tricks with cow's blood. She asked many questions about the staff especially about the tall foreigner. We all called him Tall Jack or the Little Lizard. Chastity, mother and I then laughed close to wetting at the names we called him.

We went to the funeral of my uncle who had died on a burnt train. Many relatives were angry. Our intended's parents talked in the night with ours. We thought it was Chembe. John came to see Chastity but she would not see him. The foreigner came on a motorbike to visit our house because Chastity had said to him where it was. He said he was stopping by on his way to the capital. My uncle stopped him on the road and took him to the house of the administrator who is also an uncle. This senior uncle said to the foreigner that no one had married outside of our tribe from the time of Adam. The foreigner returned home without seeing me but he left a box of sweets which I enjoyed.

He saw Chastity standing in our gold dress and head tie by the river. She was under the tree by the bad bush. It was just dusk but he had not turned on his lights in the sunset as he went slowly down the mud path from our village to the main road. I saw this from the window of the room I shared with Chastity. It was like a picture or a play.

Chastity and I still went to the same church in the village as each other despite her friendship with the priest at school and the new faith we were studying. We went back to the church in the break. But Chastity giggled at the words of the local pastor against sin especially when he said them in the foreign language. It was a mouth of dirty rags. John looked at her in the church as she giggled and then she shuddered.

She had a new song, too, which said that she would give always to God but if she had nothing she would still give her heart. She said that God was big and infinite and that it could not be held: for a woman to understand and love God it must be through a small world as a man, then the big world was hers. This is the philosophy she learned in school from our teacher. I knew she had heard it from him. She spoke like this in beauty as she sang but she cannot write novel books. It is left to me to preserve the secrets of our lives.

The bus to school was crowded and our boxes got dusty on the roof. When we reached back to the school many women had returned before us. Some teachers had returned too, especially Mister Jack. His motorcycle was before his door. Only his houseboy was home though. I wanted to give him most of this, my novel book, which I had written in our holiday. I also had made him a band of our beads for his wrist. But we had much to do so Chastity would not let me. I decided to write it more in the night as I had candles and then give it in the first morning.

We had carried our boxes with help from small girls and left them in the hostel by our beds. Then we bathed in the pails helping each other and changed to the uniforms made even tighter some because of our eating at home. We went out to the village market to buy our scents from over the border and sweets in plastic bags for the term. We could go out without permission as the school had not started.

In the village they call us toads and monkeys again as we entered the market because we dress better than they do and walk taller. It was worse than ever. From the religion of my intended a man was preaching in front of the coffee place in the market against the new sins and diseases. He was dressed in white and he had a young incomplete beard.

They also call us parrots because of our own language and how we talk to one another as we walk. They laugh at the pomade on our feet and our big radios. They say we walk like the princess prostitute of a foreign place or like someone naked as a snake on a stage as a foreign singer is. They are a stupid people and not social. The market women accuse us of harlotism with others husbands from their stalls of powders and toothpastes. Even the scent woman with her hairy arms and dirty head tie. Some show their elbows at us or wiggle their feet and bottoms from across the square.

THE BUSH

When we stopped at the beer parlour, as we did before the holiday, to talk to the taxi drivers there were shouting small boys outside but more of them than before. We put our chins up and did not show teeth. We are women now and strong and, besides, the parlour is filled with good people from our area who drive the minivans and the taxis. We enter where we please.

The men inside send news of us to our home. They are the friends of our intendeds. Our men shout at the shoeless boys who abuse us. The boys shout at the beer parlour. It is the snorting of the village pigs. When I marry I will cover myself and show no shape. My children will be tall and clean skinned and they will beat these boys and their useless brothers without work or wife, sitting all day shaded in the coffee place looking at all who pass in the heat. They are like the white thin dogs in the cemetery always in a pack but always also alone, always hungry and snarling but running when stoned. The nighttime's friends of the dead.

Their market sometimes has in it dwarfs from the mountain. Sometimes these wear skins and carry the heads of bush meat in large leaves which drip on the ground. They smell like wet maize husks and squeak as they talk like bats do. I know the villagers are marrying them. It is why they are fat and small while Chastity and I are like thick reeds.

The villagers think our tribe people are friends of the nomads who killed their small boys in the grass. But the boys were skulking there thinking of trying to steal their cows. They think that we take the fruit from their fields and have burned it afterwards. Why would we do that? What kind of people are these?

We have a woman from the local area in the school. Her head is like a pumpkin and she is as small as the dwarfs. She is always smiling in her fat little face and shows her teeth to all. Her eyes are actually blue but not like a foreign person. The lids come over them top and bottom. She smiles as blank as a test question as Chastity says. We cannot understand what she says when she talks and we do not know her age. She wanders from one class to the next. We think she has put a spell on the Headmistress and on some teachers.

THE BUSH

This little woman is probably twice our age. She was in the school when we came and the older girls then and she was there when they came. Her dress is too long and her blouse too big except where her stomach peeps through. She has the husk smell. She smells of the bush food she eats. She washes in potions. Once, when Chastity pushed her over, we could see her underwear and they were the kind that a boy has. She carries her shoes in her hands. They are plastic and ripped. But usually she is barefoot. I do not understand what she sings about. Her singing is like insects. When we pinched her she did not cry but only tightened her eyes and lips and sang. She hunched her head into her shoulders like an angry animal. How can anyone like her? But some do.

After classes, before she goes to wherever her home is through the gate, she sometimes goes to the office of the Madame. Sometimes you do not see her for days. She carries messages from Madame to the village. In the evening she brings plates of food and other things from the village through the gate to staff quarters. She has even taken things to the house of Mister Jack. On Sunday, she stands outside the church in the ferns. She steps like a bush cat in the rain, buttocks high and wobbling. She is always staring at Chastity and me. She often followed Chastity or me so we could do nothing around the corners. She should not be allowed in the school which is for learning and not for a politics for animals.

We left the village without fear and with dignity. We returned to the school full grown. There was one year to go in our loneliness and hunger but Chastity still would sing and dance on the road as we returned from the village with our sweets. And she did again with a new song for the future and to remember. I could never sing like Chastity.

She sang that she went down on one knee voluntarily before her heavenly love. Then she would curtsy on one knee. She was a bride going to join her groom. It was a lovely song and dance. It was sugar and spice. And on the way through the school gates she added to me, in a sisterly mockery, that she never, had never, done this song before, not even with the primary school Headmaster who disgraced himself *or the friend of my father who drank or John. Of course, I thought, that this was beauty, joy and magic and I was happy for her, my sister who had found what we all long for. I know how to feel the same way. She did not utter a name of her love but I knew. It was our happiest moment.*

The little cat thing stood at the gate with her hands on her hips and at her feet was a green lizard on a string the kind with the red crown and the tongue of blue foam on a string. She was cooking with her friend the gatekeeper. The lizard snapped his tongue. The eyes were evil and staring. The gatesman stared too as he tended his cooking fire which danced sparks into the sky. This is the climax of our holiday story.

I felt a tremor and a clutch at my stomach. I thought that fate would never let any peace of man be ours. We twins are the sisters of tragedy and our suffering follows every joy. We cannot escape our fate. We are killed like baby dogs in our tradition at birth. Envy pursues us like sin so there is never to be peace for us. Death is our suitor. We are bound to the destiny of each other. Two where one soul should be. Who will care for us? Who will avenge us? Who will find the secrets? Who will seek out the evil-doers? Why are we betrayed by fate and men?

Mister Jack this is my holiday story. I hope it brings you knowledge and joy as you have for us.

Jack, Jules and Hank walked talking together from the office. Hank was carrying Madame Youngo's flashlight, the one that he had gotten from the priest. The beam dashed back and forth across the ground from Hank's feet to the buildings, up to the trees and sometimes flashed behind to the nearest slope on the mountain. They had turned out the light in the office before leaving so the sandy square was now dark and shining in deep blue light, black at the sides by the buildings. The houseboy at Madame Youngo's quarters or the gateman was expected to turn off the generator connection when one or the other saw that the lights were out. The little Chembe girl darted across the square onto the dark and the beam followed her for a moment.

Hope had left much earlier. Hank carried the rolled-up foolscap pages she had given him as she had departed.

Stars and the swollen moon were bright overhead, each in their own section of sky, in the cooler night. The moon was reduced and erased, at times, behind spy black clouds, solid or in nests of wisps, streaking across the sky. There were four short figures on the path to the gate and another skipped in the direction of the left side fence. The household helps, the small boys and girls, the foreigners thought, were probably on their way home.

Jules would escort the foreigners to the staff house of Jack where the houseboy had probably made the bed up on instructions from Madame Youngo. A meal of fried eggplants, rice and roasted cow meat was expected to be waiting in candle light.

Hank was saying how the girls, each in turn, had said very little that was useful or factual, and that in fact he could not even remember very much of what the small girl had said at all. Hope on her part had only repeated the witch accusations they all knew about already and defended her sister Chastity in elaborate, subjective, often religious terms. The story to her must have to be fantastic given the circumstances and her closeness to it. On questioning, Hope had not given any new information nor had offered concrete evidence beyond the incident of the talking lizard, about which fact she had sounded quite indignant, certain she was not mistaken. She actually had sounded rehearsed really. Hope sometimes was hard to hear as she mumbled, perhaps frightened, going on, though often repetitively, staring constantly at the floor. She would not speak up and pouted when asked questions by Hank. She looked up at Hank once, seeming to be about to weep, when he asked the question about the mood of Chastity that day after the confession by the staff member at breakfast. She had spoken up about that. Hope had said Chastity had been full of anger, shame and pride. She was not guilty at all. This thought Hank was the way sisters were with each other. Hank wondered why, in fact,

Hope had not gone with her family with the body of her sister. She had said her duty was here.

The Chembe girl had swung her tiny round, wrinkled and shiny face from Hank to Jack whole time while staring, often blankly, sometimes open eyed with those strange purplish pupils, sometimes half lidded. She gave off a strange musky smell. There seemed not much there to learn. She had looked at Jules often, with a curious expression, sometimes warmly and sometimes as though she did not know him. When she glanced at Hank it was often blinking at his words as through a mist. Jack had asked no questions of her as he had not of Hope.

The small Chembe girl had maintained an odd thin, wide toothy smile constantly, through which a dark tongue tip sometimes showed, and she seemed to have said, or sighed, or nodded that she knew or had seen basically nothing and that she had no views on Hope, nor on Chastity, nor on the events at the school. She had seemed to answer eagerly but simply. There had not been too much really to ask her.

Her feet had moved back and forth in an arc swinging above the floor while she had sat perched on the edge of the leather looking chair glancing from one foreign man to the other. It was quite hypnotising in the frustration of her answers. Hank thought that there would not be much in all of this for his report but at least the school and the project had taken responsible investigative action of their own, as they must, and now it was over to the authorities. He would do his best when he wrote it up. He would do so from memory as he always thought notes were useless in circumstances like this. You needed to remember the context. He would also report to headquarters on the whole thing as part of his security report. The agency had seventy placements in the country as part of its various programs and every project had one peculiar circumstance or another. This was another. It was all to be expected especially the way things were now. Everything was getting a bit heated.

There had been an affair with a Bishop, some indiscreet social dealings with the rebels in other regions as well as two explosions, one very serious with diluted cooking gas, causing bodily harm and nearly causing a medical evacuation. Hank hated to phone parents and loved ones to tell them that someone had been killed and that they had told him they wanted to be buried in country. It was a hard part of the job. The evacuation of bodies was always so complicated with so many forms and tin boxes and so on.

As they turned towards the staff compound beyond the square they could hear a far off, momentarily pulsing kind of chanted singing in the direction of the village. Perhaps some dancers had arrived for the dancing tomorrow. Candlelight flickered in two of the buildings in the compound. There were no lights on the mountain. Suddenly a long low figure slid through the flashlight beam. It could not be made out by the foreigners whether it had legs or not but it moved very quickly. The three stopped briefly and then resumed their walk, but at a slower pace.

Jack began to talk on the theories of evolution he had read in the library. Jules had read some of the same. They discussed them as they walked. There had been some half dozen phases of evolution, in fact, distinct and unique times where the entire makeup of plants and animals had been different from that in each of the other phases. This was probably because there had been a "burn-off" or a "kill-off" between each phase. A periodic absolute big kill-off when all plant and animal life had been obliterated by some catastrophe or as part of natural development.

In between some few survivors, perhaps only one, maybe a worm, a mold or even some cell, perhaps sheltered underground in some basic place, in a cave or maybe in a surface puddle, had begun to evolve again in the new circumstances without anything alive to challenge it. It would have gone mad with life and specializations, enthusiastic and prolific so that it could develop all at once to fly in the air, whisk over the stones and swim in the sea. Some versions of itself would fight other versions and breed with them and perhaps eat them and this would create more kinds of things until you had millions of types and differences.

These would become completely distinct but have a kind of similar style and linkage and a common theme for that phase, like the dinosaurs and the ferns or all the fish and corals and they would so have naturally some common colours, shades, sounds and ways of moving. They would stay related, perhaps be able to interbreed, but end up being mutually competitive and hostile.

Jules thought that one reason for the catastrophes could be that there were too many things and too many types and too many differences so that the things trying to live together could not do it any more, they could not cope and were overwhelmed and there would be a big collapse perhaps when they all got stirred up by a comet hitting or because some species started being abominable. They would all atrophy and explode inwards. Breeding madly to no end and encouraging each other's madness.

After Hank asked, Jules and Jack spoke about the species in the area. The most common thing was as Jules explained the Chembe tree on the Mountain. This was thought locally to be a descendant of the piece of tree the Chembe had brought to the area with them. The tree bore brown and purple edible fruit. When the broad leaves fell they could be used for roofing as could the twigs. The old Chembe would wet the bark and pound it for a kind of cloth. If the leaves were boiled with a certain insect it made a gold dye. If they were ground up they were a common medicine which was slightly narcotic.

The tree was common throughout the lower reaches of the Mountain. Many thought it was all really one tree as the roots protruded from the bottom of the trunks and ran along the ground before plunging again into the earth and rising in a new trunk. The tree was usually intertwined with vines but Jules thought this might be still part of it. Sometimes a tree had its roots around it like a fence and within this circle other trees and black thorns grew. These compounds made a protected breeding ground for the baby rat deer, mice and the rat looking lizard. The priest had said once that some of the plants and insects in these bushes could be used for healing serious wounds.

The grey monkeys lived at the top in the vines and branches, Jack added. He had seen them often. They became great tribes of bucks and mothers with the little babies clinging on the back, chattering and flowing back and forth from tree to tree, in and out of the fog on the Mountain like silver rivers. Jack had seen a huge tribe of them by a pool the day he had climbed the Mountain with the Chembe girl. On another day, when he went up with someone else, he had seen what looked to be a big and bluish black cat-like predator in the bush standing at a cave mouth. The eyes shone as the sunlight hit them through ferns. The person he had been with had gotten ill so he was not able to get closer. Jack said he was really drawn to the beauty of predators. He would never forget it.

Jules had begged off at the last minute, the day of the climb with the Chembe girl, as his mother had some errand for him to do. The Priest said he didn't want to go up any more so Jack had climbed only with the Chembe girl who Jules had recommended as a guide. Jack was glad he did as he had looked forward to it for weeks and had packed a knapsack in preparation. He actually spent the night on the Mountain. It was really astonishing how few people had actually been up the Mountain to actually see the pools, the caves and the village that seemed made of tiny hives although everyone thought they knew what was up there but it wasn't actually like any of them had said.

The tree Jules had talked of was, Jack said, actually the same species as the one that you often see standing alone in the plain except that the one in the plain had deep roots that some said could go down miles for water. There was a similar species in the mango swamps on the coast which floated in tangled rafts and was the home for fish and crustaceans. It was always the same sort of tree but it had different forms and dozens or perhaps hundreds of different tribal names from all the tribes in the country. All of these names basically meant "tree".

There were hundreds of local tribal languages and dialects as well as the four regional languages and the two lingua franca. But all these languages had the same two roots, except for Chembe of course. People abroad stupidly thought that they spoke just one thing here and everyone lived in huts but then again they would have no reason to get to know the place as it was really a bush. The world had not yet come here or it had come and gone.

IV

They walked through the internal gate and reached the veranda of Jack's house. Several candles pulsed and glittered within through the Venetian blinds. There were no insects in the striped light thrown out through the window onto the veranda and past the men into the night. The porch had two blue plastic chairs. The men spoke for a few moments and the foreigners said their good-byes to Jules. Jules promised to come by in the morning and escort them to the dancing. He also promised to first call at Madame Youngo's house to receive news of the shooting and of the women before coming to Jack's. Her house, the largest of all the staff quarters, had been dark as they had passed.

Jack and Hank went into the house without closing the metal door behind them. The door had metal bar brackets on the inside and a bar stood against the near wall but Jack left this unengaged. A small boy in Khaki with a tea towel in his hand stood in the far end of the candle lit room behind a bare oblong wood table set for two at its narrow ends. The table also had two metal pots in its centre. One steamed in the brown light from the bursting bubbles from the surface of a yellow and green substance. It smelled slightly rancid. The other gave off an aroma of fruity meat and onions. Jack thanked the boy who then left the room through a side door without a word. Jack then barred the door behind him after he had been stared out into the night along the bars of light. The night glimpsed through the door was darker, colder and unusually silent.

Hank and Jack moved to the table, immediately sat down, and took up utensils. Hank studied his knife before wiping it on his military style jacket. Jack got up again and went out of the light and then the room. He returned with two brown bottles of beer. He drank from his as he set the other by Hank's plate with his left hand. He then returned to his seat, drank and spoke.

"There hasn't been electricity since the troubles started. I heard in the beer parlour the other day from one of those crew guys doing the survey on the other side of the mountain that the lines are cut beyond the Bechembe town. The old generator in the town doesn't work any more so the company was asked to repair it. They could not.

"It reminded him of the time they were working on the road here just after the war. They'd built several staff houses which are now the co-op and the police station. The administrator is in one too. They built these near to the big football field they made with their bulldozer. It had been the site of a church. They played a team of peacekeepers there. It's a general common ground now. Their houses, at the time, were equipped with ceiling fans and dozens of lights along the walls. It was really all senior staff issue but nothing ever came on or worked properly. No electricity or no parts no matter what you have. Typical of this place. It's a laugh isn't it Hank?

"Then one New Year they had set up gas lights and streamers and were having a party with the nurses from the peacekeeper's camp. And then patow! Just at midnight the generator started going in the town. It was a surprise organised by the new Governor to celebrate the new order.

"The crew guys had attached the streamers and balloons on the ceiling fans. Some were wound around hanging survey chains from the fans. These took off, spinning in the sudden glare of all the wall lights, slashing at the dancers and breaking bottles. The cords and the balloons first wrapped themselves around everyone and next some broke off, flying, and knocked over a gaslight which set fire to the sofa. Good thing they were nurses don't you think Hank?" Jack laughed. Hank stared across the candles and pots. He did not smile.

"Yes. Very interesting. Very lucky. Now, about the situation here.

"Jack, I want to see immediately your inventory of the supplies for the school refurbishment program and your accounts right away," continued Hank. "I need to make new proposals to Madame Youngo in the morning. I'll review the whole project here. I'll write my report tonight. We'll review it again with staff at my offices.

"We will leave right after the dancing for the capital. You should pack a bag tonight. We should reach the river crossing by tomorrow night for the last boat. I have to pick up another placement in the Bechembe town, the woman; I think you remember her. This will take no time though.

"What is on the foolscap I wonder?" Jack asked.

"I haven't looked," said Hank.

Jack walked over to a desk near the door. He fished a sheaf of papers from the top left drawer. He explained to Hank that this was the latest inventory of the school's refurbishment stores taken during the break. He had done it with Jules. He placed it on the desk. He said there were quite a bit of building supplies left.

There were two bedrooms. Jack went into his and was soon snoring. Hank stayed in the main room. After a while he walked over to the desk from the dining table. He sat and read the inventory. It was exactly as Jack described it. It had a column for each of goods received, costs, goods used and goods remaining by a serial number system. The goods received always equalled those used and those remaining. Hank found in the drawers two candles to write by. Those on the table still burned as well.

Hank's portable was locked into his vehicle behind the office but he would transfer the report to it in the morning. Jack had given him a ballpoint and some foolscap from a bottom drawer in the desk before retiring. Hank still had some of the beer. The dining table had not been cleared and the rancid smell lingered.

The report was just underway when the pen stopped writing in a scoured dry pit in the paper. Hank got up and went back to the dining table at the far wall. He bumped in the bad light into a hitherto unseen sofa against the side wall. Hank had placed the flashlight on the table beside his plate.

Hank glanced upward at the tiny stationary ceiling fan suspended like a bat in the upper dark. His footsteps and bump against the sofa and the candles had been the only recent sounds. He returned to the desk and, using the flashlight, began to search the drawers for another pen. There was one in the bottom right drawer. It rolled on top of a pile of standard foolscap every two or three pages of which were stapled together. In the flashlight beam he read the first paragraph of the top leaf. It was a letter or perhaps the rough copy of a letter. Since it was about security he took it up after he took out the pen. There was a sigh in the night, a gust of wind against a remote building. He switched off the flashlight and placed the foolscap on the desk.

This will be a long letter. There is not much to do here during the break; all of the students and staff are gone so I mostly read and write. Besides, I use my letters to you to express my excitement, confess my weaknesses and practice my art.

I plan to climb the mountain tomorrow for something to do and have asked the priest and one teacher, who is local, to go with me. I will tempt you now by telling you that I will write to you on everything I discover.

The motorbike I bought is running well; my houseboy maintains it and I have tried some excursions on it. One was planned to a village near the river beyond the regional capital. I missed the chance to visit some of the home villages of students last time as the machine acted up. Another was around our mountain on the road to the border. This was to prepare for the climb as I meant to descend a new way. These were really adventures.

The security situation is getting worse. Even our local village has a dozen or so young men who have returned from abroad. They are nicknamed 'The Foreigners'. Of course, there is no work for them here so they linger in the market or drink coffee at the little shop. They dress plainly and deport themselves with great gravitas but they try to pierce me with their eyes as I go by to the beer parlour or as I ride through the village on my bike. They are now the zealots and prophets of the tribe.

My friend, the local teacher, brought me a book to read on their faith. It really is similar to the sort of thing we studied in University. It is in fact a kind of invocation through prayer but the prayer can be anything as well as the official designated kind. It can be dance or chant or a simple act. The prayer redeems. The prayer requires an ascending repetition of actions or related images. It is practised in different ways by different sects. But, in common, it is designed to dissolve the boundaries of self so the imminence can be remembered through cleansed senses. In common as well is that the witness, reader, watcher or participant must participate and react with faith and imagination to a projection of those same things whether it is for good or evil. It is simply fate. It is the preordained transfer of souls.

The word for their faith occurs in the Holy Book. Several times and when translated properly it usually means something like "remember". Some of the editions of the Holy Book are annotated a great deal. We have several in our library here. Some notes call the notion corrupt and that the true divinity is not to be called up and pleased in this way but rather only seen as small things and messages in every detail of creation. The divinity is found in the normal and ordinary like cooking or love making. One footnote I read says that this and several concepts are not understandable even in a holy rage but is simply what the faithful relate. I wish I had studied this in school.

Remember that you fooled in school with the memory systems of Flood and Bruno. That was in theatre class when you were doing the paper on reconstructing scenery and stage directions or was it landscapes from old fragments? You were such a pill. Anyway, I wonder why the whole thing would not call up something that wasn't god or devil but was rather something like the spirit of my bike.

This monster was the biggest thing available in the town. It had pipes of silver and growled with the voice of God. I've had the seat covered in black and white cow skin. I have got a number plate with some of the Holy Script on it. The machine has become necessary as

THE BUSH

well as useful to get away from this tense place and see the network of roads that connects this bush to the other entire bush around here. There are old roads and paths used as shortcuts as decisive as time travel behind and around the new roads and towns. These roads are a horror of mud in the rainy season but right now they are like airport runways through the tubes of green bush. Sometimes the bridges are gone though, or are standing alone in a dry riverbed as their ends have been washed away in some previous year's flood. At some times the sand actually flows in the river beds where the slope is sharp.

I've heard that one year a van full of students was going across a river bed nearby under a bridge when a wall of water swept them away. The rains had begun suddenly in the mountains. They say the local haunted pool turned blue in pleasure that day and called to the river to flood the plains and share the deaths. I love this place. All superstition and signs.

So, on to my adventures. Another couple of stories of the exotic. I left the other day early, still in the dark, just as the houseboy arrived. I was slightly feverish, you catch things all the time here, it is part of living, you can't help it, and the only alternative is to live in a box. But I was excited. I love to court the unknown.

The school was in the exaggerated dark blue shadows in moonlight cast by the mountain. The bike started with a roar and the houseboy called out to me "Lord of the Dawn!" There were fires burning on the far parkland against the mountains. These wound in long thin lines, extending miles, the kind of fires that leap over riverbeds and burn around the towns. When the rains come they can quench these fires in an instant as they blow into the fires curtains of rain picked up from the sea and rivers, and from the mountains waving arms of moisture in great fronts from the border. But in the weeks between rains the circles of lightning that halo around the edges of the mountains at night start new ones. It takes the plain a long time to get wet. It needs a flood.

I stopped in the nearby village for coffee as the sun rose and sat on my bike to drink it after it was brought out by a small boy. Farmers on their way to the fields stopped and chatted. The Foreigners had not yet arisen even for morning prayers.

In the first light a vulture was slowly circling in the still air. It is really a season of contradiction because there can be sudden dust devils dozens of feet high sweeping across the plains like the angry, powerful creatures in the Book who reluctantly share the world with men. Or there can be sudden mysterious deathly dry line squalls that seem to rise from the earth and flatten every brown stalk in their path for a mile or so and then disappear back into the stillness. At times at this time of year you can see great trailing clouds of insects overflying our plain high up in the clear sky creating huge running shadows across the earth below.

Our plain is wide but in its expanse are hundreds, thousands, of small low compounds of one or two huts, some thorn bush fences and a bit of dusty garden. They are the same colour as the soil and invisible except at dusk when there are pinpricks of cooking fires, like children of the wildfires. There are some smaller villages than ours which are along the new roads connected to electricity, which infrequently, and on not too many nights flicker like reflected stars or memories of home on the dark plain.

I raced that day out of the village, roaring past the huts and the few houses with the Mountain off to my left and the plain on the right in the gathering heat. Small girls and boys were scurrying everywhere carrying big pots or pieces of paper. Some, on their way to the school, carried stones on their heads. I crossed the dried rivers coming down from the Mountain and flashed through the intervening parkland. Grasscutters and reptiles scrambled from the road where they were sunning themselves as I sped towards them. It is a long way around the Mountain and around its many arms into the plain, to the border and the other side.

I roared up the side of one gully beside a floorless concrete bridge into a thick black cloud on the other side, spreading ahead in the wind from a fire burning across the plain to the side of the road. I had accelerated through this wall of smoke beside the fire when two huge white moths, the size of sparrows, seemed to fall from a great height, *one onto my forehead the other into the headlight which then shattered. I was stunned and rocked back on the bike. There was blood in my eyes. I braked swerving to a stop on the side of the road away from the fire and nearest the Mountain. I sat mesmerized. The fire raged behind and along the road. The moth bodies smouldered.*

On the blackened plain beyond and behind the near wall of flame there were several near perfect circles of flame left behind, perhaps where there had been a bush or small tree. My back wheel began to smoke and my lungs burned.

I am, like you, from a background from which I have acquired all sorts of minor skills in thought and language. I can cope very well with these. I also have haunted depths of character unravelled in ordinary discourse like anyone. I am professionally a worker for good.

I have minor skills that in this place are considered extremely desirable and worthy by some, even magical, or, alternatively, especially diabolical by others but are, let's face it, banal and mechanical as a science. I exercise these skills passably well. They are nothing special really in respect of character or soul or learning. They are mechanically invoked when dealing with social events and threats and problems or when teaching, or as you must do I suppose, in an imaginary court room or assembly.

They are modern, minor, common skills used in household and family management, job seeking or in presentations for sales, and in entertaining strangers, in choosing appliances, in leading small groups or even in courtship. Here, they are extraordinary or at least a necessary exercise of power.

I have a strong ego that can bend to circumstances but which is confident in taking risks. It is based on a simple self-belief taught to me by home and school with its complimentary acting and manipulative toolbox. It is an ego built on the foundation of that of any child of our class and country. It is usually all hidden and reticent and polite.

I believe that unlike my toys I will not break dirty nor become unwanted by the world or by my loved ones. I believe I have a right to be here to be gratified and to prevail no matter what.

So I am an important, unique and ordained individual from a unique, successful and ordained society. I am a receptacle of superior experience and the creation of a rational god, one who favours me and those like me. I hold in me all the required information and all the paraphernalia and clutter of culture and required know-how, all the wise common peer opinion from home and public service which is necessary for good governance, modernity and all-round developing life. I believe all this passionately and I feel secretly superior in that belief in any circumstance and, above all, that I deserve to pursue happiness and gain respect endlessly. I feel no guilt.

So given all this and despite it I felt stupid sitting there to have had died, died in a small fire in a scraggily bush, battered to death by arbitrary moths.

This adventure may not have made me any smarter or advance my development but it made me turn back to the school. It meant that I never saw the other side of the Mountain. Perhaps, like Roland with his church, I was going round it the wrong way.

I wiped my forehead with my sleeve and turned back towards the village accelerating down the road piercing billowing walls of smoke, grey, black, sparking and swirling on both sides now as the fire had jumped the road. I rode head down while wiping blood from my eyes with one hand, steering with the other. I tipped the machine at speed down the side of the gully below the smoke and under the orphaned bridge and then up the other side, helping the machine to climb with my feet. The predator was now pursuing.

On the other side of the gully, I found myself in the midst of a herd of humped white horned cattle turning up the road away from the plain and the fire and extending down the road towards my village. They bellowed into the roar and crackle of flames. Oh my! Things never end here.

Where had they come from? From the gully which the fire had now leapt over too? They snorted and screamed and spat strings of thick saliva as I threaded between them. There were great white slabs and ripples of ribs on both sides. Some bony, rasping legs brushed my feet. I passed thick swinging tails and shit encrusted assholes. There was a sweet fetid smell from gaping mouths with protruding pink tongues. Single red eyes focussed on me to the left and to the right. I ducked under swinging and once under crashing, clashing horns. I was tight to the handlebars. Was it one animal or many? Then I cleared the leaders. There, suddenly as so often happens here, everything got better and beautiful. The sun shone from a blue sky onto a far-off village and a green mountain slope.

In front beyond the chaos behind me the sky was endlessly high and empty. The plain shimmered into the distance around small stands of bush, anthills and small castles of igneous rock. There were two isolated trees buzzing with weavers. The Mountain on my left was blue and misty as I sped along.

I was back before lunch. My houseboy cleaned the cut over my eye and put on it some healing stuff he got from a local woman. The headlight is still broken, but it never worked properly and the nights are so clear and starry that if you are riding then you don't need it.

Which brings me to my other adventure. I remember you saying to me over a beer that life was basically shit. You said the woman I would marry probably was with some greasy hoodlum hot rod driver at that moment. You said that she probably had a twelve year old mind and was destined to be the mistress of a dictator. You were pretty insecure about those things. You hated my pretensions and you were right. You said I would never find God.

Well, I climbed on my bike one day recently to visit my divine beloved. You were wrong. To really love a country you must do it through the love of a woman renouncing your own birthright and parentage. Or you must renounce your entire culture, morality and self and live for the life you see before you, no matter how dangerous a choice that is. You must posses the heat and the wet, the wind and the land. You must do it absolutely, like a storm possesses the sky or like the old pioneers in the bush, far from the faith but near god and devil, far from the hearth but near to the fire.

I set off again in the dark as the stalking Lord of the Dawn, an orphan before God.

Who knows what is the heart of a creature that goes off into the night? Who is pleased to watch it and laughs when the tombs of your family crack in the dark or the graves of your Holy men are turned over scattering their pathetic contents? Who has had their soul ripped from their body by an angel and thrown into the sky like winnowed grain?

The heaven was a dome with pathways of stars mirroring rivers under the earth. The stars sang in silence of wide spaces not yet seen, spaces to shrink the little creatures clinging below as they danced and whirled around.

A fragile thing made of a drop of blood, an accidental sperm and a bit of skin creeping out to recreate its brittle backbone and pink head in the wet swamps and puddles left from last year's rain.

The soul can be read by the night. It was reading mine as I mounted my bike in what turned out to be a pre-malarial euphoria to visit, on invitation, written on a piece of torn foolscap and thrust into my hand by a small boy in the market. It was from my secret love.

I know I should have consulted my two local friends in their fairy home on the edge of the forest or even the priest in his little museum nestling in the spot picked by the ancient missionaries to be under a constant, cooling, forgiving, sin obscuring cloud. Perhaps I should have written a letter to headquarters to ask the policy.

The bike growled to life. Perhaps I should ask the tense young men in simple white cloths who drink coffee in the market and disapprove of everything and plan its destruction. But I did not.

The ghosts of departed teachers and aid workers rose before me. There were nuns and the dedicated contracted pedagogues of all faiths from everywhere, from continents and the islands, from Holy Capitals and the enemy. All with handfuls of lace and plates of cakes burnt from antique appliances.

"Where else could we go? What else could we do?" They cried. Behind them were terrified ghosts of graduates on assignment, healers from the south in ties, wearers of pork pie hats, chequered pants and straight partings, some with tiny arrows in their breasts, some playing trombone. They all hissed "education for all" and "civilisa-

tion" or "development" to rows of hell's alumni who lamented in a chorus of second wives, disgraced pregnant first-formers, wild eyed in confusion, weeping, begging with outstretched arms for a bit of money for fees or sweets or a ticket overseas. Behind, small men with whips dressed in shins and also others with drums and pipes that were wreathed around wrist and ankle with snakes chirped "bride price" and "polygamy". There were dancers in veils both transparent and thick black. Two tall women were with them, jealous skeletons rattling, twisting and fighting in a single golden dress. There was an old child holding a red bride in the storm, rain and fire, kissing her and ripping off her wet veils. There was a gift of love to my love. They chanted "The world is the novel of the devil!"

There were small suited entrepreneurs with handfuls of unmarketable asparagus. Some carried dead and diseased chickens, empty beer crates and gutted radios. There were many toothed, large and round politicians in versions of traditional and religious dress with revolvers and flywhisks leaping up and down approaching me smiling in a line pushing around waxen faced soldiers, unarmed but wearing feathered berets and carrying shovels and bumpy squirming bags. There were aid officials with the soldiers who had handfuls of lined forms and brown plastic binders entitled "exploitation" and "output" in burning letters who were dressed in beige tailored clothes waddling, sweating, clench kneed and constipated. Behind this line was a towering black civet cat, round faced whose eyes were stars, whose body was black fire and cold rain and I heard a low voice that said that the thing that will hurt the most when the sentence is read will be the innocence of the accused. I nearly fell off my bike and never left.

I told you so. This was the beginning of my returning fever, the merciful harbinger and warning, and I must say I know it is hard to understand for those who have never had it. It is why I have been so long in writing to you as it usually lasts for days. I am quite passive when it hits. I think it may be accelerated by something in the food. It is quite normal here.

The man with the whip was really there though. He was from the mountain and looking for a goat that had gone through the fence. My houseboy went for help after I was safely in bed and the bike under lock and key in the school library where I store it. My friend, a local teacher, went later to check that this had been done and get me a book. The bike was safe. This was the second adventure. I plan more. The Mountain tomorrow and trips to the villages.

The fever outset with shivers and hallucinations lasts for barely a day and if you know what is happening you can control it and get on with life. It gives an odd detachment and speeding energy which has its powers. It is always followed by a sweating shaking and relative supine calm of several feverish days before the real outset of twelve hour dreams of terror or a kind of sleepwalking. The regular cures do not work any more.

It will be time soon again for a few days in bed. I have gotten quite used to the cycle. There is first a week of herbs, I also get an additional local remedy which is a bottle of native gin with a worm in it, I say that can't hurt, and then I enjoy lots of interesting delirium before, red-eyed and silent, I am ready to face the world again and resume my sins. The delirium is often as interesting as dreams but only as long as you remain still. Once I wandered about the buildings here at night cursing and had to be brought home by one of the women.

So on that morning, as I remember, I dismounted carefully from my bike and wobbled back to my bed. My forehead itched from the previous wound. I must have looked fairly robust though because my houseboy stayed to help. If I were going to die he would have disappeared.

It is a shame that you decided to stay at home in your dreary career. We could use you here in the project. The things you studied you would find useful here. There is a lot more past them to learn and experience in this bushy troubled place. There are opportunities for self discovery. Next letter I will tell you of my trip up the Mountain.

Hank folded these leaves of foolscap in half. He placed them on the inventory pages which he also had folded. He then took from his back pocket the other pages he had received from Hope. He read these. He then folded them as well and placed them on the desk, on top of the pages from the drawer and the inventory. After that he took up his flashlight and returned to the bottom drawer. He trolled through the other pages there, scanning them in the flashlight, finally taking up two pieces of three stapled pages from within the stack. He folded these as well and added these to his pile on the desk. Hank then returned to his report with the fresh pen he had found. When he finished writing he placed the pen back in the drawer and added the report to the pile.

Hank took up his pile of papers, blew out all the candles in the room and, lighting the flashlight again, led himself by the beam into his room but only after flashing it about the walls to locate the door and distinguish it from Jack's through which Jack still snored lightly. In his room Hank removed his jacket and folded it over the papers. He placed the jacket, papers within, on the plastic chair in the room. He then lay down on the single bed, turned out the flashlight he had placed there before removing his jacket, and went to sleep.

Hank was awakened by a persistent knocking at the door. Grey pink light streamed in his window. He got up from the bed, took the papers from the jacket and tucked them into his belt. He then buttoned the jacket over them. It was dancing day.

After the door was unbarred and opened by Hank the houseboy entered without a word. He cleared the table, making single piles, first of all the dishes and then another of the pots, into which he placed the cutlery. He stacked the piles dishes bottom-most and placed this tower on his head, steadying it with one hand. With his other hand he picked up the bottle from the table and the other from the desk by placing a finger in the mouth of each. He took everything into a kitchen adjoining the main room through the door of which Hank could see a bucket standing on another smaller table. He placed his entire burden into the bucket with several small splashes, first the bottles, then the plates and dishes. He took a rag from the table, cut a piece from a large bar of yellow soap that he took from under his shirt with a machete he had tucked into his waistband, and began to wash.

Hank sat at the table and reviewed his agenda in his mind. First he would go and open his vehicle, get his portable, put the papers from the drawer into the glove compartment, lock it, then return to the house with the portable and make his report from the handwritten version. He would then take this report, the inventory and the flashlight to the house of Madame Youngo, give them to her and tell her good-bye. He would retain a copy of the report for himself. He would then meet Jack and Jules back at the house, return to the vehicle with the portable and drive with them to the dancing which would be in the cleared area outside the village. He would play his role in judging the dancing. This last chore would really require no extra thought, work or worry as he had already delivered his report and bid Madame adieu.

She could decide herself, taking the report into account, what to do about the settlement for the shrines and about the murder if that was what it was. She had already said she would let the matter about Jack drop. Although of course Hank himself could not do this and still do his duty.

After the judging he would say good-bye to the Elders and to Jules and, with Jack, depart for the Bechembe town. There he would pick up his other troubled possibly disgraced staff member and then drive with her and Jules to the ferry crossing. After crossing they would get rooms for three in a small hotel on the other bank for the night if one was open. The next day should get them all to the capital in time for an afternoon meeting. At the meeting he would assign a staff member to get the plane tickets back to headquarters and out of the country.

There was another knock at the door. Hank opened it. Jack emerged at the knock at the same time behind Hank from his bedroom door, dressed only in underwear and scratching his head. At the door were Jules and with him was the small Chembe woman in baggy school uniform but barefoot. She was smiling broadly. Her toenails were painted an astonishing electric pink.

"There is news!" said Jules.

Jules carried two buckets of water. The small woman had a dull metal bowl in a cloth in her hands. It was filled with yellow beans and chunks of meet in bluish brown gravy. It was steaming in the cool air. It smelled of a peppery cinnamon. Jules put down the pails he was carrying. They had leaves floating in them which also were scented with a kind of mushroom sweetness. At the same time the Chembe girl walked around Hank to place her bowl on the table.

The houseboy, who had come to the door of the kitchen, saw this and turned back into the kitchen to bring out two plates. He put these on the table. Jules had taken out a small clay pipe and packed it with black leaves from a pouch he carried in his back pocket. He lit it with a safety match from a box kept in the pouch. He left the door open and walked to the sofa and sat. The Chembe girl sat on the chair of the desk and swung her legs. Jack went back into his room.

The houseboy after putting down the plates came to the door, picked up the two pails and took them back to the kitchen. Jules was drawing on his pipe, smoking in a cloud of burnt flowers and molasses.

"Madame Youngo is not here," he said to Hank, "and there are some problems with the dancing.

"Her boy said that the Governor had sent a car for Madame Youngo to take her to their other house in the Bechembe town. The governor was going to overnight in Bechembe town in that house or in his house in the grounds of the barracks after rushing up with his people from the capital. He had sent the car ahead escorted with a military four wheel drive.

"It seems that the health ministry man had flown to the capital from Bechembe town in the Governor's plane right after the soldiers shot his dog in the marketplace. The bullets had just missed the girls that the dog was chasing and the health man who was chasing the dog. The health man must have fled so luxuriously to report the trouble to the Governor with the help of Bechembe officials at the airport. The beer parlour was burned in the village too. We are not sure why yet. Some other things may have happened that we do not yet know about.

"It has been fairly peaceful overnight though and the houseboy at Madame Youngo's thinks everything is over except that vans of dancers have been arriving since last evening. They have been shouting for the beer parlour. Some others came to the school fence and then went away. The stilt walkers even went around the market. There is another armoured car arrived too. The local police are confined to quarters. But they will have to let them out for the dancing.

"This means you will have to be the master of ceremonies alone to open the dancing. There is no-one else who would be able to do it. There has to be foreigners there, if only for the formal part. This is the new propriety. We very much like the formality and protocol. We like everything in its place. It calms things and gives a modern image. I go, of course, too as I am a local dignitary. I'll guide you through everything.

"Madame Youngo left word that she would be arriving with the Governor and his people at midday in their convoy. That will be the time to start closing the official part down. I brought water for you and Jack to bathe in. There is some breakfast too."

Jack emerged again from the bedroom dressed in a towel. He walked into the kitchen. The Chembe girl jumped down from her chair and followed him there. Jules settled back further into the sofa. He continued speaking to Hank while he smoked. The bowl of the pipe glowed red and grey smoke rose straight up into the stationary ceiling fan.

"We should walk there though because it could be that your vehicle might not be safe. One of the taxis burned when the beer parlour did. It was a yellow one from over the border. There are several girls still missing but it is thought they went home to their villages with some of the other drivers. The armoured car escorted some vans to the main road early on. That was when the beer parlour burned. Some of the drivers were left behind. No-one knows where they are gone; they may have left later.

"It is not a completely terrible thing though because some of those men carry diseases. Some are really from rebel areas belonging to the Redeemer or drive things there. The Bechembe traders use the place and they cause trouble. But it is bad for the village to have trouble now especially with the Redeemer somewhere near. It makes us known. Well, please eat and bathe mister Hank. We have a bit of time." Splashing sounds came from the kitchen. Jules drew more heavily on the pipe and leaned even further back on the sofa. He smiled. "It is a no good that is blown in the ill winds," he said.

"For heaven's sake!" said Hank loudly to Jules with a snorting outtake of heavy breath. "What a mess! When will this nonsense journey to this nonsense place end? I have just about had enough of doing errands in this place for every dog and devil and your Madame Youngo. What does she expect? Am I to fix up all her problems? Why on earth don't they just cancel the dancing?"

"You can't cancel the dancing," called Jack from the kitchen. Jules nodded.

"Well, I want no bath and no breakfast. I am not pleased with this whole situation I must tell you. I just want to get going," said Hank. He spun around and stamped through the open door, turned and said, "I shall just go down to the dancing for a moment, and get things going, judge the silly thing and get out. You go ahead and relax and bath and smoke and eat or whatever. I will meet you lot at the gate in five minutes." He then turned and shouted over his shoulder from the doorframe, "I have to get something from the vehicle. Jack, meet me at the gate and don't forget your bags." Hank said this last phrase tightly but quite loudly while turning his head and flinging himself towards the square, arms pumping, stumbling on a protruding stone.

"Suit yourself," said Jack from the kitchen.

Hank was one of the first two legged animals to go across the compound that morning. It was only an hour after dawn and while it was just heating up some of the night things were still taking cover while the day things were only just beginning their hunts. There was a tintinitus of early crickets in the palms over the rattle of the weaver birds on the tree just outside the school gate. Streams of red ants were forming and reforming as they flowed down the main path between the palms and passing through the gate where beyond the gateman's fire they turned left into the pads of dry scrub moss part of a close lime scale patching the plain.

A small snouted fur ball shuffled and danced towards the back fence, an eater of ants. Behind the fence the morning sun glinted off a group of sets of yellow eyes, silent as in orchestra seats, eaters of fruit or eaters of ant eaters. Somewhere there on the lower reaches of the Mountain olive coloured snakes would be plaiting themselves up vines above the small carpet of ferns which would soon be the roofs of highways for mice, lizards and rats.

Larger rodents, some hairy and some pink and bald, would be squatting in their entrance holes of long rotting fallen trees or perhaps still stirring groggily under the fingers of fallen palm leaves waiting for the vibrations as a caterpillar or worm was driven into the open by sex or underground menace. All the large creatures were in half sleep much higher up the slope in treetops or caves or in the tall reeds by the side of stagnant and trapped pools where schools of tiny fish swirled and turned like flashing mirrors.

In the compound, at the foot of several of the palms bordering the path, and also in front of the front wheel of Hank's vehicle, were a scattering of lone lizards raising and lowering their heads and clinging with their bellies and outstretched suction toes to the cool but warming earth. Here and there a larger insect moved and darted in one direction or another. Short chaos wisping on the ground.

The gravel and earth compound was a gallery. There were stately orange and red spiders hoisted above the pebbles on white haired legs. There were troops and armies of little grey spiders moving like blown fluff. A spotted lime green worm lay partially eaten and drying, tragic and awkward with long snout and yellow spots like eyes.

In the trees beyond the fence there was a morning howl of a monkey followed by a machine gun clatter of another. Hidden birds snapped or creaked their anxieties; others blasted their potential love as sudden explosive shocks into the sky or in rising rainbows of notes in unfinished, questioning progressions. It was the season of males in heat and females mating and killing. The season of birth had ended months before in the hard dust of the dry season.

Hank hid all of his reports in the glove compartment, closed it and the vehicle, and walked swiftly to the school gate. He paused just inside, stood, waited and watched the gateman who was stirring a brown bluish substance into his pot while sitting in the smoke and steam of a small fire contained by a ring of stones. The gateman was wearing a grey blanket over hunched shoulders and sat from time to time on a larger black stone facing the fire and the plain. Today he had a long rifle with rust pitted barrel propped against the fence. A metal cup rested on another small stone beside him. The path outside the gate and the plain was dotted with the motion of figures heading in the distance towards the village. They were the same colour as the plain.

One figure approached noisily along the length of the fence from the direction of the church. Behind him came the round figure of the priest and following him the thin figure of Madame Florence. She wore a broad brimmed hat and struggled along on the stones in heeled red shoes, partially hidden under a flowered umbrella. She was in turn followed by a small boy carrying a woven basket.

The first figure was extraordinary. He wore a wooden horned mask. The horns were like antennae pronged and branched from deeply carved rippled brow and rooted to flaring red nostrils. The crown of the mask was beige leather, beaded in chains of black and red painted bone.

The figure was wrapped around in a netted cloak of woven black vines coated in some shiny gum. It was curtained above this in green and white shells hanging on strings from a ring around its neck of heavy black metal. Its legs, when the cloak flew open with its half leaping walk, were entwined with leather laces from bare lower thighs below a black leather skirt to end in leather sandals also embroidered with beads.

It was carrying an asymmetrical slab over its shoulder of highly polished wood as long as a leg and much wider, stretching a half arm's length from the neck. The top of the slab was encrusted with stones. Some sparkled and flashed in the sun, others were pointed and brown or faceted green. Some of blood red seemed to glow from inner light. There was a strong aroma, too sharp to be scented but burning cold in the nose.

The gateman flung his blanket over his head and did not remove it until the figure had turned towards the village as was some distance along the path. By this time the priest and Florence had reached the gate. The priest greeted Hank loudly.

"Well hello my dear fellow. On your way to the dancing, are you? Hope you have nothing electrical with you. Very bad luck you know. The spirits there won't like it at all. Take nothing modern, very bad form you know." Florence and he had come to a stop, the houseboy behind them. "I've brought some bread and cheese and some wine. You are welcome to share it if you get peckish."

Hank, nodding to Florence, walked through the gate to stand by the priest. "What the devil was that?" he said gesturing at the creature loping down the road away from them. Madame Florence twirled her parasol.

"Precisely!" said the priest. He was breathing heavily and grasped silver beads in his hands which glinted softly in the light. "Probably it thinks the same of you.

"That is the old father mask. He is older than the Elders and because of that it smells as bad as hell. He is carrying the Chembe memory board. Good thing you have no soul it can see or you would have had it sucked through your nostrils and into the board. Very bad luck to see him before the dance if you are Chembe. Everyone will look the other way and he'll go hide in a parked van on the edge of a field until the turn of the Chembe to dance." The Father snorted a kind of laugh and this moved into a few stifled happy chokes. The thick wrinkles at his neck wobbled furiously.

"What is the memory board?" asked Hank.

"Well, that is the soul and the mind of the Chembes, dear man. Bit of an interesting thing. Every stone is an event or a thought in the life of the tribe. The red ones are blood and are the battles. The black ones are the death of queens and the sins of siblings. The green ones are secrets of families, revenge and migrations. There are stones for secrets and stones of grievance. There are stones of blue for painful births. The mask will tell the stones as it flashes them in the sun. The Chembes will dance around.

"It links the stories and the singing by the flashes. This happens every year at this time. It is to break gaps in dying memory and link up the tribe. Renewal and animation. It happens here and all through Chembeland in every village and in every clan. They have smaller boards which they get here from the society of the mask. It happens overseas too. There are Chembes overseas.

"But the main place is here because the queen is here and so is the tree. The board here has all the magic and is the source memory board for everything else. You must remember that all the Chembes gathered dancing around the board would have seen the telling every year, year after year, just before the rains. They will know all the chants with all the flashes. They know from their mothers, grandmothers and their fathers. These are linked to the smells of the grasses they will burn, the foods they have eaten, the pipes the men are smoking, the herbal waters they have bathed in, the drinks and all the other chants and the dancing. This and the circling around for hours and hours."

Hank glanced at his watch. He looked around to the compound. It had now started to become busier. The usual routines were underway. The second day of term. Clusters in school uniforms moved in stately and chattering fashion from the hostel to the food hall. Men in white moved from staff quarters the opposite way in a collision course. Houseboys zipped around in every direction. From house to house they went, through holes in the fence, back and forth to the food hall with small packages. The mountain behind was now silent. Hank was thinking that, for heaven's sake, he had now forgotten the damned flashlight. The priest went on.

"And there will be some new Chembes there today and some others will not be there this year and some will have come back. And some who have always been there going back to Adam. Everyone has their place in the dance and for the board. Each will add to the voices some new familiarities and resonances. They will all chant their lives, selves and suffering into the board. Repeating and repeating in slightly different ways. There may even be some new stones that appear for the events just passed, or for just now, or for the future." The priest paused for a deep breath. He was now waving his arms so that the chained wooden cross rose up and down against the black surplice. Florence stared at this from his side and pursed her lips.

"The stones said last year, by the way, that the Chembes did not really come here from some other place as all had thought.

Showed the whole thing evidently. Quite a shock to some, I hear. An old black secret stone that no-one remembered seeing before flashed and started a chant which connected to bits of the chants of other stones which then caused remembering that the Chembe came from within the Mountain rising up in lightning and then went away to other places driven by fire and flood. Then they came back as they were getting evil and sick in the other places. It said the sickness followed them."

The father paused for a deep wet cough.

"When the linking is all made and all the flashes and lights and colours are done the rains are freed and they will come and this begins the healing of the earth. It consecrates the essential marriage.

"That and the metaphorical death of the previous queen and eating of her heart by the new queen, and the procession into the forest, and the death sentence of the present king. The new queen is really the old queen all along. The other one is chosen to act the new one only for the occasion. We never see her. She is killed somewhere in the preparations. Very remarkable isn't it? No kings for all that, just queens. Although kings come into it. The usual fertility stuff. The cycle of regeneration. You cannot have the king alive if there is going to be rebirth can you? The king here isn't the same person as the chief as you remember Hank. He's a married man. The chief is just part of the government administration. No, the king person is really just for a day. Just a doomed king. Not that day a priest or a chief or a warrior or anything. I guess you have to name the father. The queen's position is quite strange too. She can be a kind of memory board in reverse and mesmerize remembrance from you, obscure the surroundings and all that. This is all taken very seriously. I had a friend here who studied it and of course Jules knows the whole thing.

"I don't usually stay after the first dances which are the short pieces for the judging. No-one visiting does, wouldn't be appropriate. When the old mask comes out it is a Chembe thing only. Everyone else to leave please. I almost stayed once but well, I must keep appearances and so on. My adventurous days are past and the sins of them forgiven. Goes on into the night though. It is a wild thing. Then there is the procession up the Mountain with torches. Not on the burnt shrines side but upward on my side on the main path. We can see this from the church. The torches cast green shadows on the trees in the black. Or so I am told. They make their fires up there on the graves and ashes of other fires going way back. God knows how long. Quite something I suppose. There is talk the government wanted the whole thing stopped. There is unlicensed gin and other things. It is a defiant kind of thing."

"Thank you for that," said Hank. "That was a very nice lecture. Quite useful and informative. I might do a report on it some day. It would be useful for our orientation. Nice to hear some local colour. A very rich tradition and so on. I am happy to hear that I don't have to stay until the end of the thing. Quite a relief." He looked at his watch and glanced back into the compound. Jules and Jack were striding toward them. Jack carried a small suitcase in one hand. There was no sign of the small Chembe girl. Jack's hair was wet and his chequered shirt untucked.

"Damn that suitcase! I'll have to take that back to the vehicle."

"Leave it with the gateman," said the priest. "You can pick it up later."

The arrivals greeted the priest and Florence. Then Jules and the priest exchanged further greetings in Chembe. Jack listened to this attentively but Hank and Florence glanced around silently. The gateman was impassive. The weavers in the nearby tree spun and pecked. At the end of the greetings Jules took the suitcase from Jack and put it at the feet of the gateman. They exchanged not a word.

"Today you must not say that anything is small all day long," said Jules to both Hank and Jack. "Well, let us go."

Jules and the priest ambled ahead on the path chatting and gesturing. They were followed by Jack and Florence. Jack had taken the parasol and was holding it over Florence's head. She giggled repeatedly, at times nervously but at other times with a bright trill. Jack did one or two little dance steps but staggered slightly. Jules turned once or twice to look at them.

Then came the houseboy with his basket. After that came Hank. Far ahead the mask moved speedily away from them towards the village. Jules took out his pipe and pouch from his pocket and he seemed to offer it to the priest who shook his head. He then packed it and lit it as he walked.

The sky was pearl grey but there was no cloud except the one from the mountain which now extended over the plain to the edge of the village. The path from the school met a wider gravel road at right angles to the village entrance. This was the road that eventually met the main road to the Bechembe town. The path went through the village, through the centre of a market and past the low mud walls of compounds, some whitewashed but most light brown and mustard. Inside the compounds behind the walls were one and sometimes two storey houses, most with tin roofs but some thatched. There were sometimes a cluster of trees overhanging the wall. Here and there an unfenced house abutted a wall. Several of these had overhanging tin roofs and wide windows closed in tin shutters, locked at the centre with rusty locks through metal loops.

Past the junction, with the school path standing just off the road between two houses in the village, there was an armoured car. The car was chocolate brown, very wide and flat. From the slightly raised roof through an open hatch protruded the upper torso of a thin faced man in a red feathered beret staring over a mounted machine gun. Below him between narrow slitted windows was another barrel. A white profile of a winged bird clasping the outline of an open eye was painted on the hood over a number. The priest greeted him in a tonal language which was not Chembe. The man waved and then stared back along the road. The priest turned to Hank and said loudly, "That is the latest model. Made at home. It is as fast as blazes."

There was a smell of dust and burnt petrol in the air. The streets in the village and the winding lanes opening to the left and right of the main road were deserted. But in the distance over the roofs could be heard a buzz of many voices low and pervasive.

The market appeared, opening out and stretching on both sides of the road in an irregular rectangle. There were four rows of plastic or reed covered stalls framed on top by rough wood branches. Each stall had either a high zinc table or a low slanted and stepped plywood one. They were all empty.

Narrow paths entered the rectangle from between tightly packed houses on every side. Some were piled with husks, plastic bags and vegetable rubbish. From a few piles protruded bloody bones. Between the two central rows in the market, at the far end, the walkers could see a whitewashed building streaked with black, an open ruined box with a tin collapsed roof and mangles of burnt beams. There were heavy black carboned frames around empty windows in crumpled streaked walls and around the doorway. In front was a burned out automobile, tireless and glassless. The air around was dry and acrid with the smell of burnt diesel, paint, plastic and eggs and also of sweet thick greasy soap and rotten bacon.

They turned right and walked between the stalls past an open well encircled with concrete walls on a concrete pad and then on a wider path through more buildings until suddenly the path opened onto a very large flat field crisscrossed with footpaths. Florence still struggled, her arm around Jack's shoulder. Jack was swaying too. They then all stopped and blinked in the light.

There were grey goal posts at each end of the field separated by a flat light brown expanse. Beyond the far goal posts was a thick, tall tree with a wide snarled crown of twisted branches.

Between the two goal posts, at the far end and under the crossbars, were two rows of blue plastic chairs, some occupied, in a row behind a long table covered in white cloth. On the table was a trophy. A low whining sound, subdued but insistent, rippled over the field and hissed up to the sky. Above the crossbar was suspended a large white banner with red lettering in two languages. It said "Welcome The International Dance Festival".

The field was encircled with hundreds and hundreds of people, perhaps a thousand. More were joining every second, most from behind the tree coming from the plain. The crowd buzzed, vibrated and waved, sat, walked, stood and ran, loped, wove together and split apart and undulated back and forth, three or more deep all around the empty square field.

They seemed held back by an invisible barrier pushing tensely outward from the regular open space but heaved tightly around as a mass entwined, bobbing and slowly circulating the huge rectangle back and forth as one blurred animal. There were limping, stooped over women bare headed in traditional dresses of red and black. There were round men in grey and black tunics. There were people walking in both directions passing awkwardly with baskets on their heads. There were women veiled in black from head to foot with panels of sea green lace over their eyes. There were younger women with head ties of several storeys, tucked and folded or roped in place with many lace scarves, some wearing ground length dresses of striped gold and green cotton or of yellow and blue swirls of bees and blossoms and some with babies low on their backs tied tight in pink and blue blankets or secured at the women's waists in scarves of lime linen.

Less large figures in khaki shorts zipped and snaked between the larger ones; some of these were otherwise naked and some were gay in flapping white t-shirts hanging from neck to waist decorative but unreadable with rips through red-lettered slogans or parts of printed faces of foreign personalities. There were holstered and belted policemen in deep blue ribbed shirts and thick grey striped trousers, many bareheaded and unbuttoned to the waist, others with tall lizard peaked caps; some were carrying thin whips. Some people in chocolate and beige furs seemed to spring up from the far edges of the crowd and from the earth.

Behind the mass which was circling the rectangle in disarray and growing, splitting and moving in all directions was a larger chaotic zone of parked vehicles. There were white minivans for seven and some intended for nine with open sliding doors on the floors of which sat dozens of masks in circles dressed in coloured rags, beads and tiny bells. There were stilts leaning against others extending high over the roofs. There were large flatbed trucks with tarpaulin covered piles and stacks of cardboard boxes on which sat hierarchies of white cone headed fur clad musicians silently holding goat-skinned bagpipes or round-backed lutes. There were fleets of taxis of yellow and some of red or black. Many were without hubcaps, some without windshields, and some were hung all around inside with wine lacy fringes.

People were eating nuts while seated on woven grass carpets or white flour sacks or they were sucking on cane sugar or drinking from long brown or stubby green bottles. Some had gourds. There were stick shapes talking down to some tall conical hooded sheets and others sitting bedecked and tented with heads of palm leaves and on these the heads of small animals affixed with twine, some grabbing at small screaming passers-by in khaki. The fields around undulated with other creatures, bobbing at the edges, gliding and hunched, of the same colour as the ground but in some green or yellow moving towards the field in streams and files from the direction of the Mountain and that of the border.

There were men in white with skull caps; there were men in grey suits with narrow ties. There were men in gowns. Some had machetes in sheathes, some had naked swords with tasselled handles. Many had bows over their shoulders.

Beside the twisted tree was parked another armoured car. The hatch was open but no soldier could be seen. There were no vehicles parked at this end of the field, near the tree or the armoured car behind the rows of chairs. The crowd was also thin behind the goalposts at the far end of the field.

Jules, Jack, Hank, Florence and the boy paused at the edge of the crowd. Jack handed the parasol back to Florence. Then they each wound through parked cars and sitting or standing bodies. They reformed at the crowd's edge where it faced inward and walked into the open field. Hank took off from there far into the lead, walking swiftly. Behind him came Jules and the priest then Florence and the boy. Jules was still smoking. The buzzing quieted but rose again and then fell, soft and expectant.

Only one week to go, thought Hank, *and then I will be home where standing butter doesn't melt and you can buy chocolates. Where the milk is nearly odourless and a small tobacco market doesn't form outside your door every time you grab a sneaky smoke.*

What if the airplane crashes! There was that one regional one last year when sixty were killed. The inquiry said there were so many things that could have caused the accident it was hard to pick one. The electricity was out so it came down by flashlight. The pilot was unqualified. The plane was forty years old and was second hand from a former socialist country with several faults. It was overcrowded with illegal passengers. Some had bought illegal boarding passes from staff at the foot of the stairs. Several of the bodies remain unidentified. Revolvers were found melted in the rubble.

A week, a week, a week! Then I can wear my tie with the gold elephants and speak to women's clubs of successful lawyers around round tables of baskets of crusty bread. I can flirt at celebrity functions. I can explain the realities of suffering. I can accept cheques over chilled wineglasses. I can attend conferences where paradigms aren't discussed as a species of snake; I can talk to colleagues without assuming they are bush bunny insane. I can gossip about the competence of the executive director and argue my opinions about the quotas of national staff. I can train naïve fools. I can sit at a desk without hearing the bellowing of children or of stampeding cattle or suddenly smelling piss, puke and gin.

An end to alligator eyed calmly mad Napoleonic leading in country ministers, to endless rumours and gossips of invasions, to arch communications from contemptuous functionary stars, to interagency competition on drivers' uniforms.

I will be able to read incisive articles that get to the core of problems without getting dizzy, blurry-eyed and nauseous. Without worms on the pages. I can eat out without wondering if it is hallucinogenic lizard meat. The leaves on trees will be dark red and brown or deep green but not sun yellow and acid lime at the same time. I will understand subtlety. I will know what is now right. I will be eligible for more salary.

Focus, focus, focus. Never mind the sounds, never mind the screaming. Pay attention to the program. See the main thing. Get out.

Home, home, home without green bodies lying smiling for weeks on the sides of the main routes to the office. Tanks in the boulevards, stupid people who know military secrets.

But what if I can't get Jack into the vehicle? What if we break down before the ferry? What if my staff have run away or headquarters changes their minds?

No! Only this one more errand, one more stupid ceremony. Then one more drive. One more river. Then a meeting in an air conditioned office and then home.

From his plastic chair the main Elder rose. He moved around the table and walked towards Hank. The Elder was carrying a megaphone in one hand. The heat had increased. The high grey in the sky retreated, streaming and dissolving back across the far mountains. The sky lifted further and became high blue in roofed glaring white.

Underneath, the low cloud from the Mountain dissolved, turning back to the peak so that the immense empty field with its tiny lonely converging of six dots, four behind in file and then one ahead, Hank, and one more converging on him, was lit by the sun in a sudden yellow blaze. The grey and hued multitude throbbed and then growled suddenly sharper. All shadows disappeared. Hank met the Elder in the centre of the field.

Horns honked wildly and all the women in the crowd ululated as the Elder outstretched his free hand and Hank took it in his own.

V

The elder shook then dropped Hank's hand. He stepped away and rotating slowly to all points spoke in Chembe dramatically through the megaphone. Jules hurried up behind Hank to whisper a translation into his ear. The priest, Florence and the boy with a basket stopped where they were and stood motionless some distance behind.

"We welcome the foreign chief of the agency in the capital who repaired the well and gave the new seeds to the co-op for the farmers. He is the chief who is the new father of the school. He is here to open the dancing," Jules translated. There was another round of ululating and honking of horns. The Elder handed the megaphone to Hank.

"Just say that you declare the dancing officially open," said Hank.

"The megaphone is electric," said Hank to Jules as he took it from the Elder.

"It's all right. The prohibitions are just for non-Chembe. You didn't bring it. Now quickly open the formal part. It makes it all official."

"With the authority invested in me I declare this event opened," said Hank into the megaphone in a dry and scratchy series of quacks and then handed the megaphone back to the Elder. The Elder spoke into the megaphone again at length and rotated two more full circles to more ululations and some whistles. His sentences were measured and grave. There were a few individual shouts from the crowd as well as if of names.

"He explained your "Community Schools and Community Stakeholder Development Program"," said Jules. "He also welcomed people of all faiths and persuasions. He welcomed the farmers, the strangers, and the brides and bridegrooms."

The elder then stepped beside Hank and placed his arm through Hank's. He began to escort Hank to the other end of the field where the chairs waited under the crossbar behind the table. The others followed.

Behind them, at the end of the field where Hank and the others had entered, through the crowd came the sound of deep drumming. The entire crowd silenced as the cadence grew. Hank glanced over his shoulder to see the crowd part widely as a stream of masks poured onto the field.

They were not tall but were extremely hairy with long black and greasy strands of fur from neck to toe. Their rounded heads had unnaturally long and stiff pointed ears. They had oval red rimmed eyes and sharp open many toothed mouths dividing extended snouts held widely ajar. Each mask moved by springing in a measured flowing leap from back feet to knuckled front paws.

They were encircled at the ankles by dozens of bells that tinkled on leaping. The front paws were gloved and had long nails extending along wide outstretched fingers from wristbands of brass. All had red ribbons hanging from their teeth.

"They are the cemetery dogs of the Bechembe," called Jules to Hank from where he walked slightly behind Hank and the Elder. The dogs split into two streams as they emerged into the field. They ran, loped and sprang swiftly in these streams towards the centre of the field, alternating between running dashes and making their long leaps while swinging their heads from side to side. There were about twenty in each line. The walkers all glanced behind once or twice as they continued walking to their chairs.

Suddenly, as the first dogs reached the centre of the field all the dogs began to bark. The drumming ceased for a moment. The crowd became silent. The barking was loud and intrusive like shutters slamming. At the centre of the field, as they reached it, each of the dogs extended its long snout into the air in turn and howled. As the streams crossed one another, each one in turn snapped the long jaws with a clatter at the other approaching.

The silence of the crowd was broken by more ululating, but this time higher pitched and sharper with a rapid excited, challenging cadence. This came from small knots of spectators near the vehicles. The dogs, snouts lowered and now crouching lower between leaps, ran with quick yelps, increasing their speed until they flashed past the basket boy where he had fallen behind the galloping stream widening to each side.

Then the barking ceased as did the ululating. The drumming renewed as the two streams narrowed again and slowed passing closely on each side of the priest and Florence, then Jules, and then at their narrowest, sliding by Hank and the Elder, touching briefly. Each dog turned his head from one of the walkers to another as it went by, from walker to walker and as each dog went by the red ribbons fluttered in its mouth brushing each walker in turn. This produced stiff legged strides and frozen faces on all except Jules and the Elder who smiled and on Jack who looked pre-occupied.

The dogs continued in lines in the field to a position just before the tables where the lines then turned, one to the left and one to the right, each stream running to the edge of the field. There they turned again to return to where they had appeared, each line making its way down the length of the field as the crowd drew back. The crowds at the edges shouted at them as they passed. The drumming quickened as the dogs disappeared through a channel that opened in the thick concentration of people at the field's end. Then all was silent again. The group had just reached the chairs and table under the crossbars.

The Elder gestured Hank, Jack, Jules and the priest around the table to the chairs. He gestured Florence to stop. He followed and placed Jack, and the priest, then Hank and then Jules. Hank sat in the centre of the priest and Jules. Jules was on the very end and Jack towards the right of the empty centre. There were two chairs beside him to the left and the priest on his other side. He would be next to the Governor when he arrived. The Elder conducted the placements very slowly and with great solemnity. There was a massive cheer and ululating when Jack sat. The crowd cheered also with some laughing and applauding as the priest sat. There was an anxious murmur when Hank sat.

The Elder put the megaphone on the table next to the trophy standing there. He turned and returned past the front row's empty chairs, side gilding from foot to foot, eyes narrowed across the table to the crowd. He reached Florence who had stopped at the left end of the line of chairs making up the first row. He gestured Florence ahead from where she was waiting to the second row and then along the back row to one of the two empty remaining chairs at the far end. There was another murmur from the crowd as she proceeded to her seat.

The remaining empty chairs were on the very far right behind the four men the Elder had seated in the front. The rest of the second row along which Florence and the Elder now passed was filled, first by two white hatted men in grey suits then two in square necked white gowns and collarless shirts and the two other Elders. Then there were the two empty chairs.

Each man seated in this row stood in turn as Florence and the Elder went by them crabwise to reach their places at the far end of the row. Each in turn ducked the parasol and then sat smoothing down their clothes. The tree behind had begun to cast lacy shadows on the formal guests.

The boy who had followed Florence took the basket around behind both rows and squatted there with the basket, peering between chair legs. Passing awkwardly by the now seated Florence, who was looking at the back of Hank's head, the main Elder took his place standing before, and then sitting, in the last empty chair in the second row on the right end. This was placed behind Jules. Jules turned around and shook his hand.

Five chairs still remained empty in the front row, two in the centre and three to the left. Jack sat very stiffly, sweating through his chequered shirt. Hank slouched. The priest glanced about, eyes narrowed. The crowd had remained silent all time the Elder was settling and it had been nearly motionless. There was a gusty collective sigh as the Elder sat. Then the general buzz resumed.

Hank turned round to the Elder and said, "I have written a report to Madame Youngo recommending all that we discussed. It will be delivered to her after the Dancing." The Elder pursed his lips but did not reply.

The priest turned to Hank and said, "The dogs were quite good but like most you'll see here today there is a limited palette for Bechembe dancers and quite a lot of aggressive repetition in sound and movement. But you'll see that the arrival of the queen is sheer poetry."

At the same time Jules took his pipe from his mouth. With the other hand he took a folded piece of yellow foolscap paper from a breast pocket and passed it to Hank. Hank unfolded it. It was entitled "Agenda of the Dancing".

Past the priest, Jack started rotating his head back and forth, peering at the crowd as though looking for something. Some in the crowd were pointing at him. Behind Hank the parasol swirled around and back, fringes knocking slightly against each other as it rhythmically reversed direction. The Elders seemed to be humming.

The agenda read: "1. Entry of foreigners; 2. Greeting of foreign chief by Local Person; 3. Official Launch by foreigner of legal dancing; 4. Dogs dance; 5. Foreigners seated in propriety with administrators; 5. Dance, dance, dance; 6. Entry of State Eminence; 7. Speech by State Eminence followed by award by foreigner and Departure of officials as Queen enters; 7. Foreigners' departure through village hailed; 8. Informal activities. Marriage of the world."

The dancing began and, as it did, Hank began his judging in his mind helped by the comments and explanations from the priest on one side and Jules on the other. From time to time Hank heard a sentence from behind in his language or a sharp cry from Jack. Hank tried to focus on the movement on the field, ignoring distractions and ordering his own independent impressions towards a rationale for judgement while at the same time trying to file the comments of the others.

The dancing groups entered the field from the right, left or the end, some from all sides. Some came from behind beyond the tree. One group was on the field before Hank had seen their entrance. Many exited in a different part from where they entered often as a new group came onto the field. Some carried instruments or blew whistles. They were sometimes accompanied by drums or horns from behind the crowd. Sometimes part of the crowd chanted in response or in support of chants and shouts or the other noises on the field. From each side and behind, and beyond explanations and commentary, interpretations and similes were offered at each change by Jules, the priest and the Elder. Florence seemed to be clicking her lips. Jack was emotional.

"Here come the tall sticks," someone said, *"the grasshoppers related to give life to the Bechembe old age grade, mainly with their antelope masks that connect their minds to the animals. They are dancing that the animals and all have their own jobs but some of them are secrets."*

"They are dancing about the small kill-off after the Bechembe king and queen fled here from the big river of the empire," someone else said. *"They had had a trial marriage in the bush as children, but the grey birds and lizards saw them and, there we go. Oh no, here come the birds who are singing the story to the people...there! That one is a bird with the straw wings flapping the shame of brother and sister, my God twins as well! No wonder they fled to hide under the mountains."*

"Look!" said a voice. *"Next out are the cones with their black eyes by the top and row after row of white shells in circles to the ground sewn to brown skin. Mouthless and eyeless. They are warning that devils can walk on the bright sun and it is necessary to be polite to them on the path. Conceal what you know. You should give them water when asked. Gracious, here come the devils themselves. That is some kind of tarry paint and the hair is died orange."*

"My! How they can jump!" added another voice in dialogue. "Straight up like rockets. They are dancing messages from the future. The comets and death of leaders."

"Here is, must be, oh my! The entrance of those ten haystacks crowned in windings of coloured clothe, red and blue. Jukawa scholars think that the ancient Jukawa could only perceive a small number of colours but their language had fifteen tonal differences and separate diminutive prefixes that were taboos with some tones and they used monotone nouns for magnification. Look at them spin. Like the stars. They knew all the stars even those invisible. Remarkably they have a verb ending to obscure structure. They have another set of everything for curses which only the masks can use. They will dance against immorality with caricatures. The masks came here underground. They carry the spirits of children killed by lightning in the fields or drowned in rivers. These are children abused and dying in pregnancy. Those are the shells. The stars sing to them angry through their masks." Was it the priest?

"Look there is one bumping up and down. Listen to those drums. Ahhh exactly like a motorcycle. Oh what great fun! Another is chasing one with that old black umbrella. Look at that one waddling. Oh it has a whip. It is going into the crowd to chase women. Ahh back again. More drumming. It must be all the little drums of hell and the endless walls of rain. There they are all falling over. Bottoms up! There is skirt and skirt and skirt of orange and yellow and green and protruding bright white feet and the thick stick legs of the mask. Underneath it has its guts. Up they go."

"My, a male female from the people next to the desert with her wooden knife hooded in flour sacks. There are its familiars, the pumas. How realistic they are sitting back on their hind legs waving their black torches. They are calling to the fires and the floods to marry. They are asking the dead and the snakes to come together out of the ground. Here comes the insect to join them. It's the snot beetle and now it dances with the mud wasp. Hear those whistles whine and the rasping single stringed lute. Over and over. Like flights of locusts

again. Up and down the scale. All satire of course. Against the politics of the National Redemptionist Party. But it is calling for revenge."

"The cats are dancing like cats rising up but also moving like trees in strong winds or genies. They stop and bend. I understand that song! The king must be beheaded. Look! Now they see themselves in pools and mirrors, they themselves are the mirror of the mirror of the mirrors of evil. The dead are complaining of mockery circling around their ears but still they are to be mocked. "Do women kill women?" the song is asking. Gosh, it is one thing after another. The wasp and the beetle are mating. The man woman has left shuffling through the crowd. Ahh the cats will run right by us." Jack had not said anything for some time.

"Watch out! They are going behind the tree. This is the political dialogue of the tribes and their clans. It is also the satire of the community against neighbours. Look another motorcycle and a cow thing in a gold dress!"

"Here comes a group of Chems! Hairy red pointy things. There is a spirit for a lot of things but they are all called Chem. Chem the water, Chem the field, Chem the sky, Chem the birds, Chem the smells, but no Chem the Mountain! The Mountain is the mother of the Chems. All the Chem separates into many Chems, but look how it comes together into one big Chem. It is the same with how it sings. See they are chasing the king. Look at all their legs go! Whoops! He got away hiding behind that stilted bush. There are three kings. The one now who is to die? The one from the past, the only one who was forgiven temporarily. There is the future king, a mystery. That Chem is carrying the penis of the last king in his basket. Well what is invisible to some is different to others." That must have been Jules. It is very noisy. There is a constant chatter of explanation. I remember some of this.

"It is often we find that the king is crazy and seems to be dancing while piling up bodies like that one is doing now; it is in the dances of many tribes. He is always picking up some and snapping them like dried sticks. During the civil war here some of the bodies piled in the

plain dried while the old foreign graves and tombstones were removed from the former village cemetery to make room for the newly killed. Some administrative decision. Futile really. The new dead all ended in simple trenches, the wet with the dry. No tombstones for them. But it wasn't all bad. The foreigners should have been removed years before or been covered with concrete as you never know what can happen to a body. Some of the graves were of soldiers buried in the first war. Trying to get to the capital or escaping from something. They died here of snake bite or some other mishap. Pestilence in the night air. The old priest wrote their names in a diary. He copied the names from the tombstones even though he didn't know their faith and the administrator then too put them in his reports. Then he used the tombstones to build up his fence. I don't know who made the tombstones. That cemetery was under this field. 'Henderson, Mersault, Conrad, Haggard, Bellows and Greene'. And others. They were fragments of bone, souvenirs really, and lumps of foreign dust scooped up by shovels and dumped into senior staff boxes roughly labelled to be sent by donkey and cart each approximately and perhaps partially back to their country.

"Here come the dancing diseases. Smallpox looks quite festive. The sexually transmitted ones are over fifty. That is almost the whole Wagi clan from the Berdies."

There was a pause and all the spectators leaned back in their chairs in silence. The first dancing part was over.

"You decided a winner yet?" asked Jules of Hank. "No present exactly like the time!"

At this point came a dramatic surprise of trumpets. It crashed over the crowd slapping over any and all other sounds. It continued note after note upwards ever louder and then stopped. The diseases standing along both sides of the field and the far end stopped too in mid-manoeuvre. They then elbowed and burrowed their ways in all directions into the crowd. All eyes and heads looked out over the field beyond the tree.

From the glare of midday sun, two white pickup trucks were thundering towards the field. Between them, travelling at the same speed and slightly in front was a black stretched luxurious limousine, a flag flapping on each side of the hood. In the back of each of the two pickups were three figures in bright green tunics, red billowing pantaloons and white flapping untucked shirts. They were tall and thin, bare-headed with white bleached hair. Each had a long sword.

Of the three figures in each of the trucks, one in each truck leaned with his back to the tailgate blowing into a long slightly curved brass horn that stretched the length of the deck, one in each truck held the front of the horn over the cab roof, the final one, the one on the other side of the horn, also leaned against the cab in each truck but this one periodically raised and lowered a long gun, beribboned on barrel and stock in red and black. Each of the gunmen from each of the two trucks suddenly fired at once with a smoky blast. There were rivulets of fiery particles overhead and an instant pervasive smell of cordite.

The three vehicles skidded noses down to a halt just beyond the tree. Behind them, and from the heavy dust they had created, emerged a wider line of vehicles: five brown armoured cars, hatches closed but machine guns rattling, which, racing their engines, stopped and switched off engines in unison. They had stopped to form a line with the other which had been there quietly, unmoving, all day.

A third line of vehicles appeared behind this. They were three large six wheeled canvas sided green trucks interspaced with three high roofed black four wheel drive vehicles with darkened windows. These stopped further back from where the others rested, beyond the trucks coming to rest in a ragged curving line.

But as this echelon of trucks was slowing and stopping men were jumping from the trucks, each in turn springing forward while landing and somersaulting with the inherited motion, each in turn coming smartly to his feet, automatic outstretched. Snapping erect they then turned to the left and to the right of each truck, turned then towards the field and ran between the vehicles, forming an advancing line, shouting rhythmically, guns waving up and down. They stopped and then charged, shouting, straight at the crowd standing past the tree and behind the chairs of the officials.

As all this the nearby crowd scattered, women wailing, Jules whispered to Hank, "The Kill and Go! They love to drive across the fields and jump and go; well, here are the final guests."

The Kill and Go raced into the gap they had created in the crowd at the end of the field running to a point even with the backs of the two rows of chairs. The small boy had disappeared. The basket lay on its side in the dust. A bottle had rolled between blue plastic legs.

On sharp shouted orders and with another shout the Kill and Go repositioned, running to make two lines extending back from the chairs to the front of the vehicles. They faced outward to the crowd some still flying but most drawn back at some distance to the far edges of the field. The tuniced men in the pickup trucks put down guns and trumpets and leapt over the sides of each of their vehicles. Of the six two ran, one to each side of the two back doors of the limousine and stood there at attention hand on sword. The other four formed a line in front of the hood and unsheathed their swords. The two back doors of the limousine were opened in unison. From one emerged Madame Youngo in turquoise blue and from the other in plain black suit and narrow tie came the Governor.

The six green tuniced men then yelled a long cheer all at once, a slogan. The four with unsheathed swords waved them over their heads. The door openers each stepped behind his charge and each went forward along their side of the limousine coming together, guard and guarded, Governor and Madame, behind the four swordsmen in front of the limousine's hood. The line of swordsmen led the two forward to the chairs of the officials between the lines of soldiers, stopping at the far left of the first row, then outstretching and tenting their swords for the

THE BUSH

Governor first and then Madame to go under and then to their seats.

"It is like a wedding," said Jules.

All of the hatches opened on the armoured cars. Thin faced men in berets swung the mounted guns on their pivots and peered into the crowd. Men in black suits and some in traditional dress unravelled themselves in couples from the black four wheel drives. Two men opened the rear gate of one and unloaded speakers, coils of wires and a small generator. The crowd became silent.

The Governor, limping slightly, slid along to his chair and sat. "Good day sir," said Hank.

Madame Youngo followed, eyes down, and like the Governor sat without a word. The three chairs to their left quickly filled with two men in black suits and a beribboned officer in a peaked and feathered hat. Busy men in suits ran back and forth and around the chairs. Speakers were set up facing the crowd at both ends; a man crawled under the table wire and with microphone in mouth to the centre. A hand rose from underneath the table on the near side, the microphone grasped like a snake swallowing a rat. The hand waved the microphone about until Madame Youngo took it, and pulling up some slack, rested it in her lap. The Governor had closed his eyes and was leaning slightly backward. The suited man crawled out from the front of the table and hunching down ran along its length. He spun past the swordsmen, now sitting cross legged, swords across their laps, backs towards the vehicles. In a few seconds a generator started up.

The Governor rose. He straightened his shoulders and opened his eyes. He looked back to his right and then MadameYoungo handed him up the microphone. He snapped its head with his finger. There was a screeching clatter. Then there was a large pop followed by a gasp from the crowd. The pop had echoed from the village walls beyond the length of the field.

"My companions!" the speakers boomed. The troops and the suited men, the drivers, the soldiers and the swordsmen all cheered.

"We are putting an end to tribalism and nepotism and factions and rebellion. We are stamping out corruption and favouritism and lack of social co-operation. We are building a nation on Discipline, Faith and Unity." Another cheer came from the same men.

"He doesn't know Chembe," said Jules, "and he dare not speak Bechembe. So he uses your foreign language. It will be translated on the radio."

The microphone crawler had returned to the end of the table with a camera tightly bound around his neck. He dived down to the front of the table and was lost momentarily to those seated there, but his movements could be gauged by a small wave of turning and tracking heads in the crowd on each side. Suddenly he popped up in mid-table like a grasscutter in the fields, camera to eye, pumped several times with his finger to a whirring sound, and then popped down. He soon emerged in sight again at the far end of the table and then ran back towards the vehicles. The Governor, who had paused for the grasscutter and grimaced a toothy smile, the mirror and twin of his photograph, then continued on loudly and flatly as if reading.

"I am happy to be here at this great event of renewal. My advisors tried to stop me coming. They said I was too busy, but no, I said, I must be with my people. My administration and I, with you," he said, and turned to sweep his hand sharply at the back row, "are partners and friends in this great venture to uplift us all at last. I ask you all to continue to work with me. The fruits of our labour will soon be rewarded. Our suffering will be repaid.

"We, even this week in the Capital, will be issuing decrees and licences to create from this region an advanced economic zone. We will declare this area around the Mountain an area of significant economic activity and also a reserve in perpetuity.

You will be then a place of significant tourism. Even now the signs are being painted. We thank our foreign friends for their financial help in this and hope it keeps coming.

"With the tourists will come employment as well and perhaps more local participation in mining and wood cutting on the border. Why not? We will have education for all and eradication of diseases, even those from abroad, as the new taxes create more government and new loans create roads, schools and clinics.

"But this will only happen through our party and our movement. It can only happen through our unity and discipline. It can only happen with faith and peace. We must end all minority sentiments and all support for hooliganism and banditry. We want an end to insurrection, crime, revenge and ritual killings; to cow theft and the disappearance of women. This is a new nation.

"When the tourists and businesses come we must cherish them and not maltreat and abuse them. We cannot shame ourselves any longer. This great successful festival today shows what we can do to be modern. In place of old rubbish we have built a cultural attraction that can attract the world.

"But I appeal to you. There are few chances left and little time. Reject all conspiracies. Have faith. Let us love one another.

"To preserve our future, I must now reluctantly and in friendship promulgate a temporary curfew to curb those who wish to be undisciplined and shame our people. We will use this to catch the creepers in the night, the ungodly, the thieves, the traitors and the burners.

"The general here will read out the terms of that after we have the judging of the dances. God bless you all and good luck." The Governor ended what had been a deeper, slower monotone on a rising and animated note that boomed cheerfully into the dusty and motionless silence of a thousand sweating faces.

Many backs had turned. There was a sharp distinct shout from the end of the field. "It's coming." This was followed then by another angrier cheer from the entourage behind and then the generator stopped its distant popping. The engine of the limousine started. The Governor did not hand back the microphone but dropped it straight to the ground. He sat and closed his eyes, shaking his head.

Hank looked past the priest, Jack and the Governor to Madame Youngo and began to wave but she was already rising and turning as were the men along the line beyond her. She was stepping deliberately. One foot at a time, deliberately, head high. Another shout came from the crowd. Jules gasped.

The swordsmen were on their feet by this time. All six held their swords; blades pointed downward, standing in lines of three at the ready. When the officer, the two suited men and Madame Youngo had filed from the row of chairs and past the swordsmen the Governor rose.

The swordsmen tented their blades again but silently and he limped under towards the vehicles behind Madame Youngo. Two swordsmen ran around them and ahead to open the limousine's doors while the others clamoured back into the backs of the two white pickups. Men rushed forward winding up the wires and lifting speakers. The limousine doors slammed. Hatches on the armoured cars were closed. The troops on the left of the chairs began to walk slowly towards the crowd on their side of the field side renewing their rhythmic shouting. The troops on the other side stayed still. The crowd on the left side collapsed further down the field. Some in the crowd were waving whisks.

On the left hand side of the field the people had now been herded back about one quarter of the length. Into this space around the right of the tree and past the end of the chairs swept the pickups, then behind them the limousine in a great arc turning into that now empty corner of the field, the limousine flags flying behind the pickups whose horns bellowed, all turning in a full circle towards the crowd and then away, speeding back around the sides of, and then behind the other vehicles, vanishing into the dust of the plain. There were no trumpets. Two armoured cars then started up, turned and followed. The rest of the vehicles remained stationary, the trucks and the other armoured cars.

The troopers on the left then moved silently, stepping backwards to their original position close to the chairs. The bemedalled and beribboned officer returned to the chairs and sat in the one the Governor had vacated. He then gestured to Hank and nodded to the trophy. Jack pushed the megaphone from where it had been on the table past the priest down the table to the front of Hank.

"I will translate for you," said Jules. "It is time for the judging." The crowd was coloured stone. There was a lizard tittering in the tree.

Hank rose and took the megaphone. He spoke of how everyone, all the contestants were quite good. It had been hard to choose a winner. Everyone was a winner really. They were all remarkable in their own way. He hoped everyone would understand what a difficult task he had. Hank said that the winner was, and he turned wildly to look at Jules and then back again, the horned bear things. Jules leapt to his feet, took the megaphone and spoke into it two sentences in Chembe. His final sentence ended in the distinct word "Bechembe".

He shrugged his shoulders, handed the megaphone back and lifting his hands wide and shrugging his shoulders sat down again. The crowd roared in angry pain and disapproval. There were many loud and some threatening individual shouts. One, clear and in Hank's language was "bribery!" Another sounded like "whoredog!" or "whorefrog!"

A headless bear ran from the crowd, shelled cloak clattering. As the shouting raised and fell, it grabbed the trophy from the table and took off back to the sidelines. Small knots, groups and rivulets of people were moving at haste backward through the crowd to the vehicles. They filed into some vans and climbed onto the back of some trucks. The doors of yellow taxis closed. There were dogs, cows, and trees, men in white, stilt carriers and bow men leaving. But only a few, perhaps a hundred. Vehicles started up and scattered in all directions into the fields. A cloud of dust raised and settled. Tunnels of dust lines extended over the plain from the field in every direction but the Mountain. The officer had stood up next to Hank and drawn his revolver. The troops all had crouched and fiddled with mechanism on their guns. The crowd had not been noticeably reduced. All the dog and bear things were gone.

Then loud universal ululating began. The crowd parted narrowly on the far end and through this came six masks hung with shells topped with branched antennae, three on each side of an enclosed, tall square litter, carrying it bouncing and bobbing, shaking the hanging reeds and tiny bells on cords at its sides. The masks danced with sliding steps and chanted as they carried the litter, holding it gingerly waist high with the long white poles affixed to the sides with twisted green ropes. Inside the litter on a raised bench was a shadowy thing in iridescent brown furs reflecting back the light through the reeds.

The crowd began to sway back and forth while ululating. There began at the same time a stamping of feet, all the lefts and then all the rights, more and more in unison, more and more to measure the swaying of the litter. The front portion of the crowd began to move inward as the masks carried the litter in a circle of the field.

A second circle of crowd then formed outside this first and, also swaying but in a counter direction, moved inward. The field narrowed and the square disappeared.

As the litter passed up the field and turned in front of the table and chairs Hank, still standing, glimpsed in a sudden flash of light coming from behind the tree behind him that the creature behind the reeds, inside on the bench, was swinging short, bare legs and feet on which there were brightly pink painted wiggling toes.

The litter and bearers gave off a strong aroma of musk as they passed. The crowd on both sides moved in and closed the circle in front of the chairs as the litter group passed, spiralling inward, and vanished. The crowd moved further and further inwards a thousand swaying, waving and chanting.

This left the elders, officials, the soldiers, the general, the vehicles, the banner and Hank, Jules, the priest and Florence with parasol all marooned, staring at swaying backs rotating to the left and receding inwards, in front of which another circle of backs rotated the opposite way.

"It is the queen," said Jules from his seat.

"The glorious old fairy," said the Priest.

Jack sighed deeply, a breaking kind of sob.

Many in the crowd were wearing ropes around their necks. These were in the swaying and flashing in the centre of the circles, in the empty eye in the centre of the field where the litter now had been set down to rest. To those ropes were affixed small portable radios, beer cans, coloured bottles, a hairdryer, a frying pan, a clock, small bright boxes and plastic bags. The objects clashed together in the weaving.

Other similarly dressed dancers were sprinkled throughout the crowd. Together their clinking and slapping sounds became dominant. The sound was joined by a despairing chant. The two large circles in the field separated, the space between them grew as the outside circle danced back and the inside one danced in. This space formed and solidified between them into a wide path. Into this space, from nowhere, leaping and running on the track so formed, was the mask with the board. It circled twice and then plunged through to the centre as the dancers clanked and moaned.

He plunged past the blue shirted Chembe policemen who had emerged into the eye and formed a third much smaller circle around the litter dancing, while connected to each other in a chain of arms across their shoulders.

"They are chanting," said the priest, "that she is the only mother of the world. The pretenders are all dead. She has conceived and the rains will come. Seeds will sprout. Those destined will die. Those destined will live. The fathers will never leave the Mountain. All must guard the child and honour the dead. The fruits cannot leave the trees until the new king is chosen. It is all marvellous, quite elemental." The priest spoke out each line relatively softly in a musing voice as though reciting or remembering a text. In the second row Florence sighed and gasped. She said something sharply to the priest in her language. Jack's head swayed back and forth.. His shoulders moved in an opposite direction to that of his buttocks and hips. His plastic chair swayed too, steadied and balanced by his pushing feet. His eyes were closed.

"They are chanting too their sorrows and their anger and their frustrations," said Jules turning facing up to Hank where he stood. "They are chanting about lies and false promises and poverty and loss and abominations. They are chanting away the heaviness of memory. This is the biggest and angriest of their chanting.

"Now you should leave at once. Better never than late, as they say."

The officer then sat back down after first holstering his revolver and taking the megaphone from Hank's hand. He turned and waved his soldiers to reposition themselves. They ran around the table, some to end crouching on one knee in front of the table, some standing behind the chairs. When he had accomplished this, the officer turned to Hank who was still standing and motionless. The officer waved Hank towards the left side of the row and into the field past Jules. Hank did not move. The officer looked grim as he continued to flutter his hand. A loud roar went up from the crowd. The swaying increased and the stamping vibrated the ground.

"The Memory board has changed!" cried Jules. "Quickly, let's go."

Jules then stood and turned to his left. Hank followed Jules as he exited the row of seats and walked to the sidelines of the field. The priest followed and then Jack, who had been joined from behind by Florence. She kept her grasp of her parasol over her head and was twirling it furiously. Jules led the group around behind the backs of the circling stamping crowd, down the length of the field to the path between the houses from which they had entered.

They all strode swiftly, with Hank slightly hunched, the priest puffing and Jack staring about. They all paused and then turned back as they reached the path between the houses to stare back at the field framed between the low buildings in the harsh light. The chant had been changing to first one rhythm and enunciation and then to another, loud and soft. Humming and then a song. The pace of stamping altered too. Fast, slow, fast, fast, slow again.

"Now I will leave you now. Jack it is better you all go," said Jules and turned back to the crowd, pipe still in hand.

"Let us hurry," said the priest. He took Florence's arm and gestured Jack and Hank forward into the village and the marketplace. They turned in the market and hurried out of the main road to leave the village at the junction to the school path. The armoured car was no longer there. They turned up the path with the muffled cadences of the dancing in their ears.

"How will the poor soldier bugger ever be able to read out the curfew?" called the priest ahead to Jack and Hank. He puffed and coughed lightly. Hank looked back to the priest struggling along, his arm over Florence's shoulder. She was holding the parasol close to her head glowering as she seemed to be pushing the priest away with the other.

There was a change in the pathway. Hundreds of squashed frogs or toads had dried on the path in the sun in their absence.

Some lifted up from the ground on the soles of Hank's shoes as he strode down the path.

"Look," said the priest pointing to his left as they hurried along. There in the stubble, moving in parallel to the path, was a line of tiny furry creatures, they looked eyeless, weaving towards the Mountain and extending backward out of sight towards the village. Hank swung his head; the fields on the other side of the path were dotted with fat grey speckled birds, down and squatting, which all seemed to be throbbing and cooing.

"No!" said the priest and pointed left raising his arm. And there, at the end of the parkland, rising into the sky in a low black swoop from the invisible and shimmering horizon on one side of the plain, over the tops of the mountain rim on the other side, was a roll of boiling cloud. It was extremely distant but a prominent wall propping up that side of the bright, white dome arced above.

"It is hours away and it may not pass here," said Hank. "Let's hurry!" They walked faster. Jack glanced back and forth at the distant clouds sitting on the horizon. His eyes had widened and then he squinted repeatedly forward and to the side. When they reached the gate the gateman was gone. The tree of the weavers was still. The gateman's pot had fallen to the side off the stones and a stain had been absorbed into the dirt. Jack's suitcase was fully upright against the fence. Jack went forward and picked it up. The priest and Florence did not stop but turned immediately along the fence. The priest cried out a "Good-bye and safe journey", "we must get in" and a diminishing "hope to see you again soon."

The school compound seemed deserted. There were no sounds of rote or instruction from the classrooms. No one ran between the buildings. The pathway to the square between the palms was clear except for a few sweet wrappers. When they reached the square Hank and Jack could see that the sand was ruffled and flurried. Ridges spidered and overlapped in all directions. The door to Madame Youngo's office waved, squeaking slightly and partially opening and closing in what was now a slight fresh gusty draught from the plain.

"Around, behind to the vehicle," said Hank and quickened his pace to a short strided stiff legged run. He briefly touched Jack's elbow on the arm Jack was carrying the suitcase with to encourage speed as they crossed the square and circled Madame Youngo's office. The vehicle was there beyond the office next to the fence. It was highlighted against the shadowy and silent mountain. Leaning against the hood was the girl they had interviewed, Hope.

Hank took out his keys and opened the passenger door. He went around and opened the driver's door. He then took out two folded sheaves of paper from the glove compartment, leaving others there resting on a bed of rags, wires and fuses. He opened the back gate to the vehicle and then came around to where Jack was standing silently in front of Hope who was staring downward at the earth. Hank took the suitcase from Jack and took it to the back of the vehicle and flung it in. He slammed the gate and returned to Jack.

"Get rid of her," he said. "We have to go. We are all done here."

"Master Jack and Mister Chief," said the woman "I have come to greet you and pray for your safe journey."

"Where is all the bloody school?" said Hank.

"They are all in the hostels and in their houses Mister Chief. The classes are finished today. They are lying there since the trucks came to take away my tribeswomen."

"They didn't take you?" said Hank. Hope looked up into Jack's eyes. Jack shook his head and furrowed his brow.

"No, only my sisters," said the woman to Hank. "I hid in the toilet block. They did not want me anyway. They were the young men and my cousins. They say I am spoiled. They shouted at the other women that they were my sisters now. The men teachers stood by idly while they abused them. It was a great shame.

"Where did Madame Youngo go?" said Hank and moved to stand closer to Jack.

"She has not returned," said Hope. "They say she is in the village; she may have given up and moved to other things. Her plans have failed. We have seen many other trucks. Also people are moving behind on the Mountain."

"Get into the vehicle," said Hank to Jack and put his arm around him to push him towards the open door. The seats inside were of beige leather and cracked. Jack climbed in and sat arms folded, looking blankly through the window. Hank turned to Hope and handed her the two sheaves. She curtseyed slightly on receiving them.

"Take these papers and give them to Madame when she returns. They are an official report so don't lose them," said Hank and he slammed Jack's door. Jack rolled down the window on his side but continued looking ahead stiffly. Hank walked around and got into his side. Hope looked up to Jack and, papers in hand, brushed the front of her head tie from the front of her hair.

"Master Jack does not go now. We need you here. Who will teach us language? Who will call us ladies? Who will solve our problems? We have many wickednesses here. There is murder. There is jealousy. There are pregnancies. There is gossips. Oh please stay!"

"It is only for a few days, Hope," said Jack, still looking ahead through the windshield. "Please greet the Chembe girl for me and Madame Youngo. Go back to your studies."

"Greet Madame Youngo for me too," said Hank. "And give her that report."

"Can I not ride with you past the village onto the road? I can get a cross country taxi there. I can get a bus there. I think I must leave the school. Please help me sirs."

THE BUSH

"Sorry young lady," said Hank, leaning across Jack's chest and speaking through the window. "It is against agency policy to have passengers. Insurance you know. Well good-bye. Don't forget the papers to Madame."

He started the vehicle abruptly and then moved quickly off around the building, across the square and down the empty path. Hope remained standing still as she dropped out of sight behind the office corner. They drove across the square and between the palms. Jack rolled up the window and Hank turned on the air conditioning. They rode a moment in silence through the gate.

"How could you ever tell them apart with those uniforms?" said Hank when they had passed the gate. "How can you remember anything about them, they are so much the same? And their names? I can never tell one from another. Anyway let's beat this rain," said Hank and then, "Back to the world thank god!"

They cleared the school path and turned left onto the track heading swiftly away from the village into the open road towards the main highway. There was still no armoured car at the junction. "Not a moment too soon, I say," said Hank. "We still have a good three hours of daylight. We should reach the ferry before the storm. Gosh you've been quiet since morning. Do you need to take one of those tablets or something? Or do you have the fever again?"

The road angled and rose onto a tarmaced road several miles further which curved across the plain from the direction of the border; this in turn angled towards the mountains. The lone Chembe Mountain receded behind them. The clouds in the distance still boiled and streamed but did not advance. They seemed to be flowing up and over the mountains to the north at the far corner of the range. The plain transformed from grass into low scrub and cactus which covered short, rolling bumpy hills, interspaced with sandy valleys bowling between. In one they drove past a sharp sided green and blue pool. A slight yellowy mist rose from it. Further on there were more cacti and broad fat rubbery leaved plants on the slopes. At the bottom of some of the valley bowls were the dry flat cracked beds of seasonal ponds, surrounded by clumps of white barked trees whose tiny leaves spun black and yellow in the dusty breeze.

They passed through several villages on the valley bottoms. The houses were round made straw patched dried reddish mud and thatched with reeds. Around some were small squares of tended but barren earth. There were one or two whitewashed cement cubes of houses with tin roofs. One had a tub in front containing partially submerged bottles in evaporating water. Some thin cows filed over a far hill followed by a small boy in a white frock carrying a long cane over his shoulder. The boy wore a soft brimmed white cap.

From a higher hill top further on the two men could see a complex of several long white buildings in an adjoining valley. It was surrounded by a chain fence with a tower in the near corner. This had a square, walless platform on top.

"Eggplant farm," said Hank. "Didn't work. We did a bit better with the carrot project."

Past that hill opening up before them was a much wider valley stretching to a smoky town extending back until resting against higher hills in the shadow of the mountains. The mountains had irregular and sharp teeth against the sky unlike the almost flat rising swell of the isolated one far behind. Here and there amid these jagged peaks was a near-perfect cone.

On the road speeding towards them was a column of the canvas sided trucks, horns blowing. Hank pulled to the side of the road as they each flashed by with a zip, a sudden noise like bees or tearing cheesecloth. Each of the men silently counted twenty-five. The trucks each had two in the cab, a capped driver and a man beside in a beret. They were tightly laced up to the roof frames at their backs. After they all had passed Hank pulled back on the road and continued talking.

"You know Jack some of those peaks are volcanic. There are some trapped lakes between this range and the next one which is on the other side of the border. About four years ago, everyone in the villages around one of the lakes died one night. The people coming to trade smelled the bodies miles before they arrived for market a week later. There were bloated green corpses in the paths of people and dogs and cows. They say it was caused by gas bubbles from under the lake. Volcanic. Killed over five hundred people. The whole thing never even made the newspapers back home, not even in the little curiosity columns. No reporters this far in the bush and, after all, who cares? Things like that happen all the time. Doesn't mean anything really. New people have even moved back to the villages there, I hear." Jack said nothing.

"It was the same thing with the uprising of the saviour guy. The saviour's men actually occupied several cities. One of the agency offices there at the time could look down and see them hunting with machetes for sinners in the streets below. People were running everywhere, some holding their own arm or hand. They killed hundreds until the army went in house to house. They burned out a whole suburb of the faithful, a whole ghetto and blew up a tower. They shelled a district. They found a horrible communal kitchen.

"I had to take a taxi once around that time to see a colleague in the city. My vehicle had been in an accident. The driver of the taxi turned around to me grinning to where I was sitting innocently reading in the back. He had one of those pictures taped on his dashboard. He pulled a big stained knife out of his gown. He laughed and said I was lucky not to be an unbeliever. He waved the knife and placed it on his seat. He was with the saviour. He took me to my friend's office though."

"But, once again, not a word in the papers about the whole thing. Almost a thousand killed over two weeks. It didn't fit the current reality and agenda at home. I contacted my friends to tell them not to worry and the trouble would die down and they didn't know what the hell I was talking about. Started telling me about the local elections at home and the new Christmas shopping hours. Well, here we are."

And then Jack said, "I don't remember any of that."

VI

The town was bustling around them as they entered. Ropey yellow goats and spotted rheumy cows wandered in front of the vehicle and to the side driven at times by boys with sticks. The gutters held green stomached pigs alive and happy in the rotting floating debris. The street was initially lined with small mud cubes of houses and open air curb side stalls or enterprises on mats and blankets. Then came shops with protruding unpeeled beams to which were attached tin awnings shading open doorways leading to dark interiors. On the stoops sat string vested proprietors and naked children. Around the doorways were displayed the wares. Cans of paint, iron bedsteads, hubcaps, black headed hoes, plastic jerry cans, bathtubs.

Next came the quarter of clothing. Women in wrapped around coloured measures of flowery cloth and white brassieres, umbrellas against the heat of the day, were selling t-shirts and striped pyjamas, towels and white frilled blouses, packages of tights and yellow striped dress shirts, embroidered tunics, silk gowns of pink and green. Between them here and there were concrete taverns the clients of which drank outside on benches against the wall in the sun or were greyly framed in smoke sitting on white plastic chairs or stools scowling through door and window. Next were stalls of hanging slabs and tubes of bloody swinging, slowly rotating meat, alive with echelons and stripes of climbing insects and smeared with green and gristle. Around them stood men with cleavers wearing shorts and black, brown and pink stained aprons.

Then there was a roundabout, the raised sandy centre of which was filled with beggars of all ages in universally dirty khaki rags, each beggar missing assortments of limbs and decorated with combined cuts and sores who all darted back and forth out to the circling vehicles, back to the roundabout, filling windows with imploring twisted faces, and then back again into their own interior, a sliding frenzied circling tribe scrambling and turning, tracking the vehicles as they moved slowly around to the four exits, always ready to select and spring at one again. On the far exit to the roundabout was a squat four storey glass and steel hotel with a bright red garbed doorman and revolving doors.

They took this exit and passed larger concrete buildings, some with large windows for display and then a drive-in courtyard with two pumps for petroleum products next to which was a plywood office in front of which sat a man with a rifle on a three legged stool. Beside this, below a short fence, was an excreta field dotted with heads bobbing up and down over cloth bedecked ankles and black shoes. Then there was a series of walled three storey mansions balconied on every floor, painted in custard lemon, peach blush and moody avocado with curly white moulded surrounds on windows, pillared porches and radically gabled roofs. Then there was the school.

Hank pulled up the vehicle to the side of the road. He scattered two young men in white shirts and black pants pushing bicycles and a small boy carrying long black brushes. Trucks and cars of all ages whizzed past him and around a four wheeled wagon pulled by two oxen piled high with mattresses.

"Why don't you cheer up and help me out Jack. You are the one always saying I should be cheerful. She is going to be grumpy and nasty because I am a day late. Keep her occupied or the trip day will be hell." Hank checked carefully behind as the wagon passed and then leapt out. He gave a quick sniff to his armpit pulling the sleeve fabric towards the elbow as he raised his arm. The path on the side of the road was thronged with pedestrians carrying buckets and baskets in hand or on head. There were bloody brown packages and newspapers weeping flour. There were cartons of soft drinks and boxes of washing powder. There were fully veiled women and dozens of young men striding forcefully past everyone else carrying books or newspapers wearing skull caps or chequered headscarves.

The school wall was high and blonde and topped by glinting broken glass. There was a wide double sided wrought iron gate beside which propped against the wall, rickety, was a watchman's hut like a black discarded upturned coffin. In this was a white moustached thin elderly man sitting on a stool reading a paper. He wore a wrinkled blue shirt under a dark blue blazer holed at the elbows and with fluffy splits spitting stuffing along the front seams. Hank spoke to this man briefly over his lowered newspaper. The man then dropped and folded his newspaper, rose slowly, eyes heavenward, placed the newspaper on his stool, turned and then exited his box abruptly causing Hank to step suddenly back as he elbowed by. The guard walked to the iron gates, cupped his mouth in both hands, and called out through them. He then returned to his stool and, sitting, took up the newspaper again. Hank stood for a while and then returned to the car. He turned on the engine and adjusted the air conditioning higher.

"An hour and a half from the school there to the one here and one or two more to the ferry. We can do it if she hurries," said Hank.

"She has been complaining about the placement here from the beginning. I think everyone will be happy she is going. The security is getting bad here, too. It is still a nice place though not like your old mission compound. This has fans in the classrooms, audio visual aids, computers, sports equipment, not just a few netballs but all the equipment. It is really quite good. It is a showpiece in the project. The Governor's daughters attend here.

"Now be polite to her and don't provoke. It's only for a short time, a few hours then we're in the Capital and we will get everything completely sorted and finalised. You will feel better then. Oops, here she is now."

The iron gates had flung open to reveal two tall thin women in dark blue tunics and white collars. Their faces were completely surrounded by head ties that buttoned at the throat. Each carried a red leather suitcase. In the centre, much shorter and heavier than the escorts, stood a bare headed woman in green blouse and beige culotte skirt. She wore thick soled brown suede boots. Her hair sprang from her head in twisty strawberry mats. She stood still in the gateway while her escorts came forward with the bags to the vehicle. Hank leapt out again and in the teeth of an oncoming bicycle darted to the back gate. The women with the bags glided over to him and silently handed them over. He placed them on the deck to the sides of Jack's case and in front of his own black duffel. Closing the tailgate he followed the two women in blue back to the iron gate. Each of the women in turn strongly embraced the red haired woman. Then one went back into the walled compound while the other softly closed the gate and slid into place a bracketed bar. This woman then followed the first into the green shadows inside.

"I am sorry I am late," said Hank, "but I had to do a couple of errands for Madame Youngo as a kind of deal to extract Jack. I think she sees me as a diversion and as a cure for her own administrative mess-ups. Now Juliet, let's just get you loaded and us underway. We want to make the ferry crossing before dark and I think the rains are coming.

"Is that that horrid Jack in your vehicle Hank? I will not travel with that bastard. I've told you that. You know he's involved with his students and god knows what else. He embarrassed me when he came here with his witches for the play contest. He cheated to win. His Madame Youngo is a Nazi bitch. He's a horrible bushman," said Juliet.

"Look Juliet. I know you don't mean that. I can't make extra trips for you. The guy is probably sick. This is a kind of evacuation. You just sit in the back. It is only for a short while then we'll get you both sorted in the capital." Hank took her gently by the arm and with only a slight suggestion propelled her towards the rear door through streaming passers by. Juliet began again speaking loudly to him.

"This is the stupidest project anyone has ever heard of. I've written to headquarters about it. It is an embarrassment and a travesty. What a waste. I hope the vehicle is clean." Hank opened the rear door and closed it behind the culottes as they squeezed inside. He dodged around to his door, got in and affixed a dusty seat belt. Juliet peered over the seat at Jack.

"All set everybody. Full speed to the ferry." Hank called and started the engine. He u-turned across the face of a truck coming from the left and an old taxi to the right, rising a bit on the path on the far side of the road and then bumping down at the end of his turn. A woman squatting, selling cigarettes from a cardboard box, jumped to her feet and back-pedalled into the base of a peeling billboard along the far side of the path. It was advertising refrigerators. Jack said nothing.

"Hank, maybe you can tell me now why on earth I was placed there. I have a PhD in gender studies and that is a religious girl's school. The administration is devout clerics and the women are from the elite. I had to live on boiled eggs and squash mixes and stay in my room all the time because young men and old buggers in cars hung out at the gates. The food is all religious. Are you and the agency crazy?"

"They agreed to make a community school. Besides we were building links with the community."

"Oh yeah, the chicken farm for the Governor's sister?"

They kept silent as Hank threaded himself back to the edge of town and then accelerated down an open road along the mountains. The road began to arc and descend again into flat country, an oven broken by stretches of fenced orchard with lines of fruitless broad-leaved trees. Suddenly Juliet spoke again.

"What on earth is going on anyway? Just an hour before you arrived the Governor and his gang came wailing by the school with all horns and sirens. After ten minutes there was a convoy with the Bechembe dog dancers waving and cheering; one had a trophy. Then half an hour later just about the whole 7th brigade thundered out of town like avenging angels. I hate those animals. You know they were once sent against a rebel village in the mountains and they flattened the whole thing and then discovered it was the wrong village.

"There was a big funeral yesterday of a girl that they say was murdered. It wove all day through the streets with wailing and sobbing. They dropped the coffin once. Then early this morning a couple of trucks with young men firing into the air went by our gates and woke the whole school. It's all getting crazy."

"I don't know what is going on," said Hank. "It may be something at the border. The K and G went steaming by us, too. You never know here — ripples in a pond and all that."

"I hate it here," said Juliet. "It is absurd and oppressive. Imagine sitting up all night in gaslight telling women secretly about their bodies while the sugar daddies circle the walls whistling and drinking with the guards. Earnest, grown women at secret meetings afraid for their lives.

"They said they liked being covered up. They laughed at me like I was a child for my cloths. They said all girls are not slim. They asked me to have sense. They liked their marriages arranged because the family could watch the husband or if not ask for the money back. Some were proud of circumcision and cherished the affairs with aunts. They thought you foreigners were like pink angry babies, babbling and spitting indignations while slobbering out for nipples. They thought their men were smelly donkeys except for their brothers and their friends who were made of steel and faith and suffered for them. They laughed at me and said I will die alone when I talked of men. Where are my sisters, really, they asked. They cried when they saw comets because it meant a great saint would die. I taught them mathematics! Mathematics for what. And they were as sharp as knives. What on earth could I do here? No wonder I feel nuts. So Hank, who said they were going to kill me?

"That is all tosh. An anonymous letter to the agency. Forget about it," said Hank, "and forget those women. They do want to fly like anyone. They want out of the trap. They will be doctors." Jack had been chin on chest and hunched down in the front seat. His eyes were redder than before as he lifted his head and swung around glaring at Hank's last words.

"They do fly!" shouted Juliet and then softer "They will be doctors, as you say, and have perfumes delivered by car. They will not hoe. Some may be killed by cousins but others will shop in Paris. They will be political spokeswomen. The poor members of their extended families will beg to serve in their houses. These aren't your poor bush bunnies like Jack's. They'll get out."

"Just another note from the state house too," said Hank. "And from the diocese. We wanted to reorganise anyway because of the troubles. We'll take a more project intensive and indigenous sectoral approach. We'll cut down on soft technical assistance. Work in closer partnership with government. Juliet, you can probably be moved to the policy desk as soon as we get back."

"At least with a clan state everyone knows where they are," murmured Jack. "No bunches of people flying from reality into arrogant fantasies of their own imposing personalities."

"If you mean me Jack," said Juliet, "I still believe in equality and freedom. And professionalism. And people. I don't believe in heebie jeebies and spells."

"You two were the worst of your intake," said Hank. "I knew that at the inception meetings for the project. Always quarrelling like dogs and cats. Always causing problems and raising issues. Just joking. Don't worry. Home soon."

"I will be complaining," said Juliet.

"Me too," said Jack. Hank accelerated slightly leaning over the wheel.

Jack soon fell asleep, jerking heavily but unconsciously when the vehicle occasionally bumped over an uneven patch on the road surface. Juliet moved nearer her window and stared fixedly outside. The landscape was without any main features, the mountains had dropped behind and the long sweep of the river with its linings of twisted trees and mounds of sand was not yet visible. There were lone anthills twice the height of the car, gravelled defiles, sand patches, then scrub and episodes of fenced orchards sometimes leafless. At one stretch the road was lined on both sides with dozens of squatting boys selling huge bags of carrots to each other across the empty tarmac. They were stunned to watchful silence as the vehicle passed between them. Further on, parallel to the road at the horizon, there was a stretch of swinging irrigation hoses pumping arcing streams of mist into the heated air to create swarms of falling rainbows in the white sunlight, rainbows which swept with the mist dripping and dissolving over a narrow dark green carpet of vegetation. The irrigated fields ended and on the next strip of red desert and black rocks a circle of vultures stood in meditation over a brown and red lump at the side of the road while one of their numbers tore at it furiously.

"I am very hungry," said Juliet. "I had no breakfast with all the commotion in the town and because of waiting for you, Hank. I have to use the toilet and I am thirsty too."

"I want to make the ferry at dusk. We can just do it if we keep going. Oh, wait a minute! There is a village coming up that sells the most wonderful roast chickens. They roast them on the side of the road and sell them to the truck drivers making the run up from the ferry. I sometimes get one when I come up here on tour. We'll stop a moment and get one and eat it as we go. They'll have some flat bread and bananas. We'll get some pop. You can do what you need to, Juliet, and Jack too. Do you have some cash?"

"You are a cheap bastard," said Juliet from behind, "you always were. But that would be great. I love roast chicken. Jack looks as though he needs something, too. But are they old lady Youngo's chickens from her farms?"

"Tell me about the plays," said Hank. "What did Jack do anyway? How did he cheat?" He looked a second at Jack who slept on. Hank quickly took one hand from the wheel and nudged the glove compartment at his knee. It wobbled fixedly. Hank then returned to his driving.

"Jack brought about ten women in a rented minivan to the play contest. They had won the borderline schools contest and were here for the regional finals. There was nowhere to hold the contest inside in town. The stage had to be very big and there were a dozen school teams coming, some with parents and townspeople. The regional capital was too far and in the wrong direction so it was decided to have the contest at the barracks of the seventh brigade just outside town, beside the local airport. They had a huge indoor parade ground in a kind of airplane hanger which I think they also use for vehicles.

"Jack arranged to bring his group to my school first to eat there as guests, before he and I went on to the contest. I agreed to that as a courtesy and to show solidarity with the project. We did it to help the name of the project.

"They were loud and messy especially his two twin groupies. One sitting on each side of him nudging and laughing. The other staff he had with him seemed drunk, especially a Chembe man. My women were appalled. And their uniforms! Like militarized whores. One little woman just wandered around the tables peering into people's faces.

"We went on in their minivan which was overcrowded and rank. There were crusts of bread, sweet wrappers, plastic bottles, pots of henna, costumes, bags of sugarcane, hair extensions, underthings and the smell of stale beer. The women waved and called out to people passing on the street. They laughed and shoved one another. The other staff that was standing behind the driver kept giving berserk instructions and kept waving whenever we passed a beer parlour or a brothel.

The little woman sat next to Jack humming and snarling especially at me."

"We went out of the town and reached the gate to the barracks compound. It is a huge place with dozens of buildings and steel structures with rows of tanks and trucks. You know the Governor has a fortified house there where he stays when he overnights when in the area. There were even two helicopters. There was a big square building, way inside, surrounded by vans and busses. The gate was closed and guarded by a half dozen men behind two square little forts of sandbags, one on each side of the gate. There were squads of other soldiers running around and hooting inside.

"Two tall and heavy men with scarred faces, one with no front teeth, came to each of the driver's side windows. They were armed. I was sitting with Jack, just behind the driver and beside that little mad woman, behind the mad staff members, when I saw that one soldier had a sort of bloody hair thing hanging on a chain at his neck. It was awful. The other one at the closest window leaned in and said to the driver in a really gruff threatening voice, "Whatcha was doing here corner boys!"

"We have come to sex the Governor's wife,' Jack said and everyone inside laughed. Except me. I was scared to death. The big soldier looked at Jack and at the women laughing. You could see he was thinking it through. He gritted his teeth and spat to the side and then he started to laugh too. It was terrifying. He was like a big dog.

"We went in and were sat on plastic chairs in front of a raised open stage curtained in the back with brown tarpaulin in that enormous building. There were three hundred people there but we only filled the front half. The rear was empty but for some exercise equipment and some stores under plastic. The crowd were teachers, some officers, some ministry officials and husbands and fathers. I saw tubby Tom Hume from our project several rows back. He was in a sort of dinner jacket. He waved. There were parents too. They were mostly townspeople from the region but also a few farmers who had come in the vans with the different groups. There were some priests, a local nun and holy men. Some rows were empty at the back. I guess they were for people who didn't get through because of the troubles. I sat beside Jack while the women got ready behind the tarpaulin.

"There was a speech about theatre being important in education to teach speech, self expression, world culture and all that. There was some mention of traditional values and national culture of unity and good citizenship. The judges were introduced. One was Tom Hume. Jack said this was really unfair as Tom was also a producer of one of the plays. He is in a school near the regional capital that wins this event every year. The school also wins track and field. My women can't compete in those things of course. He is famous to everyone there because of his small enterprise projects in the capital. They are jewellery making. He also has a trade in buying and selling artefacts. The party and businessmen love him."

"We are almost at the village. Can't you smell that chicken? It always reminds me of home," said Hank and glanced at the sleeping Jack again.

"So, we watched about six awful plays all with a king and a princess kept apart by society but who seem secretly to love another. A little lizard or a bird helps the princess to fake death. But the king marries another. Then the girl is brought back to life and leaves with someone else who is usually also a king. The whole thing is very derivative although it is supposed to be local culture. It isn't but it is harmless and moral and it means the women can all be dressed up as handmaidens in scarves and bras and stand around languidly moaning. A fat one can be the king and ponce about waving a sword making long speeches. A thin one can be another king and insult someone. Maybe she can imitate the Governor. The real pretty woman can have a death scene and maybe even fake a kiss.

"There are some variations. A magic thing can be a talking lizard with painted lips and green scarves or a comical dwarf in animal skins. It is usually the short girl. Sometimes some soldiers chase the other king and kill one of his friends; these are two more tall girls in some teacher's trousers, but it is basically always the same play. It doesn't matter if it is a teacher trainer college, a civil service academy or a policewoman's driving school.

"But the next one was different. It was Tom's Bechembe girls. He had a king and a maiden but he had the handmaidens do a little wiggly dance. This caused a massive frisson in the crowd. Especially with the officers. Jack was cursing loudly.

"That play ended to sincere applause. The players from each play had returned to seats in the audience in the reserved rows in front at the end of their plays. I saw that some were weeping and others embracing. A bump slid along the back curtain and one of those horrible twins came out the side of it from behind. Even though she was in costume with some feathers and scarves she strode past the reserve chairs right up to Jack. She said, "Never mind Mister Jack. We have bottoms too!"

"Nearly everyone heard. It was like a tomb in there as she went back and slithered behind the curtain. The next play was Jack's. In a few seconds a hundred jaws had dropped. First of all, there was a hunched over queen looking for a lover. Then there was a line of three lizards who shouted what sounded like ancient curses in unison. A man was chased by soldiers in white trousers to catch him for the queen. There was also a pair of singing handmaidens, the twins. As the man was dragged to the queen by the soldiers the twins began to sing. "Eyes of blue, six foot two, coochie, coochie, coochie coo, has anybody seen my girl!" Then they began a slow traditional dance back and forth. "Turned up nose, pigeon toes. Flapper yes sir one of those." Then they turned around and wiggled their buttocks. They repeated their chorus. The lizards then escorted the queen and the man suggestively from the stage. The applause was scattered but was loud from the two officers who were judges with Tom. Many in the audience looked hypnotised. Someone shouted "exactly like that" in our language. A priest waved his fist. Tom shouted "They have changed the play!"

"The other plays passed in deadened silence. The girls returning to their reserved seats sometimes whimpered. They were all sullen except for Jack's women who did sit quietly without abusing anyone but smirking and some were noisily sucking sweets.

"The judging went to Jack. Two to one in favour. He grabbed the trophy from the table in front of Tom and stuffed it under his arm. He shook the two officers' hands vigorously. He then held the trophy over his head and motioned the women and myself to quickly follow him outside. He ran out to howls and applause with the trophy on high. The Chembe staff man had run ahead and the driver had started the engine. We piled in tumbling and the van lurched forward. Soldiers were approaching the van from all directions and from all corners of the compound at the run, attracted by the noise from the hall. The women were chanting "We have bottoms too!" The twins lifted up their scarves, pulled down their panties and pressed their bottoms against the back glass. We passed through a gate, mercifully open, with streamers of running, chasing, shouting soldiers behind. With them were some kings in costume, Tom Hume and a priest.

"We went at speed through the town. I said nothing to Jack but I was ruined. It is a conservative society. Women are protected like chattels. He dropped me and they motored off like outlaws into the night.

"What is the matter with him anyway? He hasn't said much. He's dribbling in his sleep and he smells like musk and dead flowers."

There was a silence while the vehicle jarred its way over a rough patch in the road made up of hand sized holes in dozens of even rows. On the shoulder were small piles of broken tarmac and gravel. Hank held on to the wobbling and bumping steering wheel intently. His hands, on the ten to two position, vibrated up to the wrist and then up the arm to the elbow. They then calmed.

"I hadn't noticed him smelling. He shouldn't, he had a bucket bath this morning which his Chembe friends brought to him. I did notice some things floating in it, leaves I think, when they came to the door. I'm the one who might smell. I've not washed in two days. Jack did eat some foul breakfast though. At least I think so. Can't remember, I left in a hurry. Did you notice his eyes though? I know he's had some fever but they look like two assholes of cemetery dogs. Red, tired and wriggly. He may be getting a bit bush mad. I worry a bit about that. I wouldn't blame him, really. That posting is the end of the world. One problem after another. But don't worry. I'll get you both back."

The road had continued on, now flat and even. They passed another line of irrigation hoses closer to the road. They rotated and danced water up and down into the hazy sun. This time a rainbow painted on a sheet of mist floated across the road ahead of them where the road began to bend sharply towards the south. The horizon directly ahead had a line of deep green trees above which was a stripe of bright sky and then beyond that the narrow flowing and darkening band of cloud which reached into the sky just above the level of the windshield. Juliet spoke in a whisper. Jack was mumbling in his sleep.

"Look at that rainbow. The women at my place thought that rainbows are bad luck. It's supposed to be a Mama Wuta showing all her colours, shouting in fact, while she is pointing to where she is angry. And there is the river just peeping behind the trees. It's brown. It is only a mile wide here. Just one half hour to the ferry. I really am hungry, Hank.

"You know Hank, I actually visited Jack at his school once. It was when the project was just starting and we were all excited about what we were doing and where we were and who we were. One of the wealthy construction guys, you know the ones who live in the big coloured mansions near my school, he's a patron of my school, big Whig in the party and friend of the governor and so on had told me about the Mountain.

"I met him as I was being introduced around on my first day. A big sweaty guy, smelling of acidic perfume. Staring at my chest. He told me that he had had something to do with building the main road. I think the terms of the international loan to build it required there be a local partner. It cost millions really. The main use and traffic is to transport minerals and hardwoods from the border. That and transfer Aid officials around. He said his company did the hardwoods too as well as extract the minerals. Into everything that guy. Maybe oil he said.

"The guy wore a dark blue silk suit but one of those little round striped traditional hats. He was a friend of the old general. You know the old soldier who was in that hotel on the hillside above the town. The only other guest actually. Jack and I and Tom Hume from the other school all stayed there together when we first arrived for the project. First the plane had to force land and then we had to bus from over the river to get here. No one knew we were coming although you said, Hank, that we would be met at the airport and taken straight to our postings. There actually is no civilian airport here. We arrived by bus then we went to the ministry to introduce ourselves. They didn't know us from Adam and Eve. So they put us in the old hotel for two weeks until the three schools were sorted out. The general was there.

"It had a slimy broken swimming pool and no bar. The kitchen served beans and eggs every day and they seemed delighted to do so. Small boys were the cooks and chambermaids. You remember Hank, I used to tip them out of guilt and I put "small boy" on some expense claims I mailed in, when the post worked, which you then disallowed. At one point you were so worried I heard you were going to visit.

"Great flourishes of serving beans and eggs there. Also great fun with small boy versus rats in screaming hunts between the rooms. I think the two weeks there in the filth eating rubbish was a good orientation. It should be part of your policy Hank. Anyway, I got oriented and settled in.

"And this old general lived there. He had had the same room since retiring and the construction people who built the hotel had left. It was supposed to be for the tourist industry. He was the "butcher of" somewhere. The butcher of some town, I forget which, that he had marched through and slaughtered everybody during the last civil war. They say they stacked the bodies to dry before burning them. Went to the military school at home. He said he was very impressed how we served salads at every meal over there. Jack talked to him for hours. Jack was quite sensible then. The general said no one trusted him and that the "Serpent of God", the intelligence service, was always watching him. I think he was a Chembe.

"Anyway the rich guy with the suit mentioned the Mountain at Jack's. This was about four months later. A spot of local interest. Could be a national park and tourist destination except the Chembe were nuts. Told me all kinds of stories about it. He said that the church stored all its wines in caves on the Mountain during the world war to prevent them being looted. They shipped them from Europe with precious plates and holy furniture and sent nuns and priests to guard them. He said the priests were from a church cult of Boglomites or Bashkiris or something and had to come here to redeem themselves in the church. It was some cult of marrying pagans to convert them. They had been causing some scandals in Europe somewhere. He said that in the old days some tribal rebels lived on the Mountain and they used to come down and raid the mission for materials to build their hidden camps. They took furniture and building supplies. They even took some pews and school desks. They were wiped out though.

"He wasn't sure when that happened. The Mountain, he said, may be flat topped and part of the old plateau or maybe part of the volcanic range. There is a lake up there. There is also some mining and tree cutting on the other side by the border.

"He said that the Mountain had stone aged people on the top of it that were untouched by modern life. Perhaps cannibals or nature worshippers. He said the women had many husbands, just the opposite of the Governor. Of course that interested me. He offered to take me there and show me. He was a gutsy, smelly bastard. But I sent a message to Jack instead who was just settling in there. He sent a message back that I could come and stay overnight at the house of the female teachers. What a bunch of giggly drunks they were. Native beer and wine. And their clothes! When they got out of those coverings they wore to teach in! Gold slippers! Rock chick t-shirts! They listened all night to slow blues and Hambone Jones records on a battery driven player. They cried. They kept jumping up and down with tears in their eyes to change or replay the track records because someone had stolen the remote to use it in a traditional dance.

"Jack arranged a supper at Madame Youngo's house. It was three times as large as the other staff quarters. She had a half dozen small girls and boys to spin around back and forth arranging cushions, lighting candles, filling the generator with petrol, cook, sweep. We ate pounded tubers with butter, green pumpkin and a sort of seedy spinach which was very gooey. We had some kind of rice topped with a meat which looked like a small baby. She had invited Jack, a village Elder and the Chembe teacher. The whole house was furnished in very heavy varnished sideboards and cupboards and tables. It was very dark and smelled of honey. On one table was a picture in a gold frame of a nun and a priest. Next to it was a picture of the Governor. There was no other ornament. The soft furnishings were all burgundy cracked leather. Some of the serving dishes looked like they were from a church.

"Madame Youngo talked of the time in her uncle's village when she was a small girl. She planted and hoed and cooked and washed and so on. She was beaten every day and it was, according to her, all very good for her. She said there was nothing special about the Mountain and that local people just made up stories to make their lives more interesting or have excuses to drink native beer and have dancing parties. She said the main thing was to not listen to rumours or alarms and just do your job. She was the Governor's wife.

"Next morning Jack called for me at the women's staff house. He had the Chembe teacher with him and a kind of elderly person in a flour sack but wearing a school head tie. A round-faced woman. She looked like the one at the play. These were to guide us. Jack and the Chembe guy stayed together most of the time although the Chembe man and the woman disappeared later. They kept talking the whole time about geography and history. A right couple of teachers. They babbled on about the benefits to Europe of the Black Death in strengthening the state, the church and rule of law. They talked of the mysterious declines in local populations. No one knew where people went to. They talked of types of tribal democracies. I tried to explain metastasis to them but they would have none of it. There was a big argument. The Chembe said "There is no sun over the new". What did he mean by that? Jack is a good climber and sometimes he seemed to make sense.

"These were our early days, remember, and we were enthusiastic about everything. Curious. Jack was really quite earnest, a bit attractive really, and the Chembe man seemed to want to devour everything we said. He kept asking me about dowry customs and ritual sacrifice in ancient Greece.

"We went up the mountain on a narrow path that started behind the church. The tubby little woman was first, then Jack and then me. The Chembe teacher was behind. It was gorgeous! There were green and yellow orchids in the tree tops, bean pods that were two feet long. There were the kind of cabbage palms that look like big green brains. The tree crowns were sometimes red and surrounded in clouds of insects. Sometimes they were purple and covered in grey velvet.

"I saw a huge white moth. We could hear water falling on both sides of the path. There were tiny little paths to the left and right which Jack said led to fruit trees. But along one I saw a conical pile of white stones. The Chembe man said that the local diet a few decades ago was studied and that it had over one hundred kinds of plant leaf and three hundred kinds of fruit. He said many were medicinally useful.

"The path wound upwards doubling back on itself every so often around bare grey outcrops. At one point we went under the entrance to a cave. It was no larger than my head and shoulders. The little woman might have squeezed in. The Chembe man had gone. It got hotter and hotter as we climbed and more humid. The little women in front began to hum some sort of chanting echoey thing. She then vanished too. I followed along with Jack and then I fainted. I passed right out. That was the end of my passage to the top.

"I do not remember a single thing of the rest of that day. Jack said I fell down and was only out for a moment. He said they decided to turn around and walk down but I don't remember that. I wasn't cut or anything and no bruises. Next morning I had a slight fever when I woke up.

"Jack arranged to get the minivan to come from the village to take me home first thing the next morning. I stayed at Jack's that night. Madame sent a basket of fruit. As Jack was seeing me off in the early morning he said he still disagreed with what I said about matriarchy although I don't remember saying anything.

"But then an odd thing happened. It was the season of the dust storms so that morning it was very obscure. A strongish wind was blowing and there were a few dust devils in the dark, even moving around the houses. Jack had brought a dead snake out from his kitchen to show me and even offered it to me to take back with me. What a madman.

"Jack had known of it first, after his house boy had seen it the previous night in the kitchen. Jack had hired the houseboy because he wore a traditional knife and a big skin hat even though he was just a little boy. Jack said that he wanted the boy to deal with insects, rats and so on in the house, maybe the mice. The little creature also cooked and washed.

"Jack ran to the kitchen when we heard the boy cry. He said the snake was mostly under the table but quite a bit protruded outward. The head was underneath on a coil but the eyes glinted.

"The boy was pressed cowering against the wall. When he saw Jack in the doorway he sort of squeaked "I will save you master". He pulled out his machete from his belt and rushed at the snake. He then cut off the tail.

"This of course enraged the snake which unravelled itself and slithered towards Jack. Jack said later it did not hiss but chirped. I was trembling on the couch. "It runs, it jumps!" said the boy. Jack backed into the main room, reached behind himself and grabbed the senior staff fan. With that he hammered the snake using the fan's base just as the snake came through the door. The fan was plugged in and there was electricity that night. Jack said that the fan was at the very end of the cord and just reached the snake's head as it came sliding and chirping across the threshold. I had my eyes closed. Jack had pushed the coloured light button accidentally while hitting the snake and also the speed button; you know those fans, he hit them just as he picked up the fan so the snake died in a flashing whirr of purple and red.

"Anyway there was the minivan and driver, there was Jack holding the bloody snake by the driver's window in the early dark, and there was me in jeans and kerchief sitting behind the driver with my suitcase and basket of fruit, a little dazed and hungry and confused peering out at Jack in a morning dusty fog.

"We heard a kind of chanting and stomping in the dust with some kind of horn blowing. "It is the girl's club," said Jack. "They have come to see you off. Isn't that great!" The chant was "I love you, a bushel and a peck, a bushel and a peck and a hug around the neck."

"Out of the mist marched thirty-odd women and girls in white halter tops, short skirts and frogged jackets. They had white plastic boots. They each wore high topped peaked caps with gold braid. They stopped with the first row just an arm's length from Jack and the van. There were finally six rows of six girls stepping from out of the fog. Each row came to a stop just behind the other. They did a little step from foot to foot.

"Two in the back, twins, were repeatedly blowing what looked to be an old brown brass trumpet and one old black oboe. Two in the front carried a fringed banner on broomsticks that read "Mission Girls' Club" I noticed that the apostrophe was right.

"When they had all stopped and were stepping stationary side to side, one of the twins, the trumpet blowing one, took the trumpet from her lips and shouted. "We love you Mister Jack. We welcome the good-bye of your friend from us." There was another blast on the trumpet and then the whole lot turned around at once, bent their backsides and wiggled them clucking "Coo coochy coo, Girls' club, girls' club! Rub a dub dub!" Another blast of trumpets and they marched back into the fog.

""Great isn't it," said Jack. "The club and the uniforms are a school tradition from the time of the nuns. Even Madame Youngo couldn't suppress it if she knew. The uniforms were a gift from a denominational school twinned with us on the continent. We keep them in the library. I thought it was locked but they must have a key. I love it here.""

"I think he was going even then," said Hank. There was a silence.

"Here comes the chicken village," said Hank suddenly. "Freshly roasted and seasoned, none better in the world."

The tarmac road here was built on a pad of gravel sand above the level of the plain and separated from it by a ditch on each side. At the entrance to the village the road began to be connected by little bridges to each side to wooden shacks, first in ones and twos and then built more and more densely together, perched on small stilts and some on logs and piles of gravel, each a little beyond the ditch and raised from the plain. They all were tethered to the road connected by their own little footbridges of planks, roped across frames of thin tree trunks. The ditch was dry and filled with paper and metal rubbish. It contained some brown goats. Hank slowed because of the goats and because of the approach to a main square surrounded by yellow huts. The ditches ahead of the square each ran at angles outward to the left and right and around, leaving the square as a wide island above the plain.

The road ran through the square's centre and then beyond the rest of the village straight south into the plain. There, a little distance more, a line of green trees angled towards the road. Neither Hank nor Juliet commented as the black clouds above those trees lit up suddenly grey and pink with a flash of lightening. The sky immediately above the trees was still bright blue but only a thin white stripe now shone narrowly above the cloud on the horizon. The trees were waving.

Hank had slowed nearly to a stop. There were minivans parked around the square. The huts were open faced and empty. At the far end of the square, to the left of the exit, there was a wispy column of brown smoke. Surrounding this there was a crowd of people some of whom were jumping up and down.

"Chicken, ferry and home in that order," said Hank. He sped up slightly. He and Juliet both looked to the left and right for braziers and vendors in the huts. They were all empty.

As they passed the backs of the crowd they saw over heads and between backs that the smoke was coming from a blazing minivan. A dark face was pressed against a rear window in the van, lit by flames inside but still obscure through the dense smoke in the van. Two burning hands were pressed grasping on the uncracked glass of a window. The air above shimmered and flames leapt from underneath the van and across the hood. Some of the crowd were running up to the van carrying tyres or planks and hurling them underneath. The others were drawing slowly back.

Beyond this, another van was being rocked at the very edge of the square by a dozen shouting men naked to the waist and by a few women in black. This van had a large megaphone mounted on the roof. The side was painted with the arrowhead symbol of the People's Redemptionist Party. There was a strong odour of burning rubber, yellow glue, rancid fat and wax paper.

Hank accelerated out of the square past a straggle of stilted houses where the square ended and the ditches resumed. Juliet had rolled down the window and vomited noisily down the side of the vehicle. Jack did not stir.

The car rocked over another series of bumps and then flew straight along the smooth road raised above the sunlit plain for some five minutes. Juliet rolled up the window. She then said, "I hate this place."

Hank shouted "God Almighty!" and pulled on the steering wheel. The vehicle, brakes locked and screaming, swayed from side to side on the road. A back wheel went slightly over the shoulder and onto the lip of the ditch. Simultaneously there was a heavy thump at the front, a more violent swaying, and then a bloody face smashed against the windscreen immediately in front of Hank. Its tongue stretched out to the passenger side, one eye was split and crushed. Then it was gone. There was another thump on the roof and the vehicle came to a stop.

Both Hank and Juliet turned around to see a black lump laying in the middle of the road some several lengths back. There was some glass on the road too and thick tyre marks.

The front windscreen was smeared. Jack had hit his head on the dash and was now blinking awake rubbing his brow. "I suppose this is down to me, too," he said.

The glove compartment had fallen open and papers were scattered over Hank's feet.

"Don't stop!" said Juliet loudly. "Don't ever stop! Get out of here! This is the policy. It was in a memo. Your memo. You are supposed to drive on to the nearest police post and report there. Get going!"

"We are supposed to help them, not kill them," said Jack. "Wait a minute for God's sake. I'll go back and see if he's alive." He reached for the door.

"No. No. No. Look, there are some people in that field," cried Juliet. "They can help him. They are coming this way. You complete stupid bastard, Jack. Let go of the door. Look they are looking this way at us now."

When Jack's door opened the vehicle was filled instantly with a fetid wind and brown dust. A distant but rapidly rising banging howl rattled the windows. It was some vast broken rolling thing. Through the windshield, the open door and the window immediately beside Juliet they could see a curving dark plough of cloud rising to the highest sky, racing and rushing towards them pushing ahead curtains of silver rain. Gravel hit the windscreen. Jack slammed the door closed and the car rocked from side to side. They were then instantly drowned in a crashing white spotted blackness. The vehicle's roof, sides and windows were pummelled by hailstones from all directions. Small globes of yellow light flashed horizontally by the windows and along the front hood over the top. The storm then squeezed tightly together into an impenetrable dense streaking downpour hammering head on, hammering the sides and the roof. It beat on the windshield while gusts lashed back and forth smashing into rattling window glass. The sound of rushing water started up under the vehicle and slopped heavily to the sides. Juliet cried out something but could not be heard.

All three sat immobile. The engine had stalled earlier in the collision but after several minutes Hank groped and started it again. Some water seeped around the windows and around the windscreen seams. It had gotten very cold so Hank turned on the large heater under the dash by his right knee. He also turned on the car light inside the vehicle which only produced a brown, orange and moist globe of light around the front seats. From time to time he raced the engine slightly at which the light brightened slightly. The initial wall of noise lessened and settled to a continuous rush. There were flashes of lightning to the left and right and behind. The blackness became greenish.

"It runs, it leaps," said Jack. The hammering continued.

"It is my tradition," shouted Jack suddenly, "that when the rains begin I get into them and dance. The world is renewed, the new is born."

"Who gives a damn," cried Juliet from behind. "Shut up you mad bastard." Jack laughed. Suddenly Jack opened his door to a burst of rain and howling wind. It slammed and he was gone.

"When the rain lets up we will look for him," shouted Hank. "If we don't find him in a short time we will drive to the police station." Hank then continued speaking firmly and rhythmically over his shoulder to Juliet, pausing at the end of each phrase, smiling and nodding to her and awaiting her return nod at the end of each phrase before going on. "Relax Juliet. We will report everything. If the last ferry is gone we will get rooms on this side. Tomorrow we will cross and drive to the offices in the capital. There we will sort everything out. Then you can go home. We could be on the same plane." The wind howled.

There came a loud and sharp tap on the driver's side. There was Jack's face, hair flattened on his forehead. He spun his hands crossing in front of his nose and bobbed up and down.

He then turned twice around and hopped backwards on one leg into the blackness.

VII

The road to the ferry crossing descended from a gap between two low hills to a long curving bay. The river reflected milky white and silver in the morning sun which was itself pale and small in the grey sky as through a veil. Soon it would vanish.

Water flowed in spidery braids down the hillsides and into the road's choked side ditches. A thin sheet of water flowed down the road's surface as well. The town below sparkled from tin roofs and still black pools of water in empty spaces between the shadowed houses. To the far right was the skeleton of some bridge project rising split and rusted from a shining mud bank. There were clusters of long thin empty craft, long canoes near the shore nosing franticly into the bank on straining ropes tied to partially submerged fallen concrete blocks and there were more further out, anchored in pulling and straining nests a few lengths offshore, clashing together hodge podge. A mist was tightly overhead just below the peaks of the low hills and ridges surrounding this bay in the river.

In the centre of the bay's curve were two tall square towers strung together at their tops with dripping cables. From the feet of each of these towers and into the river, lapped by waves, extended two long lines of thick wooden pylons, each line imperfect with frequent gaps.

Along the road, which ran straight down the hill from a notched gap and straight between the towers, and from there, straight and plunging into the rough water, were dozens of large trucks of all sizes. They were unmoving and unattended, glistening and dripping with rain water into black oil-streaked puddles and into silver rivulets on the road. The trucks were parked on both sides nose to tail and all pointing towards the river. Some trucks were canvas sided and some enclosed. Some had long vents and air holes. Others had refrigeration units over the cabs. A few were piled high in uncovered mounds of miscellany, heaps of scrap boarding, cable and wooden crates all secured with mazes of rope and cable.

The far side of the river was barely visible as a dark thick line over a domed central curve of water at the centre of its bloated and rapidly flowing expanse. The tops of the hills behind, topping the gap from which the vehicle descended, disappeared and appeared in fine mist. As they descended, the passing wash and roar of the river below and in front filled half the sky, seeming higher than the land. It raced south but had lateral white capped waves counter-pointing, reversing on the main direction, waves folding into each other and rolling high and over the flow as the river pummelled under, waves angling in all directions.

The river was dotted heavily with black and brown flotsam including some wildly rotating branched trees. It was living and pulsing, a white dotted scarf being drawn swiftly over a giant invisible hand. It raced out of cloud banks beyond the ruined bridgework at the edge of vision to the right, tossing and rolling swirls of vapour up over the town as it passed in a long spinning sliding curve, like fixed on a string tied to the invisible far bank. It swung back into clouds again at the end of its turn, far up in the overcast sky, at the end of the bay and at that corner of the sky, where clouds billowed up white and grey from water level blowing south as well. At each end of its visible distances, the river travelled from the lowering sky from a ground level black haze of the far bank straight across the horizon constantly vanishing. The river was in a small box of cloud, the mad floor of the whole world, everything in the world, a grey box on a silver plate. Everything immediate and close was detailed and silver; everything distant was obscure and elsewhere. The vehicle drove between the parked trucks through puddles straight towards the waves.

On each side of the two towers, towers built to attract and hold the ferry, lining the beach but on a bank back from it, and back from a gravel fringe of logs and broken waste concrete blocks, were two rows of huts, many with bright fires flashing inside their doors and some with fires burning in front on the beach in rusted oil drums. Some fires were being used to warm circles of empty hands or cookers of meat on sticks and some burned alone and unattended. Nets hung between slanted poles on the mud beach. All these seemed torn into draped windows and drooping portholes framing the river beyond. Running behind the rows of huts, parallel to them and to the beach, was another tarmaced road which intersected the main road just before the central towers at a right angle.

This side road was lined with minivans and pickup trucks and a few brightly coloured long nosed buses. There was a line of tall two-legged metal poles, at right angles to the side road, which came over the hill to join it. Some poles had hanging cables, some sparking blue flashes and small flames, and some of these had hanging, detached black boxes from their cross bars near the top. From one or the other of these pylon boxes sometimes sparks travelled in mad circles in a hanging nest of wire or flew between two wires or down the side of a pylon. The pylons nearest the road were ribboned with streamers of plastic tape extending in braids, hanging and blowing or stretched along the ground like roots to one or the other of four grey concrete buildings.

Each building was set back from the side road unevenly but in a ragged line. Each had a large generator behind it on large flat trailers painted in dark orange and each had an aerial on the roof. One aerial was incompletely broken like a green stick. One of the buildings was fenced. This one had an interior gravelled drive.

On this drive there were several four wheel drive vehicles painted dark blue. The three other buildings had none. Then at the furthest extent of the side road were two big dark green circular buildings with conical tin roofs, also connected to the poles by wires and also with generators. These were built nearest the hills that framed the bay on that side. In the centre of these two buildings was a third small square building painted in yellow, green, blue and red black stripes. All the buildings flew small flags from their roofs.

Hank drove from the bottom of the hill towards the ferry towers but turned left along the side road. He slowed on turning left to drive while searching, looking, glancing to one side or another along the side road as the vehicle crawled along., finally stopping on the shoulder at the building which was set furthest back from the road last in the row, beyond the larger fenced one and just before the circular green ones.

This building had a tin roofed veranda in front on which sat a half dozen blue shirted policemen on cane chairs; two of them were drinking from white mugs and one of those two was propping his feet on a low railing beside the two stairs leading up to the veranda. Hank had stopped the vehicle directly in front of that veranda at the side of the road furthest from the river. The river roared dully and loudly by over the roofs of the huts across the road to his right. The sky was domed creamy white and streaked with grey.

A grating metallic noise and thud shook Hank's vehicle. A small boy on a motorcycle had run into the back of the vehicle as Hank had parked. The police on the veranda all jumped from their chairs at the sound and at the sight, two of their chairs falling over, and they thumped in a clutter down the steps from the veranda shouting. Two stumbled and walked but some ran.

One by one they arrived at the vehicle to surround the boy where he lay at the back partly under his overturned machine. The first two to reach him begun to kick him and the next one bent over to slap his face. Then another joined. Hank opened his door and got out as the final three policemen ran past. "No, no, no!" Hank shouted. One policeman stopped and turned and said, "Do not worry Mister. We will punish him."

The kickers stopped after a half dozen boots each and two slappers dragged the boy from under the bike. The boy was weeping and begging through bloody teeth. The kickers straightened up the bike and began to wheel it away behind the building.

The two slappers lifted the boy up, one lifting under each of his arms, and walked him, his legs waving, along the side of the road left towards the fenced building next door. They slapped the boy with their free hands taking turns, one with his left and one with his right, still lifting as they went through the gate by which time the boy's toes dragged in the gravel drive. The slappers dragged the boy past four parked police vehicles. The door of this building was then opened by another policeman, a fat one with holster and cross belt, who came out shouting to grab the boy by the feet, raising them up with a jerk and then walking the horizontal body backwards as the other two held the boy suspended by his arms. The three carried the boy inside as he screamed.

The two remaining policemen watched all this as did Hank. Then one walked over to the rear of the vehicle where Hank now stood. The other, thinner and taller, went back to the veranda and into the office. The one approaching Hank was much heavier and older than any other had been. He had some stars on his shoulders. He, like the others, was bare headed and he alone still held his mug which he sipped from. He looked at the damage as he walked all around the car. It was a broken tail light. There was also a broken head light.

"Please sir you must come inside and make a report," the policeman said as he reached Hank after circling.

The policemen went back to the front and looked at it again. He looked at the smeared windscreen. He peered inside the car through the side window. He returned to where Hank was still standing. "Was that an animal?" He asked. "But do come in, and bring your friends with you. It is warm inside and drier. There has been a mighty storm here and there could be another."

Hank turned back to the vehicle and opened the door. He said nothing, only nodded and gestured with a curling finger. Juliet was now in the front passenger's seat. Jack was lying on the back seat. Juliet got out of her door and Hank opened the door for Jack. Jack propelled himself awkwardly feet forward and out. He was wet all over his body, especially his hair, and was shoeless. Jack slapped himself gently on each cheek. He shook his head.

"This is the right thing to do," said Juliet to Hank, as she walked by him after walking around the front of the vehicle. She then walked towards the veranda following the large policeman. Jack, swaying in his stockings, said, "Should I confess?" in a loud voice which caused the policeman to look briefly back over his shoulder as he walked.

Hank raised his hand flatly up to his own face to squeeze his nostrils. He leaned forward and whispered under it to Jack, "Would you ever just be quiet Jack? Just shut up. You've had a knock on the head maybe two and you have some kind of fever. You are raving. I will handle this. Just shut up."

The three trooped up the step across the veranda in a line and went inside the open door behind the policeman who closed the door loudly after they passed. There was a desk to the right of the entry door and an open side door to the left beyond which was a room, empty but for a rectangular green metal table with four chairs. The policeman indicated that room.

At the desk in the outer room sat the thin policeman who had entered earlier. He was now reading from a manila file. He ignored their entry. From behind the back wall and beyond a closed door there came a sizzle and hum, punctuated with mild soft babbles from an active radio. There were calendars and notices taped to the walls around pictures of the Governor.

The three entered the side room still in a file. The room was bare but for the table and chairs. It was painted green over the concrete. They sat on the chairs on three sides of the table and the policeman took the fourth facing the door and Hank. Jack was to the policeman's left, Juliet to the right.

The policeman offered nothing and said nothing but glanced at each in turn, taking longer with Juliet whose red hair was damp and explosive and briefly at Jack which glance he followed with a slight shake of his head. The policeman still had his mug. He sipped from it and then put it on the table. Then he spoke.

"In a while we will write out your statement. It may be a bit more complicated than I thought at first. Then we will take you to a place to stay for awhile while we investigate."

"Excuse me officer," said Hank, "I would prefer it if we just give the statement now and go. I will pay any necessary fine to whoever wants one and I can come back later if necessary. We just want to catch the ferry and go on today. We have been awake all night. I have urgent business with my agency."

"But Mister sir," said the policeman, "please be patient. You are too hasty. I wouldn't pay any fines if I was you. There are plenty of people who take them who aren't even real policemen." He paused and then laughed loudly. The three stared urgently at one another. The policeman laughed again.

"But don't worry. I am real. We are the regional police here. We do things properly. I think you have hit something big on the front. It may be an animal or a person. We will have to go and investigate the someplace you say it happened and see if it is the whoever you say. You must say these things to us. This is your duty. We will then follow our official steps. We are investigators. Only after we do our things, as for all things like this thing, do we do the statements to say what is to be said and do the rest to be done.

"If it is an animal you must pay for it. If it is a person you will go to our court for testimonies and blame and punishment, it may be the animal's or a person's fault, and then you must go to the traditional court for the compensation for the sin.

"If it is a person dead we have a problem because these people around here do not trust us and they hide bodies. We will have to search the village for it. If we can't find it then it will be impossible to go forward. Sometimes we find a body and bring it back but it is the wrong one. A woman or a child not a man. Someone shot not stabbed. Your claim then would not be confirmed. Then we would not do a statement. The facts would not permit it on the record."

"You mean," said Hank, "that you can kill someone and it can be as if nothing happened?"

"You could get t-shirts printed," said Jack. "They could say "The Killer". We could all wear them." The policeman looked again at Jack who was dripping from his hair onto the table. The policeman shook his head again. Jack was shivering slightly and seemed to be grinding his teeth. Juliet sighed.

"You must stay here while we investigate. It will not take long. It is a formality really. You can stay in our tourist chalets at the end of the street. They are very nice, we very seldom use them, especially to detain. They were built by an Aid program. They are in traditional roundel style, you should like that, foreigners do, and they have refrigerators and senior staff fans.

"We will not take long. And we do not think the ferry will arrive today anyway. It has been broken on the other side for the last three days. They may have to bring the replacement from up the river. The river is very high and anyone who drove onto the ferry if it did come would have to go a distance into the river to go up the safety ramp. We have the latest safety ramp from overseas. The river could go over your floorboards. Even the minivan drivers will not do that. The river should go down later if it doesn't rain again.

"But we think it may flood further upriver later today from the water from the mountains. Then it would go into the plain in which case it may cut the road on the other side of the hills. If that happens we would have trouble investigating where you came from and things could be delayed." He chuckled and shook his head. "Just relax."

A man in a white shirt and black pants appeared at the room's door from within the main building. He waved to the seated policeman who immediately excused himself, got up and walked to the door. He placed his arm over the shoulder of the white shirted man at the door and walked him out of sight back to the right. Hank, Jack and Juliet sat in silence. No clock ticked but the radio hummed behind some muffled voices beyond the walls. The river sound was very faint. A motorcycle engine started up briefly to the back then stopped. The policeman at the desk in the outer room could be seen by Juliet and Jack still sitting reading his file and pursing his lips. Hank stared ahead at the empty chair the heavy policeman had left and at the bare green behind. Another person entered the building slamming the front door and walked swiftly past their open door. He glanced in the room as he went by. He was also a policeman. He was in wet uniform and wearing his hat.

The big policeman then returned and took his seat. He had a handkerchief which he passed to Jack who used it to wipe some rivulets from his cheek.

"There has been a lot of satellite and radio traffic about Chembeland. Is that where you have come from? Trouble seems to be radiating out from there. Flying down the road like revenging witches. The small boy we think you hit in front was actually carrying a message from the Serpent of God intelligence unit in the army about it. We've now read that. We are called by them to do a lot of work. It may delay our investigation of your case. It changes priorities. I hope you understand.

"There has been a disturbance during curfew after a cultural event. There was some sort of procession on a mountain or an anti-government protest, maybe a religious one, against corruption or something, probably insulting the Governor and other religions and women as these things do. It seems the local police mistakenly fired some shots at officials or at the army or something. There was returned fire. Buildings have been burnt. A school has been looted. The whole thing seems to have started with some kind of ritual killing or the attempted assassination of an official. It seems to be tribal disturbance or religious conflict. There was an accusation of some kind of insult or abomination. Just as we have gotten used to around here lately.

"Some Bechembe nationalists and youth seem to have used the chaos and looting as a cover to commit an honour killing of a young girl, maybe pregnant, who was on the road. We will be very busy. There are some threats of retaliation. It could be as bad as the last troubles. How far behind you on the road were these things? Did you come through those places? Do you know anything about any of this?

"We are now instructed to stop all male Chembes from crossing. How can we do that, I ask you? And also a particular truck load of young Bechembe men. We are to detain them so the Serpent can question them. They may be on their way. We are also looking for a female traditional leader and her consort and an old soldier or old guard and also some local police. It seems the Redeemer has issued a bloody statement from the mountains and that the Bechembe town is under martial law. Did you see anything of that on the road coming here? Did you see any vehicles that looked suspicious?"

"We know nothing of any of that," said Hank, speaking swiftly and over any attempted interruptions. "How can we? We are Aid officials. Don't worry about our agency; it is harmless. In fact, sometimes it is barely competent. We are involved in community development. We are all with the agency and under its protection. We are not political. I now have my aerial flag in the glove compartment of the car but I can get it out. You can check. I have my identification and a letter of introduction for officials in my wallet. It is signed by the Governor and in four languages. We are under protection of my government too. We are returning to our country office. I just want to get over the river. That's all. My colleague Jack is sick and Madame Juliet is changing assignments. We'll wait in your chalet voluntarily as you ask until the ferry comes. That is all I can do. I will write a report. I'll leave it for you or send it back. I will of course co-operate with you in every way." Juliet coughed dryly and Jack stared through red eyes at the policeman. Hank clasped his hands in front of him and then spoke evenly and softly.

"Yes, yes we did hit something. That is true. It is why we are here. We have nothing to hide. It was just past the last village on the plain before the hills. It was just before the rains began. Our Jack here went back in the rain but he fell in a ditch. He said he couldn't see anything. There were some others about but they were gone. It may have been something small. After he came back to the car we sat for awhile and waited for the rain to stop. Jack was really wet so we warmed him and let him sleep. We did want to report immediately. We wanted to get away to here right away. When the rain lightened up we went a few miles on but the rain started again heavily. I was afraid we might hit a truck or go into a ditch. I found a place where we could pull onto a shoulder and we sat there until just before dawn. Then we came straight here. That is basically all that happened. We saw nothing suspicious on the road. Everything is normal. I will do a full statement. I am sure you will find nothing."

"Thank you very much for that Mister sir," said the policeman finally. He had wanted to ask questions as Hank had spoken. "I know about your agency and what it does. I believe you are from them. You can do that statement later. I will follow the regulations and then I am sure you can go. My assistant officer at the desk through there has the keys to the tourist chalet. Follow him there. You should take your bags. I will inform you when we have completed our enquiries. We have to go to that village anyway; there was some kind of incident there as well. It should all only take a few hours.

Thank you for co-operation. We must follow our procedures for everyone. This may not be complicated. I hope you excuse us." He remained seated. The thin officer at the desk outside had risen to his feet and beckoned to Juliet and Jack. When they rose, Hank on seeing them did too, turned and followed them outside behind the thin man. Hank was smiling tightly.

All of the doors to the vehicle were open. Their bags had been taken out and were placed on the gravel at the vehicle's side. Through the driver's open door Jack could see that the glove compartment was open. Juliet's brightly coloured luggage was scuffed and muddy. The thin man walked on and they picked up their bags to follow. He went splashing to the very end of the street with them following in a straggling line. He unlocked the door to the gaily striped building. It had a sign over the door reading "Reception". The flag on its roof had the arrowhead symbol. The policeman pointed to the ground in front of the door as the three arrived, Jack last, wincing and wobbling in stocking feet. The three in turn stopped at the spot indicated by the thin man. Then the policeman went inside. "Listen to that river," said Hank.

The policeman only came back outside the small striped building again after they had waited for many minutes. The policeman now had another key on a thick string which was attached to a metal plate on which was painted the number "1" in blue paint. He beckoned to the three and walked left towards the large circular green building on that side which, as the other, had a conical roof. This building also flew the party flag.

The outer walls of the building were of corrugated tin covered with many layers of paint. The roof was also of tin but unpainted. The door was of faded and splintered wood. There were round portholes spaced around the curving walls, each with white trim. The policeman opened the door, stood aside and said, "The Chalet," and pointed their way in. The three went past and in over a raised concrete threshold carrying their bags, Juliet sniffing slightly and Hank steadying Jack who hobbled in front of him. The damp interior smelled of varieties of mildew and perhaps rubbish. It was dark except for the grey spotlights cast forward onto the bare concrete floors by the portholes. There were scattered shadowy shapes of furniture.

The door closed behind with a hard thump and the key turned tinnily to lock it.

Juliet put down her bags and moved to the porthole nearest the door on the left side. Jack and Hank were both blinking adjustment to the gloom. "He is going back into the reception," she said. "The bugger has locked us in."

Juliet turned and walked to where Jack and Hank stood. In the gloom they could distinguish a grouping of chairs and a table. "Listen Hank, you had a busy day yesterday and didn't sleep much and you've been driving so why not sit down and have a little rest and a little think. We've reported now and done our duty so we just need to finish up here and get out. You just have a little think and I'll think of a way to get some food and something to drink.

"I'll shout through the window to that man or something. I'll get him as he leaves reception for the office. You, Jack, you will catch your death. Just sit down and I'll find something to dry you off with. I have some painkillers in my bag too."

"We have to go back," said Jack. Hank had moved in the gloom to a damp plush couch and had sat down. Juliet pushed Jack by the elbow to the couch and when he was close enough Hank took an arm and gently pulled Jack down beside him. Jack was trembling. "We must go back. Everything is simplifying. We are guilty." Jack said.

The room they were in was a large semi-circle as a low particle board partition had been built halfway across the roundel. This went only to the height of the walls but where the roof began, inside the cone, the whole space was entirely open above as a great dark circle with beams rising up along the inner cone to its highest point into the dark. In the partition were three doors. Juliet darted to each in turn, opened it and went quickly in. Coming out of the first she said that it was a bedroom with sheets and blankets. Exiting the second she brought with her a grey thin blanket and tossed it through the gloom to Hank who smelled it after catching it, and then standing began drying off an unresisting Jack, beginning with his hair. "We have a duty to go back. I was wrong," Jack said through the blanket.

"This room is a bathroom," said Juliet coming out of the third door. "I tested the water and it is tepid. They must have had electricity yesterday. We can each have a shower and change. Jack you need to put on dry clothes."

Hank let go of the blanket which fell down across Jack's chest. He sat down beside Jack heavily. Hank was trembling too. "Frankly Jack, I don't give a damn if everything is simplifying, whatever that means. I don't care if there is a duty. We are going over the river. I want to go home. I'll think about it when I sit by a trout stream under a tree. I want a row-boat Jack. I want jam. I couldn't give a piss about good guys and bad guys and duty. I don't care about colonial guilt and special compensation. I don't care about good development and good governance, sexually transmitted diseases or water borne ones or even space borne ones, or extended famines, infested insect bites and imminent apocalypses. I want to see double headed daffodils. I want to get out of here." As he ended he was very loud.

"Good God Hank, what is all that about!" said Juliet. "You must be tired, poor thing." She was walking through the shadows back to the porthole in the wall by the door. When she reached it she opened it outward with a squeal of its hinges. It was large enough for her to get a head and shoulder out. She put them out and suddenly shouted, "You! You! Officer! Grasshopper head! We are hungry." She stepped back from the window and put her hands on her hips. Then she reached into the pocket of her culottes and took out several notes. "Here he comes," she said.

The thin policeman's face appeared at the pothole. Juliet gestured to her mouth and made a smacking sound. "We are hungry! Take money. We are thirsty. Tea. Tea." She stepped to the porthole and handed through the money. The face disappeared.

"O.K everyone, showers and then some food. Hank you and Jack take the end room and I'll take the middle. They are drier though they are dark. Curved walls and portholes. Very exotic. But if it rains again it will be like being in a drum."

"Now cheer up Hank," She went on. "Don't be your usual grumpy thing. It was right to report to the police. Good policy. I thought you handled yourself well. I didn't like what you said about the agency but I think you confused the old fatty. Sidestepped the bugger. Let the bull go thundering by. We don't have to tell everything all the time do we? We all know that. It is O.K that we keep some secrets. We did our duty and got by. Don't blame Jack though if it got a bit complicated in there. There can be other points of view. Let's forgive each other and get on. After all, this is all normal here. Always something going on. We'll just have some food and clean up and get on with our lives."

"What do we do after breakfast?" said Jack from the couch with a higher pitch than usual. "Tell tales from our colonial fortress in the plague year? Each tell a story on the ways to do the perfect sacred murder? Tunnel to the circles of paradise? You are a mad woman Juliet, travelling with a mad man. It is mad work from a mad agency. We should go back."

There was a knock at the door followed by the tin sound of the latch. Juliet walked to the door towards it saying as she did so, "You need to have something to bring down that fever Jack. You sound like an idiot. An interesting one but an idiot nevertheless. Someone could hear you though." Hank and Jack rose from the couch. The door swung open. The thin policeman was there holding the key. Behind him were three small boys, two with bowls, one of yellow rice mixed with what could be a grass and one of meat and gravy. Perhaps eels. The third held a thermos and three forks. The policeman walked stiffly in past Juliet followed by the boys. The boys moved to the left, set the bowls, forks and thermos down on the sideboard between the two nearest portholes. They stood in front of the sideboard and waited. The policeman went further in, stopped sharply and stared into Hank's face, inches away.

He spoke abruptly and in a low voice between narrowed teeth and lips. "You will listen to me. You foreigners are also part of the law. Do not imagine anything else. I don't care what you or anyone thinks." He raised his hand and waved back over his shoulder.

"You will stay here for a good while. As long as we want. There is now some fighting in that village near where you hit something. It is all getting very close. Did you know that? We have just got that message but even so the captain and most of the others have left. But he will surely be delayed and so will be your investigation. To your pain. I am in charge now.

"The Serpent is coming here soon though to see you. They have radioed. You will behave until then. We have found some documents in your vehicle perhaps cataloguing the looted material at the school in Chembeland. You must explain these. We found some letters in the vehicle that show a conspiracy between foreigners and local dissidents in Chembeland over many years. These seem reports to people abroad. There is evidence of illegal relations, anti-social and immoral behaviour, religious interference, bribery, illegal rites. It is all disgusting and offensive to a patriot and believer. The Serpent is very interested. You were certainly there just recently Mister sirs and madams. We know that now.

"As I am in charge here now, you belong to me and to the Serpent. You will make all your future arrangements through me. You will respect me and talk to me properly." He looked behind him at Juliet who was facing away staring through and out the door.

"You will all treat me with respect always. Your situation is serious. It is very serious. I am different from the Captain you will find out. I will have no complaining. If you want anything tell those boys." He indicated the three standing in shadow by the cupboard. "They speak your language too. No need for gestures. No need to shout out windows. You are after all detainees, not guests. We will all be polite and helpful to each other. If you want to buy something you pay through me. You ask me through the boys. You must pay for the chalet too. Alright? Understood?" The policeman turned on his heel without waiting for a reply and walked through the door. He slammed it behind him. The boys remained.

"Where do they find them?" said Hank. "These northerners. Looking down their thin noses to see foreign spies under every bed causing all the problems. Terrified of immorality with women. Terrified of competitive corruption. He gets his character from gangster movies and fantasies of his religious leaders. Race of warriors. Do you think they believe it themselves? No use trying to reason with him let alone bribe him. He wouldn't accept any denials. Impractical."

"Did you notice that he didn't lock the door? Little Napolean, it would spoil the exit. Incompetent but just promoted. Typical. No focus; emotional and confused. Angry at you Juliet, isn't he? Seemed a bit frightened of Jack. Wouldn't look at him."

"Blind ambition," said Juliet. "Hank, I saw the ferry out the window."

"I still have the keys to the vehicle," said Hank quickly.

Juliet walked back to the door and opened it to a crack. "He is going all the way back to the office; no, he's going past to the building next door through the gate. He'll go into that building. Want to get on the radio, I imagine. Our vehicle is still there on the side of the road and the ferry is still coming! It keeps disappearing behind the swells. There it is! Wind is down a bit but look at that river! God it's a little dirty thing, that ferry.

Nothing on the decks. No, there are some men with long poles pushing at the things in the water. Must be straight here from its repairs. Black smoke. Loads of people are coming out of the huts to the beach." The small boys at the sideboard stared at her intently, listening. They didn't move. Over the river's rushing drone there were some crackles. "Oh my, some sort of disturbance up on the hill. There is a truck skewed across the road and a police vehicle too. Oops! The policemen are coming out of their building. Four of them. They are getting into their vehicle. Mister Thin is there. Only one police vehicle left."

"Let's go," said Hank. "Bring the cases, forget the food. The boys can eat it. Come on Jack. Let's move it. Don't worry Jack, we'll come back later after you are seen to. I promise." He stepped forward to pick up Jack's bag to hand it to him. Juliet came back to pick up her two cases.

The sky had lightened but was still entirely white and grey with a low bubbling roof of streaming cloud. There was a transparent ground fog heavy in the distances. The three lurched through the door and splashed through the puddles in front of the tin building. Hank helped the sodden socked Jack with his free hand at the small of Jack's back while swinging his own bag with the other for acceleration. Jack grimaced with each step and lurch, holding his small piece of luggage tight to his side under one arm with his free arm around Hank's shoulders and neck. Juliet marched up front, often on her toes, with one red bag lifted high in each hand. She looked from side to side and turned often back to check the progress of the two behind. The small boys stood in the doorway.

Many people now were standing on the bank overlooking the mud beach watching and gesturing at the ferry's approach. The ferry had turned almost directly into the flow and was moving upstream opposite the towers between the streaming, swelling lateral currents and its front beat with plumes of spray against the approaching waves. Some of the men who stood on the deck with the poles were now on the bow thrusting at oncoming debris. The intent seemed to be to proceed upriver and turn in an arc to reverse with the current into the gap between the pylons, this at speed since a direct entry was probably impossible due to the current.

In the notched gap into town on the hill, just below an upper border of mist and cloud, a six wheeled canvas sided truck was skewed at right angles to the road blocking it. Two police vehicles were drawn up below this in an arrowhead formation, point facing the truck. In the area walled by the arrow some figures in blue crouched behind each of these two vehicles. There were figures uphill behind the truck as well. On the road in the gap between the two vehicles and the truck there were two black mounds.

There was no sign of any activity from the concrete buildings as the three reached Hank's vehicle where it was parked. The doors to the back, front seats and to the left rear all opened easily in turn as Juliet put her bags into the rear and then taking theirs from Hank and Jack hurled those in on top. Hank got into the driver's side and started the engine. Jack hobbled around to the front passenger side. Hank opened that door from inside and pulled Jack in. Jack sat and turned groggily to close his door. Juliet after closing the rear door raced around and opened the door to the back seat, dove in, and righted herself to close the door.

All the three doors slammed almost simultaneously but were virtually inaudible within the sound of the river and against renewed staccato sounds from the hill. The vehicle leapt to a start and after a horseshoe turn spraying wet gravel sped down the street. Juliet looked behind them over their cases to see that a man in white shirt and dark trousers had come to the door of the smaller building with the veranda. He looked after them and then at the ferry which had completed its turn to face downriver and was arcing at a sharp angle towards the pylons.

Hank reached the intersection and turned into the road down between the towers. The ferry had by now turned at the downriver line of pylons at their furthest extremity, hit and then grazed inward by the upriver line and then swayed violently to the right; it was cantering and centring itself threading between the files. The ferry emitted a roar of acceleration and spewed out a churning boil of wake as it hit first the downriver row of pylons, and then the other again as it approached the shore. It impacted just behind its bow and then swung back to hit the other side almost at the front. Two of the men with poles disappeared behind a guard rail.

The sound of the engines softened as the boat eased up between the final pylons towards the water's edge where the road went under the waves and where Hank had now stopped. The ferry stopped too, held on the bottom with the thrust of quietening engines but rocking from side as it pushed in, stationary, about six vehicle lengths from the shore.

The ferry was long but squat. A big covered barge really. The wheelhouse was a yellow shack at the back. This had a small mast hung with an array of large round lights topped by a single aerial. The open top deck was only a bit more the height of a tall truck above the waterline. The deck had a dozen rows of metal benches facing forward and behind these were several rows of black lockers. The boat's front had two large doors that were now opening along the seam of a curving bow ahead of and under the guardrail above, now lined with four shouting waving men carrying long poles.

The bow doors opened just above the waterline over a curving threshold knee high above the water, raised up but bobbing although grounded where the ferry was now pushing against the sharply rising upwards slope of the bottom. From the doors, swinging open to bang on the pylons at the sides, emerged the end of a rusty steel ramp just the width of a truck. The ramp was being wheeled forward on small round metal wheels along the interior deck by four black jacketed men. It was partially suspended from a square yellow tubular frame just inside the open doors. The ramp was pushed out by the men and dropped forward suddenly into the water, held by chains clattering through round brackets at the top of the frame on its front outside edge. The frame wobbled and the ramp swayed.

The ramp fell into the water about six vehicle lengths in front of the shore causing a localised swell, a ripple, to move backwards to the ship, there to lap over the threshold of the doors into the lower deck. The men in black swayed, holding to the chains and steadying the ramp as the ship rose and fell on the river's flow.

The ramp slid back and forth, grounded but loose. The ferry lurched from side to side and the yellow frame inside on the low roofed deck jerked backwards then forwards along the deck. The back parts of the ramp bumped up and down where it had dropped resting on the steel threshold to the deck. The yellow frame squeaked, a shaking square skeleton of pipes nearly as wide as the space between the doors, chained to the front of the bouncing ramp but held together with crossbeams of moaning wood.

Some of the watchers on the beach had run to minivans; others were running now towards the trucks. Some of the vans had started up and pulled from their spots along the road. None of the trucks on the main road had yet pulled out but several had started. A large white van pulled up behind Hank.

Hank accelerated through the water which almost immediately lapped and splashed at the side doors in the wake he created. Nearing where the ramp had entered the water, while Hank aimed for the open bow doors ahead, the vehicle's wake curled slightly above the bottom of the side windows while throwing droplets further up the glass. The water sprayed in front over the vehicle's hood which was dropping rapidly as the vehicle ploughed forward. The vehicle then bumped suddenly up onto the ramp, which was then itself rising with a swell.

The vehicle's hood rose suddenly upwards, its back wheels spun and they went bumping up the ramp to fall down, front wheels crashing to the deck, then the back, splashing off the ramp over from the boat's threshold. Hank drove between the four yellow poles holding up the frame, under the low roof, straight down the deck between two rows of steel supports, past a stairway and, guided by a waving thin man in black wearing rubber boots, slowed and stopped with his front bumper a hand's breadth from nosing against a back wall. This wall was just beside a round open door surrounded by wide bolt heads. Through this door were visible through steam several large pieces of grey machinery. Just at the wall as Hank had finally braked, his vehicle had stalled.

"First on," said Hank to his passengers. "That is always great. Shall we go up to the passenger deck? It might be a bit breezy. I'm alright though. I had a bit of a fever and turn back there but it is all gone now. Are you alright Juliet? Good!" He pulled up the parking brake lever beside him and wound his window down a crack. There was a strong smell of diesel fuel. The machinery through the door was throbbing deeply. A man in a holed vest sat between two of the machines on a stool holding a large spiral notebook.

Juliet opened her door and stepped out stretching, stumbling and turning while holding on to the vehicle. She looked back down the deck and out the open doors. The boat was rising and falling. Coming into view through the open doors and then disappearing was the white van that had come up behind them on the shore. It had stopped in the water. The water was rising up and down the van's flat front with the motion of the boat. Windshield wipers slashed spray violently to the sides. The four men in black who had moved the frame stood in the opening holding the chains. One let go and began waving towards the van. The driver was shadowed behind the glass.

The empty chamber of the lower deck echoed the engine, the shouting of the men at the front and the waves. The deck was uncluttered extending to curved black steel sides, a row of

THE BUSH

brownish caged lights along each of these walls. The space was entirely hollow but for the row of supports, the stairway, the yellow frame and two large metal wheels affixed flat on the ship's wall, one to the side of each open door. The two towers on shore could not be seen through the doors, wide ajar, banging on the side pylons, but the grey hillsides above the bay were periodically visible at the top of the boat's rise on the swells as was the van visible in the water on the fall.

Hank opened his door and got out. He was holding the small flag of the agency which he had gotten out of the otherwise empty glove compartment. He closed the door, steadied himself and stepped forward to the stump of the lowered aerial on the hood just ahead of the edge of the windshield. The windshield was still smeared in beige and pink and had developed a slight crack.

Hank extended the aerial and skinned the small flag down it from the top little knob through the flag's little tube as far as it would go until it was firm. The flag drooped. Then Hank too turned around to see Juliet holding on to the roof on the vehicle's other side.

There had been a sharp whining buzz and a then loud echoing bell sound coming from a front support. The men in front were all ducking down. One spread-eagled on the floor pulling on the chain. A ringing alarm went off behind Hank in the machinery room. Two loud hoots came from above.

The engine sound increased as the prone man rose and with the men who had ducked down began to raise the ramp. They first lifted it up, two on each side, and then two left the chains to pull it back and then in. They rolled it back under the frame on its bottom wheels. When it had come down and in and was rolling back, they pushed back the frame. Two of the men left the ramp's sides. Each man ran to one of the wheels on each the boat's walls.

As each turned his wheel the doors slowly closed. There was a sudden sharp metallic bang and then pinging at the top of the left door as they did this. The two men still with the ramp crouched lower. The engine sounds changed in pitch and increased in volume. They slowly ground up to a throbbing roar. This was followed by increasingly loud scraping lurching bumps to each side of the vessel.

The white van receded on the swells and more and more pylons came into view through the narrowing gap between the closing doors. Hank could then see the van driver's face faintly through the windshield. The two men who had remained to push in the ramp and the frame straightened and ran to join the men on the wheels.

Hank then turned back see that the door to the machinery room had been closed. The door was visibly vibrating. He and Juliet were both holding tightly to the top lip of their vehicle's cab, he at the front she now at the back to the side. Jack was shouting something from his seat.

The end where they were parked then swayed radically to one side and the vehicle slid slightly sideways on the deck. There was a heavy crunch from the front of the vessel which was now closed. One man now was clinging to the front, one hand on each of two big eyebolts, one extending inwards on each side of the closed doors and one above the other, through both of which he had put one side of a hammer headed bar. Two other men had been flung to the floor from the wheel they were turning on the side of the boat of the impact. One man was still standing.

All the bumping then stopped. The sway at the end of the boat where Hank and Juliet clutched the vehicle was continued but more rapidly as part of a greater arc. The boat seemed to be moving more swiftly backward and was rotating at their end in what had become a shoreward direction. The boat had also developed a sharp tilt upward to that side while the waves hitting it echoed between the walls. Hank steadied himself, propping against the vehicle and then shouted through the noise to Juliet and with his hands showed Juliet what the boat had done and was doing: backing out, turning into the river, going forward upstream and around.

The backward sway became a spinning rotation and extended down the deck to the bow which was in turn moving in a contrary arc away from shore and the men, now on the deck, slid along the base of the wall, one flailing in the brown light. The vehicle, Hank and Juliet all slid too with the opposite tilt outer side downward and into the open river. Juliet was pressed against the side of their vehicle, Hank, grasping, slid away from it on his side. The men who had fallen to the floor came back to rest against the side of the boat just under the wheel as the boat began to right.

The tilts reversed, the boat rocked latterly and then steadied at a level. Hank and Juliet were released and straightened themselves on their feet. The boat's motion stopped, hovered and then reversed to go forward.

"Up stream," shouted Hank to Juliet. "We're free!"

There was now the sound of water rushing along the sides from the bow. The fallen men got to their feet and made their way back along the deck to the narrow staircase which ascended up the side of wall and through the roof. The others followed. There was a glow of dirty white light at the top. Finally all four vanished into the light, each in turn first by his head and then by his legs. A hand descended and pulled the last one up. The engine sound remained loud.

"I think we can go up now," shouted Hank. "All's well. Let's get some socks for Jack from his bag if he has some." Juliet nodded.

"It looks like we will be the only ones on this trip," continued Hank as Juliet pulled herself along the vehicle carefully by her hands, taking small steps on the heaving deck to open the door at the back. Hank opened his own door to talk to Jack who was now sitting quietly.

"That looked like Jules behind the windshield," said Jack suddenly and loudly over the engines.

Hank and Juliet went to the rear of the vehicle, opened it and rummaged through the bags. Juliet took a denim jacket from one of hers and put it on. She took out a brush and brushed her hair, wobbling at times, leaning against and swaying with the open door. Hank pulled out a military style jacket identical to the creased and smudged one he was wearing but bone in colour. He held it up to Juliet. "For Jack. He's now almost dry but it will be windy on top. I have some tablets too." He put the jacket over his shoulder and pulled out two pairs of white socks. Then he closed the door.

Hank helped Jack from his door and put the brown jacket on him over a still damp chequered shirt. While Jack hung onto Hank's shoulder and Hank hung onto the vehicle door Juliet, now sitting sideways on the passenger seat, lifted one of Jack's feet, then the other, to take off the muddy socks which she tossed onto the vehicle floor. She replaced each with two white ones handed to her by Hank as he held Jack up. Jack smiled down to Juliet. It was a wide smile under bloodshot eyes.

"I can't remember when I ate last," said Hank. "It wasn't at Jack's yesterday. Or did I? Or can I remember when I've had a wash? Not like you Jack, you've been in the water all day. And you had a nice assisted herbal bath yesterday morning before the ceremony. Food too. What goes on in that kitchen of yours anyway? You wouldn't believe what goes on at Jack's, Juliet. Comings and goings. Helpful fairies.

"There you go Jack, all fixed up with footwear. Thanks to Juliet and me. I have some tablets in my pocket for you. Not your usual, but something. You'll have to swallow those without water I'm afraid. And we can get nothing on this boat to eat either." Jack now had both feet on the deck but Hank still held on to him. The bone coloured jacket was very loose on Jack and short on the arms but had been buttoned to the neck. Juliet got out and closed the door. Hank did not lock it.

"Did you notice that there were no foot passengers waiting?" said Hank. "There are usually hundreds. They must all have given up on the ferry being repaired. Maybe they were kept away by the rain or something. Quite a few trucks wanting to get over though. Some had livestock. It will take quite a few ferry trips to clear up that backlog. O.K let's go up on deck. It should be warming up up there, it is nearly midday and there will be a good breeze too. Our vehicle will have time to dry out anyway. The crossing takes a while."

With Hank assisting Jack they walked carefully down the deck and over to the stairs. Juliet went up first then Jack and Hank behind with his hands on the guardrail on each side to prevent a fall. They emerged into a brightened but diffuse sky under rapidly streaming clouds still roofing the sky but higher than before. The boat was heading upstream, facing and labouring into the current about a third of the way to the mid stream. The vessel's bow angled a small way towards the centre of the river where the current was much stronger. Flotsam flashed by there at a rapid pace.

On the right on the shore side they could see the top of the broken bridge strut. The shoreline to the other side was indistinct and shadowy in a vapour haze. It was a border of narrow black lattice. The side they had left was becoming similarly obscured in heat fog as the day warmed.

A strong breeze blew into their faces, warm and humid coming downstream over the bow as they made their way across the upper deck to the back row of benches past the black lockers. They sat in a row in the middle of the middle bench. Behind them on the wheelhouse the glass reflecting the sky obscured the boat's operator and any other inhabitants.

In the bow there stood four men in black jackets, each wearing rubber boots, two on each side. Each held a tall narrow pole upright at an angle, steadying it between their feet and resting it over the guardrail. Each pole was at least four times the height of its holder and each was topped with a black metal point connected below the top to a sheath on each of which was a small hook. The men were looking into the river.

"Nothing much to see out here," said Hank. "The vision is really bad. A boring trip really. No colour, no passengers, no vehicles, not even a motorcycle. Jack you'll have to go back for your motorcycle one day. Not that I approve of that thing. The agency insurance may not have covered you. Madame told me you were giving students and local women rides. What if there had been an accident? We would have had to pay compensation to the person and you would put the school and agency into trouble. Madame Youngo would complain."

"That Madame Youngo was a real tyrant," said Juliet. "You know what she said when we had dinner with her? She said to Jack and his Chembe friend, "In any place you can have only one queen. Any queen will permit her child's father to have only one mate." It sounded like she was warning you two Jack. Were you interfering with her administration? Had you been naughty? Then she said, "Don't be mistaken, a woman is jealous and hard. She will do anything to keep what is hers." Do you think she was talking about the Governor? Mad old bitch growling away. She was really abrupt and strange but she hadn't been drinking."

The engine sound lessened. One of the men at the bow shouted and lowered his pole over the guardrail into the water. He pushed on it using the guardrail for support, and then he pulled it back. The man next to him and further along the side then followed suit repeating each of the other's actions. Both then looked back along the ship's side into the water. They next both glanced briefly up at the three sitting at the back of the benches. They finally turned their eyes to the front and back to the river. The two men on the other side had not faltered from searching the water in front of them.

"They are like kittens fishing," said Juliet.

"I should have kept to my responsibilities, played out my role," said Jack from where he sat between Hank and Juliet. His head was on his chest. "I shouldn't have left."

The boat seemed to be accelerating but the engines softened further. Hank got up from the bench and walked over to the rail. He peered over it and then returned to the two on the bench. He remained standing at the end of the bench pointing to the side of the boat beyond the rail.

"The current has really slowed," he said. "It might be that the river has gone over its bank upstream. It could mean a lot of flooding. There was a big flood here just before the last troubles. Thousands were drowned. The river actually cut a new channel. Could be a bit of a problem if it has flooded. There have been some expensive industrial plants built upstream and a refinery." Hank looked back to where the bridge carcass was disappearing.

"What could they have been thinking to try and bridge the river here even before the channel changed? Idiots! They wanted a rail bridge and something to take a pipeline across. Pretty optimistic, I think, about some finds they'd made. They even started a nuclear plant. No wonder the country ran out of money. Big waste really. All done on loans.

"We're almost in midstream. Can't see much of anything. The river is filled with floating junk. Come on, get up! Go have a look you two!" The boat was beginning what seemed a wide turn. Hank returned to the rail and Juliet followed pulling Jack up and leading him by his hand. The pole men moved down the rail from the bow towards the three to stop at the rail amidships just before reaching them. They searched the river there, where the vessel was broadside to the current, while the boat arced. The river was now only murmuring and it moved sluggishly. The current lapped with small sips at the boat's side which slid slightly downstream as it turned.

The bow was swinging effortlessly and smoothly. The three could see neither the shore they had left nor very far upriver or down nor the shore to which they were headed. There were only one or two black objects floating in the river. The river had taken on a greenish hue.

Overhead just beneath the clouds some birds were circling. They were silent. As the boat angled to point downstream the pole men moved behind the three along the rail, poles slung over their shoulders, to walk towards the stern. Two crossed over the deck so that now two were positioned on each side of the boat before the wheelhouse. The river now splashed around the stern. The men lowered their poles and stared into the river. The wind now came from behind.

"Isn't this refreshing," said Hank squinting ahead. "Our own peaceful little world! I must say those sailors want nothing to do with us. They just push away the little dangers. I hope they don't think we had anything to do with that disturbance back there. Just a few stray shots, that's all. It will probably be all cleared up by the time the boat returns. I guess they just want to get on with their jobs though. The guy in the wheelhouse seems to know what he is doing. He took the boat in and out of that docking like a fat hand in and out of a tight glove. There! I told you! There's one!" Hank pointed into the river.

Floating by in the river, pushed by the breeze just at the edge of the circle of vision, was a tall hillock of white sudsy bubbles stained brown on the bottom and caught on a raft of floating weeds. The nest of bubbles wobbled and popped, swelled and turned in on itself, expanded and contracted like a porous white plastic jelly. Behind that was another, even larger, as big as their vehicle, floating parallel and behind the boat. It trailed some smaller pieces which were breaking off and when they did bounced on the current and hopped and rolled in the wind. Juliet cried out in delight. From behind an irregular globe of suds the size of a hand had come from upriver to hit her on the cheek. Some more flew by over their heads towards the front bow.

Hank came away from the rail and turned to completely face back upstream. Juliet was wiping her cheek with her sleeve and looking back at the wheelhouse. The four pole men were faced inward to the deck behind them and were laughing and shouting while they speared overhead at swarms of flying white and yellowy brown suds in streams and scatters, chasing and overtaking the boat on the breeze. Several clumps landed on the deck, melted, and produced small brown pools speckled with yellow bubbles. Juliet pointed upward at two flying towards them above the height of the wheelhouse.

"Look, they are exactly like dogs," she said.

"And there's a lizard," said Hank.

"Oh God," said Jack deeply, eyes widened as he pointed over the rail where a great white mound, taller than the deck, was floating on a big mat of reeds a poles length off the side. Hank and Juliet turned.

"That is the mountain forest of the wicked witch," said Hank gleefully. "This is great fun, just like washing day."

"Or it could be a giant bird or an iceberg," said Juliet quickly, "and look at those colours, turn around Jack! See them there!" she said, turning herself, pointing back to the deck. Jack turned away from the side.

The clumps of suds were now landing everywhere, popping and melting. Some disintegrated into blue and green bubbles. The pools left behind shone first in iridescent flashes then became black and limpid. The pole men had all stopped spearing. The two by the wheelhouse on the far side had returned to their posts while the two on the rail beyond Hank, Juliet and Jack were pushing at the base of the large mound Jack had seen which was slipping back along the boat's side.

"Don't want that thing in the propellers," said Hank looking back and forth. "Those poor sods will have a lot of work to do to clean up these decks. Hey there is the shore!" The shoreline was emerging from the haze over the swell as the boat turned further. Only a few piles of suds floated now between the angling bow and the shore line, although there were many more floating and flying in the middle of the river behind them flashing downstream. There were two towers ahead above the mist. The engines sped up.

"Maybe we should go down now and see if our engine will start," said Hank. "At least we won't have to back out of the ferry this time. You usually do have to back out on one side of the river or the other. There's lots of yelling and sometimes a fight. They fight over who goes first, especially the truck drivers. Some have paid bribes to get on early. I know I have. It doesn't matter about the flag.

"There is often a bang or two. Once some goats got out. Vegetables spill on the deck. Sometimes there is a prostitute who has come over from the huts on the other side fighting in a truck cab to make sure to get her money before the docking so she can return for free as a passenger and not have to get off and pay to get back on.

"Then you have to back right up between the towers before turning backward in front of the waiting trucks onto the side road where they make the smaller vehicles wait. They are the ones who can go on first. At least some of them. Those chosen to fill the first half.

"Those drivers are really anxious and frustrated. They think everyone coming off is a fool or a criminal. They are counting the places that were given to the small vehicles. They want those places. They have to get over. They have sometimes been drinking beer in the huts. They swear at you. There are usually more prostitutes waiting and policemen looking to find infractions for fines and bribes, especially on this side."

"People are selling roasted maize, people are wanting rides, others are offering to drive. There are snapping dogs and gold charm sellers. Lepers banging on the window. People selling religious books, maps to heaven, pictures of saints, sinners and jazz singers."

"Come on Jack. Let's go down to our vehicle. Almost there. Juliet, take his arm. My you are sweating Jack. But the old hair is dry. We should have stolen the blanket. God I forgot to give you your tablets."

Hank led them to the stairwell. He went down first, descending backward to continue to guard against Jack slipping. Juliet's hair had become dishevelled again in the wind. It got worse in a violent gust that raged through it just as her head was going below deck. Hank led the way to the vehicle. He opened the two doors on the near side and went around to the driver's side. Jack climbed into the back closed his door and then stretched out. Juliet got in to sit beside Hank.

As Juliet got in she turned to see four men descending the stairs. They turned to walk ahead through the echoing chamber to the bow. The door to the machines in front was open but no one could be seen. Hank was able to start the vehicle easily but left the brake on. Hank and Juliet closed their doors. There was less smell of diesel fuel.

"We will make good time once we are on this side. For most of the way south we'll have a freeway. We have to worry about the trucks though; they sometimes travel three abreast and don't use lights in fog or at night. Even if we stop to eat we should get to the capital by dusk. I don't feel a bit tired. But you get some sleep back there Jack.

"I don't think I told you Juliet, but I've been asked to go home to headquarters to do some work for the agency. I'll be getting my ticket when I get to the country office. I'm going to brief the executive on the situation here. They are planning the strategy for funding the continuation of the project. I am also going to meet with the charity who is our partner and it's proposed that I meet some top government officials to discuss the policy for this place. That is impressive and exciting don't you think? Are you impressed Juliet?

"There is a plan that I give a few public speeches in the city and perhaps outside for fundraising purposes. Some public relations. Perhaps a thing for T.V. I'm really looking forward to it. There may be some others from the team going home too." The two sat silently for several moments.

"It's a stupid project. I will complain. It needs exciting management," said Juliet. The boat bumped and rocked gently from side to side. Jack took off the handbrake and reversed away from the wall swinging the rear of the vehicle to the left. He then changed the gear and went a length forward and stopped. Ahead of them down the deck the men were wheeling open the doors. The engine speed of the vessel quickened and then stopped. Water splashed along the walls. When the doors were completely open the men walked to the ramp frame. Outside the towers appeared then disappeared as the boat glided gently in. There were then two more very slight bumps and some minor rocking. The boat stopped.

"Softly in the channel this time. The water level must be down," said Hank and started the vehicle slowly forward. The men had pushed the ramp out and lowered it down until it splashed. Then the chains loosened as the ramp grounded.

Hank drove forward through the frame as the four men watched, two on each side. Hank's little flag flapped. There was a slight click as the vehicle's nose dipped down, then the slightest splash and he was on the road.

There was nobody there. The huts were empty on each side. There were no vans or trucks and no one could be seen around any of the substantial buildings. There were no chalets on this side but there was a two storey glass and aluminium building at the crossroads just past the towers which had a sign reading "Hotel". Nothing was parked near it. Opposite the hotel was a large circular structure, an oil tank much bigger than their chalet had been. From the bottom of that beside a wheel affixed on a stem rising from the ground a black pipe extended on stilts to just beside the left hand tower.

Beyond the tank was a raised open platform which ran away from the road. Along the road here was a two rung barrier, one red rung and one white. Behind this barrier, parallel to the river, and away from the platform, ran a railway line, left to the south, passing soon into a foggy wall of trees at the end of vision. No one was on the platform and there was no train.

Hank drove forward past the platform. The road began a small gradient. There were no hills. It climbed gently to head out of the depot under a sign stretched high across it, painted in gold and black, beyond which the road was bordered on each side by a row of umbrella palms with white painted trunks. These rows of palms stretched some distance and then stopped and the rolling plain began.

Between and behind the palms there were billboards, dozens on each side. Beyond these just on the plain joined a wider road coming from the north running to the south parallel to the river. Hank stopped on the shoulder just before the overhead sign. The sign said "Safe Journey".

A small green canvassed topped four wheel drive was coming towards them. A red light flashed behind its windshield. Hank and Juliet both looked behind to the ferry terminal, then forward at the oncoming vehicle. The ferry doors were still open. They had seen an orange and white glow coming through the fog from the opposite shore. It flickered and pulsed.

The oncoming vehicle slowed as it reached them. It had only two seats, each occupied by a man in a helmet wearing a beige uniform. They both stared at and into Hank's vehicle as they slowly passed. Their faces flashed in the light on the dashboard between them. Hank and Juliet looked back. Jack lay below the window with his eyes closed.

On the back of the uniformed men's vehicle was a large fringed pennant on a tall shining aerial affixed behind the covered spare wheel. The pennant had the image of a red coiled snake on a green background. It flapped wildly.

The men passed, sped up and continued on down the slope and onto the ferry. Hank and Juliet watched. The doors to the ferry began to close after they had disappeared inside. Hank put his vehicle into gear and proceeded under the sign between the palms. Juliet still looked back to the sign. The sign there said

"Welcome". They went past the trees, past the billboards showing whiskey, appliances, airplanes and clothes and turned south onto the freeway. A road sign showed the distance to the capital. There were rows of small leafy plants extending over the plain to their right.

"Hell in both directions," murmured Jack from the back seat. His eyes were still closed.

"Carrots as well," said Hank.

They drove on past the rows of vegetables, past roadside palms no longer dusty but glistening with moisture, and past fenced groves of cashew trees. The plain to each side opened up and began to gently roll in beige and purple knap of damp scrub and patches of ground fog. The plain was dotted with small compounds scattered far back from the road consisting of white square and brown round buildings enclosed in circles of brush and twig woven fencing. These compounds often flew a small green flag on a white painted pole rising from within the brush enclosures.

The landscape repeated itself for an hour. Juliet fell asleep and Jack was silent. Hank cocked his head often from side to side checking engine sounds. He held the steering wheel loosely in his hands for various distances to check the wheel alignment. He looked repeatedly at his gauges. The road was straight. There was a great deal of debris on the sides of the road: wrappers, crushed cans, clumps of straw, nests of wire, bits of rope, carrot ends, bones.

Juliet awakened as Hank slowed and stopped. On the side of the road was a corrugated tin shack open at the front. A man stood in the doorway behind a narrow wooden counter. The man wore a white skull cap and was dressed in a string vest. The counter held a display of cans and bottles.

"I'll see what I can do," said Hank to Juliet as he left the vehicle. "It's the first place I've seen." He walked over the gravel shoulder and up the small slope to the shop. The man in the doorway waved slightly and then bowed slightly as Hank approached. They talked for several minutes. The shop-keeper produced a blue plastic bag from under his counter. He took it into the shop and returned to hand it to Hank. It bulged at the bottom. Hank gave him several green and blue bills from his breast pocket and then returned to the vehicle. He handed the plastic bag across to Juliet and started off again.

"All he had was sweets, some cans of orange soda and two packages of soda biscuits," said Hank. "He says he has been waiting here for his brother for two days to bring some more supplies but the brother has not come. They each do two days on and two days off in the shop in turn. They sleep in it when it's their turn. He thinks the location is good because it gets drivers who are hungry driving to the ferry from the city or hungry after leaving the ferry. He has a farm towards the city as does his brother. One other brother is actually a ferry driver.

"He has a small radio inside. He asked if I knew anything about the trouble in the northeast. He said the radio was saying that a line of trucks had exploded somewhere else. He thought that was very funny and exciting as the goats inside would be roasted. A church has been burnt too. A rebel has been arrested transporting revolvers in the stomach of a dead baby being taken to its home village for a funeral. A man has risen from the dead in the northwest. There has been volcanic activity. Floods are expected.

"He thought it was strange that he had seen virtually no one for two days. He thought he had heard a lot of trucks go by early in the morning towards the city. Hundreds. He heard women weeping. He suspects they were from the area around the ferry or further north. The district here and the land pretty well all the way to the capital is effectively a monoculture. One faith and one tribe. He'd know if they were from around here in the trucks. They were not." Juliet had poked in the bag and taken out a package of biscuits. She then took out a carton of cigarettes and looked quizzically at Hank, raising her eyebrows and wrinkling a nostril.

"Hank I told you before that this is one reason we could never be friends."

"Don't get judgemental, Juliet. I suppose you want to report that to headquarters too. I am not smoking; those are for the soldiers at the roadblocks as we go into the city. There were quite a few roadblocks on the way out. There are several around our country offices.

"You wait and see, Juliet. There is a treat for you there. We have a new guesthouse and we've got new furniture and air conditioning in the office. The compound has been re-fenced. There are quite a few new administrative staff too. A lot more cleaners as well as more local people to fix up visas and to order plane tickets, rent houses and so on. We've really gotten organised. I commissioned a painting of the mountains for the reception room.

"So you are wasting the project money," said Juliet. "Does any get to the beneficiaries at all?" She was eating a biscuit now. The open package lay on top of the plastic bag on her lap. There were crumbs on the front of her denim jacket.

"No Juliet, there is no waste. You don't understand development management. In fact, the percentage of our administrative costs compared to delivery has gone down. All that new stuff I got is booked to project costs. It is the cost of getting things to beneficiaries. Anyway we are doing a different type of project. It is more cost efficient. We are providing expert advisors to the government. We have some people giving advice on town planning, on governance, on parliamentary procedures and so on. They are all graduates and several even actually worked at home at those disciplines before they came here. It is know-how, Juliet.

"The town planner is really interesting. He has been working at statistics. You know that the capital city here is one of the biggest in the world. But did you know that it has more miles of broken flyovers than anywhere else? You know those things where you can see through the deck to the ground? It has more miles of those broken than several developed countries have roads. It has two million child labourers among whom three hundred thousand plus are prostitutes. The slums here are one of the largest unmapped areas on earth. The city has over fifty tribal and religious ghettos. In some the majority of the population speak a common dialect barely understood in the next neighbourhood. Three thousand villages like the Chembe one and fifty towns like the Bechembe one. It has one of the world's largest ports but no one knows what is exported or imported. The total industrial capacity is less than a small town at home but it competes with our country in the sale of electrical goods, usually counterfeit. It has significant world market share in insurance sales but no companies registered selling insurance.

"There are two offshore islands made almost entirely of crushed beer and tomato sauce cans which have been piled on burning tyres, islands that have been burning for ten years. The casinos and refineries offshore do not pay local taxes. The planner we brought to advise government found several local government ministries still operating that in fact had been abolished by decree ten years ago, several governments and coups before. The city has more hospitals and primary schools than our country does but only ten per cent operate. These are sometimes depots for organ transplants. It has the lowest ratio of doctors and teachers to population on the continent, one doctor for a population as large as our capital's, but the highest paid are multi-millionaires.

"The planner guy was really depressed at his job at first but he has now arranged for hanging baskets on the road into the city centre from the airport. It is his first success."

"This road is so boring," said Juliet. "I am so sleepy and really feel dirty."

"We have another placement, a woman ecologist, who is advising on the planned national parks. She says that the river over there was once a tributary to a much larger river where the coast is now. It basically divided everything. The continents were more attached then. They have found fish in a lake in the mountains here which are unknown anywhere else on earth except in a really deep lake just below the polar cap. Really interesting. She says that this larger river in those days divided the living areas for different species. It was created after a really big flood.

"On the left bank the monkeys did not evolve. They ate fruit and lived in the trees. On the right bank some of them became cannibals. Then they developed small tools to scratch fleas and so on. Then they started to wander. You can trace their bones across the continent. They couldn't get over to the left bank so they went north. Their brain pans sometimes show signs of unequal and atrophied development. Their bones show unknown diseases. Really interesting! The ecologist wants to make an interpretation and education centre by the river."

"You are trying to be like Jack," said Juliet. "Don't bother. Let me tell a real story about a river," continued Juliet. "I got this from one of the girls at my school.

"Once upon a time all the people and animals lived together in one country and could talk to one another. The different tribes of animals made war on one another but they often intermarried too.

"Two girls, twins, were out walking one day with their friends a civet cat, a lizard and a mouse. They were looking for feathers to put in their bridal boxes to use to decorate their wedding dresses. They went very far in the forest past the various kinds of fruit trees which in those times could sing the songs of their particular fruit to make it easier for the insects and small animals to find them. Or at least then so that people could hear them. Animals always can. The five girls were talking as they walked of the husbands that it had been arranged for them to marry.

"The mouse was very worried as she was to marry an elephant. The elephants then were very hairy and had huge tusks. She asked for advice. The cat was going to marry a monkey. She said the monkey

was very small and had a fat tummy. She had seen him in the market with his brothers.

"*The lizard was going to marry a man, a holy man. She worried about how the children would look and if they would be treated too strictly. The twins had both been promised too by their parents but they did not know to whom. Their parents had not told them. They were afraid. They were worried that it might be to something ferocious and smelly. Some carnivore. Perhaps something requiring bodily sacrifice in return for a good bride price. They each confessed that they had a boyfriend already but each would not say who or what it was. The lizard suspected one of them might be pregnant.*

"*They wandered further than they had ever done before. They told each other stories about their tribes. They talked of styles in scales and fur. They actually went without knowing it into a forbidden area. This was before the mountains had risen so high or the plains had become so flat and empty. There was water and forest everywhere so you did not have clear boundaries.*

"*They came to the side of a great river. On the bank there were long feathers in all sorts of beautiful colours. Some of the colours they had never seen before. They each took some of the feathers and carried them home giggling and laughing and singing with the trees and bushes. They waved the flashing feathers by nodding and bobbing their heads, leaping in the air, as they all carried them in their teeth, even the twins.*

"*In those days there was a lot of activity that was strange. In the village of people the men talked about iron axes falling from the sky just for them. Some of the holy men found that they could see quite far into the sky to places where stars were dancing out stories. No one before or since could see so far with naked eyes. All kinds of new creatures were on the paths. Volcanoes were spouting flowery rockets and so on. All sorts of genesis was going on.*

"*When the twins had left their friends and approached their village they saw a crowd of men and women rushing towards them shouting and cursing. Some hurled stones. Several were carrying knives. The sky above them darkened and a blast of wind hurled them all to the* ground. The people heard a ferocious roaring and they all ran in every direction. The twins ran into a cave. They were followed there by an old trembling woman. After that they were joined by a few dozen terrified mice.

"Everyone rolled stones from within the cave and blocked up the entrance using the stones and earth. From outside came a great screeching as well as the sound of thunder and an enormous downpour.

"The old woman had a bag with some water in a narrow necked gourd and some flat bread. They shared some of this around. The bag also had some flints. They collected bits of wood and dried excreta they found in the cave towards a fire.

""You are the wickedest girls ever to live," said the old woman. "You have stolen from the feathered serpent. It is the world river and the rainbow of heaven. It has awoken in anger and will fly above the world. It will drown us all with its rain. It will eat us all as we float to the top. It will hunt and hunt and hunt the earth until it has found the thieves." The twins still had the feathers with them. In fact they shone beautifully in the dark.

"After a few days they all began to get hungry. A little water had flowed down the rocks at the entrance to the cave and they had collected that in a gourd from the old woman's bag. The twins began to worry the mice about how the mates promised to the twins would be heartbroken if the twins were to both die there and so reduce their new families and tribes to be. They suggested that lots be drawn to see who could be eaten to sustain the company. The mice were at first reluctant to do this as they were rarely meat-eaters. They also did not think it fair as there were so many of them and so few people. They would not believe that a twin would eat her sister either if that was the way fate went. The twins assured the mice that of course they would give their lives so that their sister might live. It would be easy to consume a sister. They would draw lots made from some of the twigs. One twin would hold the lots as the mice had difficulty in doing this and the old woman could not be trusted.

"They roasted the old woman first on a fire made from the dried dung. They carved her and shared her according to their sizes. They had found a bone knife in her bag. They butchered her with that knife. There was nothing else in the bag but a torn piece of paper with some of the first writing. No one there could read. The old woman said before she died that they were all fools as the feathered serpent would rain and coil around the world until everything was dead. When nothing floated up it would fly off to behind the stars. There was only one way to stop it but she would not tell them she was that annoyed.

"As weeks passed six of the mice were eaten in turn. This was unsatisfactory in quelling hunger. The mice voted that one of the twins should be eaten next. This was only fair. One of the twins suggested that before this happened they should check if the serpent had gone and if the flood had receded.

"They poked a hole in the stones and earth blocking the front. A mouse was selected and put into the hole. They plugged the hole behind the mouse, leaving it to burrow the distance to the outside. Then they waited and waited. The mouse would see the state of the world.

""I fear that the world is destroyed," said one of the mice after a long time of waiting. 'Then we must repopulate it,' said one of the twins. "How can we do that?" said a mouse. 'The test mouse we sent out was the last male amongst us!'

"The mice began weeping and moaning. Then one of the twins said, "Hush, my sisters. Perhaps it is better the world is destroyed. But the world is not entirely lost. One of we sisters is pregnant." The mice were quietened. In fact several congratulated the sisters. Then a mouse asked which one was pregnant. "Oh we cannot tell you that," said a sister as it would destroy the honour of the pregnant one and this would not be right as she will be the mother of the new world. This was because the mother to be was unmarried.

"They decided that the remaining mice would be eaten one by one. Then the dishonourable sister would eat the honourable one. The sister would then wait to recreate the world. And that is how our world began.

"Well Hank can you see the gender politics in that story! Can you figure out the meaning? Very revealing isn't it," said Juliet and got herself out another biscuit.

Jack then spoke up from the back. "How do you know the sisters were telling the truth? Do we know either that they would really sacrifice like that? Maybe they fought to the death?"

Juliet turned around to see Jack, still lying across the back seat eyes closed. "You feeling any better, Jack? We are almost there. You haven't missed much."

"And what about the test mouse?" said Jack. "Anything could have happened with that guy."

"Never mind, Jack. Just go back to sleep," said Juliet. "You aren't well. It's a boring trip anyway."

"You should write that story up for the agency newsletter," said Hank. "Do an analysis of it. I could get it in when I'm back home. God it's hard to think that it's only a couple of days to go."

"I am the test mouse," said Jack.

VIII

This feeling now of being in an airplane was the most favourite feeling Hank ever had. He often explained to others that it was a spiritual feeling, one of detachment and connection with the infinite. Longing was ended. It felt now like going home, back to origins, back to rewards and back to justice and sense.

All troubles of the past were now behind, on the ground; all expectations for the future lay unsullied ahead. He was miles high. The ticket and his seat number confirmed a secure place in creation. They assured progress.

Every self-assessment and anxious brooding on job or personal development was softened and then eliminated by the lift-off, the raising of the wheels, the schedule of food, drink and entertainment. The worst thing in life, check-in and boarding, was behind.

The best, stepping through the door in the thick airplane skin at the end of a good flight into a new world, being thanked by an attendant having left the old newspapers on the seat and having stuffed used plastic cups into the pouch or crushed them on the floor, was yet to come.

The pure graceful disembarking up a tunnel, the climactic event, came after for Hank satisfying bouts of helping others in their less spiritual chaos of disembarking the plane, leaving badly the secure and magic world that had transformed time and space.

He helped the other passengers to join the process with a diffident sardonic grace, an experienced diffidence, solving their personal problems with too high compartments for too short people, too stuffed for fussy, possessive people, too organised for all the anxious, hurried people, those with personal agendas, other things on their minds, those leaving putting on shoes for far too late, those struggling with seat belts, those pushing others in the aisles, asking for phone numbers, applying make-up, searching hysterically for passports. Hank, competent, taken for granted, sometimes invisible, helped them all.

All this pleasure was to come as was that later of his waiting against a wall, stretching his limbs with seasoned amusement and sharp, mature, relaxed philosophy while others rushed and shoved forming circles and hierarchies to claim luggage from as yet empty ramps, pushing and banging into crowded uneven rows, the worst ones at the front, the resentful at the back. And finally the pleasure of giving crisp important destination instructions to a waiting driver so as to depart the airport calm and alone into a busy important city into which one had arrived, as usual, by plane. The country director had returned. The world man, the global man was back. The country director from the big program in the bush was going to Global Headquarters to brief them. He was right here on this plane now.

It had been a bit of effort at the end back there. But he had got away. Got away!

Hank, Jack and Juliet had gone at the end through a dozen roadblocks before entering the city on the final part of their journey and Hank had used up all the cigarettes and a bit of money. But the traffic had been less than usual in the city streets and was almost nonexistent going up the street to the county office.

One key flyover had even been repaired in the days of Hank's absence. It was astonishing to be able to use it. But at one junction near the office a truck in flames went flying across the road in front of them and into a store front. God knows what that was about. They just drove on.

At least neither Jack nor Juliet had been rude to the soldiers at roadblocks so business was conducted smoothly and they got on with everything without military delays and searches to punish and to educate them in proper roles for civilians. The soldiers had been less sociable than usual, quite nervous actually, but more arrogant too; perhaps another coup underway. At one roadblock a soldier said that a church had been burnt somewhere and there had been a massacre. A priest had been killed.

The meetings at the office had gone well. There had been no departmental politicking. The national staff always supported their country director over any eccentricities the foreign experts raised, any attempts at manipulating privileges. The planner had been silent and no environmental or gender impact issues had been brought up. The staff decided by consensus that the country program now had a class four security level. Everyone gave good reports justifying everything which were all filed. Rationales were constructed from guidelines. Hank did not remember everything that such a level of security meant. It did mean unfortunately no flags on the vehicles, or was it the opposite?

Someone was designated to write up the report on the visit Hank had just made from the narrative he had delivered to the attentive meeting, attentive to the director of course, as well as the minutes of the meeting on security and then send all that to headquarters.

The usual brothels and clubs were now off limits. Salaries went up slightly because of the new country security designation as did the number of days that could be claimed for rest and recreation. The most important thing, however, was to evacuate people from the troubled regions. That meant the evacuation of Jack and Juliet, yes, send them home! It was a good justification they could not argue with. He would not need any other troublesome reasons. Face would be saved. It worked even though the actual act was really in retrospect to the policy.

The other teacher, Tom Hume, would have to be evacuated too, to be fair, so a message was to be dispatched to him by some means. The management committee had decided and headquarters were informed. It was all above board and normal. Everything complicated was now easy peasy.

Then he was driven to the airport in the best vehicle, the departing country director, his job well done, the flag flying, junior staff biting back tears, the final staff present to their loved and respected director clutched in their trembling hands, a present to be given on departure at the last moment. It would be some cultural artefact reproduction to be discarded at the airport (how did anyone think it would go into a bag?). Then after shouted farewells to the chief alone, as to a father, after shouldering through the line of beggars and thieves surrounding everyone who might have a ticket, after leaving behind some of the world's last tourist display leper fundraisers, after bribing oneself merrily and good naturedly through security and customs (what do you have in that chequebook sir? Is it our currency? Something for my children?).

He had gotten a museum quality plastic mask and a little stuffed monkey, probably real. No one in the waiting lounge wanted them. Then marching in, head high and calmly, settling unassisted into the designated seat and then up and up and up into the glorious international air, eating sliced beef with orange sauce.

It did not matter now about Jack or that Jack was belted in to his seat, rows behind Hank in the plane, in another class, sweating and mumbling. Jack was soon to be on his own too and back to his own world, out of Hank's hair, out of Hank's mind, out of the project, out of the country, admonished to go home and report to headquarters for final settlements of pay and benefits after visiting his doctor.

If Jack complained about his treatment and evacuation, Hank still had two of his letters, and some revealing stories written by others, perhaps by him; maybe he thought they were just personal literature but they were evidence. They were those which had gone under the seat during the collision and which had remained undiscovered when the police rifled the vehicle. These were enough in themselves to invalidate Jack's contract let alone put an end to any complaint about authoritarian and inadequate management from Hank.

Hank wondered for an anxious moment what Jack had done after he left the vehicle in the rain but it didn't matter now. Jack said he forgot anyway. What the hell. In fact all that could now have a line drawn under it including that poor murdered girl. That was all sub-consular. What was he supposed to be anyway, Hank-the-Aid-detective? Not likely.

Juliet was in the row behind Jack. Certainly no one would listen to any evaluation she made of the project or the project management. Despite what she had said, placements had been sufficiently studied, especially hers, as had the political and security situation. There were reasons for placements, political ones that she couldn't grasp. There was a real world to be managed which someone from her closeted and privileged background could not understand.

The project was well designed given the constraints. Yes, her father was an important somebody in the government, known and feared by all, but even he would know that a funded project which was meeting objectives was beyond criticism.

What would be more worrying would be if there was a complaint about political interference by someone from the agency in the country's affairs which was not in the approved program. Being caught in unauthorised spying or something. This sometimes would attract some attention of some bastard in the diplomatic sections and was not as easy to wish away as some dirty little moral outrage or minor management bungle. There was the report left with Hope. Had he gone too far in that? What if that was looked at by the police and not Madame Youngo? Where did that girl say she was going anyway?

Juliet of course would be held by the agency's main headquarters at a bit of distance. That would only be proper. It wouldn't matter about any complaint she might make. He had done nothing the agency would see as unusual.

This was partially because her father, the government heavyweight, could not be seen to interfere in agency work. Nor would he want to. But it was also because Juliet was considered a bit wet and goofy. There was that thing with the local bishop as well. The headquarters knew about that from a letter from the church. Not from Hank.

From the perspective of headquarters at home this would probably all be officially below notice. There was nothing they knew to suggest why she might be so feisty and contemptuous about Hank. It would seem over the top. Not done. Whistle blowing. Except headquarters might worry about the father on that of course. But Juliet's dad had worked with the agency when he was younger. He would be sympathetic to agency problems. Nothing to worry about there with Juliet really.

Hank knew he would see out his remaining contract time at home, at a desk, gloriously. Commuting to work, attending plays and functions, addressing seminars in nice hotels, taking office retreats in the country houses, taking holidays by bendy rivers that you could boat in, with stone bridges and grey brittle trees under which were trustworthy clean cows.

Hank had gotten a window seat. As the airplane had risen into cloudless night sky he could see the flat scattered endless flickering of lights and cooking fires of the city beneath him. He searched for the bright, clean yellow lights of his three storey country headquarters, for the spotlight on the flag. He looked for the crossing beams of the comings and goings of vehicles taking agency officers and staff back and forth to home and club. But the building was lost in the red and green glare of religious buildings and nightclubs circling the city centre surrounded by the neat gold white light lines of the embassy district. It was going and gone, fading behind. It was reduced to memory and less.

The sky had remained clear as they reached height. There was both a sliver of moon and smears of stars. When he thought they were passing over the northwest he looked down

for the Mountain but the ground was far away and black.
Later there had been threaded snakes of orange and spots of white fires burning on the plains far below as they had travelled further north, past the border where the rains had not yet reached. Beyond those burning plains black clouds appeared outside the window first in wisps and then in rags which soon obscured the ground. They passed over some lakes and then were entirely in cloud.

This all enhanced Hank's spiritual wellbeing and detachment as did the dimming of the interior lights. It was like passing a traffic accident while going in the opposite direction or hearing a crude domestic argument far behind in the crowded aisle as one was leaving the theatre by a door held open. He was somewhere else.

First go to my friend's apartment, he thought. Wonderful fellow, knew him in school but hadn't seen him for a few years; I've lost touch a bit with some. Perhaps I should have written. His apartment was really nicely fitted out with a balcony overlooking the river. Then in the morning to headquarters for oral debriefing, report to follow but not for weeks. I'll make the report a classic of its kind. It will be for the textbooks. In the meantime get to know the new job, ask questions, read the files on the new staff.

After the first morning meeting with the chief and confirming the itinerary and plan of work motor off to the ministry building with its ancient paintings and golden hall furniture. Meet the great man himself, interestingly someone coming from the same background as Hank. Meet some of the advisors. Hank fancied an honour or citation one day from this bit of government.

After discussing the future of the program he is off to see the charity partner at their offices in the converted church in the suburbs. There would be all sorts of earnest talk there. Talk about security and sensitivity to staff. Sitting in the round sharing feelings with relevant staff. He would later tell Juliet's story to the traditional lunchtime meeting attended by the whole building. There might be a celebrity board member there as well. Then the scheduled week of public meetings and private talks to raise funds.

Hank looked around for an attendant. He was thinking of a long drink but the aisles had been empty since the dimming of the lights. In the furthest aisle a small person, perhaps a child, was making their way hesitantly in the faint blue light and shadows back to where the washrooms were. She had on traditional headwear. Perhaps on her way to a good school at home.

The plane's approach was along the river. There were exclamations from those on board who peered out of the windows at floodlit familiar monuments below. It was beginning to snow. Hank saw his favourite floating restaurant and also the ministry building besides the government building for the elected representatives. The plane's directing voice warned of low temperatures and of the snow as well as cautioned against unaccompanied baggage or firearms. A version of the national anthem played for a few seconds on the entertainment system. The cabin lights came on full.

No one was beyond the final doors of the customs hall to meet Hank, although in the crowd of scented scarf-wearing, coated and suited greeters Hank believed he saw the familiar face of Juliet's father. Hadn't his staff back in country contacted headquarters? Hank always scrutinised all the names on all the cards held up by limousine drivers in the circling crowd awaiting passengers, a crowd now surging but restrained by some metal framed barriers just beyond the door. Hank walked shoulders straight and solemn faced through the doors behind some theatrically dressed travellers in broad brimmed hats and flowered shirts.

He shook his head as usual when he had finished reading the limousine driver's cards, Mister Rawlings, Mister Thant, Mister Wilson, Mister Lowry. He checked his watch and plunged through the crowd with a frustrated grimace. Some people stood aside. He was carrying on independently even though let down by some great institution within which he was very important.

Police carrying stylish multi-barrelled short firearms meandered in pairs. White faced and straw haired children in complicated electric pink high laced shoes, baggy nylon pants and striped and starred hooded tops slouched beside muscular looking black booted women with feathery collars on sparkling sweaters under the pale blue neon light of the terminal. The smell of perfume surrounding the doors that provided exit from the customs hall gave way to the scent of sweat and fried food. Organ music played above the chattering of a dark room of flashing games. It was the theme song of a spy movie. Neither Jack nor Juliet had yet emerged from the customs hall. Hank was the first.

Hank threaded the crowd and exited this part of the building into an echoing, high roofed covered pavilion through automatic doors. In this pavilion the air was cold. The departing passengers scurried across rubberised floors. It smelled of anti-freeze, exhaust and frozen mud. The cold entered his lungs like an acidic liquid as the doors to the arrivals hall closed behind him. The leather jacket he had worn on the plane from his posting seemed stiff and on the verge of cracking. His naked fingers clung to each other while wrapped around the suddenly frigid handles of his two good bags.

Hank hurried between concrete pillars and under glass overhead tunnels, those criss- crossing under the much higher roof peaked and steel beams. The overhead tunnels were to rough walled open floors of parking ahead. They pulsed with obscured quick walking overcoated shadows behind bright rainbowed but smeared panels of opaque glass. There was below, at ground level before the parking tower, a darker sidewalk and a long queue of foot stomping people, men, women and children in whispering clusters, or alone kicking and pulling bags of all sizes slowly along, crunching along the sidewalk as the line progressed before finally breaking into struggling, chaotic individuals popping through doors in twittering crouches into an opposite moving stream, a stream of eternally renewed empty crawling taxis, windshield wipers squeaking dryly on blackened glass, as the doors slammed.

Beyond a dark arch at the far end of the queue of people past their backs to where the taxis would exit through an open grey light, a portal beyond all cover and all shelter and all organization, a wall of snow slashed down in streaks and waves, a wall rising up in headlight beams as the taxis went forward, shallowly illuminating a white curved enclosing expanse fading away to dark blue, blurring and then disappearing to the left in a searching arc into the assumed road beyond the frame of the exit.

The ride into the city was along a packed freeway on ever crunching snow under tall pillared orange lights, lights which inflated into the sky greater globes of white and lime striped light pierced with tiny silver flashes, closely spaced. These lights led one after another into the city along a lemon freeway under a black sky.

Every vehicle stayed in anxious line moving at the edge of a skid but knifing along firmly and in as straight a line as possible following the way of its predecessor, a way defined by two black ribbons on the motorway, ribbons emerging and diving through the white on the tarmac, each keeping ahead its follower who was creeping or slicing closely behind barely in control.

Some predecessors and some following vehicles disappeared at one exit or another, each suddenly swaying out of the ribbonned guides of the main road, streaming in couples or alone, exiting with a bump over a small crest and then onto a glistening white tracked ramp, each carrying its shadowed souls into darkness.

When this happened Hank's taxi, still on the main track, had to make up the distance to the new car ahead without impetuousness but decisively, striving to re-establish the line or creep on in fearful expectation until the new pursuing lights conducted their overtaking advance, steadied, and then shone evenly and to everyone's relief through the back window again. Several emergency vehicles, all flashing startling blue and one flashing deep red, passed on the road opposite down its shoulders back towards the airport, outraging and slowing the labouring lines in each direction.

Snow slashed and skidded into the front windshield and glanced off the side windows. The buildings on the sides of the freeway showed through the sudden veil of white flakes against a background black, a corner, a steeple, a dome. Creamy coloured snow made rippled walls and roofs over roadside signs, snow lit underneath by the signs' own covered lights, to flash meaninglessly in reds and roses at the column of vehicles skiing by.

As his own taxi exited down a ramp into a snow covered and deserted narrow street, Hank unclenched his hands and relaxed. He left the snaking tube downtown of angry orange globes and entered a clear darkness under a strip of dead black sky. The black light seemed the origin of the snow and the snow the seeds for the darkness above.

Above the dome of the sudden emergence of snow into the headlights, just beyond the front of the taxi Hank could see small whirling grey shapes rising and falling, appearing and vanishing but hovering, darting to the buildings at street side, and there travelling along with the vehicle.

There was no answer at the security phone beside the main door to the building where Hank's friend had his flat. Hank rang and rang as the taxi waited in mid-street, waiting fruitlessly to discharge its responsibility into the warmth of the building and out of the snow. A cloud of vapour streamed from the exhaust as the taxi rumbled in cadences, stationary behind a curtain of snow.

No one was on the street. There was no street light. Very few lights burned in the squat buildings hulking nearly invisible along the street. There were no trees. The wind swirled above the street and then came straight downward. Hank returned to the taxi head bowed after a dozen silent rings.

He was taken to a small hotel further into the city known to the driver along deserted back streets. The hotel had a single light over the doorbell. Hank's ringing was answered by a very thin man in striped red pyjamas and blue rubber boots. The room assigned had an accordion radiator and a sink. It was painted pale green. Hank closed the curtains to the snow hitting the window. He hung up the suit he was to wear tomorrow in a doorless closet. The weather whispered and rattled behind the curtain. There was a damp draft.

Hank was two storeys above the street but he could hear indistinct crunching every so often as if some heavy flat bottomed vehicle was being dragged along below. Once he heard a motorcycle. It was certainly past midnight.

Hank awoke to a serious bout of "where am I?" It was still dark but it was getting greyishly lighter outside. This light produced a great gaping face at the window which turned out to be the flowered curtains. The slouching animal against the wall was the closet and his suit. The reptiles stalking him along the floor were his two good bags. A flying thing was a hand towel. The deep paralysing fear was from a forgotten dream in which he was guilty.

He washed in the sink and put on his good shirt and tie. The main wrinkles in the suit had hung out. The tie was another gift from staff for going away. It was coloured like a traditional blanket in oranges and purples. His good shoes were in the bag to be put on later after his trip to the toilet in the hall. He had time before the meeting to find an early opening discount store to buy a mock cashmere overcoat manufactured somewhere overseas. Then he would bus to headquarters for the first mid-morning meeting. He hadn't yet phoned his aged aunt at her home either.

Juliet would be now eating dark buttered toast plucked from sterling silver skeletons. Her father would be inquiring of her health. Jack was probably sleeping on the couch of his long suffering wife's bungalow. She'll do his laundry and book his doctor's appointment. Or had she died last year? No, they were separated. Where would he have gone then?

The snow on the street had not become slushy; it popped, squeaked and applauded under the first bus wheels in the street. Hank checked the weather. Everyone moving along the street outside bent with heads down and with their bodies inclined forward as they walked, like hurried monks, lifting their feet up like cats.

The bus was empty. The lightly trafficked streets smelled of deep cold and accompanying vapours of soup. The floor of the revolving door to the office was muddy in circles. The receptionist was dry faced and puffy eyed. The security guard standing near the lounge suite blinked at those few waiting. He was wearing a wrinkled blue shirt and had on a blank name tag. Hank kept his coat buttoned as he sat.

The elevator doors opened and out strode Ron, hand extended for shaking, looking to the left and right briskly, security identification slapping on his chest on a bright beaded chain, a tiny smiling Ron's face flapping there on the plastic card under a wide grin. Ron wore a dark green suede jacket and red tie. His shirt was a pale pink, tightly tailored under a brass buttoned jacket from under which peeped hints of saucy red suspenders. Ron's dark brown shoes and belt glistened as did his dark chocolate hair.

"Hank! Hank! Dear Hank! I hope you remember me. It's me, Ron. We were posted together in the wretched Magic Mountain Kingdom. Those were the days.

"It is so good to see you. Remember years ago during the bush war? King was an old bastard wasn't he? His uncle tried to kidnap the Pope later didn't he? Killed in a car crash with his own bodyguards. Poor king. Most mysterious. Five years ago wasn't it? You look cold." Hank stood and shook Ron's hand.

"How are you doing Hank? Have you been waiting long? The chief asked me to start things off with you. Everyone's tied up with an interview with the wretched media at the moment. Come with me, I have your pass." He took it from the pocket of his jacket and handed it to Hank. The pass was pink and read "Visitor". Hank shoved it into his overcoat pocket. He followed Ron after Ron had turned sharply around on a toe to go back into the elevator. The other waiting men watched. They stood in the elevator. Ron pushed a button. There was a camera.

"I guess all this security is new since you were here last. When was that? A lot of people coming in from the field don't like it. They say it sends a bad message and so on. But we have had threats lately. Hard to believe, I know. But things are changing. We're going up to floor five."

The fifth floor was open plan containing rows of cubicles but it had glass enclosed offices at the corners. Ron led Hank through the rows. Most of the cubicles contained variations of computers and young persons in dark colours and greys or in beige pastels. Some had little flags and some pictures of animals and huts. Each had a coat rack, usually with a steaming dark overcoat entwined with a bright scarf and some of them smelled of fried eggs.

Ron led Hank into a corner office containing a central table and four metal legged silver framed chairs. It had a coat rack. A white coffee set sat in the centre of the table on a tray. There were biscuits. The windows overlooked a street lined with stationary buses interspaced with taxis. There was a department store opposite. It had a seasonal sale on. There were "Big savings". The street scene was silent behind the window but frenzied with snow, taxis, buses, cars and pedestrians. It was triple glass. The bomb retarding pale white Venetian blinds had been raised for more light.

"Sit down, sit down. Hang up your coat. Have some coffee. Hard to book these rooms. Everyone wants them for meetings. Not enough space. You really brought some weather with you didn't you? Extra hour to get to work for me today. Except I stayed all night. Your fault really, but never mind, part of the job. Where did you get that coat?" Hank hung his coat, poured a coffee and sat. Ron sat opposite him.

"The chief says sorry, Hank. But it is often good to let you people just in from the field decompress for a little while before getting up to speed. It is a different perspective here. Adjust to the headquarters outlook and so on. Wanted me to sniff you out a bit too, the chief said.

"Did you know that I have the "Small Islands and Land-locked Countries" desk in my department now? Ten new country directors with that one. Department is growing, I must say. Whole agency is. Of course, I still have to pitch in at everything else too like I always did. Chief has asked me to. There is a rotational policy for the main managers. It helps perspective the chief says. I did reception once. Great fun. Sent the old visitors everywhere. Talked to some for hours about all sorts of things.

"But "Small Islands", that's really interesting. Quite a few conventions about them. Special laws and arrangements. Interesting legal framework. I mean what makes a small island? It's not like defining an "old bugger". Small to whom? We're having a global meeting on it next year. All kinds of concessions for trade if you are a small island. There are guaranteed returns. Mainly boring environmental stuff on the Aid side though. Pity. One island was made into a desert with a well drilling and damming project. Created subsidence. Good beaches, it goes without saying.

"Nasty volcanic little island. Inhabitants always complaining. But we can't boss them like you used to boss everyone when I was on your staff. We had to bring water by boat to shut them up. Reminds me of the bad old days these small islands. One step ahead of disaster. Always getting our hands dirty. But we are much better at most things now. We steer clear of sordid complications. Not like you Hank. I have the "Barely Developed Failing States" desk as well and the "Rice dependant economies". I am really the old super senior manager, Hank old chum.

"Remember that damn tomato project in the Magic Kingdom? We really had trouble with that. The farmers just wouldn't co-operate. They said red things were poison. One tried to burn the canning plant. Well Hank, you would never believe it now! It has taken right off. They are growing and canning tons of the stuff. They are even exporting it! In flavoured sauces and juices, the cunning little buggers. They must have listened to our "value added and increasing competitiveness" lectures. We've had to propose a tariff against it through the trade departments. Unfair competition that is. It's subsidized prices. We can't have that.

"Well Hank we've heard you had a spot of personal bother out there in wonderland haven't you? More complicated than the old Magic Mountain Kingdom. Bigger too, more staff headaches. Bit of a worrisome domestic set of problems for you from what we have heard. Police involved and so on. We've had a note this morning from our ministry who received a note from their embassy. We had some of your people come in very early too to talk to us. Quite a little stink there. Not saying much are you Hank?

"But that little local tangle has gone to a bit of a back burner now after this morning's coup! Lucky you, Hank!"

"What? A coup?" said Hank. He put down his cup with a clatter.

"What Hank? Sleeping in? Didn't listen to the radio this morning? Sure a big messy old bloody coup. President killed. Sultan confined to his palace. There have been all kinds of massacres in the provinces. Bodies in the river. The chief said this morning that you may even have to go back, Hank.

"Better you than me, I say. Early days yet I think though. Depends on what the chief decides about the other things. We don't want to endanger the agency. Of course, we also don't want you in the hands of insurgents with your wobbly bits sown to your nose.

"There could be refugee crises to get into though. A big one! We could invest up front in a few camps, put a couple of ads in the papers and get in on the bottom floor. Donations could roll in. There is sure to be all kinds of public money too going into this thing. Especially if it gets worse. Natural disaster, massacres, mutilations. We could pick up a few big contracts, maybe even get a special treasury vote. Perhaps co-ordinate the whole effort. Get a whopping big administrative fee. Charge the others to get in. It would be a good time for us now as things have been quiet lately since the island earthquake. I must say, Hank, I had thought some of your reports were a bit far-fetched, but what the hell. They turned out to be near as blazes almost true. Or we can say so now. We might do well out of this." Ron leaned forward and grabbed a biscuit. He munched it furiously and swallowed several times rapidly.

"What massacres? Where?" said Hank.

"Do not worry your old head about that, Hank. I think you may come out alright after all despite your problems. You got yourself some points around here, I must say, by raising up to a level four security alert a day before a coup. Cunning old Hank, very impressive! And that report on your escape! We got it last night; brilliant!

"Everyone on your staff had their little emergency plan too. Good thinking there. They all had red envelopes to open. Good image. Now most of the staff are heading across the border to the designated resort. We're bringing in temporary workers here from a secretarial agency to answer calls from their spouses and so on.

"We are going to arrange a link-up for the news to each family. Chief is doing an interview now calling for a big intervention, immediate airlift, sanctions and food supplies and so on. "Careful on the old food supplies though," I said. "We have to pay storage still for the last batch." It wasn't even looted for the markets, that food. It just sits there. We should have said it was a housing crisis. Bloody refugees ignored the camps and slept and ate at their relatives' houses.

"As for medical supplies the refugees then were healthy, mad or dead. They just weren't sick. Hardly any in between. Hard to get these things right. We could have lost money. Our surgeons sat in empty tents. They had to start dental work in the neighbourhood and even started some basketball teams. Some games were cancelled though because of the kidnappings. Quite a mess-up you remember Hank?

"Massacres all over this time though according to the news. No problem with sickness. Polluted water and so on. This is easier to call. Genocide really. Wiping out whole sections of population. There is sure to be disease and loads of bad governance. Trauma. The funds will flow in. War and rape. "War-rape!" Hey that's good. We could put that in the ad.

"Bands of murderous cannibalistic children roaming about and we might hear of worse. Who knows? Some areas are cut off by extensive flooding so we don't know what is going on there. Crocodiles, cholera. It is amazing how fast these things start. One minute everything is normal and depressing then suddenly a huge blow-up. It spreads like a wind. Flames and gunfire. Ripples in the pond and so on. It's like something from our old literature class. Remember old Empson? Bad luck for you to be missing the start. You could have written a book. Analyzing the signs and so on. Of course, you did report something but it is in the media now. That makes all the difference. You sure are quiet, Hank — headache?

"Anyway, the point is that when you see the government people and the ministry you can forget about talking about the long term situation and the projects. Forget about good governance and education or poverty or whatever. Make a pitch for us to do the rehabilitation. That's what you are well placed to do. You are the man who saw it all coming. You escaped by a whisker. You know the country inside out. It should go down a treat you being a fresh fish from the field and so on. Invaluable credibility the chief says.

"We can give a piece of the action to our main charity partner as well. I know their exec. I know you do too. He is a practical guy. He'll see the opportunity. Together we can make a good case that we have the best know-how to manage the whole budget. And it is true. But we also show that we collaborate. We can co-ordinate everything for more efficient and transparent response in line with policy. That sort of thing. Better than any other rubbishy agency or those little bleeding heart outfits with their roving hospitals and clothing collections. We'll have our advertisement in the paper by this evening. I've seen the photo. It's really great. Broken doll washed up on a riverbank. There's a smouldering hut in the background. "Where is she now?" says the hook. This should get us quite a little of our own money to bring to the table." Ron chuckled to himself.

"So we aren't going to debrief about the present projects?" said Hank. "Talk about my new posting?"

"I don't see the point, do you Hank? The projects you had are probably under water or burnt. Your assignment depends on the little issues I've mentioned. Anyway we have to focus. We must have continuity, especially in image. Stick to one approach. No use developing things in the crisis stage. This is the time for venture compassion. We can't do everything or ask for everything either. As for you, you still have a contract and we haven't yet evaluated your performance.

"The chief will want to talk about your own little downside. We need to get a line on that. How will we answer inquiries if they come in some more? The chief will be finished the interviews soon and will want to know that.

"The trouble for us and for you is that there exists a note from the embassy to our diplomats. You can't trust those sorts of people. They all have their own agenda and little tradeoffs. The note is on record and could affect our block funding from government sometime. It could crop up again officially even though their embassy staff will probably be replaced or be working for us or be brought home for terminal assessment by the new junta. And, after all Hank, it is one of those basic moral things. You can't underestimate those. It could be used to discredit us by someone public in the future. A priest or something. We could lose a donation from a whole parish.

"Oh God," said Hank in a tiny mutter.

"Cheer up Hank, relax," said Ron, "I think everything is basically fine. We're growing. We have a new thing. There are only a couple of complications but that is usual. You'll get to meet the chief. That can't be bad for you can it? Good for your career.

"The chief may tell you about our new mission statement. Even consult with you. And you are still on paid leave, you'll have time in the city, there will be receptions, some good ones, and besides you won't have to write a complete country report or at least not a complicated one. The projects out there were probably alright. But who cares now? No one can think otherwise. They might well have succeeded by this time. Who knows. All forgotten now. Bigger picture.

"But let's face it Hank. It isn't about that sort of mundane thing really, is it? You went to the same school as I did. You studied with the same people but as I remember you didn't get the doctorate did you? You know that the important thing is really that we are there at all. We are a beneficial presence.

We are the embodiment of the idea of humanity. It is by that we respond and initiate change. Us!

"It is not just the projects. It is not just that we help by employing all the local staff, bringing hard currency, buying artefacts and advising peoples how to succeed. Not even the added value that we are probably giving the first jobs to the local stars, future leaders and the kids of officials. We are creating a new class of change agents who literally love us but that is supplementary. We are giving fulfilling useful careers for ourselves if truth be told and for other bright public servants but that is a side benefit. What it is really about is drama for the nation! It is the alleviation of guilt, redemption and the justification for our prosperity. It is the commoditization of disaster and the export of our brand of common sense. Bridges of hope and hands across the ocean! Reduction of immigration! Conflict management! Securing markets! The superstructure of the future world!" Ron's voice was rising and he addressed his remarks to the window and alternatively to the ceiling.

"What we really do is even beyond all that, Hank. Think of it! We sell and export a dream. We give loans for it. We trade in systems, know-how, value added imaging. We show new paradigms. We then live them right in front of the deprived victims of injustice. We inspire. We bring a sort of new time and space. A new world of simplicities. New feelings, new attitude, new detachment. We are like poets. Not just our aerospace and so on but our imaginative space. Hope. New possibilities. Appropriate change. I would resist the notion that what we were doing was only material. It is spiritual development.

"My, I am going on! Have you read my articles on this? No? How could you, you've been in the bush. But this is what I tell all the new staff. They must never get cynical from the realities. What we do is glorious and essential. Hank, you must never lose your commitment to our mission and the agency. We all must never forget our basic mission. We must safeguard the agency as the apple of our eye. It itself is the solution. These developing places have paradigms of self-deception and palaces of delusions and dreams. Superstition and idealism. Fanaticism. Barter. The people live in a kind of fairyland of poverty. There is imaginative and administrative deception. False hopes. False histories. Vague promises. Unobtainable goals. Miracles. Caricatures. Dictators, clowns, demons and despots of the mind. Extremism. Mirrors of evil. What am I raving about? They leave the market frustrated. They don't behave like us. We must develop them. We must be firm in our conviction that they get nothing unless they govern themselves like us. Decently. But some don't want to change their minds.

"And all that's why some of them hate global ideas and efficient products on any scale or depth. Except for those few groups who have been well educated with us. But sometimes a whole people or the whole country reverts atavistically and is held together by some crazy antique fantasy of self or an agreed fantasy of their community. They become a kind of mad. They start the dance of opposition, of dreams. They are often negative and insensitive to our caring and institutions. That's what our good teacher demonstrated. Remember? We should not give up. That is the lesson history of our work, the story of our decades of struggle to build the agency." Ron sounded reverential and looked briefly downwards to his hands clenched on the table.

"Mundane moralities, Hank. Outdated memories old friend. They hold onto some barbaric psychologically nurturing myths often imposed by anti-democratic elite. Do you get it Hank? It is so frustrating. They reject our co-operative frameworks over and over. They could even develop a completely invisible economy to us. A death culture. Passivism. Non-cooperation with our peacekeeping. Unemployment in the metropolis. You don't want that do you? Remember my essay about this? Did you read it? Oh well. Listen to me. How could you? I'm not sure myself sometimes what I am saying.

"That sort of world they want out there Hank, used to work before colonialism. Sure! Create a physics defying reality, probably not a true one at that and generate some violent disordered marketplace of emotions, rituals and dreams, but Hank, it doesn't create good waste management companies with global scope." Ron had exhausted the biscuits.

"I didn't know we were doing a new mission statement," said Hank. "Will it mention educational programs and stake holding partners as a priority? Wells?"

"Well that really isn't something the field people need worry about until we publish it and have the consultations," said Ron. "We are all circulating papers. Some of the remarks I just made are in mine. They are more detailed of course. What I said was a précis. I hope you support them, Hank. They could be important policies if we restructure. Loyalty means a lot around here.

"Oh and Hank, the chief wants me to go to your meetings in the city with you. Thinks I can be of assistance. Help you to take a good approach. Well, time to go I think. It is really good to see you again. We'll have a good few days together. Remember it is for the agency. The Chief probably awaits. Come with me."

IX

As Ron led Hank to the elevators to go to the top floor, Hank noticed that in another glass walled office a man in a yellow bowtie was sitting at a table talking to Juliet and Jack. The man was taking notes. Jack had on a grey suit. Juliet wore a beige two piece.

They went up the elevator to the floor below the chief's. Entry to the chief's floor was only by a stairway through a pair of security doors guarded with a separate reception desk. At this desk Ron had to sign for Hank. Hank had to take his pink laminated card from his pocket for inspection. He noticed that it had a greenish holograph. Ron paused at the bottom of the stairs and spoke to Hank in a very low voice while grasping his elbow slightly.

"I know I probably don't need to tell you this, Hank, but since you don't know much about headquarters lately and haven't met the chief I should tell you, just to be fair, that she is an albino and she smokes.

"I know you are a sound, sensitive man, Hank, but just about everyone acts a little surprised when they first meet her. It can be embarrassing for them. I know you won't do that Hank.

"But my oh my Hank, she is better than the last chief we had. Imagine that old fool used a picture of his partner for the "Breast is Best" poster to promote natural child rearing. The scandal! And how about that seminar on the world's economic future where he said his child was the messiah! How were the delegates supposed to understand that? He took his wife and friends on quite a few inspection trips too. Chartered a plane. Didn't you say something about that once Hank? No, no, that was Peters wasn't it. Gone, poor man.

"But I think I am having an effect on her. I am straightening her out. I teach her policy. She's from the commercial sector and so doesn't yet completely understand our work. I'm getting her to see sense. These people aren't often succeeding in business because they have a strategic sense or an analysis. They just claw themselves up on their personalities. They eat those below them. They kill their rivals. Quite a few are only really shallow brutal chatterboxes. Old school and friends in high places, but other than that empty nonsense. But she's better than the last one, old golden boy of long laments. That bugger would never listen to anyone. He was completely out of touch with the latest thinking."

There was a waiting room at the top of the stairs overseen by a large desk without computer and another functionary. There was a photographic display on partitions around the walls of the various country offices of the agency. There were also pictures of beneficiaries, mainly children, in native dress carrying machetes with bold captions such as "Nutrition for The Nations" and "Bridges of Hope".

Behind the reception desk were two ceiling height wooden doors. To one side was a large wooden globe on a metal stand. They could hear a gruff voice talking loudly from behind the doors. It paused after a rising noisy glissade, hanging like a hawk in the air. This was followed by a thump and then after a moment by a phone tone, a rendition of the agency song, and then the voice behind the door resumed in anger.

Ron and Hank sat in two blue leather chairs on the invitation of the functionary behind the desk. After a quarter of an hour of their listening to more muffled, sometimes loud soliloquies without either magazine or tea but reading and rereading the slogans on the partitions from their chairs, they were finally instructed by the functionary after she had reverently answered her phone, a phone which also played the agency song, and had listened to a message silently and then had lowered the phone reverentially to go through the doors. Hank rose sleepily and placed his new coat over the chair. He smoothed down his tie. Ron opened both the doors and indicated Hank through.

The room was blue dark and wide. Both the bombproof blinds and the heavy grey curtains were closed. A table extended the length of the room to make a junction broadside with a very big desk at the far wall in front of the windows. There were some bookcases to either side or other tall doors. The desk had a screen for projections behind it and in front of the heavy curtains. On its surface were two complicated telephones with large grey speakers and screens. It also had three heavy glass ashtrays. The red pinprick of a cigarette end glowed from behind the desk.

Ron sat down at the end of the table furthest from the desk. He was nearest the entry doors. Before he sat he had guided Hank halfway along the table to sit on a chair where Hank could see in the smoke, silhouetted before the screen, what seemed a blue haired woman, bluish faced as well, in a woolly black cardigan wearing heavy rimmed glasses. The functionary from reception then closed the doors they had entered from and so the woman became black.

The room was musty and cloying with air freshener and smoke. The voice from the darkness when it came was deep and melodious with only a slight rasp. The cigarette end ribboned the air on dipping trips to the ashtray with red flashes.

"Well Mister Rousseau, Hank, if I may? You have had quite an adventure. Ronald has told me everything. The escape, the insurgency, the evacuation from the trouble spot, the security alert. I have told the media. You had a narrow escape from the extremist insurgents and under difficult circumstances organised the rational pull-out of our mission. Wonderful! I think that was terribly well done and said so to the television people. I told them all about it, just outside there in the foyer, only an hour ago. It will be broadcast in an hour. I gave them your agency photo for their items. You are our celebrity of the moment. A bit of the rough stuff.

"I told them we, you, would go back immediately with new resources and respond to the crisis with all our skill and professionalism. I said you had urgently called for resources. They wanted to talk to you but I told them you would be reporting through us on your return to your post. They took some footage with their wretched lights of our whole display out there. Not of me, thank God. I gave them some of our videos and played them the long one in here. There was a lot of gratifying interest from the journalists in our agency and how we have been on top of the situation in that country, labouring on so long despite being unheeded with all our warnings to the bureaucrats. You have done well Hank. Just what we needed. A bit of pizzazz. It comes at a good time.

"But about you personally Hank, Mister Macdonald here, Ron, says your financial reports are quite good, you are on budget and most of your expense claims will be honoured too. But I am afraid our political analyst Mister Swift and our Human Resources Director Miss Whimhurst are a bit concerned about some of the reports we have gotten from some returned staff. We don't want the agency falling into disrepute, do we Rousseau? Your contract has a clause in it about that."

"What reports are those?" said Hank.

"Well, one woman is saying that you verbally abused her, abused her Hank! My heavens! And that in an interview with the police out there you rubbished the agency. You said that we were incompetent or something. To a foreign institution! We don't want agency rubbishing, Hank! In fact our staff here is instructed to mention its work positively in every second sentence when speaking to authorities. If you did that it reflects badly on us back here Hank. And on me! We expect loyalty.

"One of our educational technical people just back from the field, Mister Jack Wesley, has made an even more disturbing report that you countenanced immoral connections by staff with local political figures. Goodness gracious me Hank, we cannot have that either!" The chief paused. The orange red pinprick brightened an instant in the dark.

"Is this a disciplinary meeting?" said Hank "The manual says I can have two representatives with me if it's a disciplinary meeting."

"No, no. Relax Mister Rousseau. No need for that yet Hank; I do take it seriously but we can talk about all that when you return from your new assignment. I think Ron has told you that after a bit of fundraising, selling our approach and so on, we will expect you to go out to arrange the relief effort. You did tell him didn't you Ron?" Ron said nothing.

"You can't be a country director, of course; the complaints against you from staff have reached some big beasts with big ears. Government ears. We have someone else for the director, anyway, but you will have the authority to go to the provinces and find out what we should do.

"I'm also worried about a formal note our government received that you were involved in some sort of accident or death or something with a young pregnant woman. There may be a charge pending. Or it was pending anyway. Of course their embassy staff has been doing that sort of thing here all the time and our diplomats have nudged and winked it away, in fact they may owe us a few, but we have been told, evidently, by two of your returned staff a few things that may confirm if pressed that perhaps something may be true about this.

"Hank. I need you to assure me now, formally, for the record, that there is little truth in these things. I know there are complex events and occurrences that happen in the field that maybe only you understand but we here at headquarters have a game to play too. We need you as our hero Hank. The man who escaped insurgents. This is what I told the media. I was shocked with what Ron's staff told me of the complaints. We don't want you to put us in trouble."

"Nothing you have described has any reality at all. Not any of it. Quite the contrary," said Hank.

"Good, good Hank. That is all it will take for me now. I can tell the government and others I have talked with you and you gave assurances.

"But Hank. Your position has changed. Others are appointed. The agency image comes first. And we'll talk about the other things when you come back from assignment. I'll tell Whimhurst and Swift. That is all then. It is settled. Ron is responsible for the rest and I am sure he will do well. I think he has a whole plan. I take it you agree now to take your new assignment after this little chat Hank? It would mean we could continue your salary at the present level for awhile. Does he agree Ron? Are you two ready to get to work?"

"Yes," said Hank softly.

"Yes chief," said Ron in the dark. "Now Hank, when you get back you will first help the new country director to bring the staff back to the capital from the resort. They are paid for; we should use them. This is our policy."

Ron continued now loudly and he seemed to be directing his voice at the chief. "The loan that we gave the country for road building stipulated that they had to take on and pay our advisory staff as well as pay for our contractors. Our government has always demanded improved planning from them and so on as a condition for our loan. This is their policy.

"It doesn't matter that there is a crisis. Their country must still pay back the loan. If anyone asks you except the media you must say so. We on our part will still pay salaries and for our office here as well as take our administrative fees at headquarters from the loan. It's partially banked with us anyway. The rest has probably gone to the beach in the neighbouring country or is being used for room service here in the city by the former government officials who have escaped. Don't you think so chief?

"We need some of the staff back to work to show compliance. Some of the others can come home but we will still pay them. Or some others here in their place. We will send new people with the new money we get to do the relief.

"Keep the two groups apart, Hank; we don't want morale undermined or roles confused. They will have different salary grades. We will be sending our own journalists and film crew right away too. We do not want bad interviews. The chief thought of that. So you better get some relief going somewhere: flood restraints, camps, something like that. Don't start a program looking for survivors and buried bodies. Those are too expensive. Say that we have given up hope and need housing for the survivors. We do better out of that. I am sure chief agrees.

"Before you go — you are listening aren't you Hank? You look a little sleepy. Before you go, as we discussed, you will visit the minister and so on to pitch for relief. You can make some speeches around the city too. Say what we tell you to.

"Remember the law. If you ask for money for stupid specific things like little old starving women in the mountains then we will have to spend some of the money you raise only for that. You can bloody find them. I won't. Don't do it. The money is restricted. It would be illegal to use it as we want. It is a headache thing for us. Don't ever do it! Be vague but sound precise as though you know what is happening.

"If you asked for money for old starving women in the mountains, we would have to ask all the women above a certain altitude if they are short and hungry and only then could we give them money. We would measure them and ask their ages. I want you to be professional Hank. This is a professional agency.

"It is alright to say money raised is being used for relief in general. That can mean that we can study the issue of relief, write a manual about relief, hold some seminars on relief, build relief headquarters and rent some trucks for relief and so on. We can also pay ourselves.

"But best is if you don't say anything specific about what we really do. Show a picture and describe some suffering and ask for the money basically because we are good and want to do good. That is the best way. People love us as a kind of institution. A therapy. We are relying on your maturity Hank. We need someone to raise funds properly. We need someone who understands reality and policy.

"We can have a bit of trouble Hank, believe me, if we fundraise wrongly especially with whispering going on all the time from our competitors to our donors and perhaps because of the law. Although we are probably pretty well placed with government now on this one not to worry as much as we used to, not like the little fellows do. O.K Hank? Understand?

"The main thing for us to do is to get people donating and worrying, then for us to get out, get going and get some government money. Real money. Then we'll have a certainty of income and a contract describing something specific for the money we get but that one we can alter every few months. Also Hank we will talk to a few of the corporations who did the roads and have the mines. They are socially responsible. They'll help us with government. They should also throw in some plane tickets and some equipment.

"Hank, I'll be with you all the time for your speeches. Chief, I think this will be a good one.

"I wish the bloody recipients and victims would pay something. Don't you chief? They are really getting the best of all this genocide and so on if you really analyse it.

"Remember the class we took on refractionary economics, Hank? The idea seemed sound to me. Standard economics operates on assumptions of value, labour, market, time and space and progressions. Real economics, the professor said, should ignore all this as humanity has for most of its existence. Real economics should, for example, take into account such things as investment made in the present by the future and in the past by the present. It should measure values changed in the past by the future and vice versa. It should embrace valuelessness and so on. Be a kind of haunted economics. This then alters, and will alter, and would alter, all transactions with hidden values. Do you follow? Quite neat isn't it? What do you think chief?

"Hank," Ron went on, "the developing world has exported to us all sorts of things like religion and abstract art and the blues and so on. They are providing a majority leadership to us already on the departmental level. What do we get back though for being their market? Nearly nothing! We are certainly not getting enough for these global crises and disasters and the work we put into them. We need more of that sort of thing of our own. Don't you think so chief?" The chief said nothing but she might have nodded. Perhaps she looked at her watch.

"Well chief, enough talk," Ron said next and stood up, a shadow rising in the distance from his chair and then standing stiffly facing the darkness. "Hank and I will be going now. Our next meeting arranged is with Jack Wesley in your foyer so Hank can hand over the country directorship to him. Then we are off to see the minister. We will see the charity afterwards. And we will see the corporations. With your permission and at your suggestion we will carry out the strategy as agreed and do what we must do to do good. It is for the agency and for our mission.

"What a world we are in chief, I must say. It is as you said in the meeting last week with your government friend a contest between the few enlightened ones with some accompanying incompetent hangers-on only aided by indifferent internationalist sludges on the one hand and legions of robust pillagers and disaster mongers on the other. It is hard to tell who is who, as you always say, chief. But that is our mission. Just like the philosophers at school said it would be. Thank you ma'am for your time. We are off!" The chief still said nothing. She had not coughed.

THE BUSH

Hank had seen Ron's hands waving and wiggling in the blackness. He wondered what Ron meant by his use of "we". Hank wanted to go for breakfast. He saw the chief turn blue again as he and Ron went through the door and closed it behind.

"I think she really listens to her senior staff. No buck passing with her. I think she agreed with all that. I think she likes the plan and approach," said Ron outside the closed doors. He seemed very excited. "She really cares for analysis. I hope I can continue to influence her. God but that must be the only designated smoking area in twenty blocks! It is a handy thing being the chief. I wouldn't mind it myself. Change the décor of course."

Jack and Juliet were sitting in the blue chairs of the reception. The receptionist indicated that Jack should go in to the chief's office. Jack did silently. Ron opened the door for him and closed it after. Ron then indicated the chair emptied by Jack to Hank. Jack had smoothed his blue tie before entering. He had been sitting on Hank's coat. Juliet's strawberry hair was calm but limp. Her beige suit was wrinkled. She looked tired.

"Hank, can you wait for me here a moment?" said Ron. "I have to talk to a few of my staff about some things and get my coat before we go out. I should only be a few moments. It is quite cosy up here. Crowded and busy below. Then when I get back we'll be off. Perhaps we will have time for some breakfast before the meeting with the minister. Oh and have a word with Jack when he gets out, turn over the project and so on." Ron nodded curtly to Juliet then he went down the stairs towards the security doors. Hank sat.

"Jack will be a better director than you," said Juliet. "He really cares for the place and the people. He is almost one of them. He gets very close to them. He knows more about the tribes than you do. He has lots of good ideas for new projects too. Cultural projects. Gender sensitive ones. He is better trained than you too. He took an educational management course once. He knows what to do."

"I'm sure he does," said Hank.

"Yes, he does. He talked about his ideas all night and then with my father at breakfast. They are really exciting. They aren't boring and misplaced little efforts like you've been doing. You always made me a bit suspicious Hank. You were cold to your staff including me. Arrogant and controlling. Except that once but that was an exception. I always suspected your sensitivities. I told you I would complain and I have. You always gave me a bad feeling. A creepy feeling."

"I'm sorry to hear that Juliet. I've always respected your views and work. By the way, I didn't know your sister was in the personnel department," said Hank. "Miss Whimhurst isn't it?"

"Yes, Cressy. We were always Juliet and Cressy, the Whimhurst twins. We used to do everything together. She is very good. My dad thought that we both should get some experience in work before joining government or going back to the university to teach. He talked to the agency about it. That's how we got in. He knows the chief from his business and of course he was in the agency himself. She is very smart, my sister. She always did better in daddy's eyes than me. Did well with the boys too. I could kill her for it. Cressy has a law degree like I do but did an advanced degree in systems management when I did mine in gender studies."

"Gosh it's a small world," said Hank. "My former assistant is now senior management here and my old professor is the minister. Well, it looks like Jack gets to go back as he wanted. He must be really happy. Is he feeling any better?"

"He certainly is," said Juliet. "It's really something what happens to you when you get off that plane and get settled in somewhere and catch your breath. You feel wonderful. Jack and I did. It all comes back to you in a rush. The best things. You long for them again really. Memories. You grasp them and feel them. It is a great discharge. And then we saw the first news too on my television in my room. We talked and talked. We had a whole new perspective on things. New interpretations. He is really quite exciting, Jack. Not withdrawn like you. No boring stuff.

"It all now wasn't so close for us but it was wider in meaning, Jack explained. We could see more clearly the real gut issues. The way the agency should be going and the country program, the relief effort. The overview. The hidden movements.

"Jack helped me to see them. Jack said that he had a whole return of deeper memory when the fever lifted. A new clarity. He saw everything more intensely. All the sickness had lifted, he was great physically, and he only had the slight whistling in the ears he's had since he left his school. We talked all night.

"Jack phoned the agency people first thing. He had their home and emergency numbers. I, of course, had my sister and dad knew some of the policy people. We rushed over for early meetings and to get the emergency going. We worked on the crisis. Wonderful. Dad gave us his driver and car. We've been talking to Ron's staff and been on the phone ever since. One meeting after another. They had your staff reports too."

"Yes, there certainly is a lot of activity going on. Everyone is quite busy. Running around, coming in early, dispatching planes and boats, giving interviews, making appointments. There is something for everyone to do. It is a bit confusing to me really as the field things aren't much different than they always were. But there is quite a good deal the agency believes it can achieve with this situation if it responds quickly. It's what they exist for after all and not just the seminars and fund raising galas. They are mobilising everything they have, scraping all the barrels, pulling out all the stops," said Hank. "Are you going back too?"

"No. Jack and I had a little talk about that and he thought it would be best if I looked for a teaching post or something good at headquarters. Perhaps assisting the chief. Dad agrees. Jack lost his job at the library when he took the assignment and we both really have no base here or career path anymore because of the time we've been away. Dad wants me to settle. We must think of the future and our roots. That's what Jack says. We can't stay bush. And, as you may have guessed, I am pregnant. If Jack goes out as director then when he completes his contract he could come back as a department head."

"Well that's all going pretty quickly with you two," said Hank. "But it should not really be a surprise; of course I suspected something was going on with you."

"No it's not going quickly, Hank. Its substantial," said Juliet abruptly. "We saw each other often in country and he used to write me the most marvellous letters. Stories really. We had mutual friends from my law school. I really got to know him on our trip back and on the plane for how he really was. He was so brave and principled with the police, not like your whingeing, and when we talked on the plane he explained the rumours. I'm really not impressed that you didn't look after him better Hank. Jack is a sensitive guy. He would have had no place to sleep when he arrived. No base. I'm very glad my father was there to meet us. There was a terrible snow."

Jack came out from the doors doing up the buttons of his grey suit. It looked new. He had left his overcoat on the chair on which Juliet was sitting. Juliet arose and after a little hug with Jack and a brief kiss went into the chief's office, closing the door behind her. Jack sat on Juliet's chair. He looked at the display of beneficiaries.

"I hear you are feeling better now," said Hank. "I hope so and congratulations on your appointment."

"Oh yes I am feeling better now," said Jack. "I feel great. I hope you don't mind. I know we don't get along but it is a professional thing. I'm better for the program. But I told you I would return, didn't I! I've left a few things undone as you might know.

"I probably won't even need the medical first, Ron says. You were wrong about that too. I know I have to get back as quickly as I can. Ron agrees. It sounds like they may really need me back there. I shouldn't have left them behind. The chief just congratulated me on the appointment and said it was critical for the agency.

"I'll probably be going a few days after you Hank. Don't you mess up then. I have a couple of day's orientation scheduled first with Ron's staff; they want to make sure I have the right policy and attitude they say, and then I have to see some other people who are friends of Juliet's dad. The agency may be sending a boatload of food supplies and some press with it. The government may pay. Juliet's dad will announce it.

"It is the "Boat of Hope". I may go with that for the publicity. Perhaps a government person too. Ron thinks my connections may be good for some other funds. But that may be delayed. It depends on how the relief effort is designed and the tone of the fundraising. I'm very anxious to return as you know. Thousands and thousands of people. I love it passionately. It feels like it is calling me home. You may not understand that. Do you think that is crazy?

"I have a stream of images in my mind, Hank. I have a vision for the place. It is almost visceral. Everything here seems to resonate with the country there. The street sounds, the creak of a bed, the whistle of the wind. It asks me to return. You must know what I mean Hank. It possesses you. Night wind in the palms, fires on the mountain. I see the faces of old friends. You must feel it too, even though not like I do. You must be anxious like me."

"Well I know that you must sincerely feel all that, Jack, I guess, but maybe you should relax a little," said Hank.

"But as for me, frankly Jack, I find a lot of places just fussy, dirty, destructive and stupid, like this whole crisis is. I respect your feelings in a way Jack, I have to, it can't be helped, and it really isn't any of my business any more, but still some things seem a waste to me, a confusion of nonsense, and I don't care so much about them. I know in your present state you can't understand this Jack, and I really can't do anything about that. But I'll do my little assignment I guess. I just do what I can and what seems best at the time. No hard feelings from me, you bastard.

"By the way Jack I have a few things for you. Some papers. They are something a country director should see. Perhaps the chief too. I'll give them to you before I go. Or I may leave them with someone. I may need them before then. Ah, here's Ron."

Ron had appeared coming up the stairs waving to Hank. Ron was carrying his camel coat. Hank got up wordlessly and followed Ron down the stairs through the security doors across the large open office downstairs and into the lift. The office was humming and barking with activity. Some people were running and dodging each other in the aisles hurtling from one cubicle to the next with papers and reports.

In the lift Ron put on his coat and gloves. He tied a yellow scarf around his neck and left it dangling outside the coat. On the ground floor the waiting area was now empty. They went through the revolving doors into the street.

The strip of sky between the buildings had become more overcast. The snow had resumed with heavy flakes. The wind was howling above the buildings but was not at that instant at street level, where the air was cold, heavy, wet and calm. The amount of street traffic had reduced. Both men paused on exiting the revolving doors to adjust to the cold and snow. Each checked his coat buttons and raised his collar. Ron took several steps forward away from the doors and Hank followed. Then Hank slipped and crashed onto his back, feet forward on the snow covered pavement.

Ron called out Hank's name sharply while turning at Hank's cry and then bent to him extending a hand. Hank raised his head and shook it. He then lay back on the pavement staring up into the snow. The wind returned to street level making swirling fogs of freezing moisture, frozen mud, paper bits and beige snow at ground level, twisting around Hank and around other people's feet.

Ron extended his hand again. Hank took it and pulled himself up, first onto one knee and then to his feet. He dropped the hand, adjusted his coat and shook his head back and forth again. Snow had melted on his face. Ron asked how Hank was.

"A bit dizzy. I think a bit of a headache. I wasn't expecting that. But I am O.K. I had a fever earlier but it's gone." Ron suggested that they pause a bit.

"No, no, let's keep going; there is plenty to do now."

"No, we'll just pause here a moment. Hank you should take better care of yourself. You've seemed tired and unfocussed and a bit quiet. Frankly I am a little surprised about how you are taking all this. Shocked really. Not being the country director any more and how your staff is behaving and so on. Most disloyal. But you seem O.K after your little meeting with Jack," said Ron into the wind while leaning towards Hank's ear. He put his arm on Hank's shoulder. "Are you sure you are all right? Are you tired?"

From where they stood they could see the length of the street and through the buildings at the end the bridge and some of the river, a brown smear in the snow. The bridge and far embankment were illuminated in the dark morning, under lowering clouds by a chain of the familiar orange globe lights which stretched along the embankment and over the bridge from along the far boulevard which was the extension and end of the freeway into the city. The reflections of the lights made pale green and brown jellylike snakes striping the water. The sides of the tall glass windowed buildings directly in front and of the little ancient preserved sandstone church amongst other buildings just down the street towards the bridge were shimmering with purple shadows as snow swirled in the valley of the street illuminated in the blue lights cast by some of the office blocks. All the street sounds in the reducing traffic were muffled, then magnified. One bus near the bridge looked as though it had been abandoned, empty, one wheel on the pavement doors open. There was some honking of horns from vehicles out of sight.

"Things are not quite going as I expected," said Hank and he flinched a little under Ron's arm. "But that is how it goes."

"Well it is not too far to the ministry," said Ron. "And it is best that we walk. My staff say that the news has mentioned that there was a power outage affecting the underground transport system and some trains are stuck between stations. Twenty thousand people reportedly. A lot of the bus system is down too due to accidents and so on. And some burst sewers have flooded and then frozen cutting off a few main routes. Let's just walk along slowly here. It's towards the bridge."

As they walked, Hank staggered slightly. He kept shaking his head. Ron stopped and looked sharply into Hank's face. He then took Hank by the arm and guided him up the three steps into the shelter of the deep arch before the dark riveted door of the church. A sign on the door gave the name and date of construction of the church and thanked the government program that had preserved it. Outside the shelter of the arch the snow swept down white and grey flecked. They stood for a moment in silence. Hank was sniffing. He shook his head again.

"It's just like the memory board," said Hank finally. "Orange and white and grey in different lines and flashes. Changes and swirling."

"What is that Hank?" said Ron. "You look a bit befuddled old chap. Get a little knock on the head did we? Good thing you landed on snow. But there was ice underneath. Perhaps we started off too soon. We could pause a bit. Do you have a handkerchief? We still have time for the minister."

"I mean, Ron," Hank spoke quietly staring out of the arch to the street, "there is no way to tell you truly how I feel about all this. I am glad you asked. Thank you. I don't know how I am taking it either. How could you believe what I know really?

What I remember? And people change, Ron, facts change, things shift around. Some sort of revolving force at play I sometimes think. Everyone seems to start thinking and believing in a different way sometimes. Things look different. Turned around, different logic. It's all part of the game really. So what? Perhaps that's the way things get new and changed. I certainly don't feel like I used to. Well forget it. The best thing is to get on with it. I can get some rest later."

"Can't hear all that you are saying in this wind," said Ron, "but yes, let's get on with it if you're felling better. Just another minute and we'll be off." Ron had leaned again to Hank's ear.

"The ministry security should be quite tight Hank. When we get there you just follow me. It may take extra time to get in. A press man may be waiting. It's all been arranged. It's an event.

"But no one may be there. My staff say though that the news had said that all the closed circuit cameras in the downtown area had frozen. An emergency was declared and the police reserve had to be brought into town quickly in armoured vehicles so they could get through the snow. They are guarding the main buildings manually. One armoured car ran over a child playing in the snow in a suburb and there is a bit of a riot on an estate. Terrible thing, mainly foreigners. I hope no one gets hurt because the hospitals are all closed because of the power even though they're running on generators except for the ones quarantined because of that strange virus, not the usual one. Airports could close too. There is a big problem with the satellites and all the electrics. We still get messages though and I have my ear thing. I can't get images though. You feeling better now Hank?"

"I couldn't quite hear you completely," said Hank loudly, looking into the snow. "I am O.K though. I think it is passing. Just a knock. Did you say that children had closed the airports? Will I be able to get out? Is it the junta? What did you say the ministry is doing? "

"No, the airport there is open. But maybe not in a while here," said Ron. "Listen to the briefing, will you Hank! The airport here if it closes should reopen soon. You'll be in a plane soon old man.

"Opening the airport is always the first thing for recovery, you know that, and the junta has done it immediately but I think you should tell the minister that we might still need to evacuate people through it. Children maybe. We could get a refurbishment contract. Yes, and I don't think I told you, but your other staff person posted in Chembeland is still missing. Tom somebody. The minister knows the press and politics of that. Tell him we need extra money to do a search. More staff. We might get your salary recovered from it and more press."

Hank suddenly plunged into the snow from the church's arch. He turned to the left towards the bridge and walked head down into a gusting wind. Ron followed in an instant, double stepping to catch up. They walked without talking as close to the buildings as they could, ignoring pedestrians speeding towards them, wobbling and squelching in the snow with the wind at their backs. Those coming relinquished right of way on the sidewalk, moving around the two determined figures, nearly blind in the oncoming weather.

They moved through two empty intersections with empty side streets, one of which had signals hissing and spluttering showing all the options of walking, on their indicators, showing caution and go ahead. The windows to shops they passed revealed inside sparsely populated aisles in harsh yellow or neon blue light. The government buildings alternating with shops were heavily shuttered all the way up their many stories. The name plates by the doors and the signs in the windows announced broad and abstract functions for the departments within as "Transport and Commerce", "Communications and Energy". The plates were streaked with shimmering frost; the windows were mud and snow spattered. They passed the entrance to an underground station which was closed by a heavily woven steel gate.

It took ten minutes to reach the ministry. Ron's hair was wet and dark; Hank sniffled heavily and shook his shoulders frequently. Ron's camel coat hung stiffly while Hank's eyes were slitted and caked at the corners. His coat glistened with droplets. They both stamped their feet on exiting the revolving door into the ministry's robustly heated public foyer.

A tiled mural covered the opposite wall at the end of an expanse of marbled floor. The mural showed three-masted schooners, trains and bi-planes. There were depictions of overseas religious sites and fields of square topped wheat. Someone was showing a woven cloth to someone else and an ambulance drove behind them with a broadly smiling woman nurse at the wheel. There were two separate groupings of students and teachers. One was under a tree and the other was in a laboratory.

Under the mural was a large crescent shaped reception desk of an opaque white material lit internally. There was a receptionist standing there flanked by two armed police with short guns hanging from shoulder straps. To the left of the desk was a bank of three elevators separated from the room by a guardrail broken by three square archways. Beside these were grey boxes penetrated by empty but moving conveyor belts. A woman in black uniform sat beside each box past the guardrail on a backless stool and each was looking at a flickering screen.

On the other wall, to the right of the reception, a large shining slab was mounted which announced the ministry officials who had department members who had given up their lives. There were over a hundred. Ron and Hank walked over to the receptionist who was also dressed in black. The two armed guards, three elevator gatekeepers and the receptionist watched their progress. Ron's and Hank's shoes slapped wetly. There was no one else in the hall.

Behind the receptionist to his left a free standing board of double his height and bottom-lit listed in a tall column the various departments of the ministry and the floor on which they each could be found. There were ten floors and perhaps fifty departments.

Ron announced loudly and crisply that they were here to see the minister. The receptionist did not consult the screen before him which was imbedded in the desk. The screen was in any event blank and light blue and said nothing. The receptionist nodded and pressed a button under an overhang on the desk. Ron made a comment on the weather to which the receptionist nodded again. One armed guard shuffled his feet. Hank unbuttoned his coat and Ron followed suit. Ron then unbuttoned his jacket underneath, shrugged his shoulders and pressed them back to loosen the jacket. There was a slight scent of lilacs. Hank and Ron looked over to the arches. The women looked back.

The furthest of the elevator doors opened. A tall woman in a long black pleated skirt and a short, waist length corduroy black jacket strode out. She wore a white ribbed blouse on which hung her security card on a black shoelace. The woman carried a clipboard tightly to her side, walking swiftly through an arch, her ponytail flapping, to the reception desk. She called out Ron's name in full with a pursed lipped laugh and while hugging the clipboard to his back gave Ron a peck on each cheek. Ron pecked each of her cheeks back. The woman then stepped backwards and then to Ron's side and firmly shook Hank's hand while looking a bit over his head at the corner of the mural where a camera was mounted. She spoke to Ron after dropping Hank's hand.

"Ron, Ron, you sure brought the weather! Nice to see you; the minister is waiting. The man from the paper is already here and Doctor Malati. They are waiting in the tea room. You can see them after the meeting. We can go up right away. The minister hasn't much time as he must go to a cabinet meeting in an hour and transport is almost impossible. There are several more meetings before that. I would say you have seven minutes. She turned to face Hank.

"You must be Mister Rousseau, the man from in-country. I am Elizabeth. It's your first time here isn't it? Just a few things first, Mister Rousseau.

"I hope you don't have a written report. He hates that, especially the sound of paper rustling. And I certainly hope you don't have a visual presentation. It gives him headaches. He doesn't like the humming either. Whatever you do don't bring up the subject of trees or of fish. And do not make a speech. It might be a good thing though to tell him how you like his refurbishment of the building. The deputy minister will be at the meeting. Don't address any answers to her and don't take notes. I will take the notes. That all right? Good, then let's go."

They filed through a security arch putting nothing on the conveyor and walked into the end elevator. It had mirrored walls but no controls or indicator of floors. Elizabeth passed a card through a small wall mounted box and then the elevator rose suddenly and quickly. She asked Ron how the chief was and if the chief had given up smoking. She also asked how Cressy Whimhurst was and her father.

From the elevator, they walked down a wood panelled hallway with doors to either side. Each door had a nameplate such as "Communications Room", "Deputy Minister", "Tea Room", "Crisis Group", "Stores". Elizabeth knocked at the end door, "Minister" and was answered by a female voice which said the word "In". They entered a wood panelled room, three walls lined with leather backed books. The fourth wall had a large iron fireplace protruding from the wall on a black tripod. There was a bubble of glass over a blazing fire.

In the centre of the room were two long green couches facing each other over a very low green tiled table which was bare. On the other sides of the table were two armchairs, also green. On the couch, with his back to the noiseless and heatless enclosed fire, was a heavy man in a dark blue suit and boldly striped pink and green tie. He was wearing gold rimmed half glasses. Beside him sat a young woman, tanned orange, in a white double breasted jacket over a burgundy dress festooned with small white spots. Her brunette hair was short and tightly curled. Elizabeth stopped at the door and introduced Hank and Ron with their full names. She spoke slowly. The minister stared at her intently. She said Ron was from the agency and that Hank was just from the field. She led Hank and Ron to the couch facing the minister and the deputy. She sat in the chair to the left. Her clipboard had a small sheath for a pen attached to its side and she took one out and licked the nib. She then nodded to Hank.

Ron began to speak. He stared smiling at the deputy minister who was adjusting her legs on her the couch. "Minister, there is a grave situation in the country which needs our intervention and an increased use of public money. The country is a good trading partner struggling for democracy. It has oil reserves and is a potential major purchaser of our equipment and expertise. We have a duty..." Ron stopped. Elizabeth was glowering strongly at him. She had coughed and said "Sorry" for the cough. She had not written anything.

The minister then spoke in a sleepy voice; he was looking at his deputy but asking if the Hank Rousseau from the field that Elisabeth had introduced was the same one who he had taught before he had been taken into government. He chuckled. Then he turned and looked at Ron warmly and leaned back in his chair. His glasses slid along his nose. He said he remembered that it was the year of his best class. His classes were always full. He said that one of the leaders in the new junta had also been in that class. Another time he had taught a king. He seemed startled when Hank replied.

"Yes I am," said Hank. "I took politics and economics, but only for one semester."

The minister peered at Hank intently through his glasses and then shook his head. The deputy minister seemed to swallow a giggle and then asked in a sharp voice what it was that Hank thought was needed given the situation and based on his expertise in such crises. Ron sighed and sat forward on the couch. He swivelled to look at Hank. Hank cleared his throat. He spoke to the minister.

"Well the first thing is to refurbish the airport," said Hank, "in case we need to evacuate our nationals and others. We don't need a food supply project but we should take a radical and innovative approach to rehabilitation. We need money to finance a search for missing staff. We need four wheel drive vehicles. Perhaps some motorcycles too. We should refurbish the villages. Dig some wells. The other things we need are to fix up the schools that have been destroyed, perhaps with new fences, then we should staff some of them and also we should organise some economic projects to get the rural people back on their feet.

"We should do some cash crops such as carrots and eggplants. We'll need to do some urban planning in the big city, rebuild and support some good governance projects and some gender enhancement projects; we should support cultural events to help rebuild the society. We should send advisors. Later on we should do capital projects like bridges and further tourism." Elisabeth wrote furiously.

"Do we need to send in peacekeepers?" said the minister. "There are all sorts of criticism in the party about the defence budget. Not enough expenditure or purchases. We could send my old regiment. We could beef the budget up a bit for that, perhaps move some money from transport or health." He seemed to be addressing Elizabeth. "Do we need to protect pipelines or anything?" Elisabeth looked thoughtful and said slowly to the minister that the pipelines were not yet built but the junta might be helped by peacekeepers. She then wrote something down.

The deputy minister asked what the press was saying and what line the agency was going to take. Ron answered, speaking to Elisabeth, that the press had as yet no real picture of the crisis or how long it had been going. They were showing a picture of Hank on the morning news and that picture was also in the morning papers with the escape story. They had no analysis of the coup or the junta.

They did have some quotes from the chief with some general ideas on the amount of hardship and also rough appeal. Ron said that he and Doctor Malati would work out a statement after this meeting giving a joint view of the agency and the charity on the severity of the crisis, outlining its nature and praising the government for its response. They would say of the minister and of the deputy that the fact that this meeting had taken place showed the government treated the situation correctly as a matter of urgency. They would work out some figures on casualties and so on. This would all be general. They would need a new picture of the minister for the press.

They would say nothing about the junta, nothing political. The government could then talk to the junta through the day about the airport and the other contracts outstanding and so on. The minister could announce the detailed Aid program the next day.

Ron asked Elisabeth how many points the minister's statement would have. She looked at her notes and said it would be six, counting the carrots and the peacekeepers, plus the recognising of the junta. Ron said that he would be going to some of the defence corporations and health companies that operate in the country for more donations which would then be announced after the minister's statement and be part of a response and appeal. This would mean another day of news just on donations. The deputy minister nodded her head at this. The minister was leaning back in his chair but looked to Elisabeth from time to time and at then at Ron pursing his lips. Elisabeth wrote notes. The minister then closed his eyes. Hank noticed that he had a hearing aid.

The minister suddenly opened his eyes and said loudly to Elisabeth that she should write a note to other ministers and department heads causing it all to be done. Elisabeth nodded. The minister looked at his gold watch. He then said that it was now done wasn't it Elisabeth. He looked again at Elisabeth and raised his eyebrows. Elisabeth nodded. The deputy nodded too. He added that all that was needed was a figure. Elisabeth said slowly that it was only a medium sized crisis but that there was a lot of sympathy for the country amongst immigrants. She would ask the treasury and put the figure into the statement.

The minister then turned and said to Hank, "What sort of trees and fish do they have there?" When Hank answered that he didn't know but would send a report from the field as soon as he got there, the minister squinted at Hank and said, "Pity," and then leaned back in his chair again. Elisabeth smiled and rose.

The deputy minister looked at her watch and rose too. Ron told her that she had on a lovely dress and asked if that was an appropriate thing to say to a minister. She said that of course it is and they smiled at each other. Ron kissed her on both cheeks. Hank shook her hand and then the minister's, who had remained seated. Hank said that he liked the way the foyer had been done and waved his hand in a sweeping gesture. The minister smiled and then looked at his deputy. The minister seemed to smile smugly and then curl his lip. The deputy frowned.

Elisabeth stood in the door looking at her watch. Everyone said goodbye. Elisabeth closed the door. She then said thank you fellows and wasn't that great it only took four minutes. The crisis was confirmed. Ron smiled. Elisabeth told Ron to send her a copy of the press statement and that she would send him a copy of the minister's statement with the figures and a new photo of him.

She said that he should say hello to Doctor Malati for her and that when they were finished they should use the phone in the tea room to phone reception for a guard to see them out. She waved them towards the tea room along the hall. She then re-entered the minister's room. Ron and Hank had not removed their coats. Ron was sweating.

X

Hank felt a constriction of the throat and a bubbling in his nose as the airplane descended. There were only five other passengers in the economy class. They were scattered and isolated. It was one small woman in a head tie and four large men. Jack was ahead behind the curtains in the upper class, which on this airline was called "The Chief's Class." The landing announcement was of a very hot temperature and recent rain. The morning sky was red and orange outside the window. The night was retreating across a lightless city.

Ron had decided yesterday in the restaurant during the lunch and writing of the statement that the supplementary fundraising could be done by himself and Doctor Malati alone. Hank was not really needed, or not best used in that capacity, especially given his image as a derring do field man. There was a consensus on the staff that Hank was of better use to them to be seen to return immediately. It also had to be seen that a search was on for the missing staff member in the field. A proactive search, a responsible, caring search.

One newspaper had evidently asked "Where is Tom Hume"? There was an interview to go with that storyline and a picture of a grieving mother and also of an attractive sister who was proud of the work Tom Hume had done in Chembeland. The sister had outlined the play Tom Hume had produced with the children of his school. She told of his collection of artefacts and minerals. The play was thought to have been quite professional and interesting. "Is Government Doing Enough?" the paper was asking. "Why has Government not Recognised the Junta?" This was in a paper that supported the government.

Ron's staff had also worried that that evening's flight, if it was able to take off in the snow storm, might be the last flight able to land in the city in crisis. After this it might be necessary for people to go into the country by boat from the neighbouring country. They also had a concern that no one had the slightest idea what was going on in case further positions had to be taken and descriptions given in regards to the media.

So Hank landed into the morning sun as it flashed yellow and orange through the porthole into the deserted airplane. There were tanks at the airport. The plane touched down between two sets of two of the heaviest turreted, longest barrelled vehicles, a model produced by his country, best in their that class, the most expensive, standing on each side of the runway, barrels raised in welcoming salute. The airplane taxied past a large burned out helicopter broken backed on a muddy grassed verge. It stopped, whining softly down the scale, settling at a point on the runway unusually distant from the terminal, almost at the outer fence of the airport, the tall linked fence which separated the airport from a refuse dump of hilled cans, bent wire frames and feathery matting.

There were no cabin staff to say farewell at the open door. The agency four wheel drive with flag and driver was parked engine running at the foot of the steps which had been wheeled to the door by several small boys. Jack was already getting into the vehicle as Hank emerged from the plane. As Hank descended the steps the four wheel drive sped off, flag waving. Had Jack not known if he was on the plane? In any event Hank had decided to let Jack come to him if he wanted. They both had a lot on their minds. Now was not the time to talk.

Hank walked to a smoky, low and wide bus which stood, engine running, looking as though crouched under one wing of the plane. It sounded terrible. Only two passengers from his class followed. The other three had remained on the plane. There were black columns over the city rising through the brightening yellow sky and there were periodic distant heavy crunching booms. An army patrol spread, fanned, regrouped and scurried over the hills of cans beyond the fence. They had dogs with them. Small grey clouds puffed up as their feet fell. The dogs were barking hoarsely and continuously.

THE BUSH

Hank sighed as he grabbed the hot metal pole in the centre of the bus. He swayed in the thick, moist, diesel scented morning heat. He was back. The investigator and rescuer was back. The bus responded to the last passenger's entry with the expected wrenching lurch and a dramatic, swaying, swinging accelerated complete turn, bumping over potholes in the runway to straighten and hurtle towards the terminal building. The bus driver was enclosed and protected in a rattling steel box in front. He shouted something.

Hank was wearing his khaki pocketed military style suit which he had changed into in the washroom of the airplane, a secure, private, personal, washroom of a bank of six, but he was still sweating heavily like any newcomer. He was very tired. He would need the cloth he had thoughtfully transferred from his other trousers to wipe his sweat. Ready for anything.

Yesterday, on the day of Hank's departure, when they had gone into that tearoom down the panelled hall at the ministry, that unheated bright tearoom at the top of the tall ministry building, Ron had been greeted by a very tall woman who had risen swiftly from her chair and had quickly bent to peck him on each cheek. Snow flew against the windows like little kisses. The tea things clouded and cleared from the air that circulated as Ron and Hank had entered.

Doctor Malati had then nodded to Hank whom she knew from a past job interview. Seated on one of the six leather chairs around a low glass table was a thin man, the only other person in the room, Adam-appled with sparse straw coloured hair, tieless, in a blue cloth pea jacket. There was a dark varnished counter at the wall which had silver tea things and a classic multi-buttoned phone. Doctor Malati introduced the thin man as Skip, the journalist. Skip licked his lips and slightly inclined his head to say a kind of wet "hi".

"Well boys, how did it go?" said Malati, smiling broadly. She remained standing and began to button her coat which was hooded and fur lined. The outer side of the coat had a short-haired sheen on a rough hide surface. The hood lining was a holograph of black and white long, soft bristles which shifted colours as she moved her arms. "Did you get the money? Very dangerous work talking to ministers." Ron had laughed.

Ron had said that they had got it. Malati suggested that they should go immediately out of this boring repressive place and have their meeting at a restaurant owned by a cousin which was just around the corner from the ministry. She knew they would be more comfortable there. It would be a sort of celebration. No need to be tiresome bureaucrats all the time. They phoned for a guard to escort them out. The journalist became animated in the elevator's descent and began to talk about the weather. He thought he might be called to cover a story of flooding in a suburb which had disrupted both power and water. He talked of the trade in human organs that had been discovered and implicated someone in the health ministry. He thought no one should be surprised at just what these people were really like.

They ploughed their way around the block, swaying and slipping as floating shadows in the blizzard. The few cars which still meandered and struggled in the street now had their lights on. The street was a dark rainbow of whites, greys and creams in the swirls of snow, swirls lit and punctuated with an infrequent hostile flash of pure light where a headlight or streetlight beam hit frosty glass or a patch of clear ice. The howling wind sounded deep, relaxed, rhythmic and permanent.

The restaurant door had closed like a clap of thunder. Each of the four immediately began to drip on the black tiled floor. A tall bowtied man and a woman in multi-seamed jeans exploded from a far kitchen door, rushed to them and took their coats as they circled and buzzed around the group with laughing cries of greeting and sympathy. The restaurant was deserted. All the tables were set with clear glass plates and transparent handled silver cutlery on dark red tablecloths. There was a circle of black woven grasses and cane on the far wall hung over a short bar with a mirrored surface.

Hank, Ron and Skip sat while Doctor Malati went arm and arm with the woman in jeans and with the bowtied man through the portholed doors into the kitchen. When she had taken off her coat she had revealed white wool cabled dress, veined with silver thread and three silver loops of chain. Her braided hair had silver tips on the coils. All of this sparkled in a cloud of vapour as the kitchen door opened.

Doctor Malati returned alone to the table moments later. Ron held her chair. She announced that she had arranged for her cousins to make something special. Skip began to talk about a pancake with fish slivers, soft bulbs and pickles he had had when overseas. Ron mentioned a stew made from pounded leaves, layered with tomato, mangoes and boiled beef with halves of sweet peppers. Doctor Malati told them of a traditional dish of yellow bean rice only made in her village cooked in rancid fat which had been buried in a pit and flavoured with a drop of blood from the cook's finger. Ron asked her how the charity was doing. He wanted to catch up with all the details and gossip. He was interested in this, not only because they were partners in this crisis with the agency but because he was an old friend of the Head. He thought he might actually work with the charity one day if things didn't move on at the agency. Ron laughed and looked at Hank.

Malati explained that the Head Executive, as they all knew, had contracted that tragic debilitating nerve disease and she had noticed that now he got more decisive every day. It was a frightening environment. He wouldn't be long there everyone said. Wasn't it tragic? The head had sacked the special projects officer, the blind woman who had helped start the charity. He was now flying everywhere with the Chairman of the trustees visiting the charity's projects abroad and the offices of the Chairman's electronics company. He was having a book written on his life. The charity would publish it.

The Head looked a sight these days. He could be seen at dozens of airports with his sunken cheeks, shaking limbs and black luggage festooned with privilege travel cards. He sometimes wore the foreign order, with false diamonds he had been awarded by the dictator in the islands, hanging around his neck like a tie. The Head constantly visited embassies, agencies, ministries and other charities. He was doing his rounds. He haunted receptions. He himself had held receptions for the anniversary of every event in the charity's history: the founding, the initiation of the health program, the telethon, becoming one of the biggest five charities, his appointment and so on.

The charity had now moved to new offices, a big country house with attached church in a park in the suburb where the Head had lived as a boy. It was a long drive to get there from the city and very inconvenient. The roads were often gridlocked. The Head's brother in law had fixed the place up, restored it really. The Head's brother owned a big construction company. There were dozens of new staff now, quite young ones, mainly in the public relations department. Quite a few staff had gone.

The charity had used the money from the children's show, the one where it had been named "Charity of the Year," to buy the headquarters. The kids had all been asked by the show's presenters to set up stalls on their local streets and sell the things they had that children overseas did not have and to send in the money to the charity. This educated them, didn't they think? The children had been wonderful. Some had been interviewed on television at their stalls saying how much they hated those worms hurting people in foreign countries.

There had also been a televised program with popular singers and others who had asked for bigger donations. Some were the people who acted the roles of super heroes. There was a bishop too. He played guitar. It had all been an enormous success. They had shown pictures of the damage done to children in remote villages by the main water borne worm. It looked so ugly. They showed that the evil worm could be forced from the little bodies by a simple, cheap pill which needed to be taken once a year for ten years. The pill needed to be delivered by four wheel drive vehicles and administered by doctors. There had to be storage buildings bought and studies made.

The restored church was quite cold even after restoration. Doctor Malati knew because she had sat in it many hours to watch with the other poor staff the slide shows of the Head's visits overseas, often with his wife. Doctor Malati had had to wear thick white tights. The Head also had shown some movies of their holiday trips and some slides from his youth, at least it seemed so. It was hard to understand. The Head had said coveted that church since he was a boy. He had sung a few bars of "Amazing Grace".

The two women, almost celebrities, who had founded the organisation had left the governing board at the Head's request but, thank God, they were still fundraising. Ron must have heard of them. They were paid salaries now by the charity. They charged their expenses too. This was mainly taxis, hairdos and wine for forming committees with their friends. Quite a bit of wine. Doctor Malati asked the diners not to tell anyone the last bit of information. It was just between professionals. Hank, Skip and Ron nodded agreement.

The charity often held galas, launches, parties and celebrations with celebrities and the leading corporations who had to pay a certain amount for seats at each table. The founders were very creative in fundraising as they knew so many of these people, especially the top men. Skip and others would go to the galas to take magazine photos and sometimes television shots of all those attending. The tables were photographed and shots were taken of the brands supporting the event with their donations of food, wine and so on. There were goods for auction such as the around the world plane tickets some firms donated. There were often corporate sponsored tables from the big electronics people, construction and oil people and some others for visiting customers. Sometimes the founders auctioned a date with someone. Then someone important would sing their old hit. There was a list of these people provided to the charity by publicists. The co-founders held these events in major cities all over the world. It made the charity international. They also opened restaurants and attended plays.

The former founders would collect money at events, especially with auctions, from the really rich guests to finance a school or hospital to be named after the guests or their partners. It would be really funny if they actually tried to do this in a religious country. It would be burned down. People in some countries were so tiresome about this sort of thing. But it was all good fun.

One of the founders or someone from one of their families, someone in government or something, perhaps in the trade ministry, would conduct the auction. One man wanted the school to be named after a famous cartoon character one time. Imagine. Another wanted it named after Doctor Malati, she didn't know why, although she often spoke at the galas. Sometimes she would dance when part of the entertainment was a traditional dance troop. Doctor Malati named some of the celebrities and business leaders who had come to the galas. Ron said he wished he could meet a certain few of those. Doctor Malati laughed. They were not what you would expect; they were boys and girls really.

At the last gala, Ron must have seen it advertised thought Doctor Malati, each table was decorated with little flags of what was then the latest poor disaster country and each seat had on its back the name of the tragic little destroyed town where the Aid would go. One day the charity would go there to do something too she was sure even though the crises had been long over by then.

THE BUSH

The founders had both wept and sang at that evening. They had worn matching wine coloured dresses and shown slides of when as girls just out of school they had impulsively travelled to a disaster instead of to the resort their parents had booked as a celebration treat. There they had been kidnapped by drug dealers and had met the president who was in fact a distant cousin of one of them. The story had been originally told in a fashion magazine. This was when they had started the charity. There had been so much press. There had been a famous T.V documentary made of the founders called "The Sisterhood of Mercy" and subtitled "From Chandelier to Cholera." The main scenes were recreated. Ron had seen this documentary he said. Skip said he had helped make it.

There was the screening of another documentary film, a hard hitting experimental one, at this recent gala made by a friend of Skip's. It showed the typical scenes of burning things and of mothers. Skip's friend looked as though he was gaining weight. It would be released in longer form soon, perhaps commercially. Skip nodded at this.

The founders had been leading socialites of their day Doctor Malati thought. They were the "It" girls of the last decade. One was the daughter of a legendary race driver and the other of a merchant banker. One of them now had a fashion company which sourced goods in some of the countries where the charity worked. She often displayed her fashions at the galas. Everyone raised thousands at these things. Ron asked who was the "It" girl now and laughed. Doctor Malati laughed too.

Some of the new board members now appointed by the Head now that the founders were staff, Doctor Malati informed them, were once with the foreign services or were from corporations operating overseas. They were getting more helpful each day. Doctor Malati was extremely grateful to them because of her own case. She now had a house here as well as in her own country. She was a dual citizen.

It is true that she actually had not practised medicine for some time but she was one of the few qualified doctors from her country still with a residence in that country. Yes, her uncle was a major landowner and she was now his partner, but she still identified projects for the charity to take up. She regularly did consultancies for the charity too, funded by the government, for which she was paid fees above the money paid as her salary. She often travelled with the Head to places in the world she would not have seen otherwise. World capitals. She also rented to the charity some offices on one of her properties in her own country. The training of locals like her was one thing the charity had successfully raised money for. She herself was an example of successful development.

Doctor Malati laughed when she explained that the Head had just fired the operational director on her account. The Head was so jealous and paranoid. The silly little operational director had tried to change Doctor Malati's arrangements with the charity by sending out an actual administrator to her country. As if a boring administrator could understand the medical necessities! Doctor Malati had entertained the fellow. She took him to a local jazz concert and to several restaurants. He wouldn't go to the beach. She introduced him to relatives and government officials. She had a big reception. He stayed at her house. She brought him breakfast. This was just as she had done for the Head when he first came. The Head had had a really, really good time. Completely enjoyed himself. He had been healthy then. Not that little functionary though. He was an ignorant thing.

The administrator then had criticised her that there were no projects actually running. Criticised her, a medical professional! That tense little creep from an oppressive developed country. What could he say to her from the developing world! Naturally she had complained to the Head as well as to colleagues in the teaching hospital in the city here from where she had graduated. This hospital had a unit actually in the same town as the new headquarters. It was a good institution. She had such fun as a student. The Doctors were really fun.

The school now provided all the consultants to the charity for studying the worms and so on. She had very close friends on the board of the school and now on the charity as well. You couldn't mess with her. The administrator was soon gone. The Head had after all even given her a loan from the charity to fix up her house. What would she do when the Head was gone? Doctor Malati, tight faced, at that point passed the bread dish to Ron which he declined. Then he changed his mind and took up a roll.

Ron had listened avidly to Malati's discourse and gossip. Twice he had giggled and he had nodded often. Skip had laughed at the fate of the administrator but he was now looking at his watch. The food was coming from the kitchen. It was glass plates heaped with a pale brown meat, a kind of jelly covered in a purplish black sauce. There was cola for everyone.

Ron said that they should get started with the statement.

"How many people at risk?" asked Skip with a full mouth.

"How about two million?" said Doctor Malati. Skip had a small black notebook in a breast pocket. He put down his fork with a sigh, took out the notebook and wrote something down in it with a pencil which had been in the notebook's coil. He also had an electric device in another pocket which he ignored, leaving it to peek out and wobble over his plate.

Skip had first placed the notebook with a slap on the red tablecloth and had then swivelled to write in it. The notebook sat to the side of his plate next to where his fork had gone down. The colour of the tablecloth bulged up through the fork's glass handle. Skip wrote his note and watched by all returned to eating. To do this he had hurriedly taken up his fork again. There had been splashes and dribbles.

Then after two bites and a swallow, Skip sighed suddenly, rolled his eyes and putting his fork down again heavily, returned to the notebook.

"At risk of what?" asked Skip.

"How about water borne diseases, starvation cholera and the usual, wait, no, let's add at risk of freezing. That way there are heated tents," said Ron.

"We will need to build three, no four, camps, one in the remote northern district. Is there a northern district, Hank?" said Doctor Malati. "Good, there is. The charity and the agency will build these together. We'll need money for a joint film of this too. We will call it "Hands Together". Make sure we say how dangerous it is in the statement." Skip only nodded at this and kept eating. The notebook remained closed.

"This is such a good time for our partnership," Ron said to Doctor Malati, swallowing. He was smiling broadly at her. She smiled warmly back. "With the agency and the charity co-ordinating the crisis response we have a much more efficient, attractive, clear and simple presentation for the public. It will be a chorus of compassion. All holding hands. Everything can be included and expanded. The donors won't be confused like last time, or Skip's readers either. There will be one story. Government will be singing too. People really trust you there at your charity, Doctor Malati. Many of them grew up with your appeals. They expanded their minds about the real world. And it is the end of everyone's budget year at government too. Lots of slush around. We could even visit the country together when things had settled. Do a retrospective. We could call it "Memory of a Crisis". Make another appeal." The restaurant light was sparkling on Malati's chains. Skip was chewing noisily. Ron passed the bread dish to Doctor Malati.

"This is good food too," said Hank although he had not touched much. No one spoke to that.

Hank had never seen the statement of the program before his departure nor the details and description of the crisis that were eventually drawn up, nor even read the newspapers he had heard had been published with his picture before his departure in the airplane — it was the last one they said — up into a snowy sky. He had not seen the television or heard the news. He had barely eaten.

Ron had told Hank in the restaurant after Hank had returned from the trip that he had made to the restaurant's washroom that the agency's staff were arranging a ticket for Hank to depart that evening and that all plans had changed. Hank had to leave before dessert. Doctor Malati regretted that. It was a special dessert.

Hank was told by Ron that it meant that Hank must immediately take a taxi to the airport where a ticket would be waiting. More information might be sent to Hank in the field on his tasks. Hank must also do what had been discussed, Ron had said. Hank must begin work immediately upon landing. They would brief the press that he had returned for the rescue.

It was a slow ride to the airport. There was one stop en route at Hank's hotel to pack, pay and pick up bags. Hank found when packing that the restaurant serviette was still tucked in his collar. He put it in his pocket.

Once again, as when he had arrived, as he departed, Hank did not see his driver in the front of the cab clearly. It was a dark afternoon, getting darker, as after they left the little hotel they crawled, nudged and slithered in the ruts in the continuing snow to the airport. Hank could not make any conversation as the wind shook the glass. He could only shout his destination and sit back and make his plans. He thought of how he could do his job in the easiest way. He thought of everything that had happened and why. The journey took two hours but there was still time at the end of it to catch the plane even if the departure was not delayed. The staff had thought of this.

At the airport departure hall Hank had seen Jack in the boarding line to the upper class. A group of leave takers made up of Juliet, her father and what must have been Juliet's sister, were to one side of Jack's queue where it inched towards the fast boarding check-in desk. Juliet looked as though she was crying. She wiped a sleeve across her eyes. Her shoulders shook; once she stamped a foot. The father looked very grim glancing at the high ceiling or at the slot machines. The sister, it must have been Cressy, so much like Juliet, stood a little apart and looked pouty. Her eyes did not leave Jack.

Hank's queue was several times as long as the one Jack was in. It was the lower class queue. The queues were to all destinations. To company audits, disasters, resorts, family reunions, funerals, sales presentations, quarrels and affairs. Everywhere you could think of. People getting out. People going back. There was still lots of motion spinning around the city despite the snow.

Hank tried to wave to the group seeing Jack off. He especially tried for Cressy. They must not have seen him, nor probably had Jack. Hank remembered again as he waved that he still had some of the papers from Hank's desk. This made him smile.

The bus from the airplane jerked to a stop in front of the open terminal glass doors under the early hot yellow sun. One of the doors was cracked; stuck under the other was a yellow rag. Heat and machine vapours rose from the tarmac between the bus and the doors. Hank was the first of the bus into the arrival hall. He wiped his brow with the serviette from the restaurant. Hank clenched his teeth to the heat now in his lungs. He slapped his pant leg and strode purposely forward.

The terminal hall was nearly empty. There were no customs men in the array of booths, nor lepers, nor people offering other services, salvations and explanations in exchange for spare hard currency. One woman in a head tie was mopping the floor. Some small boys were sitting on some luggage. No one was selling food. There were no echelons of extra bureaucracy in livid uniforms to ask for forms and fines. Hank walked through the customs hall to the front entrance of the terminal and through its unguarded front doors. An army four wheel drive sat isolated in the parking lot. Its four uniformed passengers looked at Hank through glassless sides; one raised a large camera, pointed it at Hank and put it down. One of the other passengers was in the uniform of a soldier from Hank's country.

The only other vehicle in the parking lot was a cross country taxi. It was a model of a station wagon over twenty years old. The vehicle had a shining purple door although the rest was a faded white. The driver leaned against this door in his light blue shirt which rose up and down over a protruding stomach. He was quite short and smoking vigorously with rapid frequent puffs to a stubby cigarette which arched back and forth from his lips to his side. He stared at Hank intently, blinking, as Hank walked to him. He was chewing on something and he spat.

"Taxi? Where to Mister Plane?"

"Chembeland. How much?"

"Chembeland! You are joking of course! Chembeland! My God! That will cost you thousands. You cannot get there! You cannot get back! No one will take you! What will you pay?"

"I don't need to get there really. Forget it. You can find another customer. I was only asking."

"Wait Mister! It could take days! There is a flood and a war! Why do you have to go? Is it important business? It can't be the regular price for Chembeland now. Do you have hard currency? Would I return empty?"

"I thought I would see some friends. I could stay a few days but never mind. I can go another way another time. I just was there recently anyway. It was quiet. It just took a day. It wasn't so bad a trip. I was able to buy carrots and chickens and bring them back. There was some good beer."

"I can take you to the far north instead. It is much more interesting. There are beautiful animals there and a lovely lake. You will like it. There are mangoes. You can't get them here. The animals are mysterious and behave in strange ways. They make you laugh. I could guide you and guard you for no extra.

There is hardly any trouble ever there no matter what the radio says.

"Or I can take you into town. There are some streets and neighbourhoods open and I know where they are. I can get anywhere in town. To hell with the army. Did you miss the people here? The women? Were you gone long? Where have you been to? I know an open jazz club. It is hidden from the army and it goes day and night. This would be for the regular price. For Chembeland though you must pay by the day. A special price. You must also pay for fuel. Who knows what the prices are doing there with the fuel? People hide it, sometimes on purpose. The big people are hiding all the things everywhere now to change the prices. They burn the warehouses. They are stealing gold." He spat again.

"I don't care about all that. I only want to go to Chembeland to see my friends or I can go back home too. I could pay by distance if you like. But I don't need to go anywhere at all really. It is really bad management to wander around without reason. There are some people in town who could pick me up here and I could stay with them. They have a vehicle with a flag. You could find another market for your taxi, although I don't see one. I could give you a little above the ordinary rate and pay for food."

Hank paid a deposit in hard currency. The driver went back in the terminal with some extra cash to bribe someone for Hank's bags which he said on returning he had found unaccompanied where they had been unloaded to the middle of the terminal floor. The driver gave back the bag money.

Hank was still sweating heavily as he finally sat into the back seat. He mopped himself with the serviette. The driver urinated into the parking lot and then eased himself into the front seat. He had thin legs for such a protruding stomach. The steering wheel rested on that stomach. On the seat beside the driver were several packages wrapped in newspaper, some leaking yellow grease, and a blue plastic thermos. There was a religious object on the dashboard. The vehicle smelled of several types of smoke. Hank's seat was stained. The exhaust was blue and sparked.

The driver turned on his radio to a spitting erratic military instrumental fanfare. This ended suddenly and a female voice began a guttural wailing song. It was of lost love or lost country or perhaps a lost child. The driver sighed and shouted back to Hank that the streets in days gone by would empty to bars and the city would not breathe when this singer had her regular program but today there was also the bloody army music, roadblocks and the announcements.

The driver asked where they could buy the chicken that Hank had mentioned and still had received no answer as they left the parking lot to take the road to the expressway bypassing the city. The driver said there was no chicken in the city today. He asked Hank if he was sure he was not on any serious business as they entered the freeway from the bypass. Hank told him that no he wasn't. He was just visiting.

Hank listened at first to the singer and to the frequent announcements made in a regional language that he could not understand as the station wagon sped along a nearly deserted freeway. One door rattled quietly. The vehicle had a slight sway and bias to the left although the steering wheel was held straight. It seemed to be travelling in two directions.

The driver grunted at the announcements delivered in a tinny gruff voice as they interrupted the songs. Once he barked an angry sentence and hit the dash board with his fist. He sighed often at the singing and would sing a phrase in a satisfied, sad way from time to time when the singing voice got particularly deep and weepy.

Hank felt an easing in his muscles, a light feeling. His tiredness had become a heavy drug and his eyes closed and opened to the vehicle's vibrations. Hank knew as he closed his eyes finally and decisively that rows and rows of citrus trees were flying by on each side of the road. Many of them would have withered brown oranges or wrinkled lemons left by fate, rain and mechanical pickers for grey birds. There would be irrigation ditches, narrow ones, leading from the gutters on each side of the freeway which were once part of a river.

Hank had seen no people alive or dead and only one or two taxis like his own but going towards the city. There were several wrecked vehicles and one burning one. There were also two chimneys on the horizon at this point in the road which usually let out white smoke. Hank wondered if they were doing so now but kept his eyes closed anyway. It was nice. He needed sleep.

Hank began to think of a story that Jack had told him during the first week Jack had been here. It became easy to remember as he neared sleep. They were drinking beer in the evening after a day long orientation session on the culture of the region which had been presented by the local staff. Hank remembered that Juliet was there too. It was supposed to be a well known story but Hank hadn't heard it before. It was about a city or a country or somewhere. Perhaps this place. Hank tried to reconstruct it and tell it to himself as the vehicle sped along. He added some things because it was hours to the ferry. It was fun and restful.

There was a city, which was at times a village or a town and once a nation and which had been destroyed six times. Nothing but some birds and lizards had been left between times, the trilling type of lizard, and a few grey chattering birds in the rubbish. When they rebuilt the city the seventh time no one quite remembered the other six times.

The prince of the city didn't care much about this history. In fact he didn't care about much at all so everyone thought. He had as a boy wanted to be a singer and play a lute. His singing had been quite bad and the lute playing worse. The other children laughed at him behind his back. They would request the most horrible songs for fun. Some encouraged him to put on performances for which, when they were still alive, he would get his parents to arrange sweets and treats for the audience. The children were given gifts when they left. Some children would pay others to use influence to get themselves invited. He was always being tricked. They called him "The Lute Man".

As he grew older the prince then asked people to pay for entertainments. The children laughed less. The parents of those in his audiences had to pay for their children to attend and force them to do so because those parents wished to please his parents.

The prince's parents were killed when out hunting by an assassin from the enemy or so it was thought. Or it could be that a hole could have opened in the ground to swallow them up as so often happened. The prince started to rule immediately after the parents had gone missing and soon after that gave up his attempts at singing and at entertainments. He just did his job as a prince. He just collected taxes and when he entertained he did so normally. People marvelled.

What had happened was that he had gone alone one morning to the place where his parents had disappeared and had sat against an orange tree. He had taken the lute and some paper to write a song. He kept trying to think of words and trying to get the lute to play but it sounded bad. He shouted at it. He put it down and spat on it. This commotion caused birds sitting between the trees to fly into the sky and then to settle back into the tops of the trees. He said to the lute, "Sing you bastard, sing." It didn't sing.

The prince then sat thinking against the tree. He fell asleep. He opened his eyes to see some grey birds and colourful lizards trilling and carolling and chirping and whistling to one another in the trees. Amazingly he could understand them, not their sounds exactly but the vibrations. Their heads bobbed up and down. Lizards on the trunks, the birds among the leaves.

They were saying that the prince was a complete fool, an ass, a monkey and a smelly fish. He could not sing, he could not play. He sounded like a howling cat. He was as thick as a buffalo turd dried in the sun. He was a mommy's boy. Everyone could fool him. He should get on with his job and not cause either trouble or mirth to everyone.

You can't play a lute by shouting at it. Words do not come from nothing.

They then changed the subject and trilled and chirped about how the rebuilding of the city was going. They thought it was an awful place with rubbish and bad food. They then remembered the other six times there was a place there. This memory took all day until evening to elaborate as the birds and lizards had to sing the memory as they of course must. Sometimes they disagreed. The prince listened and found it all very interesting.

For each place built of the six places and for each time there were hundreds of verses sung; each had seven hundred lines and each verse had a song. Some verses were about long wars, others were about the weather and fashions. Some verses were about streets and others about each of the hundreds of rulers, their character and their motives. Some verses were about fools who were smart and some about wise men who were very stupid.

Some of the songs attached to a verse were about lovers and some were about betrayals. Several verses were sung in so many tones and with such dark vibrations that it felt like they would boil the blood or cause a faint. When the songs came for these verses they seemed to call the dead. The leaves of the trees twisted and turned. These were about very black things thought the prince. Other singing was of green and leafy things and places to hide in dry caves. They sounded sad.

The verses went through building all six places and all their destructions with all the causes, and at the end of each line of each verse and of each song of all the songs, the heads bobbed up and down in a chorus of harmony of lizard and bird song. It was their own language but a bit of the prince's too. The chorus was "oh, fadder, simla, oh."

Each time "oh, fadder, simla oh." It was a regular beat, a monotone, repeated "oh, fadder, simla, oh!"

Sometimes it sounded like laughter, sometimes like an angry shout and sometimes like a sob. Oh, fadder, simla, oh.

At the end of the songs of the sixth city of all the cities before this city, the creatures put their criticisms of the prince into song. They said the lute would never sing as the prince was just a prince and was not a poet or a bird or a lizard. He was really a dirty stupid thing. Oh, fadder, simla, oh!

At the end of the story of the sixth city and of the criticisms of the prince the birds and lizards suddenly stopped. It was getting dark. The prince rose to his feet, opened his eyes and stretched his legs. There was a mutter in the trees. He slung the lute on its strap over his back and went home. He did not try to play it again.

From time to time as Hank told himself this story, reconstructing what he could remember of Jack's and adding some things of his own, he fell asleep. When he awoke periodically he started all over again from the beginning as it was relaxing to do so and he liked the sleep it produced. It was better than proverbial sheep counting or the reconstruction of buildings that he sometimes used to get to sleep. Once during an interlude of sleep the driver had awoken him by shouting "Many dead!" after an announcement on the radio. Then all was silent again except for the awry wheels, the rattle and the radio.

The prince returned to the city, some said a new man. He married and had seven children. All of them were daughters. Some of them were beautiful but bad. Some were short and round. There were twins. There were some very clever ones who could perhaps rule, perhaps one was a liar and there was a baby.

The enemy attacked the city. It attacked and attacked again. There were constant bloody battles. The crops failed and the animals departed to the mountains. There were none of the healing people left alive so casualties of battles and of starving diseases all festered where they were lying in the city's religious buildings. The routes of escape to the mountain were cut off. The city was infected.

The prince led his army into battle. He had a large horse and heavy armour but he also wore the lute on his back. This showed his position to everyone. It showed who he was. The troops were constantly defeated and the prince was becoming ill. He was becoming silent. He read secret books. He was thought to be trying to practice spells. He was quiet about everything. He thought he would die and wondered which of his daughters he would name to lead the city after he was gone. Would it be the true or the clever? Would it be the liar or the beautiful? He knew he would have to teach them the sort of realities of life he had heard from the lizards and birds. He knew that when they were not innocent of the world their characters might change. They could be duplicitous. He would test them.

So in turn over seven battles he took each of his daughters from the eldest to the youngest separately into each of seven battles fought seven days in a row against the enemy, carrying each in turn on the back of his horse. He gave each one in turn a sword. His advisors thought him mad. The people grumbled and some bitter ones laughed.

Each of the first six daughters, the twins, the beautiful, the true and false were killed, each in her turn, each in her battle. Finally the prince took the baby into the last battle wrapped in gold cloth, strapped on his back next to the lute. Drums rolled and the city's army roared as they flung themselves at the enemy more bravely and wildly than ever before. An enemy sword plunged into the child. Another severed her head. Blood drenched the prince, his armour and his lute and he and his horse fell to the ground next to an orange tree. He saw creatures scurrying around its roots.

And then the lute began to sing.

Oh, fadder, simla oh.

XI

"We have reached the ferry," said the driver.

It was a completely different place. There were no towers and no paved road. There was no sign. A short dirt road veered from the highway suddenly and then led down immediately to a lime green, scum bordered lapping shoreline passing through a narrow gap between two spreading vine laden grey trees. The trees were also full of rope, broken boards, wet cardboard sheets and long fat snakes. The far shore seemed a spinning mirror reflecting into the sky less than the pale bright light of the midday behind them.

"It looks as though there was flooding but it's gone now thank God," said the driver. "We are a ways downriver from the regular government dock. Perhaps that was washed away. Who knows? The radio didn't say. The other side is still flooded though."

The ferry was a different one too. It was very small and open topped, able to hold only a few vehicles. It was painted olive green. It came over the bulge of the dull yellow river slightly upstream at the same time as the taxi drew to a halt next to the water's edge. Hank looked back to see that the snakes were settled. The driver did as well. Neither of them liked to say the obvious. The driver turned off the radio.

The ferry came to shore at an angle, turned sharply and ran itself aground, engine coughing, with the rear pointing slightly in the direction of the current. The front prow then dropped down into the shallow water almost at the shoreline. There was only one man aboard behind a small cabinet at the rear of the deck. There was a wheel there and a large lever. There were no vehicles.

Hank stretched out along the back seat in the taxi after they had driven onto the ferry. The craft reversed and turned into the stream. The driver of the station wagon turned off the engine, got out, lit a cigarette and went to talk to the driver of the ferry. Hank could not see over the green painted steel sides of the craft through the windows. He could see a band of blue grey sky. Periodically the side facing the current thumped with a deep ringing tone. Hank was jarred. The door rattled. The radio was off.

The driver returned smelling of his cigarette and mouldy spray. He sat and said to Hank that the ferry driver did not know what it was like on the other side. He just went back and forth. Back and forth all day. There had been no other vehicles since the morning.

The ferry driver had explained that the large ferry had been lost at the end of yesterday's flood. No one knew where it went. This ferry was an emergency one which was used by the army. It had been stored at a base near the chemical plant upstream. The army had brought it down early this morning. He had been awoken by his wife and told by soldiers to begin his shift early. He lived near the regular dock.

He was driven to the spot they had boarded at and the ferry was waiting. There had been a large fire in the depot on the other side. Lines of trucks had been burned. The new road was closed. The crossing was moved down so traffic could use the old road going around that area on the other side. The taxi driver thought that the government was really incompetent about transport and pocketed the money that should go for it despite what they had said in the election. Taxi licences had gone up and there was so much bribery. Good thing there is a coup; now he wouldn't need to pay for weeks.

Things were always going wrong. He also thought that one day they would hide so much fuel that the orange picking machines would stop, the taxis and the generators and hospitals too, and everyone would die. The radio had said normal service was restored. The taxi driver thought that they should give the ferry driver some extra money although the service was supposed to be free. Then he changed his mind and told

Hank not to give any money as this would spoil everything. Hank only listened and took no position.

Hank was thinking and remembering about how peculiar it was that the chief at home had thought that he was behaving like Jack. Perhaps they thought that of all field people. Well they had their little ways and their characters and we have ours. We are what we must be. The driver hoped there was not too much flooding on the other side. This might mean more time. Perhaps they should discuss the price again.

The ferry ran aground on the far bank and the prow dropped. The taxi driver waved out his open window without looking back and accelerated, splashing onto shore. The road here too was a mud track rising up onto a ridge or bank about ten car lengths from the river. The road turned left at the crest of the bank and ran along it. The river was on one side and a shimmering unbroken plain of water on the other.

They drove along the ridge for less than an hour when it widened and turned into the flooded plain towards Chembeland. A narrow bank branched from the ridge and continued north along the length of the river which was running swiftly, yellow green and broad. Not much further upstream the river was almost the height of the bank, now a muddy dyke. There between the bank and widened ridge was a narrow mud pool and puddle spotted lowland strip, becoming wider, and in this, nearby, a hut which was stark and backlit from the river and delineated by the pool behind it. The sky was turning pink behind the haze.

They turned on the ridge top angling towards Chembeland, with the flood on one side and the river lands on the other. There was an occasional blue smear of mountains ahead. After a few minutes the road curved further and descended from the ridge. They bumped down what seemed a bulldozed trench dotted with clusters of protruding black stones, the vehicle twisting to the right and left as the driver cursed. At the bottom of this file the road extended into the plain. The road was slightly elevated with grey, white and pink glaring water on each side. In places it was two dark tracks with water shining between. The ridge was behind and the mountains ahead had disappeared. There was no horizon and the far extent of the road was invisible.

"This might cost extra," said the driver.

As they drove they could see parts of palm trees rising out of the water in the distances on each side and tufts of tall grasses. They passed a section of rows of leaf heads poking just out of the flood in square watery fields extending from the road bed. Far on the left side there was a circular grouping of huts, black and slightly raised from the surface. The shapes were rounded and irregular as though melted.

The driver shook his head and made a clicking sound. He explained to Hank that he had learned about plants in school. He had a foreign teacher. A good one. She said she was a biologist. A biologist, tremendous, in his little school. The driver wished there were more of these sorts. She had left the school suddenly which was too bad although she didn't stick to their assigned books when she taught. He knew from that class that if living things were stopped from normal growing they went mad. They forgot how to grow and even their seeds were crazy too. The seeds would remember to forget the same way next time. They lived funny and died rotting. Animals were like this too. He remembered the sentence the foreign woman had said, it was wonderful. He used it to the bloody licensing man in the market. "Addicted to disorientation." He had written it down from the blackboard. His father was very impressed. Good man, his father, from the village, but he had been a driver too. There was another sentence too: "Seeking physical death to avoid a living one." Tremendous.

The driver thought everyone was going to starve or be killed by crazy animals soon. He blamed the government. He wondered where the cane cutters and the rats had gone. Probably to the mountains. He believed the whole world was made up of people who were smart and stupid at the same time. Smart buggers on some things, crazy stupid on others. Just like local people, only worse. He told Hank that the village he came from would seem crazy to Hank and that Hank's place would seem crazy to him. Especially how people lived and died. He laughed.

More and more of the landscape was appearing above the flood as they drove. There were larger islands and archipelagos and bigger watery grasslands. The road wove now from one to another hill. It was the old route of horses and cows. The clusters of huts were more frequent but there were still no people. They then climbed a distinct hill that arose suddenly in an island of palms where sounds of birds and the hollowness of water suddenly passed into heavy air with a new low buzz. On the other side of the hill there was no flood. The road passed there between tight, dark, tall rows of date trees in furrowed light brown sandy soil lit by bars of blue grey light.

Along the sides of the road through the palms were scattered prone short lumpy shapes. Some arose unsteadily as the station wagon approached but others remained still. Further ahead there were two trucks parked lengthwise across the road. They had torn canvas sides. From behind these trucks streamed a dozen bicycles heading towards the station wagon. Some other shapes appeared and lined up in front of the trucks. They seemed to be dancing or leaping. There were animal cries. The taxi driver stopped, looked behind and said, "Oh, bloody bother." Some other figures were running towards them from out the shadows of the palms and onto the road behind.

The windows filled with the faces and arms of children. The driver's far door opened and a child, naked to the waist wearing khaki shorts, spurted in, grabbed the thermos, and slid out. There was then a gunshot and the faces at the windows disappeared as the children withdrew in a circle from the vehicle.

Most circling the vehicle were in khaki shorts and t-shirts; some were in torn dresses, school uniforms or coloured wraps. Some had chocolate stained khaki strips as bandages. Many carried knives but some of the bigger ones had short barrelled guns with straps. The shot had been fired by a child standing in front of the station wagon with a revolver which was still pointed in the air as the others moved away from the windows. He had a bicycle held by the seat with his other hand.

A shorter boy standing beside the bicycle pushed around the station wagon to the door on the far side of the driver. There he clubbed the semi-naked boy who had the thermos on the head with the flat side of his machete. This boy fell to the ground below the open door and there began to weep. Another seemed to kick him.

The child with the gun dropped his bicycle and pushed around to the driver's side. Gaps opened and closed in the circle of children as they moved even further back. Through these gaps Hank could see some of the shapes that had remained prone. The two nearest were in army uniforms One had a head caked with dried blood and covered with flies. Beside him was a crumpled blanket and a boot. The weeping at the driver's far door stopped.

The boy who had come to the driver's window leaned against the car and spoke to the driver in a forced angry voice. He rested his gun on the doorframe in the window, his other arm on the roof. The driver had a calm voice as he spoke back. The driver gave the boy the religious object from the dashboard; he did so slowly. The boy took it with the hand from the roof, stepping back and then pointing his gun at the driver. The boy looked at the object, turned it around and handed it behind him to another. He smiled and leaned on the station wagon again. Both then looked at Hank.

"These are the God's Redemptionist Front," said the driver. "They are warriors of the true Divinity. They speak the language of my mother although some can speak yours from school. They wonder what you are doing in an old taxi here on a day like this. They wonder what you have. Are you a doctor? Do you have drugs? Do you have their diamonds?"

One of the children at the back of the vehicle started to shout. The boy at the window turned to listen. Then many of the children shouted the same phrase and some jumped up and down, dancing with sloppy, knee lifting steps. The shouting became for a second a chant. One child, laughing, punched another in his shoulder just outside Hank's window. The punched child turned and slapped the puncher, then others grabbed the arms of these combatants and restrained them. The shouting stopped.

"They know you," said the driver. "They say you are lord of the carrots."

"Yes, I am," said Hank.

"They think you are mad. Some used to sell your carrots."

"Please tell them for me," said Hank, "that they can have everything I have. I am not a doctor. I have no diamonds. I am going to visit friends in Chembeland."

There was another conversation. Hank was asked what friends he meant. Hank said it was Jules and some others although he did not know Jules's last name but he was from the village and the school. He did not mention the names of Tom Hume, Father Buchanan, Madame Youngo or Florence. When he mentioned Jules the boy stared straight and unblinking into Hank's eyes for several seconds, inclining his head through the window. Hank wanted then to take out the serviette from his pocket but did not know how this might be interpreted. The boy's pupils had been almost entirely dilated and as reflective as the flood they had just left. The driver let out a restrained pressured breath.

"I will tell them you cannot give them the money you will give to me," said the driver.

"That's all right," said Hank.

There was a further short conversation and then the rear end of the station wagon was opened. The gate dropped down heavily. With a sliding, scraping sound Hank's suitcases were removed. The gate was slammed shut. There was a ripple of voices from behind and then silence.

A boy smelling of burnt maize and vomit opened the far door of the back seat and slid in beside Hank. The door closed. While Hank sat stiffly immobile the boy searched him and removed the serviette and the leather wallet Hank had bought in the Magic Kingdom years ago. The money in the wallet was removed and counted by the searcher as he sat next to Hank breathing erratically between each sequence of counts. This process was watched intently by the driver and by the boy at the front window. Several faces came to Hank's window. At the end of the count there was a brief loud exchange between the driver and the armed boy at his window.

The searcher beside Hank put his hand on a machete handle protruding from a green canvas sheath that he wore at his waist and grasped it tightly. He tensed. Then an instruction was shouted to the searcher from the window. The searcher counted out the majority of the notes and stuffed them into Hank's breast pocket. He exited the taxi with the remainder and the serviette.

"It is not a fair price," said the taxi driver softly.

An arm returned the thermos through the opened door on the far side of the station wagon and the door was closed. The boy at the window stepped back and waved them forward as the circle at the front of the vehicle parted. The driver went forward as a few hands slapped the vehicle's sides. The chant resumed as they moved towards the vehicles. The driver was able to get around the roadblock on the left shoulder of the road. The wheels crackled on the brown stony soil. The road ahead was clear but there were still lumpy shapes for a little distance on each side.

"We are lucky they were in a good mood and not hungry," said the driver.

The old road took them through the palm groves and over low hills into the afternoon. It emerged from the hills onto the scraggly plain to join the new road just a few miles before the Bechembe town. The change from the bumpy track was calming to Hank as the vehicle hissed along. Hank felt relaxed and rested. Hank told the driver that they would have to make one stop in the town. They could also look for fuel there. After that they could go to the Chembe village.

The driver turned the radio back on. The driver had been silent since they had left God's Redemptionist Front. He seemed reflective. Then he said forcefully that he hated taking the old road but the government kept messing things up so much that the new things could not be used by ordinary people.

Bechembe town had been burnt. The rough mud buildings on the outer edges were untouched but deserted except for several wandering goats but some pickup trucks had been burned there. Some of the small shops further along lining the road to the centre had tin shutters hanging or missing. There was a lot of broken glass, glistening by several open doors and pools of spilled liquids, some soapy. The station wagon drove over ripped burlap sacks with aurora of grey and white dust. The first body was burnt and wetly split open by a thin length of pipe propped up in intersection.

The market area in the centre of town was black, ashy and twisted broken rubble. The mounds, some higher than the vehicle, were damp from the rain. Rivulets of black water moved slowly from under the various heaps into clogged gutters at roadside. The district was colourful with waving ends of sheets of scorched printed fabrics fluttering in the rising smoke and steam amongst bent and woven frames and beams. Some thin dogs stared through the wisps as the station wagon passed. The mounds were dotted with bodies.

The main roundabout was unscathed. The hotel beyond it seemed so too except that the lower two floors were windowless above a circular drive empty but for a half burnt armchair and a wheeled trolley.

"Just like the city," said the driver. "We won't get any chicken; everyone is hiding."

Hank instructed the driver as they went past the hotel to continue on the roundabout and leave at the exit past the one he had taken the other day to Juliet's school. After this exit they travelled down a street of high walled single storey homes which were intact. They passed a clothes shop with large plate glass windows unbroken, next to which there was magenta stucco and stone building with no windows but red double doors. A sign was above the doors said "Hambone's".

Hank instructed the driver to park and wait. After the station wagon stopped on a slight verge before the magenta building Hank got out, stretched, and walked towards the building. The driver kept the engine running but turned to pick up the thermos which he shook by his ear. Satisfied by the sound he opened it to drink. Hank knocked at the double doors and waited. Then he knocked again.

"Who is it?"

"I'm looking for Tom Hume. Is he there?"

"Are you with his company?"

"With his agency, yes."

The doors opened. Hank stepped into a dark room lit by two gas lamps fixed atop two blue canisters sitting on the edges of a black bar along the far wall. His eyes adjusted to see about twenty men, most in t-shirts, sitting in ones and twos at round tables between himself and the bar on white plastic chairs in a large room. The doors closed behind him and a voice behind said, "For you, Tom." Many of the men at the tables had their heads in their arms on the tables. Others were sipping from tall glasses. There were sleeping bags on the floor. Some tables had carcasses of one or two chickens and piles of orange peelings.

THE BUSH

There was a row of clear plastic bottled water glasses along the bar. Only a few men looked towards Jack. A man sitting at a table alone stood up and waved and then sat down again. Hank went to that table and sat down.

Tom was a fat man with very short hair. He wore a long sleeved shirt buttoned to the neck. His table had a notebook open on it. Tom shook Hank's hand.

"Well I knew you were around here somewhere, Hank. Come to be rescued, have you? Someone saw you at Juliet's and I heard you might be pulling that scumbag Jack from his school. You've heard how he cheated at the play contest, haven't you? Well just relax here with these pigs. You look tired. Look at them. They drink like suicidal pigs. Two of them are priests. I expected the construction men to be animals. But the priests, really! What kind of people do they send out here anyway? Did you expect there would be so many? When will the rescue come from the embassy anyway? Do they have many collection points? You wrote the plan didn't you?"

"Yes, I did but I'm not sure that it was the one finally adopted for use. It was one of many. What happened here anyway?"

"Well Hank, it was a lot like it was before when I was in the islands. I've written it all down; I might do an article later. I'm keeping a record of everything. I know you told me once you don't keep notes because they aren't accurate but I need the detail for my recollections.

"My houseboy came first and knocked on my study door and told me not to go into the town. I wasn't going to go anyway. I was tired with sorting my artefact collections.

"I had just got back from across the border on my walking tour. I got some lovely plant specimens. Remember I told you I would be gone in case you were in the region and called on me for an inspection or something? Then I heard some gunfire and I looked out to the school compound and everyone had gone. Well, I knew what that meant so I got in my vehicle and drove to the collection point here in town as you instructed and named in your security memo. I would have rather been nearby the Governor's place but I do what my agency says. What an irony that you end up here to be rescued yourself.

"You must be tired. Where did you come from? Juliet's school? I had no trouble getting here. There were some roadblocks but I had cigarettes. I wasn't frightened.

"I took nothing but my papers, my clothes and sleeping bag, water and some food. I must go back for my collections. The things I brought are mostly in the collective resources pool here but I have seen some jam since at least. Can I get compensated for what I contributed? My mother sent me that jam.

"By the time I arrived here there were already about ten vehicles parked in the back. The fellows were covering them with palm branches. There was smoke on the edges of town. People kept arriving in ones and twos. Some said that the seventh brigade had gone by them on the road leaving town. Others said they had seen it returning. Towards the evening we could hear a roaring in the market. There were screams like hunted things. The sounds came and went in the wind." Tom was now breathing shallowly and one of his hands on the table shook.

"The seventh brigade evidently defended the official district from the roundabout on up the hill but there was slaughter in the town. Then came the rain but we could still hear firing going on. Some sounded like artillery. The pigs in here were drinking and shouting. They gathered under the picture, on that wall over there, of our Head of State and sang some sports songs. They sang them over and over again in a most aggressive way with their fists in the air. Terrible drunks, big boys really, children. They did it again when the radio said we would send peacekeepers.

"A couple of locals, officials, knocked at the door and asked to be let in. That fellow over there in the red t-shirt cursed them and even punched one as the door was closed on them. The poor official cried through the door that they were killing us all. Did you see the town? I haven't, but it is supposed to be terrible. Everything has been quiet for a few hours now though. The man in the t-shirt crept out an hour ago. He said when he came back that the town was ruined. He brought some whiskey back from his own compound which is just down the road. He said that was fine. We had told him to stay inside. Some others took their vehicles and left in the night. We have heard nothing from them since. Where did the army go do you think? You are quiet, Hank." The gas light flickered on Tom's sweating face. There was a snore in the darkness.

"We have a really good radio here that someone brought. You didn't advise that in your memo, Hank. We only play it every hour to preserve batteries. Just now there was a man on the news service from our country that mentioned my name. Tom Hume. Everyone cheered and a few booed. I'm a celebrity now. He mentioned my play. This chap on the radio was being interviewed for the agency. Ronald something. He said that even now measures were underway to find me. Find me. Isn't that amazing? Do you think he meant your rescue plan? I hope so.

"He said that the army had restored transport to the worst regions and that the agency had information those insurgents had used a natural disaster as a deplorable cover to create a crisis. It was to be condemned. There is a temporary junta now in power evidently which took over to safeguard foreign interests and deal with the problem of democracy competently. Our government has approved an Aid package for them. What do you think is really happening Hank? Did you know that about the transport being restored? One fellow heard a broadcast on another station that named the people on the junta. He's one of those doing the exploration on the other side of the Mountain. He said that one man on the junta was O.K. He was on the local board of his company. But do you know any more of what's really happening? You are the country director after all." Tom's voice was a little high and his throat sounded dry.

"Oh, hard to say, Tom. It is the eye of the storm and that sort of thing. The usual stuff. You've seen it before. Nothing unusual going on really. No mystery. A little confusion and chaos. We just keep our heads. The true situation will come out." There was a moment's silence. A bottle rattled by the bar.

"Say, Tom," Hank said suddenly, slapping the table with his hand, "can you lend me some money and do you have some spare clothes? I've got nothing with me. I had some bad luck getting here. I want to go and see what is happening now in the Chembe village. I think I must."

"Duty always calls, doesn't it Hank?" Tom now sounded cheerful. "Harsh mistress you have. A man must do as he must do, mustn't he Hank. Going after Jack are you? Even though I know you don't like him. Neither do I. I half expected him to turn up here. Some of the fellows here think he is a bit wet. He'd get a cold reception. I'm surprised he hasn't though. Do you expect he will be there at his school at all? Knowing Jack, he might be up his Mountain or carousing with one of his local so-called friends.

"Why do you do it, Hank? I've often asked myself that about myself. Maybe we are all as crazy and driven as Jack. Follow different laws and so on. There is a lot of bother in it, this life, isn't there? Is it worth it? I think once the rescue comes I'll end this contract and go home. I'm telling you now, frankly, I'm getting quite discouraged. The romance is gone. I hope I don't disappoint anyone if I do that, Hank. I can just about afford it now, I've put something aside. I can live at my mother's for a while. I collected some valuables here too. I'll sell those. I'll take the plunge. But what makes you go on Hank? Is it the adventure?" Tom's voice had lowered and as he peered at Hank as his hand shook again. The table was still.

"Well I just do the job as best I can and go home, as I can, as you do Tom. There was a buzz sometimes but now I just try to do what I have to, and finish it, and do what I must to get home. Wherever that might be or where it takes me. That's all. The same as you. Quite normal really. You have to deal in the meantime with what comes, even the unexpected. It's just the usual sort of thing. So cheer up, Tom! You aren't alone. You aren't disappointing anyone." Hank's voice had gotten louder and prompted a shushing sound from the dark.

"I am expecting Jack at the school as you say Tom," Hank said softly. "I really am. I have to finish with him especially now that I know where you are and safe as can be expected. There are one or two other things to do too, I now realize. I hope we all then get to go home. So I need a bit of money and a change of clothes."

"Listen to us," said Tom. "We are like two old persons in a play on a sinking ship. We are having deep realisations about our lives and predicaments. How silly. I certainly can let you have a little money and give you a change of clothes. Not much, but something if you have to stay overnight. And good luck to you Hank! I have some hidden jam too. You might get peckish. My suitcase is by the sleeping bag under the table. I'll need a receipt from you though, Hank. On agency paper if you have it. I'll get the stuff out for you but can you wait a minute? I'm just going to the washroom. I really must go immediately even though that place smells to make heaven cry." He rose and went into the darkness past the bar. Hank looked around for some food on the tables. There seemed none uneaten. He wanted to search Tom's bags but decided not to risk it.

Hank took the change of clothes, the jam and a small amount of money from Tom after he had returned from the washroom. Tom smelt worse than when he had left. The money Hank put in his sock. The other items went into a plastic bag Tom had taken from a pocket in his luggage in which he had several. The bag was also itemized in the receipt. It was a soiled blue bag from the shop in which Hank had bought his coat. Hank asked Tom to not tell any rescuers who arrived where he was or even that he had seen him. Tom raised his eyebrows about this and looked confused but them winked excitedly at Hank and said that he always had suspected that Hank may have an extra role. Hank winked back and then smiling left Tom in the darkened room.

When Hank returned to his vehicle he found the driver sleeping. The driver awoke with a start as Hank opened the back door. He immediately started the engine glancing right and left and then forward into the empty street. Finally he turned around to Hank. He smiled at seeing the plastic bag. Hank nodded to him and said to go to the Chembe village. The driver turned the vehicle and they proceeded at speed back the way they had come. They went around the roundabout, past the ruins and out of the town. Then they turned onto the road to the village. The lone Mountain was visible on the plain. Some of the bodies they had seen on the way in were now gone but not the one in the intersection. The driver thought that some of the people might be hiding the bodies from those who might try to collect them.

They drove through the little hollows and then onto the plain. The driver was driving slowly, peering ahead for potholes and obstructions or other things in the road. He said that one never knew what might have happened. It was hard to drive when there was no traffic as you couldn't see the people ahead avoiding things and swerving or bumping. The Mama Wuta pool as they passed it was pink, reflecting colours in the setting sun. After driving on the deserted road in fading rose and blue light, they turned onto the road to the village. When they reached the turn-off to the school the village was in darkness. There was a glow from some fires in the direction of the market.

As the station wagon bumped along the path to the school gate they saw a fire ahead at the gate. When they reached the gate and stopped they found Jules sitting on a pile of luggage. Beside him on a stand was a motorcycle. It had no tires and seemed to have a twisted frame. Beside Jules, facing the good fire, was the Chembe girl. She squatted, legs askew, holding a long stick on the end of which she was roasting something. There was a pile of bits of wooden planks beside her. She waved to Hank. The nearest palms on the path behind them and the fence had been burned. They stood upright, but shattered to half length like broken pencils.

Hank got out and walked to Jules. Jules rose to meet him. They shook hands. Jules called greetings loudly out over Hank's shoulder to the driver. The driver called back. They then conversed for a moment. Jules then turned to Hank; he spoke softly so that the driver would not hear.

"You must pay him now Mister Hank. If you don't, he will leave. If you do, he will think you still have money and will stay overnight. There is still some beer in the village and he has relatives near here."

"I didn't know he was Chembe," said Hank.

"He is known to us. His mother was Chembe. His father is Bechembe. That is why they went to the city. It is a common thing there. The mixed marriage people always leave. There is one who is even a driver now in your city. He writes that he hates the cold." Hank went over to the driver and paid him. The driver said he might return in the morning to see if Hank wanted a return trip which would be extra. He said he would be looking to see if there was anything he could take back to the city that night. He thought he might find an extra paying passenger in the morning but Hank would have to pay full price anyway. The other thing he might do was to drive to the border and see if anyone was waiting there without transport because of the disruptions. He drove off singing to the radio.

"We thought you might be coming," said Jules as he led Hank back to the fire. "Yes, I see you noticed that those are your bags there. They are not bad children, God's Front. When you told them you were coming here they decided that if that was the truth they would do no harm to deliver the bags to us. They are full of respect and honest. They brought the bags by bicycle on the old paths. They thank you for your donation too."

"Well that is very nice of them," said Hank. He sat on a bag and indicated the other to Jules. The Chembe girl was smiling and humming. She sat on a stone. She threw a stick in the fire to be lit suddenly to her eyes in the eruption of sparks.

"My passport is in those bags, Jules. But more importantly there are some critical papers. They have key information. I wasn't sure how I would replace them. I came here because of that. And to see how the project was, of course."

"Mister Hank, the project is finished for now. I am sorry. The school is destroyed except for some of the library. Many of the girls and teachers were killed. My tribeswoman, Mama here, and I have spent the evening finding the bodies and covering them from the animals. There was some help. We used some roofing material and stone, heavy sand and pieces from the classroom walls. They are in rows in the square. Mama here said a prayer." Jules indicated the Chembe girl. She smiled at them both.

"Jules, your shirt is wet. You could become ill. I have a coat in one of those bags if you like."

"Never mind Mister Hank. It is just water. I have just washed it. Mama helped me and we did my trousers too." Mama was now chanting something and swaying on her heels. She was still smiling broadly.

She is disabled isn't she, Jules?" said Hank and smiled back to Mama.

"Well not from our way of seeing, Mister Hank. She just has the old ways of thinking, more than anyone else. She settles us. We all love her very much — that is why she is our queen. And she is very capable. She not only sells beer and gin but she makes medicines and she attends the school year after year. She also travels to all sorts of places. She roams around everywhere, sometimes with the small boys. She disappears for weeks. She is mysterious, moves and waves."

The Mountain was black but faintly outlined in silver from a sun setting far behind and across the border. The air was heavy and cool. It smelt of soot. There were reedy calls from the mountain

"What happened, Jules?" said Hank.

"Well Mister Hank I am afraid you will think we have all misbehaved. The Chembes and Bechembes have always fought. This time it was more awful and faster because of the politics and because some of us are deciding what our religion should be. The religious people burned the beer parlour. The soldiers shot at the ceremony. Bechembe boys, some religious, and some of the soldiers burned the school but they also killed some of our small boys working there and two Elders who defended it. We saw them taking their women away first. We took away some materials before they came back though. We all went after all that from everywhere, all our villages, and we burned their market. We were urged. Everything comes to those that hate.

"The killing was not clean. It wasn't just over land or cows or just about bad men or women. Everyone did their own. They went down the roads to attack the politicians and religious they did not like. The religious and politicians shouted to the people and urged. More urging came from the radio. The soldiers shot at everyone and then they ran to their villages. They will come out soon because their chiefs have got the city. Our people went back and forth on the roads and paths until they were stopped by the river and the mountains. I did it too. We all did bad, even Mama. People were cut up and hacked to death even if they were found already wounded. They did terrible things. We had all felt the killing was coming. We all felt the season. Not just here. We couldn't stop it. Nothing held us together.

"Where is Madame Youngo?"

"We think she is dead with the Governor and his other wives in the barracks. Their politics didn't work. They sent out some people to negotiate with the crowd but the people hacked them to pieces. Some thought they were always with the Bechembes and the soldiers. It is said they offered some money and a position. The priest is dead too. He was burned in the church with some of his girls and an old woman from the village who was still of his faith. Madame Florence we don't know.

"We will sleep up there tonight Mister Hank. Mama's little house is burned but one of Father's rooms is still intact and has a roof. I think it may rain again. There is a bed for you but no mattress. There is nowhere to go in the school. We can't go to the village as there are people there not yet finished. Many are just hiding and sleeping and relaxing their guilt. There are those who want to give the killing a new shape and ride it in a direction forward. We expect some others to come from the capital. We are safest near the Mountain, Mister Hank. Better safe and sorry.

"Mister Hank, I don't mind that we killed the soldiers or burnt the Bechembes. From our perspective that is understood. Please forgive us. But some of the other things are evil.

They sat in silence. There was a smell of roasting meat. Mama took some from her stick and placed it on a broad leaf she had on the ground by the fire. There were several chunks already on the leaf. On another leaf beside her on the other side were some pieces that glistened dark red, wet and rubbery in the firelight. Mama took a knife from the waistband of her school uniform skirt. She used it to cut each of the cooked chunks on their leaf into smaller pieces. It took only one or two strokes for each.

She stood, replaced the knife at her waist and then bent down to pick up the thick and ribbed leaf, holding it on arms and palms. She stepped over to the seated men and offered her platter. Each took a piece. She stood standing and watching as they chewed and swallowed. When Hank had swallowed, for he was the last to do so, she offered again. When the platter was finished she returned to the fire. She took a raw piece from the other leaf and put it on her stick to roast.

"I read Jack's papers from your bags," said Jules. "They aren't as good as some of his other writing. One is a kind of confession. Do you think he ever expected anyone to see them?

"I also read your report to Madame Youngo. One of the boys brought it. They found it on a woman by the road. I think it is really good. We should put it in the library."

XII

Jules had with him what looked like Madame Youngo's flashlight. When they had finished eating they followed the beam along the fence and across the gully up to the church. Mama carried one piece of luggage. Jules had the plastic bag Tom had given him.

The steeple stood but the roof had collapsed into the shell. All of the walls were scorched and broken down to a third of their height. The ground was black around, as were the stone pathways. Even some of the ferns on the sides of the clearing had been burnt to brown lace. As Jules played the flashlight beam over the building, Hank thought of the cinema in the town he grew up in at home.

The house behind now had a roof which slanted to the ground in front from the back. The big room had collapsed. They walked around to a rear door in the middle of the back wall. This opened into a kitchen. There were some broken plates, cups, and a tray on the floor which they walked carefully around. Jules opened the door from the kitchen into what had been the main room. The ceiling, slanting to the floor, left a space to the left and right, a tunnel which connected to the doors on each side. They went to their right, Jules and Hank hunching over although it was not necessary. They stepped over some broken gramophone records. They opened the door on the right and Jules shone the light in.

"We came in here to look for Father and Florence," said Jules. "Mama and I were very anxious. But I think Father ended up in the church. There was some looting and raping here too, but not much, as people were frightened. Also there was a fear of the fire spreading from the church. It isn't as bad as the time of the mission."

The bedroom floors were scattered with bits of torn clothing, a red surplice, a brassiere. There was a floppy hat. There were also a lot of scattered papers; some of it was music scores.

"We looked for copies of his sermons but they were not to be found. People here like to take away papers that they think are special. Some are used in charms," said Jules. "Father wrote some comic songs which he would sing in the voices of some of the people here — the sister, Madame Youngo, some of the girls — but I couldn't find them. It is a great loss.

"Hey there mister!
Call me sister!
I'm very smart,
With the purest heart!

"I fear no clouds
Nor empty shrouds
Because every day
I sing and pray."

Jules sang in a kind of high voiced blues. Mama hummed along with him. They both smiled.

"There are many more verses," said Jules, "each about a different person. You should have heard him sing them! Well here is the bed. Mama and I will sleep on the floor in the other room. We are used to that sort of thing. I think Mama wants to check the church again first. There are some blankets under the bed there that we found in the other room. They are hardly burned at all but they smell a little. We have taken two already; it is cold at night in the rainy season. We will leave you the flashlight too. We don't need it."

After the Chembes had left, Hank went to sleep on the floor under the bed staring up through the pattern of springs. The mattress above had a hole burned through the centre. He had used the flashlight to take his overcoat from the bed to use as a mattress. He did not need the blankets.

Hank set out the t-shirt and shorts he had gotten from Tom Hume at his feet for the morning. The t-shirt was an old one with the name of Hank's university. Tom had gone there too. Hank put the flashlight after he had extinguished it near his head. He ate some jam with his fingers in the dark. Once he awoke hearing voices outside his door but otherwise slept well with no remembered dreams. It was the first good sleep in several days and the first time as well that he hadn't gone to bed hungry. The papers had been returned to his luggage. They had been smeared.

The morning came in through cracks in the walls through the hole in the mattress and the web of bare springs. Hank had a new spell of "where am I?" and sat up to hit his forehead on a bottom slat on the bed. He rolled out from under the bed and stood, stretching and rubbing his head. Then he changed from his military-like outfit to the t-shirt and shorts. Some wind was blowing through the walls and under the roof to rattle papers on the floor. He repacked his luggage and put it in the corner of the room.

There was a knock at the door.

"Come out Mister Hank, it is a fresh day. Mama has found some eggs and she is cooking them."

It was late in a clear and breezy morning. The cloud from the Mountain was overhead. Hank followed Jules past the church to the edge of the hill overlooking the plain and the village. The burgundy couch was there, cracked even more and tilted into the earth slightly from a shortened leg. There were some pieces of cloth and a holed tin washing bucket lying on the slope down the inline from the lip of the hill where the couch sat.

Mama was beside the couch crouched over a small smokeless fire which was confined in a circle of black rocks. At her side was a stack of palm leaves and twigs. She was cooking eggs in the lid of a pot which she held in the fire, her hand wrapped in a rag of flowered cloth. The eggs suddenly smelled as though burning slightly. She pulled the pot lid from the fire and dumped the eggs onto a leaf. There were four.

Jules sat down on the couch with a sigh and said that they could see the world from there. The village, and all the plain, and most of the school. It was a good spot. Mama gave them each a palm leaf which they put on their laps. She returned and scraped egg from her serving palm onto their leaves with the edge of her knife. They ate with tightened, scooping fingers. Mama was still wearing her school uniform but was barefoot although with her customary painted toes.

Then Jules stood, clutching his leaf in the palm of his hand, and pointed to his left. There on the path to the school was the agency vehicle, flag flying, approaching the gate. Mama stood up too from the fire, an uncracked egg in her hand. Her lips drew back from her teeth and she let out a kind of hiss. She dropped the egg directly into the fire where it sizzled and burned.

The vehicle stopped at the school gates. Someone, a man, got out and walked over to the ring of stones and the damaged motorcycle by the gate. There seemed to be no one else. He did not return to the vehicle but walked through the gate and between the splintered palms toward the square. He stopped midway down the path to turn and look to one side at the former staff compound, now fallen walls and rubble behind the poles of an absent fence. There were some dogs near one of the poles.

"I guess we had to expect him," said Hank. "He couldn't stand not knowing what had happened." Jules sat down again beside Hank on the couch.

"Mister Hank. Just look at that view. In the eyes of beauty is the beholder." The mountains on the rim of the plain were purple but lit yellow on their tops. The plain was still shadowed on its floor but bright just above. The village was indistinct but glimmering in yellows, browns and reflecting blacks from the streaking shadows created as the cloud above the Mountain extended towards it.

Hank and Jules had some more eggs. Mama left them for a moment and went through a gap in the side wall of the ruined church. She returned with a yellow bowl full of water and two cracked white porcelain cups. She heated the water on her fire and then poured it into the cups. The bowl had blackened.

Mama gave the cups to the men and then forked earth over the fire with her knife. The men sipped the water as the final shadows rolled back from the plain, leaving only that from the cloud. The village was partially destroyed but people were moving in it and some vehicles. There was a wall of cloud rising on the extreme horizon.

Jack emerged on the path from the school which came up from the gulley. He was wearing a shirt of a different check. He said that he had wondered where everybody was as he walked over to the couch. Jules got up and embraced him. Mama moved quickly in front of the couch and sat beside Hank. She stared ahead, unsmiling. Jules dropped his embrace and then shook Jack's hand. He looked into his eyes. Jack dropped the handshake and spoke to Hank.

"Well I have found you at last, Hank; I thought Tom sounded a little coy. Hank you continue to be a figure of secrecy and mystery. More clever than you seem. Are you doing it for the press?

"Tom was really upset to hear I was the country director, Hank. He even told me he had already been rescued. He wouldn't say by whom. He didn't look rescued. So it was you. Still doing a sloppy job, Hank? Tom said he didn't want to be rescued again by me. He didn't know why there should be a second coming. What a stick he is! He told me he had to get his collection first before he went home. I left him with the soldiers."

"Did you have any trouble at the river?" asked Hank. "Is the ferry still running?"

"Yes it is. You can still get out. I think the big one actually sank with passengers so we won't see that again. I came with a good sized convoy and we all crossed on a small one. Several vehicles of God's Serpents coming to order things. No, their name has changed to People's Research Bureau now. The ferry could only take a few vehicles at a time. We had to wait around for each other. The flood was glorious."

"So your plans were altered then Jack? Best laid and gone astray? I don't suppose Ron decided there was no crisis after all and changed his mind about the wonderful Boat of Hope. Did he think it was better for the agency to forget about the whole thing and send you to do real development? Being country director is not all smooth sailing, is it Jack. You get pushed around. Well has the agency's idea of the situation changed? Do we have different assignments?"

"No. The idea is still the same. The fundraising is going ahead in full swing. It is still all based a little on your last reports Hank, you should be proud of that, you remember the reports and minutes that got us evacuated.

"Actually it was Juliet's father who thought I should come out as soon as possible, you know Hank, the one in government. He thought I should come right away. He spoke to the chief." Jack's voice was dry and he swallowed frequently. He stared at the church. He then looked at Mama tight by Hank's side on the couch.

"Not Cress's idea? Or Ron's then," said Hank.

"Cressy has been reassigned to be in the field at one of the islands. Part of the staff development thing. Juliet and her father like the idea, keeps her out of trouble. I guess you know Juliet and I are scheduled to be made official, as they say, on my first leave home. I hope you can come Hank." Jack turned back to Jules who had been listening attentively and quizzically.

"Jules. What has happened to everyone?"

"You have seen most, Mister Jack. Her relatives and the others came back. They murdered some of the staff and the girls."

"Was Hope brought back?" said Jack.

"Hope is Bechembe really," said Jules. "What did you think would happen?"

The Chembe girl shouted a single word in her language and then she pointed down to the school. The agency vehicle was burning in the sun. They all turned to look. Jack cursed.

"They must think it is you come back," said Jules to Hank. Jules spoke in a measured way. "Or your taxi driver has told them. It will be the young devoted men from the village. They will search around the school and then come here. They are a great danger to us all.

"They fear nothing, those men, and have no respect. Killing is good for them. Our best plan is to go up the Mountain. They may even follow us there but it will not be easy for them. Please follow me. Mister Jack and Mister Hank, you must trust me on this. The path starts behind Father's house."

Jules put his arm momentarily on Jack's shoulder and then turned towards the Mountain. He walked quickly towards it. Jack followed immediately. Hank then got up and followed them past the church and the house. The Chembe woman came up close behind him, always a half step behind.

The path began behind, concealed at the entrance by wide leafed ferns. It broadened immediately after the ferns had been parted and then rose abruptly between grasses and other thin leafed ferns, swinging to the right. When climbing Hank twice slid back and had to use his hands.

After a few moments the path levelled and crossed through what must have been the same gully as that down by the church, but up here the gully was narrower and bordered at its rim by black mosses and grey grass. On the other side of the gully the path rose on a more gentle slope, not directly up the mountain side but along it. Here there were trees with tall trunks and high crowns standing in small clearings around their bases but separated by tangled ferns, vines and a mire of earthy fallen branches. Between the trees in the ferns were speckles of small white flowers and large rubbery yellow lilies. As they went on they could see the school below them over the foliage through gaps between the trunks. The crowns of the trees began to merge. More and more vines hung from them and it grew darker. They were all panting except the Chembe woman. They had been moving very quickly. Jules stopped and whispered.

"We will rest a moment here." They stood quietly, their breathing slowly easing. As they stood sound began in the trees. It was first a light twittering, then a heavier buzz. A monkey howled ahead and upwards.

"We will have passed over the school soon," said Jules. "Further along, the path goes up another gully. This one will have water. It will be brighter. This is the gully that goes down to the other side of the ridge beyond the school to be a brook. We must leave it if we hear rain on the trees. From there we will get up to the main path." He cocked his head. "I do not think they are behind us yet." Mama picked some small blossoms from the side of the path and put them in her mouth. She was standing close to Hank, beside him on the side away from Jack and Jules.

"It is beautiful up here," said Jack. Hank grunted. Jack's eyes were still bloodshot.

A gust blew along the forest floor from up the slope of the Mountain. The air suddenly cleared. Hank sniffed, finding that the smell of soot and boiled cabbages that had been in his nostrils since the Bechembe town had left. It was strange how you forgot strong, constant smells and odours after first realising them, that is, until they are gone. Hank could now smell the large red petaled flowers on the slope above him, the odour of peanut oil and bacon. Hank whispered over to Jules and whispered to him a sound completely submerged in the growing chatter of birds and whirring of insects.

"Jules, where are the shrines that were damaged? Will we pass the place where the procession goes after the dance contest?"

"Mister Hank, there are no shrines behind the school. There was a grave just below us of one of the God's Front. The girls spoiled that. The Front had brought the boy back to the Mountain to heal but it was too late. Madame Youngo knew there were no shrines. She sent you to negotiate to try to end the growing troubles with a little bribery. You nearly did. There are some real shrines further up.

"The Father didn't really like any foreigners to know but the procession actually used to go up the slope to end on the little shelf the church stands on. It always did. The people stand on the slope and the queen and Elders dance just where we sat on the couch. That is where the fire is built. After his own ceremony the Father even paid for meat and beer for the Elders for a few years. He would come out to serve it and I would help him, but Madame Florence when she came stopped him. She was always jealous.

"I don't know why Father used to think that the procession would stay a secret; you can see the torches and fire across the plain. You can see they are not anywhere else. When the soldiers fired on us from the dark all of Chembeland could see what was happening.

Jack spoke out in a normal voice which caused Hank, Jules and Mama all to flinch.

"What are you two nattering about? Don't you think we should get on?"

They walked around and up until they could no longer see the school below through the trees. The path was sometimes joined by others and it sometimes forked. They always took the rising fork. The crowns of the trees had completely merged and the trunks were now more frequently joined by vines. The spaces between trees had narrowed and the vegetation there was denser, piled with thicker rotting boughs speckled with green and red flowers, and webbed with fallen vines. There were no palms and the grasses had vanished. Moss bordered the path which was a narrow groove in red earth.

They emerged in bright sunlight over a deep gorge. The gorge was sloped with sand around grey outcrops. At the bottom white water rushed around large honey coloured boulders in a blue clay trough. There was a path up the Mountain along the trough. A distance above them, the path and the river came down between two large grey outcrops which stretched from the top of the forested slope almost to the water. There the path was a smear on a sloping beige rock, a shelf into the water.

They slid and bounced down the side of the gorge on a river of sand. Hank fell once on his knees and roughed them in pink suede but got up almost immediately. His t-shirt was soaked with the humidity and heat from the forest. Jack stepped in exaggerated lengths, as though weightless, his thin body erect. Jules, leading, had gone down first in small crab-like hops, carefully jerking from foot to foot, and then walking sideways down turning from one side to another as he descended and the others watched. Mama did the same in her turn, close behind Hank, but stopping to wait as he stumbled.

At the side of the river there was a warm spray. The path was a dark and muddy purple. Jules told Hank when he arrived that the river was mostly underground and only ran off on the surface after rains. He said that deep water runs still. He said that when water came to the surface it formed permanent pools. You could drink the water even though it smelled of sulphur. It was healthy and came from the largest pool at the top of the Mountain.

When the group had collected they moved upward between the two outcrops. There the gorge widened. Some trees at the top of the gorge had fallen along the slope so that flowered vines trailed down in the sand. There were small bushes growing in the crevices of the outcropping stone buttresses around which the path wove as it climbed.

Ahead of them at a distance at the top of the slope arose a curve of high crumbling black cliffs, a broken wall flecked with clumps of trees, from which the river flowed swiftly through a gravely crack, almost a waterfall. At the foot of the cliffs and before the crack the river came from, they crossed over the water, there turquoise and opaque, on large black stones fallen from above which widened and slowed the river and cut it into channels, channels which joined down the slope in a white swirl.

The path led along the face of the cliffs curving around the Mountain and edging the forest below the cliffs. The cliffs shortened, softened and ended in a pile of black rubble where their path re-entered the forest, forking away from a narrower one which led downward through the trees and vines. They were climbing again on a track which was more and more emerging from the earth as a dry ribbon of stone. They heard a rumbling harsh roar below them. They all stopped. Jules said that that meant they were still alright. Then they went on.

The path emerged after some time into sunlight across a lime green meadow which footed flat and shingled yellow cliffs. They could see the path zigzagging up the face like a child's scrawl.

"This is the farther side of the Mountain," said Jules, "and that is the main path up."

"Do we need to go there?" said Hank.

"I think we do, Mister Hank. Those chasing will feel as though it is a hunt. They will feel that to get the game will be the greatest thing for them. It will be a big story in a big story. They will forget to fear the Mountain. They think fate will be with them.

"It is a big mountain," Jules went on. "It has many sides and all kinds of valleys and caves. It has many animals and more are coming back here all the time. It has many kinds of deep bush but it is all connected; it reaches to the village and there is intercourse and information back and forth. They know there is a main path where animals are fewer and that it is here. They will know that someone on the Mountain must be helping. Everything must go a certain way.

"I remember that path," said Jack. "It is where we came with Juliet. There are some caves." Mama was looking into the dark green grasses and reeds. A wind was blowing over them so that they rippled like the surface of a lake.

The vegetation was knee-high to Hank and the path ran straight through it, a dark stripe under the grass brushing their legs. Jules' white shirt glared in the sun as they crossed the meadow but his black trousers became streaked in yellowy green. Hank's legs felt wet below the hem of his shorts. They all watched for snakes, especially ahead where the grasses parted and the path was open to the sun, but also to the sides to the running roots and tendrils under the tangle of stems.

They paused at the foot of the cliff where in sloping steps the way was carved upward into soft and pitted chalky rock. Mama was wet and stained to the waist of her royal blue skirt. Her dark red blouse was missing all the buttons but the lowest. She had her knife in her right hand. She was breathing in short gasps while her heavy lidded purple eyes opened and closed slowly. She swayed as she stopped behind Hank. Jack stepped around Hank and extended a hand. Mama stepped backwards and waved the knife. Jules came up behind Jack and clutched his shoulder. Jack spoke to Jules as Mama muttered in her own language between her teeth.

"Mister Jack. Do not try to touch her. She is connecting you now to discomfort and pain. It is natural that she wants you away."

"But the wedding?" said Jack.

"She was happy then because of the conception. But she knows the rest too. She is beginning to get sick. She will birth in the dry season in the dust storms. This is what you mean to her now."

"What goddamn wedding!" shouted Hank.

"Mister Hank, the dancing always was a wedding. It was never an international contest with Bechembes and every dog. It was the time and it was before the tree. The child was offered to the Mountain by the tribe. To her it was wonderful, a perfect wedding. Everyone came. The new groom was seated where he should be and the one giving away and the new groom. Everything arranged as it should. The other queens settled."

"Why wasn't I told!" said Hank.

"Mister Hank," said Jules, "be calm. You've behaved really well in your role. And Jack and the agency wasn't really the important thing. The king never is. In fact he is sort of a villain. But Mama was really happy. The other thing is that Jack being there and you made all the Chembes content. That is why Madame Youngo and we agreed it. There had been complaints. It made things proper."

Jack was staring straight at Hank. His jaw was tense and fists balled.

"Jack you are a bastard," said Hank.

"What do you know, you boring slug?" said Jack stepping forward.

"I know you can never be a country director. I know you don't know what to do and need to ask me. I know the agency is going to do whatever it wants to no matter how much you create a chaos. I know you take advantage of vulnerable people."

"I have never done that," said Jack.

"Someone who just wants to get out of her life and into the world, someone who wants to secure themselves, another who just wants to mate!" said Hank.

"Please be calm," said Jules. "Mister Jack is my brother. To us he is a legend. We love him. He is a poet king. We will dance him next year surrounded with swarms of predators and queens as the father of queens and chiefs in many tribes. He is the man of sacrifice." Mama stepped up close to Hank, facing Jack with her knife held steady on her hip pointing outward.

"We must climb quickly," said Jules. "We have no time for this. For every season there is a thing."

It crunched underfoot as they climbed, the dust covering their feet and ankles. Some dust blew into their faces and onto their clothes in tiny erratic winds curling around the cliff face. At times one foot had to be put carefully in front of the other but at other times the way widened, several times passing behind slabs of rotted cliff rising from the face like teeth. In three places there were caves above the path; one with straw piled in the mouth and another closed off at the mouth with roofing material. That one could be reached by a ladder of toeholds cut into the stone.

They went up at a steady incline to the left in a relentless sun, walking and walking, heads down and then after a long time surprisingly turning sharply left, walking slower and less steadily upwards for a timeless period, seeing only the chalk and small stones at their feet, looking up only if the path changed, adjusting to the new width, once walking with backs to the cliff sliding along and then zagging at last to the right, moving upwards as a shadow shot up the cliff from the ground and the air cooled suddenly. The meadow far below shimmered in deep green.

The top was sudden. There was a tuft of grass, a small treed field, the sky and more mountain behind. Standing back from the lip where the path came up into the field were five small people in furs. There were burlap bags and a dozen large gourds at their feet and scattered around them. Hank and Jack stopped behind Jules facing the furred party. Both men were gasping and Hank was coughing. They had swallowed some yellow, chalky dust.

Mama went forward laughing and talking. She was yellow. She sounded like the river below did as it went around the black stones. One of the greeting party shouted to Jules. Jules was waving to them vigorously.

"These are the hill people," said Jules to Hank and Jack. Jules was laughing too. "They have seen us coming. They are almost alone here. They say most of the God's Front are gone too down into the forest. Some of them were still moving around by the flood. They say we are big bananas." All three men were yellow too.

Mama had taken off all her clothes. She washed her face and feet with water poured from a gourd. Then she drank. She took what looked to be cheese and a dried piece of intestine from one of the bags and ate it. The people in furs were laughing and talking to her. She beckoned to Jules as she talked. From one bag, the biggest, she took out a burlap dress sewn with fur pieces and a cloth and fur vest. The furs were blonde and long haired. She dressed in this.

Jules took Hank and Jack each by the hand and pulled them forward. He indicated the bags and the gourds. Jack undressed and washed immediately. The smaller people all stared at Hank. He undressed more slowly, leaving on his underwear. Unlike Jack he was not thin. The smaller people all laughed a sort of gasping, high bark as he took off the t-shirt and another as he lowered his shorts. The smalls Hank wore were orange flowered. After this, Mama went off into the field with two of the greeting party. She vanished behind some trees. One other, a woman, moved past the men and disappeared down the path.

Jack was in a burlap gown open to the chest and furred at the collar. Hank and Jules had cloth jackets with short sleeved, furred arms and patched khaki shorts furred at the buttocks. Their former clothes were three yellow piles. One of the remaining two greeters gathered up these piles and put them in the now empty large sack.

All three men drank from the gourds. All three ate the white foods; the cheese was sweet and the intestine peppery. There was unleavened bread too. After the men put their gourds down the other person from the greeting party gathered up the gourds into a large net which he had been holding at his side. He closed the net, stooped and hoisted up the bundle on his back. It was raised only a tiny space above the ground but it bulged over his head. He turned and was gone; the men watched as the bundle wobbled away beside the person who had the clothes. This one was now yellow armed as dust seeped through the burlap. Jules said that the three men must wait here while things were prepared ahead for them.

In the distance behind some tangled leafless trees, some cacti and a copse of palms with clusters of red fruit, there were three bee-hive huts, and beyond them through tall ferns glimmered a pool. The wind blew down from the narrowing, flat top of the final stage of the mountain. It came across the field into their faces. To their left, from the Mountain's top, the cloud extended away from the Mountain connected to the slopes by shimmering curtains of moisture and a half dozen rainbows.

"What happened to Hope? Tell me everything Jules. Where is she exactly?" said Jack. He was looking around intensely staring into the field and up the Mountain. He still had a piece of the intestine in his mouth pushed into his cheek or chewing it.

Jules did not answer Jack. He turned to Hank and spoke evenly. His eyes were looking over Hank's head and back over the cliff.

"Mister Hank the bush children bring me all the papers they find, especially the official looking ones. I use them sometimes to write the scripts for the Redeemer broadcasts from across the border. I can tell you a secret now Hank, as you are almost one of us. There is no Redeemer really. Or there are several. We all take turns to be him when it's needed. There is numbers in strength.

"The boys and girls usually have papers from dead soldiers or from the offices of the companies on the Mountain's edges by the border. This time they had a report authored by you addressed to Madame Youngo. I was amazed. They said they found it in the luggage of a badly hurt girl in a field past a Bechembe village.

"Some Chembe roaming around had seen her by the road earlier but had ignored her to go into the village where there was fighting. They came out across the fields from that fight later; that was when they met her. There was an idea raised by someone to bring her back because we can heal people here on the Mountain but she was a Bechembe. She was gone in the rain. Water is thicker than blood.

"It was a great tragedy because I had taken the school van to roam around to find people as part of the trouble. I was near there. In any event the van like almost everything got lost.

Jack was coughing as though weeping.

"I thought your report was very good Hank," continued Jules. "It was so logical. You gave the objectives of your two missions: first, to negotiate a settlement peacefully and prudently to budget and second, to find out if the possible causes of a death affected the project and the agency. This is the kind of thing you people are so good at and we need to learn. You are so unemotional and objective.

"You itemised what the project had, what it needed and then recommended what be given to the Elders. You did not go into the causes of the incident or affix blame. It was wonderful. When we took the things from the school we took only what you had recommended." Jules paused. He still avoided looking at Jack who had been shaking at the shoulders but was now tight lipped.

"As to the death you said that there was either a supernatural cause or a natural one. You said that only these could be the direct causes and only these, not indirect causes, would be part of your role to investigate. You listed who you met and their positions. I think this approach is wonderful.

"If it was natural then you said the girl Hope must be involved as she slept close to her sister. She had a traditional motive to kill her as well as a modern one. You mentioned Mama was suspected but it was unlikely that she could naturally creep into the girl's dormitory and would not naturally have the strength to pierce a strong heart. You said how tall and strong Hope looked. You said that perhaps a staff member could be suspected or a jealous woman but that too was unlikely given the proximity of the two beds in the crowded dormitory. You mentioned that you heard of an instance where Jack had gone wandering in a fever and he had been spotted and brought home by a girl. This showed how close a community it was. Nothing escaped notice." Hank had closed his eyes. He was scratching at the ground with the toe of his damp shoe.

"If there was a supernatural reason as some had suggested, you said Hank that the person most materially involved would also be Hope. She was the main one who reported on supernatural events and seemed the closest to them. You said Mama was named as a suspect. But that was not relevant as we did not want to go into supernatural inspirations, only into the agents animated by them. In this case Hope was, because she was there, the only likely person animated in regards to this case. I would have used the example here of the ministry of health man's dog to illustrate the principal you were using, but perhaps this would be too complicated. But it would have shown how cause is established.

"You recommended that Hope was expelled from the school and the authorities be informed. You said the agency and its staff were not involved in any meaningful way as you had shown. You said the intervention continued to have good relations with the school authorities and the community.

"You did not specifically report on Jack or on any other thing. You said all other issues or complaints regarding the project, its staff, and future were resolved, were being resolved, or could be resolved. This was really a good conclusion. It made me hopeful.

"It was interesting that you trusted Hope to deliver the report. I guess you had to leave things to fate. That was a sort of Bechembe thing to do."

Mama was coming back across the field with two women and with two tall boys in khaki. They all had machetes in their hands. She had a goat with her tied with a rope. It was also blonde. A cloud had risen up behind the top of the Mountain. Jules then turned to Jack and spoke to him softly. Hank looked away and then stepped closer to the cliff.

"Hank has some things you wrote, Mister Jack, in his luggage." Jules was speaking in a whisper carried away by the breeze over the edge of the cliff. "The luggage is down in the priest's house. You might want to tell him about them and what those papers mean.

"And here comes Mama. Let's stop talking about Hope Malati for a while. Hope and her sister used to both torment Mama all the time. They would wait on the path to your house Mister Jack. You never disciplined those two. You know Mama did not like them. She thought they were witches.

"I am glad you left, Jack; you needed to. Hank was right. We were all right. I could never have thought to keep you even though you are my brother and I love you. We will always be grateful but you should not have come back."

Jules shouted over to Hank standing at cliff's edge. "Let us go now quickly Mister Hank. Leap before you look!"

He then turned and left Hank and Jack to walk to meet Mama and the others. When he reached Mama he took the rope tethering the goat from Mama's hands. He beckoned to the men and turned to walk towards the huts.

"Do you think those people following us are really dangerous?" said Hank to Jack. "We don't even know if they ignited the vehicle. Perhaps they are coming to rescue us or perhaps just to kidnap us. I certainly don't want to do any more climbing."

"I think, Hank, that they do think in their own minds that they actually are a rescue party. They are hunting devils and saving souls from their point of view. And Hank, we may be technically kidnapped already. God's Front sometimes has people's trials. They may think we are here to accuse them of something or to support Bechembe.You never know with Chembe. That's the beauty of them." Jack walked forwards towards the huts and the pool following the group with the machetes leading the goat.

"Is there anything else you didn't tell me, you damn airhead?" said Hank, stumbling behind. The fur on the shorts was itching. "What did you see when you left the vehicle into the rain? Had that girl been able to get transport and get ahead of us when we stopped to get Juliet?"

"It was raining and I was ill. It is hard to remember. I did want to find her here well though," said Jack. "It was my fondest dream. I had no reason to think otherwise." Hank was just able to hear this as the wind was now blowing steadily and briskly from over the Mountain. It carried small clouds over the summit and seemed to dash them on the slopes just before the brim where they disappeared into vegetation, trees and rocks.

The goat was tethered to a broken grey tree, a tall stump beside a hut. The hut seemed to be a dome of rows of woven reeds tied at the top. The entrance was small and covered by a grey blanket like those used in the school dormitories. Near the goat past the tree a rectangular pit had been dug and filled with rocks. On top of the rocks was a sheet of tin roofing. Smoke came from the pit.

Mama stood by the goat. The smoke was blowing around her. The others sat on short backless stools around a small fire just before the reeds and the pool. There was a pot on the fire which was steaming. The fire pulsed red with gusts coming from over the pool. Clouds ran across the sky. Jules met the men at the hut. He smiled and gestured to the pit.

"It is a good example of the relationship of form and function," Jules said. "Father and I discussed this kind of thing. If you think it is a roof you would never think it could be a grill. But here the reality of cooking is more connected to the mind and the idea of roofing has not just caught up yet, or it is settled in the mind with something else, so it is a perfect grill. It can't be thought otherwise. Unless of course you remember seeing a roof somewhere. Then everything changes." He laughed.

"Alright you two. Go sit by the fire with the others. The boys have made something to drink. We will greet you according to tradition with a sacrifice. Then we can all eat scorched meat, which is a fine thing.

"We have someone checking on what is behind us and there may be a new storm ahead for you, so now is the time to take care of the body and soul."

There were stools for Hank and Jack. They were each served by the tall boy a tin cup full of the liquid from the pot which he ladled out. Mama cut the throat of the goat with her machete. Jules had joined her. He too now had a machete. The pumping spurt from the goat's neck did not touch either Mama or Jules who stepped back at what was exactly the right moment. Some blood did hit the grill which sizzled; the strong aroma blew away quickly in the wind. The goat fell first to its knees soundlessly. It then collapsed to its side. The legs ran in the air. Mama picked up her knife which was at the foot of the tree and put down her machete. She knelt and seemed to cradle the goat. She plunged the knife into its side between the two first protruding ribs. The goat jerked and the legs stopped.

Together Mama and Jules made incisions and cuts along the legs back and stomach of the goat. They peeled back the fur, sliced it, and stacked it to the side in irregular pieces. Underneath the goat was a fatty white, now tinged pink and crossed with many small veins. When all but the area of buttocks of the goat around the anus had been peeled of fur, Jules cracked and sliced away the head with two strokes of his machete and placed it at the foot of the tree. Mama began to cut off a rear leg. This time her cutting only produced trickling ooze. The leg pulled away as Mama twisted it back to break the bone and she then cut away the last gristle. She then took the leg over and placed it on the grill. The air was getting cooler and so the fire became warmer.

"I am helped in this by what I learned in school," Jules shouted over. "There were all sorts of techniques in the books we had. No need to stick to the usual."

More chunks of meat were added to those cooking on the grill. The boy by the fire had a pot at his leg by the stool. It was covered with a white cloth. He took off the cloth and placed the pot by one of the rocks surrounding the small fire. The pot held slices of green bulbous vegetables. Two small women dressed in furs joined the circle at the fire. One carried four stools and one carried a bundle wrapped in leaves and tied with green tendrils.

The women set out the stools between the others already seated. They each sat in one leaving two empty. The shortest woman unwrapped her bundle. It was a stack of palm leaves interspaced with large round pieces of unleavened bread. It looked damp. The woman took off each leaf from the pile in turn and passed it to her right. She stacked each alternate piece of flat bread in turn on a hot rock in front of her.

When the leaves had gone around, two being left on the empty stools, she took in turn each piece of bread from the rock, beginning with the one on the bottom of the stack, stood and handed that piece to each of those sitting around the circle. She left one each on each of the leaves on the empty stools. The tall boy then stood and took the empty cups back from Hank and Jack. He ladled fresh liquid into them and passed this to his left and right around the circle. Each person there sipped from one cup or another, including Hank and Jack again. The last two who drank a sip placed a cup on each of the empty stools.

Jules and Mama then joined the circle. Mama had a wooden board which served as a platter for pieces of smoking meat. The tall boy took it from her. Jules and Mama sat down, one on each of the empty stools, each taking up the leaves and bread having each first sipped from one of the cups and then each put that cup down at the side of their stools.

The tall boy had put down his leaf and held the board between neck and shoulder. He took his machete from his waist and walked around the circle to shovel a piece of meat onto each piece of bread on each lap over each person's shoulder. He returned to his seat and put a piece on his bread there. He thrust the empty board into the fire between the two stones in the centre on which the pot there rested, took up his leaf plate and sat down. The fire glowed and flared with the board. No one had begun to eat.

The goat lay half carved on the ground by the tree overlooked by its own head. The grill was now empty but still sizzled. Hank felt a drop of rain fall on his head. Jules using one hand ripped a small piece of bread from where it lay under his piece of meat. He used this as a holder to pick up the whole piece of meat by a protruding bone and bring it to his mouth.

"Let us now remember absent friends," he said, looking around the circle nodding and smiling; everyone nodded back. He took a bite of meat. There had been no dribble of grease or anything else. They then all began to eat. Jules said that Chembes were always good with knife, fire and cooking pot. Hank between bites thanked Mama and Jules and praised the goat.

As they ate, the cups went back and forth with the tall boy doing the ladling. Apart from requests for these in both languages there was no conversation. The sky grew darker. A woman in furs came from behind the hut and walked to the edge of the hut behind Jules. She spoke in his ear. Then she turned and walked away. The meal continued until all had finished and the leaves went into the fire and lay smoking there giving off a smell of cinnamon.

"The hunters are behind us at the river," Jules said. "They are many. A pack of them, more than we thought. They may stay at the cliffs tonight and build a fire. We can watch this from here. You two must go higher up the Mountain. They will not know Mama and I are not part of the people here. Everyone here will say they have not seen you.

"We hope they will then decide to go back. We will listen to their sermons and agree with them and feed them some goat. My brothers here from God's Front will get behind them and then go back down the Mountain ahead of them. I will find you to tell you when it is safe and then we will try to finish this whole business."

The others at the fire rose one by one and went about the task of clearing the detritus of the meal. One returned the pot and cups into a hut. Two went to where the goat was. They lifted the roofing over the pit and threw the remaining carcass in. It was still bleeding from the neck. The limbs waved white tendrils in the air as the goat fell into the sparks. The tendrils were both ropey and filmy, made of the muscles and ligaments that had been cut while the shin was peeled back. Only Mama, Jules, Jack and Hank remained at the fire.

Jules went on. "They have gone to get some excreta and offal from another goat which was eaten last week. We will rub this over you two. The Mountain is full now with animals and the part you are going has the biggest. Reptiles as well. The main predators will avoid you if they think you are dead. The jackals and others will avoid you if you are moving. They have other things to do. This is the same trick our women and girls use when the Bechembe rapists come.

"There are other things up there that you must ignore no matter how terrible. The Mountain is a living thing and many things have life on it. Just carry on. If you do that they will think you are one of us as they know we always have reverence for the very strange and weird. We revere any grotesque and unknown thing. I don't think you people do that do they Hank?

There are many, many persons in the bush too. They will stay in their little clearings away from the path. Do not ask them for water or take their directions if you see them.

"If one of you is killed and being eaten the other one should join in to save his life. The animals will growl at you and drive you off but they will not see you as prey. The important thing is just to keep moving and stay focussed on your goal which is a cave near the top of the Mountain. This cave goes through to the other side of the rim and there you will overlook an island in the centre of a lake in the centre of a circular rim. The lake always steams. If I am not there in a day or so do not eat the fish in this lake. We will give you food for several days. Do not eat the insects that try to eat you. If you are hungry eat the others especially the ones that die in numbers.

"Do not lie down under a tree. There is a tree which covers the side of the Mountain and which has roots in some of the caves. This tree also has branches which seem as vines. It is the weeds in the lake. It transmits sound at distance and it is the biggest consumer of the dead.

"Do not go from the path I show you and always take the fork upward and to the left no matter how small and narrow. Do not go into any cave or among any rocks roofed by school roofing or surrounded by school fencing woven with vines. These are places for the others on the Mountain. Do not go down the Mountain by any other path. By the time you reach the cave you will have forgotten the path anyway and what you remember is not to be trusted. The cave is really a tunnel through the rim. If you go to the end be careful not to fall down on the inside in the dark.

"Thank you, Jules." said Hank. "That sounds alright to me. I think I can handle that."

Jack suddenly got up from his stool and walked to the reeds bordering the pool. He walked around the pool beyond the reeds into the greying light. The pool reflected black in the extending shadow of the last part of the Mountain.

THE BUSH

"I love that man," said Jules to Hank "We had such life together! You must love someone filled with life and energy like that. I think now he has become thoughtful and confused. But he is wrong. Nothing has happened that anyone was surprised about. Nothing will happen either which is unusual. Did the goat look surprised? Does the pool look surprised? Jack is by the pool now thinking of warm nights with animals howling and people moving around in the bush. He is thinking about bathing in the pool. He thinks about the motorcycle and strange villages. He is thinking of long jewelled lizards and fat thrumming birds. He is thinking of bodies in the dark like gourds smelling of musk and fat, burning herbs. He may be thinking of ripened fruits and terrible queens. I hope he doesn't fall in."

Jack came back to the fire and sat down on his stool. He had brought a reed back from the pool with him which he pushed into the embers. Mama was hunched into her fur in the breeze. She looked to the side of the field where people were moving. There were insects twirling and dancing in the last wisps of smoke.

"I have some ideas for projects," said Jack. "I think we should not rebuild the school but instead start a co-operative factory to employ raped women. The ones raped in this last disturbance will never be able to find husbands. Their brothers and uncles will want to kill them. Others may want to rape them some more.

"We could manufacture tourist items from wood from the hardwoods and bones and feathers. These could be sold when the tourists come. We could set up shops on the road. If they have some income these girls could start their own households and perhaps find a husband.

"The other thing we can do is start a transport company and employ the God's Front people as drivers. They may be young but will be becoming the right age soon. That whole age grade is now basically without work. We can give it to them. The other thing we could do is grate and can the carrots and add sugar. I'm sure we could grow sugar in the plains. The cans could be sold in the capital. If we rebuild the school we shouldn't make it a teacher's college. It should be a training school and be co-educational. We could build another unit where the church is to train disabled people as equals. We could start a literacy program there and a chicken farm. What do you think Hank?

It was Jules who spoke. "Jack you must understand that these boys have become what we call "the against the against". Remember that Jack? They are for God and against everything that is against them. They now won't imagine anything that you do could give them a direction away from God or their own destinies. They like to cut the hands and throats. They like the raping. They like to find diamonds in pockets. They love to shout slogans about the Redeemer. They feel no guilt. Everything happens as expected. It pleases them and makes sense after what they have seen. Jack you used to understand this and even said some of you are like that. Jack you said all stories were part of all other stories. That is true. Over and over again. But for these boys all the stories they know have changed and their bones that held what they knew have dissolved into other things rising out of them. Their souls have shifted around.

"The world is permanently different to them and is in a kill-off against them. They want terrible justice and they do not like strangers and abominations. They will not train; they will only become skilled. They would miss the ritual sacrifices and mutilations. Eating their enemies. Leave them to me Jack. Let us do the school. Mama was tired of the other school and Madame anyway. The church too for that matter. Their time was past. The God's Front are very respectful boys, Mister Jack. They will respond to a traditional training. They will do as they can. Some broken things cannot be fixed, Jack. Jack you are breaking your heart with these ideas."

"Jules you will be head of state one day," said Hank with a laugh. "You are always so sensible about the local realities. But I think there are some good ideas there too, Jack," continued Hank, "especially the co-operative and the carrots. Once we get down from this Mountain and away from all this foolishness. When everything is over, then we'll look into that. I'll show how to budget for it."

"Mister Hank, you will be head of state too one day," said Jules and laughed. Jack and Hank laughed too. Hank's laugh continued into a smile. Jack's had been loud and brief and seemed to startle Mama. Then Hank said that dusk this high up was quite cool and pleasant.

A small woman in furs came from the edge of the forest across the fields carrying two burlap bags, one dripping wet at the bottom. As she approached the wet bag smelled more strongly, cutting over the smell of the reeds and that of the sulphurous pool. The woman stopped, put down the dry bag and held open the wet bag with both hands. Mama went over, reached in and scooped out some of the contents. She walked over to Hank and, giggling, stood on tiptoe and flung the handful over Hank's head where he sat. Jules took several handfuls one after the other and smeared them over Jack's face, his hair and his robe. He worked carefully and deliberately trying not to miss a patch.

Mama and the other woman then took the bag and poured it over Hank's head. Then Mama handed the bag to Jules who emptied the last wet bits and a few heavy lumps onto Jack. Together they smeared the contents over him, under his arms, around his crotch, behind the knees and onto his shoes.

"Now you are well and truly dead," said Jules happily. "You look like the abominable twins from the grave!" The two women were laughing at Hank who still had not opened his eyes. There were small white worms on Jack's head. An organ had dropped off his head to the ground and smeared his face with a purple stripe along his left cheek.

Jules pointed to Mama where she was laughing and now embracing and dancing around with her furred companion. "There is only one Mama. Isn't she wonderful? There can only be one queen. Look at her Jack! She is happy and so are the Chembes. Don't doubt it. Things are going properly. Everything is going to be fine. There is no doubt, no splitting of soul."

Jules turned to Hank. "This is our law of "onlys", mister Hank. It is what I wasn't able to finish when we talked before about us. There is only one tribe, one memory, one queen, one king and one child of the tribe. We all try always to go back to oneness. There is only one soul. It is this that keeps us clear about what we are. Also there is finally, after all is done, only this Mountain, and it is ours. Come with me, it is time to go."

Jules picked up the other bag which the woman had brought when she brought the goat remains and walked off around the reeds and then around pool towards the far edge of the field where the last slope of the Mountain began. Hank and Jack followed while Mama and her companion stayed by the fire.

When they reached the edge of the forest Jules indicated a fairly wide path between grasses and low, wide trunk trees. It only went a short distance ahead before it turned left to go into dark trees and twilight around a fallen trunk, the height of Hank, grasped in grey vines and resting on a mound of red rotting wood. Jules handed Hank the flashlight which he took from his pocket. He gave Jack a bone knife which he took from the waistband of his furred trousers. He then gave Jack the bag he was carrying. He whispered to them that it was mangoes and some dry meat. Jules next whispered good luck in Chembe twice as Hank, followed by Jack, set out on the path. In a minute they had left Jules' sight.

Hank reviewed the instructions mentally. He was to stay on the path. If it forked he would take the climbing one to the left. He was not to seek help from anyone in the forest and was to ignore things that seemed strange, perhaps showing respect, while sticking to his task. If Jack was killed and eaten, he was to join in, but creep off when growled at. He was to keep moving.

He was to go to the cave and wait. He must not eat fish in the pool beyond the cave in what must be a volcanic crater. He could eat dying insects. After Jules was sure they were safe he would meet them at the cave. Then he could go down the Mountain. All problems would be sorted out so that they would be dropped. He could find a taxi or the old Serpents Tom had come with. The ferry was probably still running.

Tom had been rescued by the new People's Research Bureau and, if truth be told, by Hank. Jack had been assisted on the programming for the new country program. The old project's name was in the clear and so was the agency. There was no reason not to go home. He would be able to write a good report; he had all the facts and evidence to do this. The chief should be happy no matter what influences were on her. It was doubtful whether that accident, nò matter who was to blame or anything else from before the crisis was declared, would come up again. Hank had been everywhere and could not see how. And besides, the crisis was declared, the frameworks were altered and rationales would change. Ron would be doing that all the time. Hank also was thinking how lovely the two huts and the women had looked beside the fire over the pool as he had begun to climb the last of the Mountain and how bad Jack looked in the dirty robe and wiggling hair. It was good to be going.

"Did Juliet know everything about Hope and Chastity?" Hank said turning to Jack walking behind him in the murk.

"She may have, but that sort of thing didn't bother her," said Jack. "I think she may have been curious. What really bothered her was a thing that happened with Cressy. Her dad was mad too."

Hank suddenly said, *"The maidens wove splintered bones into souvenirs."*

Jack said, "God, Hank. Where on earth did you get that?"

"It just came to me, from nowhere," said Hank. "It must be this Mountain. You really have been a bastard Jack. Do you feel bad?"

"Do you?" said Jack abruptly and stopped. Hank turned back and snapped on the light in a single flash to see the next stretch of path. He walked on and Jack followed. The path was climbing steeply around large rocks and between the wide trunked trees. The sky flashed a brief red fan overhead from a distant sunset and then it became suddenly dark. Their eyes adjusted so that the flash was not needed except when the road seemed to fork. Once in the path ahead there stood what seemed to be a small wolf or bear, perhaps an anteater. They stopped and it leapt to the side into the bush. The insects were few after it darkened. There were some long brown worms in the path when the light was shone. The night around was full of shuffling and scratching. A steady breeze blew.

"The idea about the Front was a good one," said Jack in a whisper behind Hank.

"I don't think so," said Hank in a normal voice as he walked. "Not unless they stop attacking the army and murdering women. You might have to get them to confess as well before they got the job. Otherwise donors might not buy it." Something squealed and gurgled to the right and below. There was a bark and a high bleat. An insect or lizard laughed and chattered.

"Which letters do you have?" asked Jack. He stopped and Hank stopped too but spoke without turning.

"I have one which seems to be something like a resignation letter. It lists all your sins. You do have a complicated life, Jack. Much too complex I would say, even historic. I am not sure how it could be simplified. I am not sure the letter is all that sincere either to be quite frank.

"The other one is a printed love letter to you. I don't know if you wrote it or copied it out. But it is annotated with some comments about culture. These two letters were attached together. I lost the others that I found but I read them. I thought of giving them back but then as things happened I thought to myself why not keep them in case they are needed to recollect anything, or something new comes up about the management of the project. You never know.

"I know the letters you mean," said Jack. "You can keep them."

It was late afternoon the next day when Jules reached the cave. Hank was sitting at the far end in the cave mouth overlooking the crater and the steaming lake with the island plug in the centre. There were silent birds with wide wingspans circling around the crater's rim on what seemed constant updrafts. From time to time a splash would take place on the lake and a silver belly would twist or somersault around just on and below the surface. The central island was heavily treed with ferns and spreading palms. The vines on it were yellow so that it looked covered with a shedding wig on a green skull. When Jules arrived Hank was squatting in the narrow opening to examine in the light some brightly coloured stones he had found on the cave floor. Beyond the crater rim and above it was only sky, grey in one direction and bright in the other.

Jules squatted down behind Hank and looked out over his shoulder. He greeted him.

"The flashlight ran out in the early morning," said Hank. "I heard you coming into the cave but I thought I would best wait for you here and not go through to meet you."

"That was a good idea Mister Hank," said Jules. "If you had come down the path on the slope on the other side you might have gotten lost. The Mountain changes in the light."

"Jack went out at dawn to see if he could find another way down the Mountain," said Hank. "He said there was a side of it he had not seen. Maybe he was looking for something. He seemed anxious to get back to the plain. Maybe he wanted to check his vehicle or something. I don't think he wanted to face that cliff again."

"That was not wise," said Jules. "There are really no safe ways down the Mountain."

"You know how Jack is," said Hank. "He was going on about how the landscape was. It was like photos he wanted to see but hadn't. That sort of thing. Stage directions for the sky and night. Plots in the water."

"Mister Hank," said Jules, "some people in the forest as I was climbing told me that there had been some killing below the rim. I think it is something we need to face. The Mountain is a deadly thing full of deadly things. It may be a sorrow without words. A sorrow on all our others. There is not any way that Jack could get down this Mountain safely. It rained last night and this morning. He would need God with him and not against him to get down." Hank and Jules were silent a long time. Hank looked at some more stones and Jules watched the birds. Hank tried his shorts for pockets to put the stones in but the pocket places were sewn shut.

"He took the food so I can offer you nothing," said Hank.

"I have eaten," said Jules, "and we can go back. The hunters have left for good. I think the God's Front will teach them not to come on the Mountain. It is terrible when we split in the tribe but that is how we can get a oneness. What else can we do? Mister Hank you were right to wait here. Learn and Live. I will take you to the meeting field now.

"Mama and I will then take you down the Mountain. Mister Hank, your clothes are washed but you need not put them on until you are sure you need to be clean. We have them in a bag. You will be smelly until you have had quite a few baths. You cannot use the pool like that. In any event you will get dusty on the cliff. How does that sound?"

"That sounds alright Jules. I'll need to contact the agency as soon as I can. I have to bring them up to date. I'll avoid the village. I wish I could get that motorcycle going. Maybe I'll borrow a bicycle to get to the Bechembe town. Can you help me with that, Jules? Then I'll try to find the People's Research people to see if I can get a ride to the ferry. I hope they don't recognize me. I'll be quite strange by then. If the ferry isn't running I can rent one of those canoes." Hank stood and dusted down his shorts. He was bending slightly under the low cave ceiling. He threw down a red stone he had in his hand. The stone flashed in the sun as it rolled down the inside rim of the crater and splashed into the circular lake. Jules stood too.

"I'll lead the way through the cave back to the outside slope Mister Hank," said Jules. "You have to be careful because the cave actually twists and there is a hidden fork facing you going back. Mister Hank, do you think you will ever come back here really after this? We don't like to lose people. Will there be another project?

"Yes, there always will be one Jules. Don't worry. I have some ideas. And I do think I will certainly get back here sometime for an inspection. Things don't just go away and anyway I would like to see all the known faces again.

"I have a good feeling that when I get back to headquarters I'll get a headquarters desk job at home which has responsibility for this country. There is a man there now, Ron, who has made some mistakes with this crisis and cost the agency money. He has told everyone the events were in the wrong place and were the wrong kind. Poor fellow. They will have to do something internally about that. I think there is a chance I'll get his job, Jules. I should have a good reputation now, especially after this tragedy.

"And Jules, you remember Juliet don't you? Didn't she visit and come up the Mountain? She's an old friend of mine. I think even she might want to come back here for a visit sometime. She will want to remember old times. I think I'll probably go to stay a while at her house when I get back. I'll need to tell her about Jack. That will be difficult. I don't know quite how to tell her that. I think I'll put it in a poem or something."

"If you do come back Hank," said Jules, "make sure it is in the dry season. Mama and I would like that."